T

HAS

NOTHING

TO DO

WITH

YOU

Lemay 2020

LAUREN CARTER

this has nothing to do with you

Freehand Books acknowledges the financial support for its publishing program provided by the Canada Council for the Arts and the Alberta Media Fund, and by the Government of Canada through the Canada Book Fund.

 Canada Council for the Arts   Conseil des Arts du Canada   Alberta Government   Canada

Freehand Books
515–815 1st Street SW   Calgary, Alberta   T2P 1N3
www.freehand-books.com

Book orders: LitDistCo
8300 Lawson Road   Milton, Ontario   L9T 0A4
Telephone: 1–800–591–6250   Fax: 1–800–591–6251
orders@litdistco.ca   www.litdistco.ca

Library and Archives Canada Cataloguing in Publication
Title: This has nothing to do with you : a novel / Lauren Carter.
Names: Carter, Lauren, 1972– author.
Identifiers: Canadiana (print) 20190130555 | Canadiana (ebook) 20190130571 | ISBN 9781988298542 (softcover) | ISBN 9781988298528 (html) | ISBN 9781988298535 (pdf)
Classification: LCC PS8605.A863 T45 2019 | DDC C813/.6—DC23

Edited by Naomi Lewis
Book design by Natalie Olsen, Kisscut Design
Author photo by Heather Ruth Photography
Printed and bound in Canada by Marquis

Epigraph from ALL THE LITTLE LIVE THINGS by Wallace Stegner, copyright © 1967 by Wallace Stegner, copyright renewed© 2001 by Mary Stegner. Used by permission of Brandt & Hochman Literary Agents, Inc.

FOR TIM

"There is a sense in which we are all each other's consequences."

— WALLACE STEGNER —

part one

1.

THAT MORNING, just past dawn, my brother sat in the driver's seat of the minivan, reading the liner notes from *Kiss Me, Kiss Me, Kiss Me* by The Cure. The sky infused with pink like the wash you'd use on an Easter egg, to get that bottom tint of colour.

"Ready?" Matt asked when Lara, Josie, and I came out of the cabin, leaving our sleeping friends. The windshield was splattered with dead mosquitoes, dark smears of blood, and he hit the wipers before manoeuvring the van between somebody's pick-up and a stand of birch trees. Dust billowed from our tires and he asked me to squeeze some calamine lotion into his palm, then rubbed it on the bites spotting his skin from the hungry bugs that had come out in the night, during the party for the Hixon River High School Class of 1991. My grad.

Now, nearly three years later, I still remember how I felt right then: this deep, steady calm, fringed with an eager excitement, like a quiet morning spent waiting on the platform for a train to arrive with its promising rumble. The rest of my life was just beginning. Matt would be heading back to university in the fall, and this time I'd follow, starting school to become a vet. Lara was moving, as well, to go to art school out West. Only Josie would stay behind, but she was getting married in a week. I said nothing to break the quiet as we drove, until Matt shoved in a tape and Springsteen growled *Glory Days,* and I said, "Good choice." Behind us, Josie started to talk, rambling on about the flowers for her wedding, changing her mind again about using the white lilacs cut from the tree in her parents' backyard.

"They're full of ants," she said, and in the side mirror, I saw Lara roll her eyes, then swivel her head to look down the steep sandy bank at the brown river.

"Seems fitting to me," she muttered, and I would have shushed her, but Josie hadn't even heard, was going on about how much nicer roses would be. She was worrying the ring that Bruce had bought her, the gold band with the tiny diamond chip that hung on her slender finger, stopped only by the jut of her knuckle bone. Lara glanced back, let out a sigh, then reached over to still Josie's fidgeting. When they were clasping hands, Josie looked at me, grinned, and wiggled her fingers, beckoning. Lara groaned. We all knew what was next, the familiar chant from our childhood, the club call we'd taken so seriously when we were eleven, gathering in the loft in Josie's garage to add scratch-and-sniff stickers to our communal collection book or read the dirtiest parts out loud from Judy Blume's *Forever.*

"Come on, Mel," Josie said, when I hesitated, and I don't know why I didn't do it. Fatigue, maybe, or maybe because I'd already noticed what was coming up ahead: a red glaze streaking the dark pines in the parking lot of the Happyland Campground. Sirens blaring.

Three police cars blocked the entrance, throwing light across the familiar sign with its worn yellow paint, a garish red smile spotted with pitch that dribbled from an overhanging spruce. Past that, the old log cabin, a luminescent neon sign that said *Office* in its grimy window.

A single police officer stood beside the highway, his handgun a black lump on his hip. His serious gaze slid over our windshield, and I stared back before my eyes drifted to Matt's face, gone pasty so the dark stubble on his jaw stood out, the calamine lotion dried to a flaky white powder on his chin. He imagined what I did, I figured: a poor alcoholic dead in his mouldy trailer, or a man who'd beaten up his wife. The campground was full of people down on their luck, living in broken-down motorhomes and rusty camper vans, and our mother used to make fun of it, calling it Sadland whenever we drove by on the 143-kilometre drive to Sault Ste. Marie, the Soo, the nearest big city, to go see a specialist or shop for Christmas presents or see a movie at the mall.

For a split second, it was Mom's Electra I thought I saw — the same burgundy colour, a dent in the rear fender — when one of the cops pulled back to let in a screaming ambulance. But that couldn't be, I thought, and quickly enough the car was hidden by the boxy vehicle coming to a stop beside a wide lump on a carpet of pine needles, covered with a sheet, soaked in blood.

I pushed my fingers against my lips. None of us said anything as we rolled past. All we thought to do was stare, and now, in my memory, knowing what I know, I also imagine her.

Wrapped in the plush purple robe she always wore, the hems of her pajama bottoms flapping around her bare ankles. Her heels bent slightly in, those collapsing leather moccasins. A gun in her hands.

2.

THE MORNING BEFORE, the day of my graduation, my mother slept until eleven. I worried she wouldn't be ready in time for the ceremony in the high school gym, but then Matt went to her room, helped her get up and put on some clothes, and together they left the house. Through the front window I watched them walk down the steep driveway, turn right towards the path to the beach. They moved slowly, my mother stopping every few steps while Matt talked. They didn't go far. Soon they were just standing on the side of the road, Matt clutching her arm as my mother held both hands over her face, then turned away from him, turned back like she couldn't decide which direction to move in.

"What were you talking about?" I asked him later that night at the party, the two of us side by side on the dock, facing the lake.

He stood there fidgeting, shifting his weight from one foot to the other, ripping the paper label off a bottle of Canadian.

"Tell me," I said, but he wouldn't.

It had been his idea to escort us, to drive Lara and Josie and me out of town, past Copper Bridge, down the dirt road to the cabin on Lake Mattawa, and I was glad. He was my big city brother, into things nobody in Hixon River had ever even heard of — the Violent Femmes, booze cans, protests at the U.S. Embassy in Toronto, which he called the "grey fortress of Imperialism." For three years, he'd been away at school, although it would take him five to graduate because he'd switched his major from biology to political science and seemed to be more focused on his volunteer job escorting women through demonstrations at a downtown abortion clinic. Every spring, he came back North to work at the Ministry of Natural Resources, the job he'd started the summer after Grade 13, the one he hated, still does.

Part of me was relieved that Matt wasn't talking that night. I didn't really want to think about my family. Besides, it wasn't unusual, my being kept in the dark. Most of the time it seemed my mother couldn't see me, that I wasn't much more than a shadow cast by Matt. He was bright, living colour, the love of her life. So I turned away from his silence, wanting only that moment: the two of us standing on the dock, watching the sunset bleed into the deep neon blue of dusk. The stars blinking open like tiny, watchful eyes. Josie and Lara plunking down the boards to join us. I looped my arms around their shoulders, one best friend on either side.

It was a perfect time, before the night came on, before Todd picked up Lara and threw her in the lake, before the rest of us stripped down and waded out past a fringe of reeds and lily-pads to swim, one girl screaming at the sight of a blood sucker and running back on shore, forgetting she was naked. Before Charlie got so drunk he set fire to the dry, yellow lawn, and we watched it smoulder, sending up fat, noxious rolls of smoke, beers loose in our hands until somebody shouted *fire*, and we all looked around for a place to set our bottles down. It was nearly three a.m. before we got to bed, escaping the bugs and the stench of the grass, crisped to charcoal, to stumble into the cabin to sleep. I couldn't have known what would be waiting when I woke up, that I'd spent the night on the rapidly diminishing surface of my childhood, that last patch of solid ground.

WE DROPPED LARA AT her uncle's place in town, then brought Josie home. Her wedding was the following Sunday, and I was her maid of honour, Lara her only bridesmaid. Josie sat sideways on the back seat of the van and swung her feet like a little kid while we sat stopped in her driveway.

"What do you think?" she asked. She meant about the roses.

Matt shut off the van, and as if he'd suddenly remembered something, popped the rear door, leapt out, and went around to the back.

"Too expensive." I knew the budget as well as she did.

She sighed. "We might not have a choice."

I liked how she said "we," because I knew she meant her and me, as if the two of us were getting married, not her and Bruce. We were probably a better match. Since Grade 10, she and Bruce had been on again, off again, until he proposed after the Christmas formal. I knew the story: down by the marina, six falling stars in a row. Lara and I assumed he was afraid that if he didn't hold on to her she'd leave along with us. We tried to talk her out of it, but it didn't do any good, and I remember how astonished I felt to be witnessing the first big mistake that one of us was making, at least according to me and Lara.

"Roses," Josie said, a decisive statement, then leapt to the ground as if off a swing. In the side mirror, I caught a glimpse of my brother holding a shiny thing to his face. A bottle. The vodka from the night before. He capped it as Josie leaned in my window to kiss me on the cheek, happiness coming off her like a vapour. I smelled the wood smoke in her hair. "Sweet dreams," she said as the front door opened, and I watched as her mom took Josie in her arms, gathered her up, drew her inside.

Our own house was empty. The only sign of life was Frankie barking at our arrival, scampering around our feet to be let outside. I opened the back door and watched as he rushed through the long grass that needed mowing, to the garden at the edge of the woods. He peed on a crooked wire cage around a tomato plant that already needed its suckers snapped off. My mother's boots sat at the top of the basement stairs, orange Cougars, the laces loose like collapsing spider webs. I saw them as I hunted for Matt in his room, then in hers, and finally downstairs in the family room. It took a moment for my eyes to adjust to the darkness, and then there he was, scattering orange flakes of fish food into the aquarium. A cloud of red cardinal fish poked at the surface while the shimmering angelfish made its way up from the bottom, its fins drifting like fallen streamers at the end of a party. Garbo, he'd named her, after the movie star from the 1940s.

"Where's Mom?" I asked.

"How should I know?"

I had a lump in my throat. The glimpse I thought I'd caught of her car stuck in my head like a dream I didn't want to admit having. Any moment now, I told myself, she'd walk in, glance at me, push by to get to Matt.

I walked to my father's bedroom. When I knocked, the weight of my fist pushed the door open. The bed was unmade. Two glass Pepsi bottles stood on the dresser, and when I lifted them, I saw they'd left intersecting rings. His smell was in there too. Cologne he'd started wearing that winter, which had saturated the air in the house. My mother had complained about it while they were out for a drive, and it was that fight, the one about the pungent, spicy sweetness of his new odour, that led to his spontaneous confession.

I shut the door. I carried the pop bottles to the stairs. The silence hummed in my ears as I watched my brother's back in the large mirrors that my father had installed, back when my mother was still dancing. Matt had one short sleeve pushed up onto his shoulder, and his arm was fully immersed. He moved the fake sunken ship with its overflowing treasure chest, the fake stone archway, while the fish nibbled at his skin.

He was trying to be normal. If we were religious, we might have gone to church, since it was Sunday, around nine in the morning by then. Instead, we stayed put and I stayed down there with him. I thought about putting on a pot of coffee, but I didn't think I could drink it without throwing up. Not because I was hungover, but because I was aware that we were waiting. At ten, almost on the dot, the doorbell rang, and Matt's eyes bounced over to me, ricocheted away. When he opened the front door, there were the police, Frankie with them on the concrete steps like he already belonged to somebody else.

I fell to my knees on the living room floor when I heard, pushing my face into the carpet like an animal needing to burrow. Matt above me, his hands on my back, and the cop, launching the story into the air. My father, dead. His mistress too. My mother, their murderer.

part two

1.

I DON'T LIVE WITH Matt and Angie anymore, but I'm over there a lot. Sometimes I babysit, other times I'll go for family gatherings when her parents are in town from the Soo. That's where Angie lived when she met Matt, when I was out West. He frequented the same diner that she did before our mother was sentenced and sent to the Cornwall Prison for Women. Angie ordering cups of tea before her morning hairdressing courses; Matt picking up double-doubles to take to the jail.

"Come for dinner," Angie said when she saw me at the library this afternoon. It's only April 14, but it's one of the first warm days of spring, one of those balmy afternoons that remind you the grip of winter has loosened, and summer's beckoning up ahead. I told her yes, but it would have to be quick, because I had to go to the animal shelter where I volunteer.

"You're still doing that?"

"I just started."

"You keep yourself so busy."

Working with books was her idea. It's not that I'm ungrateful. She helped me get the job when I moved to Norbury in January, but my dream isn't to spend the rest of my life cataloguing articles about long-ago accidents or binding hardcovers in cellophane. I like to read as much as the next person, although not nearly as much as my mom and Matt. It's just that I like animals more.

THREE BURGERS ARE SIZZLING on the barbecue when I walk under the carport and into their backyard. Angie hands the baby to me, and Ellie immediately starts wriggling, swinging her arms, kicking her pudgy legs.

"Where's Matt?" I ask, although I know. The rumble of the news is leaking through the open basement window whose glare of glass reflects a grey heap of snow and a purple crocus sprouting out of last year's mulch. I can't see Matt, but I imagine him: sitting on the edge of the sofa, one knee jumping up and down, ripping at a thumbnail with his teeth. It's been about a week since rockets shot a plane out of the sky in Rwanda, killing the country's president and the president of neighbouring Burundi, and triggering what they're calling a bloody civil war. Matt's fixated, and I'm not surprised. I remember him like this: leaning towards newscasts about the embassy bombing in Beirut or absorbed in the coverage of the *Challenger* space shuttle explosion. My mother and him linked by a phone line while they watched the televised bombings of Operation Desert Storm when he was away at school. The screen showing a red star over Baghdad, then the strange, smeared view through the missile's green eye until the blurred shapes of houses turned to silver static.

I've seen the news, seen the maps of the East African country, white against a green continent, nearby Lake Victoria coloured bright blue. We are extremely worried, one reporter said a couple nights ago, the last time I had the television on, the last time I could take it in, that and the suicide verdict on Kurt Cobain's death.

"Do you have the news on?" Matt had asked me that night, on the phone.

"Yes," I lied, because I'd already snapped off the set.

"We should do something."

His voice was clear, reminding me of happier times, when we'd hatch schemes to carry our camping equipment to the beach or walk the tar-smelling train tracks all the way into town.

I hesitated. "Like what?"

He muttered something about writing letters or planning a demonstration, but I felt myself pulling back, growing distant, like my father did when faced with Matt's plans to change the world. Once I remember him telling Matt to save his tears for his own life, and how mad Matt got, how he turned to me later, in the middle of an episode of *The A-Team* and said, "Is there a paucity of tears?"

I didn't know what the word meant. Like scarcity, I found, in the dictionary. Scarcity I knew. Scarcity of emotion, even of breath, as I moved so cautiously around my parents, limiting my weight, trying not to catch their attention.

"Matt," I said, interrupting. The clock on my ancient kitchen stove ground closer to midnight. "We both have to work in the morning."

"People are dying and you..." My hand twitched to hang up. "We can't just watch," he said. I picked at the broken chrome edge of my kitchen counter, imagined Angie beside him, swinging Ellie in her arms, trying to get her to go to sleep. "Hush," she would be murmuring. "Hush."

"Goodnight," I said, and hung up the phone.

NOW I WANT to talk to him, want to give Ellie back and go downstairs to see him, but Angie's holding a spatula in one hand and a bottle of Corona in the other, a folded lime wedge stuffed down its neck, so I stay. I jostle the baby, pushing my nose into the sweet mist of her soft, blonde hair. My mother's hair was blonde at birth, I know from old photos now packed in boxes in Matt's basement, and so was his before it darkened to a deep brown, a colour which sets off his blue eyes. I've got my father's hazel eyes, his auburn hair in my short mop, still growing in from shaving my head out West. But these are thoughts I try to avoid: what we received from each of them, both Matt and me.

"Get the potato salad?" Angie asks, pulling open the lid of the barbecue. She unwraps the plastic on a cheese slice, sets it onto a patty. "And there are paper plates on the counter."

I look around, trying to find a place to put down the baby when Matt slides open the glass door. Ellie reaches towards him, grabs at the air. I want to give her to him, but his face appears dull, unfocused, like he's looking at something none of the rest of us can see.

"Nice of you to join us," Angie mutters into the spout of her beer bottle, but it's like he doesn't hear her. He starts talking; I check my watch. I have to leave in half an hour. My mind drifts to the dog who's waiting for me. Quiet in his cage, huge head tucked between his paws. A mastiff mix, with drooping jowls and big brown eyes that usually look like he's about to burst into tears. I've already fallen for him. When I walk him on the leash, his big brindled body sways; he struts like a lion. His name is Sunday, and if I tell Matt about him I know exactly what he'll say: Isn't your place too small? Are dogs even allowed? As if he can compare my eighth-floor apartment to the ideal place of our childhood: the forest in our backyard, the beach a short walk away. *You can't give him the life we gave Frankie.* But if I waited for that I'd never get a dog, and I need to start over, make new memories, because thinking of Frankie hurts my heart, how he ended up living at Josie's aunt's farm after I left, when Matt was too overwhelmed. Probably happy, I tell myself, wandering the fields, sleeping by the wood-stove, until the coyotes came one evening. Sometimes I wake in the night, full of cold guilt about that. Reading has taught me things I can't forget: dogs need their packs. Like humans, they grieve sudden absence. What would he have thought, in his last days? That we'd abandoned him. That we were never coming back.

"Did you hear me?" Matt asks. I didn't, and Angie is staring down into the red-hot embers, poised to pull the burgers off the grill. I see how her lips have tightened. Matt looks at her for a few seconds, then quietly slides the door shut and retreats.

"You know he's taken over my room," Angie says, as soon as he's gone.

"What do you mean?"

"I don't know what I mean," she says, hitting the barbecue with the spatula so the grill clangs. "Because the door's always locked."

I say nothing. I use the need to fetch a plate as an excuse to get away, to disappear inside, and when we're settled at the dining room table I eat as fast as I can. When I finish, I wipe the ketchup off my lips with a napkin, glance at Matt's untouched burger, and finally ask her, "So what do you think he's doing down there?"

this has nothing to do with you

"Beats me," Angie says. She holds a piece of potato in front of Ellie's mouth, waiting for her to grab it. When she looks at me, I see a sinking in her normally sturdy face.

"This situation in Africa," she says. "He's always watching."

Ellie grabs hold of the potato chunk, touches it to her lips, leaving a smear of mayonnaise. "He's taking it so personally when nothing we've ever been through can even compare."

I look down at my empty plate.

"I don't mean..." She reaches across the table to touch my wrist, but I push my arms under the table, hunch forward. I know what she's going to tell me — I'm not trying to be dismissive, to discount your loss — but I don't want her to go there, to talk about it at all. Of course they aren't comparable: all that bloodshed versus my mother's spent rage, two measly deaths next to an accelerating massacre we're powerless to prevent. I know that. You think I don't know that? I stand up to head downstairs to try to talk to my brother.

"He went down there after you moved into your apartment," Angie says. "I haven't been inside since. He says he needs it. He needs a space." We stare at each other. Angie's little home salon is the only way she can make any money, with Ellie to care for. She shifts in her seat and shakes her head, as if refusing an offer I haven't even made.

"It doesn't matter. I'm so busy with her." She gestures with her fork, accidentally knocking a knuckle against Ellie's nose. The baby's face scrunches in slow motion, flushing red, and Angie stands, swoops in, lifting her out of her chair. Then she raises her eyebrows at me as if to say, See?

DOWNSTAIRS, in the den, games from Matt's old Atari system — *Donkey Kong, Pac-Man* — are strewn across the carpet in front of the TV. On the coffee table, there's a pile of newspapers, neatly stacked, and three empty beer bottles. To my left is the laundry room, and I glance in, hoping I'll find him folding clean clothes, doing a task that's productive and helpful, even normal. He isn't there, so I turn towards Angie's room. The door's closed, but I know exactly what's inside. A chrome and red vinyl barbershop chair she found in the newspaper classifieds, a large mirror fastened to the wall, even a sink with a dipped edge for washing hair and a tall jar of blue Barbicide that holds her combs. And Matt, as well, although I don't know what he's doing. I stand so close I can see the grain in the wooden door and a familiar, sweet odour leaks through the cracks. It surprises me. Matt — my straight-laced brother, who never did drugs, who never failed to warn me of their dangers, to remind me of the fact that our grandfather, our father's dad, died of lung cancer at fifty-eight — is smoking up in there. I remember a guy he told me about from his dorm who got heavily into pot and started thinking people were after him, even the CIA, and when he went home at Christmas break, he never returned. Too fragile, Matt had said. His brain.

My hand reaches for the doorknob. I twist hard, but the lock holds.

"What?" Matt shouts.

"I'm going now. Come say goodbye."

He doesn't answer. I hold my breath and lean in. He could be disappearing in there, fading away, and this makes me think of stories we'd loved as kids, about time machines built by amateur scientists and teenagers stumbling into portals, disappearing into fantastical lands. Maybe that's what he's doing: inventing stuff, trying to alter his life, building a secret path. I tap my knuckles softly against the surface, but he says nothing, and part of me is tempted to sink to the floor, stay there, keep a kind of vigil until he opens up, but the other part, the part that wants my own life, my new dog, a future severed from the past is the one that wins. I step backwards, moving softly like I'm sneaking away, and find Angie upstairs at the front door.

"Weird, right?" she says. I shrug.

"Do you think we should be worried?" she asks, like I'm still as close to him as I once was, closer to him than she is, like I can answer that. The truth is, that worry hasn't even occurred to me. Matt's the one in charge, the mediator, the counsellor, the caregiver, the one everyone can count on. "I'm sure he's fine," I say, and I leave.

2.

MATT WAS THE ONE who rescued me. Three months ago. After I ran away, I lived in B.C., and then, for a long time, in Arizona. My only friend a hobo named Robert who had blue eyes and long white hair and spoke mostly in rhyme. He'd built a shanty beside the creek and let me stay in a nearby cave carved out of a red rock cliff. He was kind. He helped me shave my head so I wouldn't have to worry about lice and could more easily clean myself in the river. He taught me the correct way to meditate, cooked for me, and after a time I shared with him what had happened to me, to my family. He told me his own awful stories of jungle wars, and eventually they helped me grow up a bit, to realize I wasn't alone in facing tragedy. It was a start.

Other things happened: the ashram where I worked for a while, my job making sloppy lentil burgers that always fell apart, the brief love affair with Marcos. I drifted through days, weeks, months, passing through seasons, past birthdays, not even speaking to Matt, and then, one morning, I woke and stepped out of my snug cave to find a thick frost on the river banks, lit white by the sun. The brightness made me squint, my head still throbbing from the previous afternoon's magic mushroom trip.

"What's today?" I asked Robert.

"It's a day to play," he said, grinning, a familiar twitch in his left eye. He rolled a joint on the dried out saguaro cactus that acted as his table.

Eventually, I found out it was January 14, a few days after what would have been my dad's birthday. I realized how much time had passed, how lost in a blur I'd become. For two years, four months, and five days I'd been on the run.

That evening I called Matt collect on a gas station pay-phone. It took me a while to get his number. When there wasn't any listing for him in Hixon River, the operator suggested searching for a Matthew Barnett in both the Soo and Norbury, the biggest cities east and west of our hometown, both a couple hour's drive away. I sagged with relief when she read out the digits.

A woman answered, a baby wailed in the background. I almost hung up but then Matt's voice sounded in the background, its deep timbre, so I simply said his name, started to cry, was still crying when he came on the phone.

"Her name's Angie," he told me. She got pregnant the second time they slept together. That baby miscarried, but by then everything was decided, they were living together, and had bought their house, a split-level with wooden siding, on a narrow lot that backs onto a forest.

The MNR — Ministry of Natural Resources — where he'd worked summers for years, had given him a job at their regional head office in Norbury, so they tried again, embarking on a life not even close to the destiny our mother had often told Matt was his. He was supposed to be someone special. A famous author. A lawyer. Even prime minister. Instead, he pulled on a pair of green pants and a khaki button-up shirt every morning, climbed into a pick-up truck, and went out into the woods to count trees or keep track of fish stock, to bushwhack into marshes deep in the boreal beyond the hydro lines and take water samples, tasks he'd complained about a lot when he was doing the work during summer breaks.

I stood in the phone booth in Sedona, and he told me: "Wait there."

Like I could remain in that pool of yellow light drawing in moths and desert flies for a full night and day until he got on a plane and crossed the continent to get to me. I went back to the cave. A couple of days later, I woke to see him picking his way across the flat brown river stones, stepping wide over cold pools, heading straight for my hole in the earth as if he already knew exactly where I'd be. Hidden in that blood red crevice, tending to my wounds.

3.

THE ANIMAL SHELTER is on the edge of town, at the top of a rock slope overlooking the highway and a forest flushed with pink and yellow buds. As soon as I pull into the parking lot, I hear them, the dogs, launching into a frenzy of barking, and something settles in me, as if it's been floating all day, look- ing for a place to land. I clutch the wheel, close my eyes, listen, and feel the love I had for Frankie, his tail wagging, ready to rocket out the back door and into the woods, to gobble up pellets of rabbit poop or race along that narrow trail strewn with loose sticks he'd drop at my feet. It's almost enough. It's almost enough to crack me open, send me away, but then one dog howls above the rest, the most mournful sound, and I'm out of the car because I hear how much he needs me.

Liv, the manager, stands at the tall desk, looking through a stack of application forms. The baubles on the elastic bands holding her braids shine like gum balls under the fluorescent lights. She grins when she sees me, her dark face beaming. "He's been waiting for you all day," she tells me. "Every time anybody came in, his head would fly up, then fall down when he realized it wasn't you. Seriously," she says, "that dog is in love."

A grin tugs at my lips. I cross in front of the desk, walking towards the wall hooks strung with leashes. Down the cat kennel hallway, there's a woman and a young girl gazing through the glass at a skinny black cat we've named Starburst, who's flicking the white tip of her tail. That one's a biter, I think, but I won't tell them that. Even biters need a chance.

"I'll take him out," I say, but Liv taps the pen she's holding, gives me a pinched look, then reluctantly speaks. "Somebody's coming to meet him."

I turn, the leash a limp string in my hands. "What?"

"He's a challenging case. We can't wait forever." I don't answer. I think I know what she's doing: prodding me to take a chance, to step forward. "This guy's a trainer."

"But he isn't ready," I say, slumping against the wall, a red burn of frustration rising into my cheeks. Really I'm thinking: How can you do this to me? Don't you know he's mine?

Liv wags her pen, instructing. "Nobody's ever ready. There's no perfect time. Not in this overrun home of heartbreak."

"Liv," I say, still arguing. "You just said yourself that he ..."

this has nothing to do with you

27

But she interrupts me, lifting both hands like she's balancing heavy stones.

"Honey, what do you want me to do? You've got to decide."

I frown, fiddle with the clip on the end of the lead. She doesn't know. Not about my small apartment, the no-dogs-allowed rule, the fact that it would just be me, on my own. We barely know each other; I've only been volunteering here for a few weeks. I haven't told her anything.

"He's a great dog," Liv says, shifting her gaze to the bulletin board behind my back, full of lost animal notices, a list of the top ten reasons to spay or neuter your pet, instructions on how to relinquish an unwanted animal. "Underneath all the crap."

SUNDAY WAS NAMED by the woman who rescued him. That was the day of the week that she freed him from the tree he was tethered to, that he'd been attached to for God knows how long. She kept driving past him, on her way to and from her own farm, watching him leap up to bark at her car, sometimes knocking over his plastic bowl of water.

Finally, one night after dark, she parked twenty feet up the gravel road and carried a cookie tray loaded with half a pound of cooked bacon, still hot. At first, he barked, and she stood frozen in the shadow of the tree, waiting. Through the lit living room window, she could see Much Music on the television set, one video playing after another, the back of a man's nodding head and a hand tapping a cigarette into an ashtray on the window-sill. She tossed a slice of bacon over, then slid the whole pan into the dog's range and Sunday lunged at it, gobbling ferociously. The woman unclipped his chain and attached her own leash, and then he nearly bit her, she said, because his skin had grown in around his collar. There was pus and blood clotted in his fur. He was skin and bones, dehydrated, flea infested. The vet had to put him under just to cut off the collar, and now he's got a tough grey scar around his neck like a noose.

He's been with us for just over two weeks, after a stint at a shelter further north where he came close to having a home when a man took him for two days then brought him back because he refused to go inside. Sometimes he panics in his kennel, pacing frantically. He pants almost constantly, tucks his tail between his legs whenever anyone approaches, and usually growls at men. But who can blame him? The tips of his ears are polka-dotted from frostbite, and there's a constellation of scars along the ridge of his spine. From burns, the vet said. From people butting cigarettes out on his back. She said she's seen that before.

When he first arrived, I crouched by his kennel, holding dog treats through the cage until he finally took one. He swung his big head close, his brown eyes wary, and carefully grasped the Milk-Bone with his front teeth to pull it inside his wrinkly black snout. The next day, I entered his cage and sat on the floor, on the far end, ignoring him. After a while, he came over, and eventually let me touch his flanks, even though I felt him bracing. Then one day, he gave in, sighed, let his weight loosen to the floor. Only for an instant, and he was up again, the moment quickly gone, but that was when I knew it was possible, that he could relax, could trust, and soon he started letting me squeeze the thick brindled fur along his spine. Now I pour all the love I can through my hands, trying to teach him that I'm not one of them, the humans who've done him harm.

Two days ago, when I opened his cage, he swished his tail, and I felt it, the deep gushing pull of my heart, and I knew.

What exactly?

That he needed me. That this was a new beginning, a chance to start again.

this has nothing to do with you

LIV TELLS ME to hope for the best. "If this guy takes him," she says, pulling out the adoption form, "it wasn't meant to be." I turn away and roll my eyes. I had enough of that way of thinking when I lived out West, when people would tell me that we attracted bad things for a reason, that all the shit in one's life had some sort of meaning we just had to figure out. I don't really believe that anymore. Lara would be proud of me. If we were still speaking, that is.

Out in the yard, I toss a ball for a miniature schnauzer named Captain Jack whose one eye is a blind white bead. As he's running to fetch it, a blue car pulls into the parking lot on the other side of the fence. I watch as a man gets out, and I try not to notice how cute he is, with his dark hair, nice face, strong build. I don't want that; I want to hate him.

A few minutes later he comes out with the leash in his hand, Sunday eagerly leading him. My heart sinks. I thought my boy might have scared him off, tried to take a chunk out of him, at least pulled his lips back in the growl I've seen him give some of the male volunteers. But they seem okay, although Sunday's pulling hard, and the guy's arm is hyperextended as they move down the driveway, heading for the forest where we sometimes run the dogs. Soon, they're gone, and I pick up the ball, damp with Jack's slobber, and throw it as hard as I can.

LIV BRINGS SUNDAY BACK after I've put Jack in his kennel and started to clean. When he sees me, he bucks on his leash, and Liv can hardly hold him. I lean the mop into the corner, crouch, and beckon him. His toenails clatter across the linoleum; frantically, he licks my face, and I dodge his sloppy tongue and flapping jowls, laughing. When he's calmed, I hug him, hold him, ruffle his fur, then gently unclip the leash he's dragged along the hallway.

"Good boy," I say, and turn to Liv, heart beating, waiting for news. If the man wants him, I'm not sure what I'll do. Kidnap him maybe, grab him and run.

Liv smiles. "He said he'll sleep on it. He'll let us know tomorrow."

Relief floods through me, followed quickly by fear. Am I going to do this? Should I do this? Down on the floor, Sunday groans and pushes his big paw against my shoe, and both of us look at him. "Sometimes you don't choose them," Liv says. "Sometimes they choose you."

4.

THERE'S A LETTER from my mother in the mailbox when I get back to my apartment. I don't read it. I never do. She sends them every month, sometimes twice, and when I returned from out West, Matt had a stack of them wrapped in a rubber band so old it quietly broke in half when I tried to take it off. I'm sure Lara also has a bunch she hasn't forwarded.

I ride the elevator up to the eighth floor carrying the envelope, and in my apartment, I walk straight to a shelf full of novels and non-fiction books about exotic places, photography, animals of the sea, edible plants. One of the books — a green hardback medical manual from the 1800s called *Detection of Poisons* — isn't actually a book at all. It's been hollowed out and varnished into a box. I found it at a craft fair, and inside is where I keep the letters, so many that it's starting to bulge open. I stuff this one inside, not thinking about it, ignoring it, because I'm busy trying to come to a decision. In my little kitchen, I put the kettle on to boil.

I wish I could talk to my brother, I think, as I stir a mug of hot chocolate spiked with bourbon, like my dad used to make on Christmas Eve. But Matt seems to have turned away from me, changed from the brother I knew to someone who locks himself away during dinner. I suppose I started seeing those changes when I first got back: how Matt seemed withdrawn, robotically following a routine that I knew didn't satisfy him, carrying a battered metal lunch pail to his pick-up truck in the early morning, not arriving home until dinnertime, when he ate in front of the television set, leaning towards the broader world as if hoping he could step through the screen.

Having a baby, I thought. That's what it does.

From my narrow balcony, where I stand with the steaming mug, I see the light snap on in Ellie's room, and I recall the day I moved into this apartment, a one-bedroom in a high-rise rooted into a granite slope that looks down over the back of their house, their yard, the narrow strip of forest that edges their property.

"Now you can always keep an eye on me," Matt said, and I didn't respond. When we were kids, it was he who watched me, took care of me, but things have changed. There's a distance between us now. Only in the very beginning, during the long flight home, had we touched on things, and one other time when he hung up the telephone in the dining room and said, "She asked about you," sending me scampering back to the guest room where I stayed, feeling that familiar twitching need to get away, to run, lest he open his mouth to challenge me: to actually talk about the situation with our mother, about how I'd up and left him in Hixon River, the small town we grew up in, just a two-hour drive west of Norbury, where Josie still lives with Bruce. Even to tell funny stories from our childhood or difficult ones.

But I needn't have worried. He left me alone. Although I knew he spoke to Mom every week, he didn't mention her to me again.

Way down at Matt and Angie's house, the light in Ellie's room is suddenly extinguished. The dark building sits in a pond of dim amber from the streetlamp, as still as a painting of a shadowy stranger's home. I sigh and turn away, retreating from the chilly evening, still wondering what I should do.

BACK IN THE EIGHTIES, my mother started looking for signs. She'd find a queen of spades face up in the supermarket parking lot, assume it was a warning, and drive back home. Cardinals became what she called her spirit bird because they seemed to show up whenever she made up her mind about something, affirming her choice. When she spotted that blot of red crossing over our white, snowy lawn, it meant she was on the right track. Never mind the fact that there were loads of them, that our neighbour filled his three birdfeeders every week.

I'm not sure what the right track would have been for her. A cure for her unhappiness, maybe, or even a path back to the life she felt she'd lost because of Matt's arrival when she was only eighteen.

During my time in Sedona, I fell into this habit too. It was hard not to. Everywhere you looked there were posters advertising *I-Ching* readings or street vendors selling crystals on hemp cords that swung in circles for yes, stayed still for no. I bought myself a deck of tarot cards and used them regularly until one day I was shuffling them for the fifth time in a row, asking over and over whether or not I should go with Big Bear to the Rainbow Gathering in Colorado, and Robert spoke to me.

"You won't find what you need in there," he said. "You have to have the guts to dare, to do what you want and do it with flair."

He sucked on his mullein cigarette with a trembling hand. I stared at him, waiting, and finally he cleared his throat, levelled his eyes on mine. "Trust yourself," he said. "Then make a choice." I put the cards away. I decided just to go. It turned out to be a mistake. For the whole night I lay awake in the back of the vw, armed with a heavy bottle of rye after coming to consciousness with Bear's hand shoved under the waistband of my pants. I escaped, but I had to hitchhike back to Robert's. I arrived back at the river and he said, "See? You had to flee. But you made it through because you knew what to do."

I SIT ON MY COUCH, staring at the few things I own, most of which I took from Matt's, from the boxes in the storage room. My eyes scan the books from my childhood — *Doctor Dolittle, All Creatures Great and Small,* all of the Narnia books, which Josie, Lara and I read together — and finally settle on the figurine Lara gave me for graduation. It's St. Francis of Assisi, the patron saint of animals. An orange tabby curved around his sandaled feet, a hand resting on the head of a German shepherd. The dog gazes up at him, their eyes connecting, both creatures totally at peace. It's enough of a sign for me. Sunday needs me, not some guy who just showed up, who will probably fail like that other man who couldn't even figure out how to entice the dog inside. For better or worse, he's chosen me, he's already mine. Softened by the bourbon, I go to bed with love filling my heart, and a future appears where I'm happy, where we're happy, where we're living a different life. I'll make it through, I think as I fall asleep, because I know what to do.

5.

THE NEXT DAY, the day I'll adopt my new dog, is Friday. First thing in the morning, I call the shelter to leave a message for Liv.

"Don't let him go," I instruct, and tell her the phone number of the library in case she has to call me. By nine, I'm at work, and Teresa, my boss, says if I stay at my desk through lunch, I can leave around three. "Although that's still a bit early," she comments, but I'm already walking out of her office, and I pretend I don't hear.

My job is to scan all the clippings from our vertical files, using a state-of-the-art scanner donated by a professor at our local university who believes in the digital future. By now, I'm up to the Ns, and because of where we live there are a lot of clippings in the Nickel, Natural Resources, and Northern Lights files. All day I lift the heavy lid of the machine, slide the brittle articles onto the glass plate, and listen to the slow motor grind out an image that appears, pixilated, slightly blurred but readable, onto my computer monitor like magic. As I repeat this tedious task, my mind ricochets between fears: that Sunday will always be a nervous wreck, that I'll be found out and evicted, that I can't possibly love him enough, that I'll have to give him up. While my body moves on autopilot, the negative thoughts rise in my mind.

Once I leave, though, I spring into action, heading first to a pet store to get supplies, including a giant bag of kibble that I wrestle into the back of my car and then into the lobby of my apartment building and the elevator. Then I drive to the shelter, where I take my time, waiting for Liv to return from an errand. I change the cats' litters; I walk a dog named Champ, who was left abandoned in an apartment after the tenants moved, like a stained mattress, and I wander past Sunday's cage a few times, watch him watching me. He's on his best behaviour, quiet, eyes imploring, big face lying between his paws. It's like he knows. When he presses the black pads of his fore-paw against the chain-link, as if reaching out for me, that's it. I'm ready.

I find Liv at the desk, the phone pushed against her ear. She's half listening, jotting a To Do list on a steno pad. When she hangs up, she chuckles and shakes her head. "That lizard climbed into the walls again," she says, and I roll my eyes. This is the third time it's happened: an iguana an old man is hous-ing in his spare bathroom chewed its way through the holes for the sink pipes. He keeps calling us for advice, then hanging up when we suggest he relinquish the animal.

I pick up a pen, turn it over in my fingers, uncap it, cap it. "Did you get my message?"

"Yes," Liv says. I expect her to congratulate me, to eagerly hand me the adoption form, to give me the bag full of coupons and dog biscuits that everyone else gets. Instead, she fixes me with a serious stare and says, "I know you guys are in love but you know what you're getting into, right?"

Impatient, I nod.

"You remember that other guy? Had him, returned him." She reiterates the story as if I don't know it, including the part about how the shelter up North had then sent Sunday to us because they figured he'd be a long-term resident and they didn't have the space.

This seems less like a warning and more like the workings of fate. As she's talking, I walk around to join her on the staff side of the desk, grab one of the forms and start filling it in. She turns to the filing cabinet plastered with stickers printed with sayings like *My Rescue Dog Rescued Me* and *I Heart My*

Labrador Retriever, and pulls out his file, flips through the pages, including one that says that his original owner — the one who'd chained him to a tree — had fifteen days to claim him before relinquishing his rights by not showing up. I know the other parts too, but she runs her finger down the list anyway, reading out loud: serious separation anxiety, issues with men, needs behavioural intervention.

While she talks, I write my name and address. The pen scurries over the paper as I lie about the rules in my apartment building. Pets aren't allowed, but I know there's at least one other dog in the building who lives on an upper floor and barks constantly, who I've never seen outside, who must live a miserable life.

Liv goes on about challenges, about needing a plan in place, about rehabilitation. I sign my name with a flourish and count out five twenty-dollar bills, the last of my savings from the sale of my parents' house. Happily, I hand over the money. Finally, I think. A dog of my own.

Liv takes the form, skims my information, and dampens my joy with a brief lecture on being a good dog parent, telling me things I already know, that I've told other clients. Finally, she's quiet, and I see a smile twitching on her lips. She leans forward, surprising me with a hug and when she pulls back, she grips my upper arms, stares into my face and says, "You're sure? Because you have to be sure."

This could be a warning. It could also be a chance to express a little bit of doubt, to ask for help in advance, but I don't take it. This is me, I think, the one who adores animals, the one who was going to be a vet before her life got derailed, who can gaze into their yellow or brown or green eyes and read their minds. The one who ultimately earned Sunday's trust. I'll fix him. I'll show him that there's nothing left to fear.

6.

SUNDAY SITS IN THE front passenger seat all the way through the city to my place. Black tongue hanging out, nose smudging the window. At a stoplight, a man in a jean jacket and an orange hunting toque crosses in front of us and the dog goes crazy, barking so ferociously that spittle flies all over the glass, his head lunging at the windshield so I can almost see the invisible chain holding him fast. I say his name, the one he has right now since I'm still thinking about my choices — Sunday, Sunday, Sunday — and touch his bristling hackles with my fingertips. He's unresponsive, the light turns to green, a truck honks behind me, and I carry on, Sunday swivelling his head to follow the man, his barks ringing in my ear. For a split second I think about turning around, about driving him back to the shelter, sticking him in his cage again. Panic tingles in my chest. I tap the steering wheel with one finger. I breathe. I carry on.

"What'd they do to you, buddy?" I whisper as he calms down, whimpering a little bit, returning to a quieter watch of the world passing by.

AT MY APARTMENT BUILDING, I check to see if anyone's around and then open the car door, holding his leash as he jumps out. All the supplies — his food, feeding bowls, treats, and toys — wait in a heap on my living room floor. "This way," I tell him, and he follows me slowly towards the building, casting glances, licking his lips.

"Come on," I say, encouraging, and he moves more eagerly, tightening the lead, tugging hard so I feel the extension in my arm and have to grip with both hands. Across the parking lot, a man walking a kid to a pick-up in a visitor's space glances at us, then grabs the child's hand. I know why: Sunday's strong, muscular body is intimidating, his friendly eyes lost in the black of his broad face.

"You walking that dog or is he walking you?" the man calls nervously, and Sunday lunges towards him, booming out a bark. I run, I actually run, hauling him through the front door and into the lobby, praying we won't be seen. There's no one inside, but Sunday is afraid of the elevator. He freezes when the door slides open, stiffens his front legs, and refuses to move forward. Quickly, I change course, and guide him up the stairs, all eight flights, until both of us are panting. "Cookies," Liv had said before I left, handing me a new dog owner bag and a blurry Xerox titled *Adopting a Challenging Shelter Dog*. Number three on the list: don't expect miracle changes overnight. "Use liberally," she'd said, digging into a box to add a few extra, and I think about how maybe I'll build a trail into the elevator, like breadcrumbs, like Hansel and Gretel's path through the woods.

SUNDAY LIKES HIS BED, a stack of folded blankets on the floor. He lies on his side while we watch a rerun of *Magnum P.I.* I brush his fur, one stroke at a time, letting him gobble a tiny treat if he stays still and doesn't try to grab the comb with his teeth.

When the phone rings, he jumps, and when I look over at it on the kitchen wall, wondering whether I should let the answering machine pick up the call, he lunges at the pile of treats, gulps them down all at once.

"Sunday," I quietly scold, and leap up.

It's Josie, and as soon as I hear her, I remember our plans. I was supposed to be there by now.

"Oh, shit," I say.

"Mel," she whines.

"I got a dog."

"A dog?" By her tone, you'd think I'd said ostrich, hippopotamus, sea lion.

"You know, man's best friend." There's a long pause. "Woman's, in this case," I mutter.

I hear clattering, a spoon striking the side of a mug. Josie and her endless cups of tea. A drizzle of milk, lots of honey. "Hello?" I say.

"Isn't it just... Aren't you just getting settled?"

I sigh, disappointed. Why can't people be happy for me? Isn't that a crazy thing for you to do, she's really thinking. You, who couldn't even help your own brother, who took off when the going got tough, who alienated your best friend. So I shock her. I tell her Sunday's whole story, emphasizing the gruesome details, how they figure he had lived like that, abused and captive, chained up, for years. The cigarettes stubbed out on his fur, the dehydration and mange, the collar grown into his skin, the whole deal.

"That's awful," Josie breathes. "Poor thing."

"That's just it, he's not a thing," I start to say, but I'm distracted by Sunday getting up, stretching out his front legs with his butt in the air, then disappearing into my bedroom. I stretch the coiled phone cord as far as it can go to try to see what he's up to, hope he isn't peeing somewhere like Frankie did that time at a neighbour's house, into the potted lemon tree they'd grown from seed.

"And that didn't..." Josie says.

"What?"

"Wreck him."

"What are we supposed to do, Jose? Euthanize him?"

"Of course not. It just seems like a lot for you..."

I change the subject. "How's your hand?"

"My hand?"

"Yeah."

"You mean my wrist."

I nod, although she can't see me. In the winter, she slipped on a patch of ice outside her house and broke it.

"Still sore, can't use it much. They took the cast off last week but it's at this weird angle..." She keeps talking, her voice growing tiny as I pull the receiver away from my ear to lean towards my bedroom door. Sunday's curled into a tight ball against the end of my dresser, underneath my cracked-open window, asleep. My heart swells.

"You should see him," I tell Josie, interrupting.

"Come tomorrow," she says. "Bring him. Bruce loves dogs."

I don't really care what Bruce thinks, but I don't say that. She's always defending him, trying to make us like each other.

"I don't know. Maybe I should just stay home, let him get used to my space."

"You haven't been up since Valentine's." She's bored, I know, had to take time off from the video store to wait for her wrist to heal. "We can eat some good food, rent a movie, go to the Riverside and get a pitcher."

"Not with him I can't."

"Maybe we could find a sitter," she says, and chuckles. That's Josie's dream: to be a mom. The last time I was there she told me they'd been trying since Christmas.

"What's his name anyway?"

Not until right then do I decide. I've been thinking about it but when I say it out loud, my mind is made up. "Grommet."

"Oh," she breathes. "That's perfect."

There's a sudden tenderness in her voice, a soft nostalgia, and I think we must both feel the spirit of Lara, but I nudge her away, prod her out of my mind even though it was her brother who came up with the nickname for us. Little grommets, baby surfers. That was his dream: to go to California, to crest the Pacific surf, but he made do with the north shore of Lake Huron on windy days. I haven't seen the big lake in a long time, not like it would be now, breaking up, loosening to blue. "Okay," I tell Josie. "I'll come."

7.

GROMMET LOVES CAR RIDES. Not so much in the city, where people make him nervous, kids belting down sidewalks on their bicycles, mail carriers in official uniforms invading every home, but out on the highway. Once we speed up to head west, passing the *Thanks for visiting Norbury* sign, *Road Apples* by the Tragically Hip popped into the tape deck, he settles back. His breath fogs the window as he watches the stone cuts, the forests, the bits of marsh with drowned trees poking out of the punky ice. Soon he's stretched out on the back seat, quietly snoring.

A couple hours later we arrive at the subdivision off the highway where my family used to live. On the edge of the road, a large wooden sign says *Spruce Grove* in black letters against worn green paint. If I turn left, then left again, then right to cross the railway tracks, I'll end up rolling right by our old house. I don't do it. I don't need to. Not right now.

"That's where I grew up," I mutter to Grommet, as we fly past the turn. I see the place in my mind: the bungalow at the top of the sloped gravel driveway, the exterior clad in walnut–stained barn board, the minivan, my mom's burgundy car hidden in the garage. Shadows that are us moving in the windows: Matt, my mom, me, and my dad, playing out our lives as they were back then, the drama that's somehow never ceased.

Back then, that July, Josie's wedding went ahead as planned. Despite it all, despite everything. I didn't want to go. Lara came to my house, pushed me into the shower, zipped up the back of my peach taffeta dress that Josie's mom had made, which matched Lara's exactly, with the wide bow on our backsides and the big puffy shoulders. At the ceremony, a hush hung in the air, an expectant quiet, as if everyone was waiting for me to give an explanation, or at least that's how it felt. When it was time for photos at the marina, when I stood beside Josie, my best friend since she'd moved there in Grade 4, I had to tell her it was okay to smile. Her lips looked severe, a waxy red streak on her face. Behind us, the lake glittered bright blue, spreading out from our shoulders in the picture like a cape.

At the reception the air felt hot with whispers, and I could feel all the eyes on me. Matt had not come. He was in the Soo, I think, with my mom, or else trying to make arrangements. Earlier, he'd called from the funeral home to ask if I wanted to see our dad, our dad's body, and I said no. Matt went silent for a long time, so long I thought he'd hung up but then he said, "Okay."

The day was perfect. You couldn't ask for a better day. The string of good weather went on and on that summer, lasting through Josie's wedding and the funeral and into August when our aunt came from Saskatchewan, and we sat together in the living room trying to decide what to do. I'd never actually met my Aunty Doreen, and I'd expected someone different from the woman who arrived. My father had described her as strange, distant, "not a nice lady."

"You don't even know her," my mother said once, and he snapped back, "Don't pretend you were close," angry at her contradiction, at how she seemed to be taking sides.

One summer, my mother wanted us to buy a camper van and drive out West so Matt and I could meet Aunty Doreen, our grandparents, and the rest of our prairie family, but my dad insisted that we take a trip to Michigan to go to an air show instead. They fought about it for weeks, my father badgering, demanding, threatening, until my mother did what she always did: gave up, shrank inside herself. We went to the air show, the interior of the van thick with tension. Matt held my Barbie doll out the window so her golden hair was tangled and ruined, but I pretended not to care. Any tears, any complaining, would only aggravate my parents. My grandmother died in a car crash that winter and then my grandfather had a massive heart attack. My mother didn't go out for the funerals. My father encouraged her, but she set her cold eyes on him and said, "What would be the point?"

"Don't blame me for your regret," he said, and the next time Aunty Doreen came up in conversation was when Matt had to call and tell her what had happened.

She lived in Prince Albert, a place I pictured glowing with canola fields, capped by a broad blue sky, because that's what Saskatchewan looked like in the films we watched in geography class. But during conversations over breakfast, she explained that the Canadian Shield jutted out of the earth in the upper northeast corner of the province. "In fact, it looks a lot like here," she said, but I didn't listen. I couldn't yet imagine a fracture in the myth, even that myth, a stupid one about geography. Too much was already broken. Instead, I hummed to myself as I pushed down the soggy cereal Os, sinking them, letting them pop back up, almost drowned, because I wasn't hungry. By then I'd lost six pounds and felt guilty for appreciating how slim I was starting to look, when my father had been buried and my mother sat in a cell, waiting for her arraignment.

In late August, I went back to my job at the Three Aces, serving rice and gravy and chicken balls with that neon red sauce that matched the colour of my uniform, to teenagers who now buzzed with whispered gossip. The place was busier than ever, because everyone wanted to see me, speak to me. The jukebox blared April Wine and AC/DC while kids set fire to sugar packets, leaving a huge sooty mess on the tables.

I had a plan, but I couldn't tell Matt.

He hadn't gone back to school, but I barely saw him between his job and his constant travelling to the Soo to see my mother.

I knew, though, that he'd try to talk me out of it, and I also knew I had to go. I was drifting through the house, frissons of rage shooting through me, so the piles of things my mother had been dividing for my parents' separation ended up scattered and broken from the casual swing of my foot. I couldn't help it. The easy destruction gave me satisfaction, a quick crackle of relief, like a pine log popping in the fire.

It's resin that makes that snapping sound.

The same resin that solidifies into amber, trapping tiny insects.

And that was what I was afraid of. That what had happened would get stuck inside me, my life hardening around that single point in time.

In September, after Aunt Doreen left, I emptied my bank account in secret, the one full of university money. As the teller slid over the thick envelope, I wondered if anyone had even told the registrar's office I wasn't coming, but then I thought, irrationally, as if I were famous, surely they must know.

"I don't care," I told the travel agent. "I don't care about the cost."

The ticket was 456 dollars. I put the money on the counter, and within a couple of days a fat envelope arrived. Inside was a one-way ticket to Vancouver.

"I'm pretty busy," Lara said, when I called her.

"You don't have to entertain me."

"I've got two roommates."

"I'll sleep on the floor."

I heard her nodding, then the rushing exhale. "You're going to love it out here," she said.

8.

IT'S AROUND LUNCHTIME when I pull into Josie and Bruce's driveway. She's just arrived home, sits in the driver's seat of Bruce's truck, and we both get out at the same time. She comes over and hugs me with one arm because the other's wrapped in a tensor bandage, then holds a finger against the glass, peering in at Grommet. I expect him to freak out, but he doesn't. He sits inside, panting, and I open the door and clip on his leash as Josie gathers shopping bags from the trunk. I reach for one with shaggy, green carrot tops sticking out.

"Soup?"

"Curried chicken stew," she says. "Blueberry cheesecake for dessert."

Josie loves to cook. Whenever I visit, she feeds me fancy meals made from recipes she gets off a listserv on their new home computer. Asparagus risotto; fish pie. I bring wine, a few bottles usually, and it's all gone by the time I leave on Sunday afternoon, even though, with almost every glass, she says, "I shouldn't be drinking." We stay up late. Sometimes we sneak into the garage or go out onto the side porch for a Colts cigar pulled from Bruce's pack in the freezer. I like it: being drunk with her, feeling close to who I used to be back then, before, because obviously I'm different, while Josie seems the same. If I squint my eyes, I can push away the slight changes, bring back that brown mole on her left cheekbone that she had removed last year, leaving only the shiny round circle of a scar.

"Sounds delicious," I say, as I lead Grommet over to her. Immediately, he pushes his snout into her crotch, and Josie laughs, looks down, then quickly up at me, eyes bulging.

"He likes you."

"Well, I wish he didn't like me quite so much," she says, nudging Grommet's head away with her knee.

"What? Bruce won't mind if you get a little extra on the side."

Josie purses her lips. Instantly I'm sorry. Those were the words he used, after they got engaged, when he was getting cold feet. Josie hadn't told us about it until a month before her wedding when she, Lara, her cousin, and I were drunk in Norbury, at the Water Tower Motel. "Years from now," he'd said, "when we're bored, would you mind if I get a little extra on the side?" I don't know what she expected, why she even told us. She worked quickly to counter our astonished calls to cancel the wedding. Soon enough the subject was changed, and we all knew there was no turning back; it was simply too late.

Now, in her driveway, I mutter an apology. Josie turns, and Grommet and I follow her around the house to the back door that opens into a mudroom beside the kitchen. Past their washer and dryer, Bruce sits at the table eating a sandwich, and as soon as Grommet sees him, the dog stiffens. The hair on his back rises in a puffy ridge. A low growl starts in his throat, and his black lips pull back from his teeth. He looks terrifying, his gaze fixated on Bruce, who stops chewing, then swallows with a gulp.

"Now there's a face only a mother could love," he says, his eyes on Grommet, and Grommet explodes into barking.

this has nothing to do with you

Front paws fixed, he bucks, lunging towards Bruce as I hold tight to his leash.

"Sit," I cry, but he ignores me. I say it twice more, then switch to his new name, then his old one, shouting even louder, but he keeps barking, spittle flying off his lips.

"Shut him up," Bruce hollers, half standing.

"I can't."

The chair shrieks against the floor as Bruce pushes it back. Quickly, he walks over and Grommet goes quiet with surprise as Bruce reaches down and flips him hard onto his side. I hear the thud of my dog's body against the linoleum, like a suitcase dropped, a bag of heavy trash, and then I see the crazed look in his face, how wide his eyes have become, how white, and I don't even have a chance to warn Bruce who's still holding Grommet's shoulder, before —

"Fuck," Bruce shouts, whipping his arm back. There are puncture wounds in the fleshy part of his hand, and blood, streaming. Beside me, Josie sways. Josie, who's never been any good in a crisis, who fainted dead away that time a guy we knew tossed a handful of shot onto a bonfire at the beach and was sprayed with it before he could dive behind the picnic table. There was blood then, too, seeping through his Guns N' Roses T-shirt, and Lara drove him to the hospital while I dampened a beach towel in the cold lake and held it to the back of Josie's neck.

My loyalties go to Grommet, even though Bruce is standing there holding his injured hand. I crouch beside my dog, press my palms against his ribs, keep him there. He pants, then opens his mouth in a huge yawn that shakes his whole face and ends with a whimper. Bruce jogs the few steps into the kitchen and whips a tea towel off the stove. It's an Easter one and the pink eggs and fuzzy yellow chicks are soon stained from the gushing bite.

"Great dog," he says. "A real charmer."

"It's not you," I tell him. "He doesn't like men. He's scared. You shouldn't have —"

"What was I supposed to do? Let him bark at me like that? He has to learn." He bends his elbow so his hand is up at his shoulder, then juts his chin at Grommet. "That thing'll be a nightmare if you don't teach him."

Bruce, always the expert. I resist asking when he last had a dog, because I've never actually seen him with one, or heard him talk about any family pet, all the time we were growing up. "Maybe if you gave him a cookie or something." I glance at Josie, who's covering her mouth with the fingers of both hands. She's stiff with fear, like some of the animals who come into the shelter, arriving into that new, stressful space full of other panicked creatures who might do them harm. Under my hands, I feel Grommet's lungs bellowing.

"Kill him with kindness?"

"No, Bruce," I say, annoyed. "Lure him, seduce him."

They're both silent, and I feel a gush of embarrassment. Bruce hasn't had to seduce anyone ever. Josie threw herself at him, starting in Grade 10. She didn't stop until she got him, even when he drifted off, picked up another girl at a community centre dance one winter, asked someone else to prom.

"Give him that," I say, gesturing towards the remains of Bruce's sandwich.

"My lunch? No fucking way."

He turns, grabs a glistening pickle off his plate, and shoves it into his mouth. Then, hand held aloft, blood flowing down his wrist, he finishes chewing and asks, "Any chance of rabies?"

I shake my head. I'm not sure how to proceed, what will happen if I sit back, let Grommet go. "Or anything else?" Bruce says. "Maybe this is really your secret boyfriend? Do I need a silver bullet?"

It's a jab. I glance at Josie, but she's pulled herself away, slides a Styrofoam tray of chicken into the fridge. At their Valentine's Day party, they'd invited a few couples over and a friend of Bruce's, a guy nicknamed Jacko. We were the only single people, and it was obvious that Josie was trying to set us up, probably imagining the four of us going on double dates and maybe even — if I know Josie like I know Josie — having babies together, living next door to each other. He was cute, in a hillbilly, small-town, Skidoo-riding sort of way but after he made some crack about my short hair, called me Mrs. Clean, I ignored him most of the night.

Not that I'm a virgin. I've done it a few times; the first was out in Vancouver, in the tiniest bedroom you've ever seen, at somebody's place near Chinatown. A guy my friend Daisy knew, who insisted on walking everywhere barefoot. His name sounded fake, like Flame or Arrowhead. He touched my face a couple times and then it was over as quick as it started, a few small jabs of searing pain, which was surprising because otherwise, I didn't feel much at all.

It isn't that I don't want it. Love, romance, a relationship, or even just sex. But in order to get it, I'll probably have to talk about things I don't want to, answer questions I'd rather not be asked. About my parents, my family, my life before now. Live in the moment, Daisy said to me the first time we met, when I resisted her invitation, and that was the first thing that lured me to her.

In the kitchen, Bruce is still staring at me, waiting for an answer about whether or not my dog is diseased. If there was any risk, I wouldn't even warn you, I think. "You're fine," I say, and lift my hands off my dog.

9.

BRUCE IS GONE SO FAST, he practically leaves a blur. I don't expect to see much of him over the weekend. But it's not my fault. He could stay. Grommet doesn't even move when I ease up on him, just lies there as Bruce darts out of the room. When the front door slams, Josie and I watch the dog get up, sniff his way over to the table, stand on his hind legs and turn his head sideways to gulp down the crust of the sandwich. I start laughing, but when I look at Josie, her face is tight with concern.

"I hope he doesn't need stitches," she says, pushing her thin blonde hair behind her ears. "I hope you're going to apologize."

"I'm sorry."

"Not to me! To Bruce."

"I didn't bite him."

Suddenly I think of Lara, Grade 10, during her brief goth phase, the winter no one knew what had happened to Pete. Bite me, she shouted at our law teacher in class one day when he asked her to stand up on a desk, do a twirl, show off her outfit. She got detention for a week. As usual, when I think of her, shame balloons inside me, fat, crowding out everything else.

Josie opens the fridge and pulls a green pepper and a brown bag of mushrooms out of the crisper. I'm tired of how things are, I realize, how they always stay the same. Me, in her kitchen, watching her cook, trying not to think about certain people, certain times. She lines the vegetables up on the counter, starts breaking the orange skin off an onion with one hand. My gaze slides over to Grommet, stretched out on his side on the floor like he's moved right in.

"What do you want to do?" I ask.

"I have to get the stew on."

"I'm sorry," I tell her, sincerely this time. "I didn't know he'd do that."

this has nothing to do with you

"I just wish you'd give him a break."

"Grommet?" I mutter.

"No," she says, rolling her eyes. "My husband. My soulmate." I nearly scoff at her choice of words, but I don't, because I don't want to talk about Bruce and his failings, what an idiot he can be. Snowmobiling drunk in high school, hydroplaning over open holes on the lake until one day he went through and would have drowned if his buddies hadn't snapped to alertness and managed to drag him out. You don't see him like I do, Josie whined back then until eventually we stopped bothering to protest. Well, maybe Lara still does, calling from Vancouver to talk about the ocean, the mountains, art parties, and exciting dates, the big world that Josie's never seen. I don't ask about those conversations. When Josie brings Lara up, I usually change the subject. Now, she turns towards my silence, points the tip of a big knife into the air between us. "The future father of my children."

I'm grateful for the change of subject. "How's that going anyway?"

"It'll happen," she says. "When it's time."

She slices the onion in half and starts chopping, slower than usual because of her injury. Grommet lifts his head at the sound. "Want to go for a walk?" I ask, and he's up on his feet and ready. "Wait for me," Josie says, glancing at me with tears in her eyes. She blinks hard and tips her head back to stare up at the ceiling.

JOSIE LIVES ON Colonization Road, and we walk until we get to the curling rink, then turn right to go up the hill. Piles of dirty snow lie in the shadows of houses, slumped against stacks of wood, and the street is full of dust from the winter's sand trucks. At the top, we pass the community centre and the marina, and my eyes travel over the lake, skimming across the distant, dark humps of islands and a closer bulk of rock that's white with ice and guano from the gulls. We stop at the narrow beach beside the old hospital. The building is empty, built too close to the lake so the ice pushes against its concrete foundation. In my last year of high school, a bunch of us broke into that hospital one night in February, ran up and down the hallways with jumping flashlights, but now all the windows are securely boarded up, a large *No Trespassing* sign posted on the front doors.

"When are they going to tear that place down?" I unclip the leash from Grommet's collar, let him loose.

My mother ended up in there, the summer after Matt's first year at university, when I was sixteen. The hospital was eerily empty because they'd already started the transition to the new one by the water tower. We were allowed to see her, but they had to buzz us in. In the hallway, a woman cooed to a Cabbage Patch doll cradled in her arms, her face beaming, and my mother's expression seemed so dull in comparison when she looked at us, her real, live children.

It was Matt who found her, lying on her bed, the window wide open, pills scattered across the covers like candy so he couldn't be sure how many she'd taken. After they pumped her stomach and she slept for a while, she told Matt she hadn't meant it, while I listened from the doorway. It was an accident, she said, as if you could trip and swallow half a bottle of Percocet. But it had made her realize how much she wanted to live, she told him, casting a glance at me that barely made contact before sliding away.

She hadn't even left a note.

Matt offered to stay home from school that fall, but my mother refused. She was the one who told him to go. My father seemed angry, fuming behind his newspaper when he wasn't absent. His face a flat countenance at the supper table, worried about the layoffs at the uranium refinery where he worked. He only said one thing to me about what had happened, and that was, "Your mother can't leave me." But what if she did, I remember wondering. What would that mean for me?

"How are your parents?" I ask Josie. Her family always amazed me; I loved the bustling Sunday suppers with her two sisters, her parents, and her grandparents. Homemade perogies and fresh whitefish and everyone laughing and happy.

Before she can answer, I say, "Remember when your mom made us those costumes? The lion, the witch, and the wardrobe?"

"Yes! And you guys made me be the wardrobe!"

I laugh, and she bends over and picks up a rock.

"I couldn't fit through any doors, and nobody knew what the hell I was!" She tosses the stone into open water near the shore. Grommet looks over at the plonking sound, then sniffs his way along the sand, investigating a chain of paw prints from another dog. It's warm enough out that I peel off my thin black gloves, stuff them into my jacket pocket.

"The most humiliating night of my life," she says, and I laugh, but I'm thinking, Wow, you don't get out much. Then, casually, almost as an aside, she asks, "How's your mom?"

I think of ignoring her. I think of saying, Don't. Or shut up. Or mind your own beeswax, as if we're eight. Instead I tell her the truth. "Don't know," I mumble, and her eyes leave their worry all over my face as I turn away and call for Grommet. He's over by a red metal garbage can, head down, nosing into a small heap of trash. I take a step closer and when he lifts his head, I see that he's chewing something.

"Oh, shit," I say, hoping he isn't eating chicken bones that'll splinter in his gut. When I get to him, he leaps away, but I'm able to grab his tail. I pry open his mouth, thrust my fingers over his slimy tongue, trying to pull out the object before he swallows but it's too late. It's gone. All I can do is await his fate.

"Gross," Josie says, as I stand there, gripping Grommet's collar, holding my filthy hand away from my body, fingers covered with bits of what might be mouldy bread. "You must really love that dog."

"Take him?" I ask, clipping on the leash and handing it to Josie. When she has it, I cross the beach, crouch down, and sift my hands through the water, which is clotted with ice. Behind me, a car horn sounds, and when I stand, breathing again after the shock of the cold, I see a red pick-up truck disappearing up the hill, towards the highway.

"Who was that?" I ask.

"Bruce's cousin." Josie lowers her hand from a wave. I nod. Dwight. Bruce's best man at their wedding, eyeing Lara as we stood at the front of the church. "You know it'll be three years soon," she says.

I don't answer. I think, I know that. Do you think I don't know that?

"We're thinking of going to Quebec City."

"Who?"

"Me and Bruce."

I stare at her and there's a blur between us for a second like we're watching different channels until I realize she's talking about their wedding anniversary. My gaze drops to the dog. I point to a piece of wood that's bobbing in the light swell. "Look at that stick," I tell Grommet. "Get it."

Josie lets the leash go, but he doesn't move.

"We might even fly," she says. I look at her.

"I didn't know he doesn't like water," I say. "What kind of a dog doesn't like water?" Frankie would take on the whole lake in a heartbeat, swimming twenty feet from shore, soaked to the skin whenever we took him to the beach. But Grommet stares straight ahead like he's got no idea what I'm asking him to do, like he doesn't speak my language.

THAT NIGHT, Josie and I watch a movie that took us an hour to choose at the video store and isn't very good. I drink half a bottle of wine while Josie has just one glass then downs cup after cup of peppermint-licorice tea. At eleven, she says she has to go to bed. Grommet and I stay in the spare room. Since I was last there a couple weeks earlier, she's painted the walls a soft yellow, edged them with a border of dark blue wallpaper printed with smiling full moons, pointy stars. In the corner is a wicker shelf full of stuffed animals and kids' books, some with their golden spines worn down to the pulpy white paper. Grommet prefers the floor, but he stays close, so I hang my arm over the side, hold the rough pad of his foot in loose fingers. When Bruce comes home, late, after midnight, I wake and hear the quiet thump of their voices through the wall, then Josie's tinkling laughter, Bruce's deep chuckle. Grommet lifts his head, growls, and I call him up on the bed. When he doesn't come, face pointed at the closed door, panting, I drag a blanket down and stretch out on the floor beside him, squeezing the skin between his shoulders, smoothing his bristling hackles, until he settles, letting out a sigh, and sets his big head between his paws. For a long time, I'm awake, wondering what Josie and Bruce are talking about, trying to make out their words. It's an easy conversation, I can tell, and as I lie here, hip aching on the hardwood floor, I feel a flicker of uncertainty. Maybe she's happy, I think. Maybe they're even a good match.

"You're too hard on her," my mother told me once, back then, sick of listening to me gossiping with Lara on the phone. "People don't live their lives to please you."

10.

IN THE MORNING, Grommet wakes me with a single bark. A dream is floating in my head, or part of one anyway, the last flickering remains. My father, swimming in a lake. I haven't dreamt about him in a long time but there he is and I'm with him and the water is so clear that I can see huge green pike with their pointy snouts and sharp teeth, the red-speckled flanks of brook trout. My arms move through the water, touching the slimy skin of the fish, and then, I'm back on land. Standing on a slope of red rock, listening to an orchestra play the *Star Trek* theme song, trying to remember something I forgot.

When I wake again I smell coffee and bacon. Josie frying pancakes in the leftover grease. Grommet smells it too, snout lifted, wildly sniffing. He claws at the door. "Okay, buddy," I mumble, and I get up, pull on the robe that Josie always leaves out for me, and peek through the curtain. Except for my car, the driveway's empty. Bruce is gone. The coast is clear.

Grommet trots along with me into the bathroom, then through the living room to the kitchen. Josie's standing in front of her avocado-coloured stove in yellow fuzzy slippers, jogging pants, a royal blue sweatshirt with frayed cuffs, from our high school days. *Class of '91*, it says on the back.

"Morning," she says, turning, and I see our old mascot — a bug-eyed lion — embroidered on her chest.

"Where's Bruce?"

"Helping a buddy open his camp."

"That's a good excuse," I say as Grommet jumps up, sets his paws on the counter's edge, pushing his nose towards the bacon. "Off!" I yell, sweeping my hand towards him, but he doesn't move until I push past him to pick up the platter and carry it to the kitchen table.

"Maybe he thinks it's for him," I say. I snap off a crispy end, pop it into my mouth.

"Doesn't he need to go out?" Josie asks, as Grommet licks my fingers.

I glance at my dog. How could I forget that?

Outside, feet stuffed into Josie's rubber boots, I walk Grommet around the backyard. The earth is soft, and the air is filled with the cold, fresh smell of the lake on the other side of the hill. Grommet pees on the new plum tree Josie planted last spring, after they'd moved in, and on the fence near the spot where she put the enormous rhubarb plant rescued from an abandoned farmhouse where we partied back in high school. A tiny fuchsia leaf is sprouting, wrinkled like a forgotten apple. It looks so vulnerable, I lead my huge dog away.

In the front yard, Grommet takes a crap, and I look right, then left, as if I'll find a plastic bag floating in the air, but of course there's nothing. I leave it, steaming on a skim of snow.

"WHAT ARE YOU doing today?" I ask Josie as we eat, Grommet devouring his bowl of kibble oiled with bacon grease.

She shrugs, then stuffs a forkful of pancake into her mouth, talks while she's chewing. "What do you want to do?"

"I don't know."

"There's a matinee on at the show."

I jerk my head towards the dog.

"Oh, yeah," she says. A silence fills the space between us, and by the time she says, "we could..." I know what's coming. I know by the way she casually pushes a hunk of bacon through the syrup on her plate, staring down. I know because in the winter, after too much wine, I told her that in the spring, as soon as the snow cleared, I wanted to go to my dad's grave. Because I haven't been there, not since the day the dirt closed in, swallowing his coffin, when my brother stood stiffly, closed up like a cabinet, like Josie in that ridiculous wardrobe costume. Lara's dad rested his hand on my brother's shoulder as if letting him know he'd be there in case Matt had to teeter backwards, but he didn't. He stood tall. Surrounded by my girlfriends, leaning in to their scaffolding, I wept, a slide show of childhood images in my head: my father cracking jokes, piercing a worm with my hook, making a papier mâché wasp with me for my Grade 5 science fair project, teaching me to shoot a gun.

I'm turning the option around in my mind, trying to imagine what it would be like, leading my beast of a dog through Sunday mourners laying down hopeful clutches of imported tulips, when she shrugs and says, "Go to some yard sales."

I look up at her, surprised. Grommet's come over to me, is leaning his weight against my thigh, so I put my hand on his back, knead the loose skin around his shoulders, careful not to get too close to his scar.

"I think I should go," I say.

"Already?"

I nod, wipe my sticky lips with a napkin. "Matt hasn't even met him yet."

"Who?"

"Duh," I say, standing. "My dog."

Josie pushes her lips into a pout and I can tell she's going to start working on me, trying to convince me, but I'm still thinking about the graveyard. Even now, almost three years on, it still feels too soon, like I'll get out there and find a heap of fresh dirt, summer all around, my father hiding behind one of the mausoleums built for the wealthy Hixons, the lumber barons who'd founded the town. That would be so like him, pretending to be dead to make us show our concern, to prove that we love him. He used to do things like that, once letting out a long scream

from the forest behind our house when he was out cutting fire-
wood. We found him bent over, clutching his leg, the chainsaw
cast aside. Matt, Mom, and I out of breath, adrenaline sparkling
down my arms as he stood up straight and said, "I just wanted
to see if you all cared."

The phone rings, saving me from my thoughts and Josie
trying to convince me to drive around and dig through other
families' artifacts. While she answers, I wash the dishes in hot
water running from the tap, not bothering to fill the sink. It's
her mom, I can tell, and I listen as they make plans, something
to do with helping Josie's grandmother finish a quilt.

"You can come if you want," Josie tells me when she hangs
up, but what would I do with the dog?

11.

I TAKE MY TIME leaving town. Put gas in the car. Stop at the
fishery to treat myself to a bag of frozen pickerel cheeks. I'm
not certain I'm going to do it, but then I'm taking those turns,
crossing the railroad tracks, pulling over across the road from
our old house. I haven't seen it since I left, since that September
day when the taxi's tires crunched down the gravel driveway to
take me all the way to the airport in the Soo. I sat in the back
seat, window cracked to let out the sour smell of old cigarettes,
watching the place recede, wondering when I'd be back.

There's no one around. The yard's empty, the grass over-
grown around the front-yard apple tree that my dad carefully
pruned every spring until the last one, that last year. No cars in
the driveway. The paint's faded on the wooden siding. Matt had
a hard time selling it, and it went for much less than it should

have, but my parents had managed to pay off a chunk of the mortgage over thirteen years, so there was cash for my father's funeral and my mother's legal bills, and a bit left over for each of us, my portion of which he gave me when I came back.

"So there it is," I whisper to Grommet, but he doesn't care. He's looking in the other direction, eyeing a kid on a bike who's stopped on the side of the road, fiddling with her loose chain. When I swing my gaze back to the house, Grommet starts growling, and maybe he's right: maybe there's something frightening here, something I should run from once again.

Before that June, no one had ever died on me, except our grandparents out in Saskatchewan, and Pete, of course, Lara's brother. After his death, she had moved around like a sluggish zombie, her normally sharp retorts slowed, a dullness about her that was scary. The day after my graduation, I felt like that too, like I was sunk in a jar of water, and I stayed like that for a long time. Blood slow in my veins, the world wrapped in foggy plastic, although every now and then a memory would tear through, puncturing the skin. Sometimes I wondered about the other family too, what they were thinking, what they were going through, and if we'd ever have to meet them. Matt told me her name, and I read it in the newspaper too, saw her picture. Celia White. The other woman, the dead woman, my dad's lover.

I sit there, staring at the house. It seems like an image from a dream or a memory I can't quite place. Sometimes the past is like a wide, soft marsh that looks deceptively solid, but with every step water floods your insoles, soaks through the skin of your shoes, and the sensation of sinking shakes your solid footing.

Yours, meaning mine, of course.

My past, my shoes, my swamp.

Because we aren't talking about you.

This has nothing to do with you.

part three

1.

LARA LIVED IN East Vancouver, around the corner from the poorest postal code in Canada. We bought our groceries at busy sidewalk markets in Chinatown, where smashed tomatoes smeared the sidewalk and the smells of fish and rotten vegetables and delicious cooked meats hung in the air. Coming from a small town like Hixon River, we discovered many foods we'd never seen before or eaten: durian, with its surprisingly foul aroma, hot pink dragon fruits. Even avocados were exotic, because we didn't have them in Northern Ontario. And then there were the junkies. Milling around outside the hotels or gathered on the wide front steps of the library at the corner of Main and Hastings, their coats flung open to the autumn damp, a twitchy desperation in their skinny, striving limbs.

Lara's apartment took up the first floor of a house. She had two roommates and they were all busy with school, creating colour wheels or writing essays or making sculptures out of clay, chicken wire, egg shells, old electrical components, and whatever other junk they found inspiring. Lara was mostly into drawing though, filling pads with careful sketches of hands, and in her bedroom, where I hid out most of the time, she had a wooden model with moveable joints that stood on the dresser, head cocked, hands on her hips. I called her Tabatha and talked to her as I tried to figure out what to do. I could tell Lara felt guilty about not being around, but she also defended herself, talking constantly about the intense school load and all her assignments. Eventually, I started thinking that she wanted me to leave. Stubbornly, I resisted. Where else could I go? I settled into my nest of blankets on the shag carpet in her room for a few weeks and then, when I needed money, I got a job at the ice cream parlour, which was where I met Daisy.

Right off the top I'll tell you that Daisy was odd. She dressed in a crazy assortment of patterns and textures, and I picture her wearing a paisley wrap skirt over faded bellbottom jeans, Birkenstock sandals, a pale blue *My Little Pony* T-shirt with navy piping on the edges of the sleeves. Her blonde dreads piled high, held with beaded hemp cord. At the ice cream place, which she visited a few times a week, she feigned decision making. She asked for sample after sample, and Andy, the guy I worked with, the two of us dressed in our matching pink-and-white striped shirts, would glare at her as he handed over tiny pink plastic spoons of coconut, green tea, soursop, and other exotic flavours. But she wasn't stupid. When you could almost see the steam shooting out of Andy's red ears, she'd order a single scoop of plain chocolate, paying with coins counted out on the counter, pennies and dimes and crumpled American one-dollar bills that I later learned she earned from panhandling downtown.

One day, when I finished my shift, I walked up to Commercial Drive, looking over at the snowy mountain peaks as I headed to the Co-op. I needed to replace Lara's lavender deodorant, because I'd used it up, and that morning we'd had a fight. A ring of drummers in the park was playing within a thick mist of pot smoke. I eyed them, intrigued. Feeling, I guess, like they would understand me. Like them, I was an outcast. The ties binding me to an ordinary life had snapped but still hung there, frayed and awkward. I wasn't sure where to attach them.

Lara looked down on nouveau hippies, as she called them. Lazy, she said, looking for easy answers, believing that *going with the flow* was more meaningful than figuring out what you wanted and working your ass off to get it. "Those are the sorts of people," she said one day, as we walked to the movie rental place, "who wake up in a decade realizing how much time they've wasted."

"It's the ice cream lady," a voice called as I moved past the park, and I turned to see Daisy prancing towards me, barefoot, the hem of her skirt flapping over her bellbottoms. They were filthy, I realized, the cuffs a deep, muddy brown. She lifted her hand in a sort of flat-palmed wave, and, unintentionally, I repeated the exact motion as if we were saluting. She laughed and then I laughed. When she beckoned me over, I hesitated. "Live in the moment, sister," she said, and I followed her back to her group.

IT WASN'T LONG before I started dressing like Daisy and doing the things that she did. I set up a shrine in the corner of Lara's room, made from an upside-down cardboard box covered in turquoise fabric, with a white porcelain Buddha on top.

"So you're a Buddhist now?" Lara asked, when she saw it. I shrugged. It was something Daisy and her friends talked about, and in the park, cross-legged under the long, snaking arms of some type of pine tree, I was trying to learn how to meditate.

It was hard, the not-thinking. When I shut my eyes and tried to focus on my breath, tried to hit the off switch in my brain, faces swam up through the current: Matt's, my mother's, my dad's, even Lara's, eyebrows raised, irritated and asking questions. Most of the time, while Daisy chanted, I played mental games, working to remember the lyrics to TV theme songs I liked as a kid or challenging myself to name every teacher I ever had or writing imaginary letters to Matt that always started with *I am fine, how are you?* and usually petered out into blank pages. Sometimes I got so tired I fell backwards and went to sleep, ignoring the ants that crawled all over me.

"It isn't supposed to be a battle," Daisy said, scolding. Later, when Robert taught me, he told me it wasn't possible to stop thinking. That instead I needed to learn to stay calm and just watch the thoughts that flowed by in my head. "Don't try and stop them, watch them," he said. "Try not to fear it. Not by might, but by spirit."

I pretended to listen to his instructions too, but really I just kept doing what I had to: filling my head with whatever swarming thoughts I could find. Anything to block out those faces I didn't want to see.

2.

GROMMET LICKS MY FACE until I wake up. The green numbers on my alarm clock say 6:14. I groan, shove him, and he lies down, panting hard, staring at me. When he barks, I'm up, throwing the covers off, stumbling as I pull on my jeans, hauling a red T-shirt over my head. I get my jacket on and shove my feet into my Doc Martens, but don't bother lacing them.

We take the stairs, and twice I have to stop him when he lifts his leg on the landings to pee. Outside, we wander the edge of the parking lot, where he sniffs at patches of snow in the surrounding granite slope before leading me onto the street. For a second, I think of turning right, walking the few minutes to Matt and Angie's, surprising them, letting myself in with the hidden spare key and putting on a pot of coffee if they're still in bed. I didn't call them yesterday, hadn't arrived on their doorstep with the pickerel cheeks as I intended to do when I got home. Something held me back: Matt's distance the other night, and the thought of their serious faces directed at me, at Grommet. Angie, who never had pets growing up, and Matt, judging me: what's she gone and done now?

BACK IN MY APARTMENT, Grommet watches me as I dress for work, the radio on, the D.J.'s jabbering voice echoing the early morning noises in the building. Head on his paws, lips drooping, eyes studying my every movement, he looks like he knows that something's up. I talk to him, tell him the plan.

"I have to go to work. I'll be home soon. You can do it. You'll be fine."

I don't bother with the dishes from the night before and from breakfast, leave them heaped in the sink, the sides of the saucepan covered in sticky white foam from a poached egg, crumbs all over the cutting board. Before I go, I dump a scoop of kibble into his bowl, make sure he has enough water, then close the door with a soft click, as if I can disguise my disappearance, as if he won't notice that I've snuck away.

AT MY DESK in the glassed-in office in the library that looks out at the reference stacks, I spend a couple hours processing a pile of new books, then leaf through the weekend newspaper and cut out a few articles. Finally, I return to the tedious task of scanning, and when my boss, Teresa, pokes her head in and asks me how it's going, I smile as if I'm having the time of my life.

"Great," I say, and ignore my rumbling stomach as I lift a clipping off the glass plate.

"Lunch soon?" she asks.

"Working through," I tell her. It's easier for me to leave an hour early than to race across the city at noon to walk Grommet and have to turn around almost right away. She raises her eyebrows but doesn't say anything. I'm not sure what that means.

I SUPPOSE IT ISN'T surprising. I suppose I should have expected it, but after I race home to my building and swing open my apartment door, I'm still stopped in my tracks. There's a puddle of yellow urine on the kitchen linoleum, and the living room carpet is covered with a spread of demolished books. Even the *Detection of Poisons* box is there, one corner chewed to its pulpy interior pages. The letters have slid out and are sitting in a neat stack by the wall as if Grommet set them there, as if this is a ploy to get me to read them. It would have been easier if he'd eaten them too, their ink blurred by his slobber, paragraphs mashed in his sharp, strong teeth. Instead I have to touch them, hide them away once more, refuse all over again to read them, to allow my mother her excuses.

Grommet doesn't seem to know he's done anything wrong. There's no hung head, no slinking away, no tipped up, apologetic eyes. Instead he races over to me and shoves his body hard against my thighs, panting so hard that he drools onto my boot. I reach down and lightly touch him, feeling a cold ball in my throat. Then I clip on his leash, make sure the coast is clear, and take him outside.

THE NEXT DAY, there's more destruction. My bathroom towels shredded to ribbons, a puddle of diarrhea on the red carpet in my living room.

On Wednesday, I find my bougainvillea plant overturned, soil tracked everywhere, the blooms a mash of bright pink petals like torn up party streamers. Grommet runs away as soon as I come in, pushing against the glass door that goes out to my balcony like he's hoping he can melt right through it, find freedom, run away.

That evening, we walk. We walk until my knees ache, until he's too tired to pull, until the sky has stopped pulsing neon blue, and all that's left is blackness. And still, we keep going. Inside the chain-link fence of a baseball diamond I let him off leash to fetch a ball. He watches it fly overhead, bright yellow like a finch, and barks, lunging angrily when it hits the ground and bounces. He doesn't know how to play. He runs over to sniff it. I wait, a cookie clutched in my hand, ready to reward him when he picks up the ball in his mouth and brings it to me, but he doesn't.

"Come here," I call. He just stares at me from across the field. I can't take it anymore. I jog over, crouch down and grab the ball, jerk it aggressively back and forth between our faces. "This is fun," I snap, startling him. He flinches and tries to pull away, but I'm holding firm to his collar, knuckles rubbing the tough scar. Right then I feel a crack in my heart, remembering our time at the shelter, how he'd slowly let me get close to him, when he trusted me, when he loved me. Now his eyes are wary, watching me, the one who's imprisoning him. It's like he's been waiting for me to show my true colours, to snap.

Could that happen?

Could I be transformed into an animal abuser, swinging a boot into his ribs, extinguishing a cigarette on his fur?

Anything's possible, I think, from the deep well of my frustration, the betrayal I feel. I sit cross-legged on the damp, cold ground, cover my face with both hands, picture the gun in my mother's grip.

3.

I DON'T KNOW what to do. All I can think is to keep trying, keep my head down, push forward, hoping sooner or later things will click into place. Grommet will get used to being home alone. He'll sleep instead of destroying my stuff. We'll settle in together, a happy family.

This is, after all, what I learned growing up: don't admit there's a problem, pretend everything's fine, lie if you have to, don't rock the boat.

So I hold to the bucking hull, and the next day, Thursday, I come home to find Mrs. Slater, the old lady who lives in the apartment next to mine, standing in her open doorway.

"You've got a beast in there," she says, jerking her head towards my apartment. Her coiffed white hair does not move. I clamp down on the frisson of panic that surges inside me and pull out my key, playing dumb, sliding my eyes from her face to the wall like I'm looking for whatever creature she's talking about.

"I've got a goldfish," I lie, "and I might have the left the TV on, for him."

She crosses her arms. Dark arrows of rouge colour each of her cheeks, and I wonder if she applied it just to talk to me. Her lips gleam with a fresh coat of lipstick. We stare at each other until, thankfully, her phone starts ringing, and she pulls back, shuts the door. But she's still there, I know it, know that the phone cord can stretch far enough that she could be standing on her tiptoes, watching me through the peephole. I move slowly, pretend to be sorting through my mail, mostly flyers, the telephone bill, until a few minutes have passed and she's hopefully moved on. When I shove my key in the lock, I hear Grommet gallop towards the door, and my heart sinks. Every day I try to enter quietly, hoping he'll be sleeping. When I hear him race away, I turn the key, bracing for whatever destruction I'll find.

When I flick on the light, my mouth drops open.

My couch has exploded. The upholstery ripped apart, torn bits of foam erupting out of holes dug deep into the cushions. A powdery yellow drift spreads across the living room carpet, the kitchen linoleum, and the air smells pungent, like dirty feet.

Grommet stands in the corner beside the bookshelf, his fur spotted with flakes, his eyes tipped up nervously to meet mine. He's trembling, I see, and I realize that he's becoming used to this moment: me coming home, getting upset and angry. He's growing afraid of my reaction, of me. So far, this is the only training we've done.

Consciously, I uncross my arms, then lick my lips, imitating the body language that dogs use to diffuse tension, that I've recently read about. He yawns fiercely, his face quaking, and I yawn back. Slowly, he plods over, pushes his big body against my leg.

"What happened here?" I whisper, touching the velvet softness of his ear.

Shoved between the couch arm and what remains of one of the cushions, I find the scrap of a plastic baggie holding a scattering of parmesan cheese. Grommet found it on the counter, I deduce, dragged it to the couch, ripped it open, and dug in, soon unable to determine what was parmesan and what was yellow foam from the couch cushions, coated in a delicious cheese scent.

Surrounded by the mess, I pluck the phone off my kitchen wall and dial. Liv answers right away.

"Norbury No-Kill Animal Shelter."

"It's Mel," I say. "Grommet ate my couch."

"Who?"

"Sunday."

"What do you mean?"

I explain what happened and she starts laughing. Then when I say, "last weekend he bit my friend's husband," she laughs even harder, once I tell her it wasn't serious, he didn't need stitches, although I don't actually know.

Behind me, Grommet barks. I turn, trying to shush him with my hand, knowing that Mrs. Slater is probably leaning her ear against the other side of my wall. He's on his hind legs, pawing at the glass as a seagull flies by. I stretch the cord over to the TV, and turn it on to Much Music, playing a video of the Cranberries.

"I don't know if I can..." I say, and realize right then that I'm actually really close to tears, but Liv interrupts. "It hasn't even been a week. You knew it wouldn't be easy."

But the confession erupts out of me. "I'm not even allowed to have pets here, and I have to go to work during the day, and I can't leave him at night, I can't go out anywhere, I can't even keep volunteering with you..." I take a breath, expecting her to say something, to ask for clarification. What do you mean dogs aren't allowed? The shame of the lie — or, more specifically, the lack of full disclosure — has heated my cheeks, and I chew my bottom lip, waiting for Liv's anger. But all she does is sigh.

"You have to figure it out, Mel," she says.

I try again. "But maybe I'm not..."

"Jesus," she says, all laughter now gone. "Really?"

Neither of us speak. I rip a fingernail with my teeth. I want to say: he isn't at all like Frankie. He won't even let me scratch his belly. He doesn't like water. I can see the panic in his eyes.

"I have to go," Liv says. "Somebody found a litter of puppies in a garbage bag at the dump. He got them out just in time, although the one at the bottom was dead."

The horror of that sits in me for a second, and then, puppies, I think. Maybe I should have opted for a blank slate, a dog I can...I fumble to find the words to say this out loud, to present this as an option, but she's hung up before I can even tell her that I won't be there tonight for my regular Thursday shift. The dial tone bleats loudly and in the corner of my eye, I see Grommet's ears perk up, twitching to locate the sound.

When the phone rings again, I lunge for it.

"I'm sorry, Liv," I say, ready to tell her that I'll try harder, that I still love him, that he's still my dog, but I don't hear anything on the other end except the distant rumble of my brother's voice, saying something about mushrooms and extra cheese. "Matt?"

"Mel?" Matt says, too loud, nearly shouting. I pull the handset away from my ear.

"Can you do me a favour?" His voice is loose and sloppy, like a braided rope that's sat too long in water. I tense, alert to strangeness. "Can you tell Ang that I'm a good guy?"

"What?"

"That I'm a good dad. That I'm not like our dad."

"Okay," I hear Ang say, stern, and then there's a fumbling rustle for the phone, Matt laughing, a high-pitched cackle I've never heard before.

"You're a good dad," I say, but neither of them hear. He is a good dad because he's a good person. You're the best of us, my mother said to him, her slender hand clutching his across the table so hard her knuckles were blanched. That was the last time I'd seen her.

"Mel?" Ang asks.

"What's going on?"

She doesn't answer.

"Has he been drinking?" I look at my watch. It's 4:46.

"We're planning a party," she says, as if that explains his behaviour. "At first he didn't want anything and now he does."

She sounds tired. I pinch the skin on my forehead, close my eyes. "Shit," I mutter, because I missed his birthday. It was yesterday. I'd been looking forward to it too, to taking him out for dinner, doing something fun. The last time I helped him celebrate was in 1990, after Mom had driven down to Toronto to get him, to bring him home for the summer. Mysteriously, they came back sick and injured, Matt with a purple and yellow bruise on his jaw, my mom claiming she had food poisoning and disappearing into her room for days. "You should see the other guy," Matt joked, but I never found out what had happened. Maybe I asked, likely I asked, but neither of them gave me an answer, and my dad said nothing about it. That night, April 20, I stuck a candle into a bowl of macaroni and cheese and gave him the new Sinéad O'Connor cassette that I'd actually bought for myself. We watched the tribute concert for Nelson Mandela that Matt had taped, ears alert to movements in the house, listening for potential arguments.

This time, though, I don't even have a gift for him. For a split second I think of giving him Grommet. They have a backyard, a big enough house, and Angie is home most of the day. But she's already told me that she isn't a dog person. In the winter, we heard about a toddler mauled by a husky in Alberta and had an argument over who was to blame.

"Dogs give signals," I said. "It's not like they just attack."

"This one did."

"It didn't. There would have been signs. We don't know the whole story."

Angie went quiet, her jaw hardening, reminding me of my father, and also my mother, because of how Angie retreated. She stood up, pulled the plates off the table, carried them and the remains of the casserole into the kitchen. We didn't continue the conversation, but the next time I was alone with Matt, I tried to talk to him about it. "Leave her alone," was all he said. So I did, because I could tell she wanted to hang on to her fear.

Maybe a fish would be better. A lonely Siamese fighting fish with bright, fluttering red or green fins. A couple of silver tetras. Something to remind him of who he used to be, how much he'd enjoyed keeping fish when we were kids, how our mirror-lined basement den had glittered with the colour and light of his aquarium, filled with blue-green chromis, orange and blue Australian Damselfish, the Lubbock's Fairy Wrasse, that magical red and yellow creature with twinkling blue eyes that we called the fairy fish.

Josie, Lara, and I had played Mermaid in that room, running around until my mother stomped on the floor upstairs, warning us. Different from other mothers, who'd bring us celery sticks stuffed with raisin-studded peanut butter or bake chocolate birthday cakes filled with saran-wrapped quarters. She'd rather we hadn't been in the house at all, I'm sure, that she could have kept the space to herself, danced away the hours in the room my father had lined with mirrors for her when I was seven. For what? So she could practise and stage a solo dance performance in the high school gymnasium, selling tickets during the annual ice fishing derby? Raffle off a snowmobile as a door prize? None of that mattered anyway, because it wasn't long before he'd taken the room away, filling it with furniture and a second TV.

"The party's tomorrow night," Angie says.

"I'm not sure." I already know I can't possibly go. How can I leave Grommet that long on his own?

"Short notice, I know, but like I said."

"It's not that. It's . . ."

She waits. When I don't continue, she says, "And wear eighties clothes. It's an eighties party."

I roll my eyes. "Already? Whose idea was that?"

"Whose do you think?"

"The eighties were only five years ago."

"And yet things are so different."

I'm not sure what she means: fashion, politics, music, or herself. Her own life or Matt's. "There's so much more, Midge," Matt said to me the first time we talked after he moved to Toronto — a seven-hour drive south of Hixon River — to go to university. There was a breathlessness in his voice, an excitement, his future beginning while I stayed behind, hiding in my room.

"Come for him," Angie says. "It's your brother's birthday."

Guilt surges in me. I take a deep breath. "I got a dog," I tell her.

She's silent. In the background, I hear Matt playing a boisterous game with Ellie. Throwing her up and down or swinging her around. She's shrieking with glee.

"Go easy," Angie says, muffling the phone. Then, "What kind?"

I pick at the loose edge of my counter. "A mastiff mix."

"Aren't those really big dogs?"

I look over at Grommet, stretched the length of the glass door onto my balcony, chin on the floor, black lips sagging. His copper and pitch coat littered with cheese he hasn't completely licked off. I'll have to bathe him, I realize, and I wonder how that will go. I think of telling Angie his whole sad story, but then there's a dull thud; the baby starts to scream.

"I'll see about the party," I tell her, but she's already hung up. I set the phone into its cradle, refill Grommet's water bowl, and when I turn back around, he's up, lifting his leg in the corner of the room.

4.

GROMMET'S SO TIRED when we return from our walk that he lies down on the landing of the fifth floor and won't budge. I try to lure him with a Milk-Bone, but he ignores me, his face flat and bored. I prod his butt, pick up his hind end, shove him forward, but when he snaps at my arm, I stop, plunk myself down on the cold step and start to cry.

"You win," I tell him, when my tears are done, and still he just stares at me, an unreadable expression in his eyes. I push my knuckles into his flank. "You little fucker."

I know I need to talk to someone. I wish Robert had a phone in his shanty, if he's even still there, squatting beside the creek. I'm a failure, I'd say to him. I can't do anything right.

And he'd say: Failure is relative to what you desire. Find an alternative and cut loose from quagmire. Or something like that. Or maybe he'd ditch the rhyme scheme, which he did when he got comfortable, when it got in the way of what he needed to say.

Truly, though, it's Matt I need to talk to.

Matt who knows me, who can help me get grounded and figure out how to move forward. He's the one who's more or less always had his shit together, the most together person in our whole family. It's obvious, isn't it? By how he's managed to build a solid life with a loving wife, a baby, while I still seem to be sinking.

But then, he's different now too.

Hiding out in Angie's room, smoking pot, drunk in the afternoon when he should be at work. If I'm honest with myself, I'll admit that he's no longer the same person, the brother I long to lean on. It's a bit like he's been taken over, like in a science fiction movie where only a person's true intimates can see that their soul's been swapped out, that an alien is hiding in their skin. Where's the real Matt gone?

"How can I ask him that?" I mutter, and Grommet's brown eyes flicker between me and the dark stairwell as if he's trying to figure out the answer. He doesn't have the solution, and neither do I, not right now, not stuck here, in this limbo between floors. We sit there for another twenty minutes, and in the echoing space, I practise what I might say to him: I think we should talk, we never talk. Long awkward silence. Then, "What do you want to talk about?"

He used to talk. Back when we were kids. Spinning stories at the dining room table about his day. Debate club, a mock trial in law class. Excited about his life. My mother would ask him questions while my father sank further and further into a pout, jealous at the attention Matt was getting, I suppose. Eventually, he'd pick a fight, ask pointed questions designed to play devil's advocate, to challenge Matt beyond what he knew. I'd sit there, shrinking into the background, wishing I could leave. Why didn't I? Sometimes it was easier to hide in plain sight, wait for the moment when no one would notice as I slid underneath the table.

Other times, my mother leapt up, escaping into her bedroom, and Matt flicked his fingers at me, instructing me to bring her food. A spaghetti dinner I'd made that was watery and disgusting, one night, late in our story, that my mother glanced at dismissively, her face red and tender with anger that sparked easily into rage over stupid things, like how I hadn't properly cleaned the kitchen counter or taken Frankie for a long enough walk.

Back in the dining room, Matt stared down at his food, letting the noodles slither off the tongs of his fork. My father ate mechanically, quickly, slurping the sauce. When he finished, he said, "I've got things to do," and pushed back his chair.

"Like go see your mistress," Matt muttered. My eyes lurched up, but if my father heard, he ignored him, was already halfway through the kitchen, sliding his plate onto the counter beside the sink for one of us to wash. I lowered my meal to the carpet for Frankie.

MY MOTHER HAD told me a couple months earlier. "Affair," she said, and I looked all around the room, at the orange velour chairs and the antique grandfather clock, things I'd lived with for my whole life, and said, "I'm sorry."

Her laugh was sharp, a cutting cackle.

"Don't do that," she said. "It's got nothing to do with you."

But of course it did. They were my parents. I don't know what she thought: that she'd raised me separate from her, strung me up in a chrysalis. That once I broke through, I'd flap away, never to return. As if. Even back then I knew I'd be snagged in those branches for years.

Three months later, in June, my father still hadn't left the house. He was sleeping in the bedroom in the basement while my mother had begun sorting their shared property. There were piles in every corner of every room — china dishes, books, records, photographs stripped from old albums leaving clean white squares on the pages where no dirt or yellow age had adhered. Everything was shifting, and I felt like I was living at the bottom of an ocean, attuned to the echoes of sound all around, the surging movements far above, but largely in the dark. A little bit like now, sitting on a cold concrete step in the hollow space of the empty stairwell with my stubborn dog.

"Oh, Grommet," I say, massaging the muscles around his spine, calling him a good dog. I stand, but he still won't budge, so I sit again too, rub my fingertips against my cheekbones, cup my hands over my short, soft hair.

"Why are we here?" I ask. He groans, settles his chin on his front paw.

What am I doing? Working a job I don't like, trying to care for a dog I can't manage, forgetting my own brother's birthday.

For ten more minutes, we sit there. Then, I hear voices rising, smell pot smoke and pizza. A group of teenagers comes around the bend of the stairway, one of them swinging in a wide arc with her hand on the railing. They hesitate on the landing below when they see me, and a girl quickly drops the roach she's holding, smears it to charcoal with her shoe. A boy by her side holds a pizza box like a tray, a jean jacket draped over it. They were laughing but now they've stopped, and a growl starts in Grommet's throat. I can feel the vibration in my leg; I lay my hand on his back.

"Just visiting my grandmother," I lie. "She loves my dog."

Slowly, they climb towards us, then scurry past. When they've started ascending to the next floor, I get an idea and call after them to ask if I can have a slice. The girl's black eyebrows pop up on her forehead as she looks at me, but the boy jogs back down, whips the box open like a magician. Further up, I hear giggling.

"Help yourself," he says, and I do, realizing when I bite into the hot cheese and salty meat that I'm famished. I gobble half of it, then dangle the rest in front of Grommet's face. He follows me eagerly up the rest of the stairs.

5.

ALL NIGHT LONG, trying to sleep, I'm haunted. By my father, Matt, my guilt around Grommet. I'm only twenty-one, but already I feel like I'm messing everything up, like mistakes are piling around me, and I can't shake the shame of the past week. The way Grommet's looked at me every day that I tensely entered my wrecked apartment, before quietly starting to clean: picking up the mangled pages from books, the chewed up TV remote, the garbage dragged out from under the kitchen sink. This is all your fault, his expression seems to say. Not enough exercise, attention, fill in the blank. Abruptly, I sit up, switch on my bedside lamp, and look at him, curled in the spot he likes, against the side of my dresser. Is my place too small? Is that it? Is he so used to being outdoors — the branches of the oak tree spread over him, his back against that sturdy trunk — that he feels claustrophobic, closed in? I get out of bed, go into the living room, and position his blankets beside the sliding glass door so he can lie there during the day and watch the clouds. It's something. But I doubt it's enough.

IN THE MORNING, when the sky's tinted a deep rose, I get up. It's just after seven. There's a heavy weight in my chest as I pick up the phone and dial, expecting to have to leave a message, not sure what to say. I'm surprised when Liv answers. Before she can dismiss me, I say, "I thought we wanted what was best for the animal."

"Yes," she says. "And you convinced me that you are the best for the animal, and I saw by Grommet's behaviour that he thinks that too."

"Well, I think you might be wrong."

"Maybe, but maybe you could try a few other things before you give up."

I don't answer. Grommet wanders out of my bedroom to stand beside his empty kibble bowl, already adjusted to that part of his routine. Regular food, something he wasn't provided in his previous life.

"He isn't a new car, Mel. You can't drive him around the block a few times then decide he's not for you."

"I know," I say, because I do, but committing to Grommet has made me realize my own limitations, that I'm not much more than a kid without parents. If I knew Liv better, I might tell her that, and also how scared I am of screwing up, and how I'm not sure how I'll live with myself if that happens. I'm struggling to find words for all of this when Liv says, "Give it a few more days, okay?"

I nod.

"Okay?"

"Okay." My voice is choked. I want to be agreeable, enthusiastic, but I have to ask. "What about that guy. The trainer who took him for a walk?"

"What about him?"

"Maybe he . . ."

"He said no. He thought he needed too much rehabilitation." I hear the curl of irony in her voice. He, a certified dog trainer, thought he couldn't and yet I . . .

"There is a woman near Massey who fosters though."

I nod, eager. "Yeah?"

"But that would be relinquishing him again, and you don't want that, do you?"

I look around at the wreckage of my apartment. "No," I say quietly, after a long pause.

I GET OFF THE PHONE knowing Liv's right but still not sure that Grommet and I have a happy ending ahead of us. I love him, I do, but the whole thing feels like a huge mistake. After a quick shower, I bring him outside for a fast walk, then sneak him back upstairs and have to wait for the hallway to clear before we can make the mad dash to my apartment.

"Fuck it," I say, grabbing the phone again when we're both safely inside and Grommet's gobbling his breakfast. It's Friday, and if I can stay with him for three whole days, maybe we'll turn things around. I call the library, and when Teresa answers, I tell her I'm not feeling well.

"Oh, no," she says. "That came on quick." The day before I'd been fine, standing outside the back door of the library during my break, face up to the throbbing spring sun.

"I know. I'm sorry." I flinch. Sick people do not apologize.

"Well, I hope you feel better," Teresa says. I hear the touch of pity in her voice, the easy acceptance, and it makes me remember. I'm the girl whose mother murdered her father. I can do whatever I want.

GROMMET AND I don't do much. We lie on the floor together, watching *Polka Dot Door* on TV, and then I do the dishes and flip through the yellow pages looking for a pet store, still thinking about getting that fish for Matt.

Around eleven, Angie calls me. "I was at the library," she says. "Teresa said you're sick."

I groan.

"Are you really?"

"Food poisoning maybe," I tell her.

"Can I come over? I'll bring you some ginger ale."

I look around my place. It's still a disaster: a leftover drift of dirt that I haven't swept up, the couch's pitted cushions wrapped in black garbage bags, the leg of my coffee table chewed to splintered wood.

"I don't want to pass on any germs."

"I thought you said food poisoning."

"I'm not sure."

Angie sighs. "Well, I hope you're still coming tonight."

I close my eyes, press my fingers against my forehead, wish it really was hot. How much I'd love to crawl into bed, burning up, and not have to take care of anything, anyone.

"You haven't even called to wish him a happy birthday."

"I know, Ang, I'm sorry. This dog..."

"The dog ate my homework?"

It's a joke. She won't understand. She's never had pets, not even a gerbil or a cat. I can't tell her anything.

"It would mean a lot to him if you even just made an appearance," she says, and I can tell by her formality that she's pissed off. I grab the phone cord and turn around, leaning my lower back against the counter, and see that Grommet is on the blankets that I put by the door, belly up, legs splayed. Relaxing, maybe? Maybe getting used to his home?

"Okay," I tell Angie. "I'll try."

6.

MOST OF MY STUFF from before is at Matt's. He and Angie kept what they thought I would want and packed it into boxes that are stacked at the end of their laundry room. I haven't opened any of them. I don't need to. I have x-ray vision and can see right through the cardboard walls to my hot pink Barbie corvette, Winnie the Pooh piggy bank, Shamu the killer whale stuffed animal, and all those Xeroxed band posters Matt had stripped off telephone poles in Toronto and mailed home to me. Clothes are in there too: jeans patterned with floral prints, skinny leather ties, desert boots, fanny packs, plastic banana hair clips.

I could find a costume there, but I don't have it in me to open them, so I load Grommet in the car and head out to search for eighties clothes like the neon orange sweater I'd bought with my allowance one shopping trip to the Soo. When I'd held it up to show my parents, my dad had shielded his eyes. "Getting ready for hunting season?" he asked, and then ordered me to return it. I argued. It was my money, but he said I couldn't have an allowance if I wouldn't spend it with good sense. I hated him right then. His control, how he'd bring us to Dairy Queen after something like that, pretending nothing was wrong, and I had to smile, be happy, be appreciative, with rocks in my belly. In the store, I got a refund, then used a bit of it to buy a bright yellow tank top. Before I returned to the car, I went to the washroom near the food court and put it on under my clothes. It was a secret. It didn't matter what he did, because I knew. Deep down I was radioactive, deep down you couldn't touch me because I burned like the sun.

I DON'T KNOW HOW Grommet will be, left on his own in the car, so on the way I stop at a pet store. There's a shelf full of Siamese fighting fish in tiny glass bowls, cardboard between each one so they can't see each other and hurt themselves trying to attack. I'm in too much of a hurry to decide between the one with the shimmering blue fins and the orange one puffing its side gills at me, so I just grab a treat for Grommet. In the Salvation Army parking lot, I unwrap the meaty cow bone and set it on a sheet of newspaper on the back seat.

"Look at that, Grommy," I say. "Yum!"

He doesn't even glance at it. He looks at me like he knows I'm trying to trick him, refusing to eat it but betrayed by the drool that runs from his lips.

"I'll be really fast," I tell him. By the time I reach the store, he's already barking.

My hands fly through the racks, hangers clattering. Within ten minutes, I've got a pair of acid-washed jeans, a green cable-knit sweater with a wide neck that will droop over one shoulder, and a long string of white plastic pearls to knot between my breasts. I don't try anything on. The outfit costs me seven dollars and putting it together, remembering how I used to dress, is even kind of fun.

Grommet has not touched the bone. The newspaper beneath it is shredded. Grease spots speckle the grey fabric of the seat, and there are gnaw marks on the gear shift. I touch him lightly on the back of his head, and he cries out, a high-pitched plaintive whine that sounds to my ears like I'm sorry, I'm sorry I'm like this. My eyes smart. I toss my clothes in the back and drive all the way across the city to let him run along the frozen beach as the ice, broken up near the shore, tinkles like chimes. By the time we get to my apartment, he's calmer, and has discovered the bone, and I can barely manage to carry it, and everything else — my bags, the handle of his leash — because he keeps leaping up, convinced I'm now taking it away.

"Stupid dog," I say. "Dumb dog. You have to wait!"

I picture Frankie in a neat, square sit, waiting for my father to give him the command to eat his dinner, saliva sliding from his lips like thread. How did he do that? For a quick, stabbing moment I wish that I could call him, say a few forced niceties to his girlfriend, listen to his footsteps as he walks to the phone.

"I'll come right over," he'd say. "I'll show you how it's done."

But of course he wouldn't. Even when I was a kid he didn't

have the patience to show me. The few times he helped me with my homework I ended up in tears because I couldn't grasp the math equation or keep my cursive on the line. And if life was that different, I wouldn't even be living here. I'd be down South; I'd have finished three years of university. I'd be well on my way to becoming a vet. I'd know so much more than useless facts like how dogs' nose prints are as unique as fingerprints and every dog's skeleton has 321 bones. I'd know how to help Grommet get better. I'd have a fulfilling life.

I GET DRESSED while Grommet is on the living room floor, in the dead centre of the room, gnawing. I put on a mixed tape of eighties music that Josie gave me for Christmas, smear blue eyeshadow on my lids, use gel to spike my short hair.

When I'm ready, I do an experiment. I pull on my jacket and move to the door, and instantly Grommet is up and alert, the bone abandoned, staring at me. I put my hand on the door-knob, and he charges forward, pushing to leave as I do. I stop. We stand there for a minute, and then I let out a long sigh and say his name. When he sees how I'm defeated, something in him releases. He moves back to the living room, lies on his belly, returns to the bone.

"Psych," I whisper, watching him chew, listening to the crack of the bone. I turn the doorknob again, and he's beside me in a flash.

Angie answers the phone. "I can't come," I tell her.

"Mel."

I rub my forehead, touch my crunchy hair. "I want to, but the dog."

Ang muffles the phone for a second and says something to Matt. Ellie gurgles, then shrieks happily. "Hang on," she tells me, and I hear the phone clunk onto the kitchen counter. A second later, Matt picks it up. "Midge," he says, and he hasn't called me that in so long I thought I'd never hear it again.

"Matty," I burst out, blubbering, and everything comes out, everything about the dog. When I'm finished he doesn't speak. I push my fingers against my eyes and they come away black and blue from my makeup. "I'm sorry," I say. "Happy birthday."

"Listen," he says. "Do you remember when we'd take Frankie over the border? When we didn't have his papers?"

I nod. I'd started nodding as soon as he started talking, reading his mind.

"I guess I could try that," I mutter.

"See you later then," he says, like it's decided. Angie's voice is a muffle in the background. "And pick up some ice."

I HATE THAT I'm going to do this. Liv would hate it too. If she ever found out, she'd probably take Grommet right back, no questions, no complaints. I think about calling her instead to ask if she'll look after him for me tonight, just this once, but the thought of her frustration with me on the phone this morning makes me cringe. I can't keep trying to negotiate with her; I have to make this work on my own.

I crush the pill, mix it with peanut butter, stir the sticky mess into his regular bowl of kibble, add hot water from the tap. All the while I sing to him, moving my body in time to the music. Just before I put the bowl down, I say, "This isn't a long-term solution. This is only for tonight. This is only the one time."

He doesn't care. He's drooling.

He eats it all in less than ten seconds, and I go to fix my makeup, taking my time. When I come back, he's passed out on his blankets. I turn on the television, put the knee bone beside him, and leave.

7.

ANGIE MEETS ME at the door. She's holding a martini glass, the drink inside it glowing a deep pink, a plastic sword skewering two maraschino cherries that still have their dark stems.

"Did you bring the ice?" she asks, talking loudly over Tears for Fears. I lift my hands because they're empty, and remember suddenly that I also forgot to get Matt a present, even just a card.

"It was one thing," Angie says.

"Sorry." We stare at each other.

"It's not like I don't have stuff on my mind," I say. Angie tips her head, eyebrows raised, and I know what she's thinking: Try having a baby.

"Well, you can help me with other things," she says, and turns towards the living room. I follow her gaze through a clutch of people slugging back beers, and there's Matt. He's holding a green Jägermeister bottle in one hand and a TV remote in the other, and he's facing the small black and white set on the stereo cabinet that used to belong to our parents. On the screen, the talking news anchor is followed by the still image of a man with a wide face, a thick moustache, a beret on his head, who I recognize as General Dallaire. I can't hear what's said, but Matt shakes his head, points the neck of the bottle towards the TV, then guzzles. When he drops his arm, the dark liquid pours out on the carpet in a stream, and Angie swears, fumbles her drink into my hand, and springs away, running towards the kitchen for some towels. I take a sip; sweet, cold vodka sings in my mouth.

Matt's made an effort. He's wearing bright pink MC Hammer pants with the crotch hanging down, a black mesh shirt over a white tank top, and gold chains, lots of them, when his only jewelry in the eighties was safety pins, fastened to his favourite jean jacket. There's a guy standing near him who didn't dress up at all. He's definitely currently in fashion with his black pants, billowy white silk shirt, hair dyed white-blonde and slicked back with gel. He's the one who takes the bottle from Matt and sets it on the dining room table, where *pour some sugar on me* comes bleating out of a ghetto blaster beside a pile of scattered cassettes. The ribbon has come out of one of them, is splayed over the wooden surface like a loopy black squiggle of illegible script.

Carefully carrying my drink, I push into the crowd to snap off the television set. Angie and I arrive at the same time and she drops a tea towel onto the puddle as I step closer to Matt. When I take the remote control out of his hand, he stares at me, and his sudden, surprised grin is startling but then I remember how I look: spiked hair, blue eyeshadow. A little bit like back then, minus the permed and feathered hairdo I had through most of the eighties. More punk. He, in contrast, seems very different. Apart from the weird outfit — one he never, ever would have worn back then — I've never seen him so drunk.

"Midge!" he calls, grabbing me in an awkward hug so more liquid drips on the floor, this time pink. Somebody plucks the glass from my hand as Matt curls his arm around my neck and bends me into a headlock like we're kids. I'm pushing on him, trying to get him to release me, when he shouts, "You know what my crazy baby sister did?"

He's talking to the guy with the bleached hair who's standing so close to my lowered face that I can smell him, a mix of clinging cigarette smoke, spicy cologne, but everyone else gets quiet and even the music seems to fade.

"She drugged her fucked up dog," he hollers. I close my eyes, wish I hadn't come. He's laughing now, a crazed, hysterical cackle that's about a lot more than being drunk, and I pull back my elbows and shove him as hard as I can, feeling, as I do, how skinny he is. The hard, pronounced edge of a hip bone.

"Whoa," he cries, as he stumbles back, losing his balance. His friend catches him, pulls him away, and I slip free from the loop of Matt's arm as if a link's come loose, been broken.

8.

MATT'S FRIEND COMES outside while I'm on the back porch. A few other people are out there — girls on the lawn, one of them pumping her bare legs on the squeaky swing in the corner of the yard, and Angie's cousin Beth who I've met a couple times — but I'm alone, standing at the deck railing, arms crossed. It's warm enough that I'm not freezing, but I'm glad I wore the sweater and jeans.

Silk shirt guy is holding two beers, and he hands me one and starts to say something, but his voice is drowned out by screaming as a crowd rushes inside to dance to Frankie Goes to Hollywood. Beth's teased her hair so it's huge, her bangs an inch tall and erupting out of the pulled-up hood of her sweater, and her friend's dressed like Molly Ringwald in *The Breakfast Club*. It's a weird flashback, seeing all these costumed people, turning the eighties into a caricature. The Cold War, I think. Prince Charles and Diana's wedding. The start of AIDS. Real life things we witnessed, mostly from afar. It's only been a few years, but it feels like a lifetime ago, even for me, barely out of my teens.

"You're Matt's sister," I hear when the patio door slides shut, dulling the inside music.

"Unfortunately," I say, still pissed off.

The guy shrugs. "He's cutting loose. It's his birthday."

"Two days ago."

"Close enough." He gazes at me, and the attention spreads warmth through my body. "What'd he mean though, about the dog?"

"I've got no idea," I say, taking a long swallow of the beer.

He tugs a pack of Camels out of his pocket, flips it open and holds it out to me but I shake my head. "You just got here, right? From the desert or some shit?"

"Yeah," I say, and I start to tell him about Sedona, as the flame from the lighter refracts in the mirrors of his deep brown eyes. He cuts me off. "Why'd you come back to this shit town?" He waves an arm, gesturing at the pines around us, the city beyond. "All I've ever done is try to get away."

I shrug. "It's not so bad."

"Can't get ahead though."

I look at him.

"As a musician, I mean." His hand rises, fingers tapping his chest, the bare spot beneath the few undone buttons at the top. "As a writer."

"You're a writer?"

He glances to the side and shrugs. "I write a bit," he says, looking down as ash scatters across the worn boards of the deck. Spontaneously, I reach for his cigarette, and he hands it over, ember pointing up. Smiling, he watches me.

"Well, I could tell you some stories."

"Could you now?"

"I'm Mel." My name leaks out with the smoke. My head swims, and I step a tiny bit closer to him.

"Owain."

"Owen?"

He shakes his head and his gelled hair doesn't even move. An earring glitters in his left lobe. "Owain," he says. "It's Welsh."

"Welsh. From Wales."

He smiles, a sexy smirk he's really good at, and doesn't bother answering. That, I think, was a stupid thing to say.

"I'm quite the world traveller," I tell him, sarcastic, but hinting at what he already seems to know about me: that I've seen things, I've been around the block. I'm practically holding my breath, waiting for whatever will happen next, how this flirtation will develop, realizing how much I want it. This is the first time in a long time that I've met someone who seems interesting and it's on the tip of my tongue to tell him about Grommet, make my confession, but right then the glass door slides open and Beth steps out. She's stripped off her black hoodie to reveal tight layered tank tops knotted at the waist, gold crosses and chains tangled in her sweaty cleavage. Owain swivels his head towards her. When she whispers into his ear, he nods, looking past me towards the woods at the edge of the backyard.

"Walk?" he asks, pinching his thumb and pointer finger together. I'm tempted. I haven't been high in ages. Not since that last night with Robert, when the bed of coals in the fire-pit opened up and inside I saw Matt's face, knew I needed to get home. The drugs had started affecting me unpredictably by that point, sometimes making me scared. When I smoked, I would shiver so much that I'd end up wrapped in all the sweaters and blankets Robert and I owned between us. Even then my body leapt around in a frantic, spastic trembling I couldn't control.

Has it been long enough? Am I cured? If Matt can do it, why can't I?

Another image from the eighties pops into my mind. That egg sizzling in the frying pan. *This is your brain on drugs.*

I turn to walk into the forest with them but am stopped by a rapping on the door. It's Matt, a bottle in his hand clattering against the glass. A woman pulls back his arm, and I see her glancing around just before Matt lurches sideways, then drops to his knees, starts crawling under the dining room table.

"Are you your brother's keeper?" Owain asks as I brush by him. The words sound rehearsed, like a question he's spent the whole night thinking up. For a moment, I'm torn. But it's Matt. "Rain check," I tell him and go inside.

MATT DOESN'T WANT to come out. He's sitting cross-legged, shoulders stooped so he'll fit under the table, rocking back and forth. Angie's on the phone, answering a question from the babysitter who's looking after Ellie at her house, and she flicks her fingers at me as if I need to be told what to do. This disappearing act was always my trick when we were growing up, and the space feels familiar, the ceiling of pale, unvarnished wood, and my initials, still there, scrawled in a heart with O.Y., Oscar Youngfox, the guy I had a crush on in Grade 8. I point at them, but Matt doesn't follow my finger. Closing his eyes, he leans his head against my shoulder, nuzzles into my neck. Acting like someone else, not Matt, not my brother who likes to keep his distance lately, it seems.

"Midgey," he says. "Innocent Midgey, always in the dark."

His words are slurred, bleeding together, but still mocking. I feel myself harden.

"What do you mean?" I ask, hesitant, whispering beneath the loud music and the party crowd singing along. I wish I was in the living room with all of them, feet pounding, jubilant. He doesn't answer, because he's already slipping away, sliding out of consciousness.

OWAIN AND BETH drift inside the forest, their clothes standing out against the dark pines. Like fireflies, I think, watching the flicker of his pale shirt through the kitchen window after I've helped Angie and her friend's new boyfriend get Matt upstairs to bed. I should go too, walk home, check on Grommet, sleep beside him in my lonely, wrecked apartment, but the thing that's drawn me towards Owain hasn't yet settled. With Matt acting so weird, nothing feels normal, everything feels on edge, like a hole has opened, the size of that Jägermeister stain in the middle of the living room, and none of us yet know what's down there, least of all me.

This sense of impending doom is familiar. I grew up with it: always ready for my father's temper to flare, to find my mother up to her neck in a quagmire of depression. What I need right now is distraction, I think, so I wait her out, Angie's cousin Beth, the Madonna look-alike, and stick around as Matt and Angie's other friends start to leave. I wipe spills off the furniture, wash glasses, gather drinks, and around midnight, I follow Owain downstairs.

I'm a bit drunk, so it's easier. I go right up to him, put my face in front of his, eye to eye. For a split second, I worry that I've read him wrong, that I'm about to be dismissed, but then his hands are on my waist, working under my loose sweater, and he leans in to kiss me. It's been so long since I've been touched that I find myself sliding fast into the moment, falling easily onto the couch. Something hard presses against my hip, and he pauses, pushes me back, tosses a black pager onto the coffee table, then fumbles for my sweater again, reaching into the warm space between the fabric and my skin, and then there's Angie, shouting down at us over the thumping, shivering sound of the Smiths' *How Soon Is Now* sinking through the ceiling.

"Matt says don't forget about the dog."

this has nothing to do with you

I bolt up, pull my hands out of the silk of Owain's shirt.

"Mel?" Angie calls.

"Yeah," I holler. Owain's still got his hand under my bra. Over his shoulder is the orange and brown pattern of our old couch, the one that used to be in our living room, where my dad would sit and read the newspaper, set his coffee on the back edge, leaning it against the wall.

"I have to go," I say.

"I could go with you."

I almost agree, then I think of Grommet, sinking his teeth into Bruce's hand.

"He's challenging. My dog."

"Did you really drug him?"

"He doesn't like men."

"Did you?"

I hesitate. "It was only Gravol."

Owain gives me his sideways, flirtatious smirk then squeezes my nipple so hard I suck in my breath. He pulls his hands out of my clothes and shifts around, adjusting his pants before shoving my arm.

"Get the fuck out of here then." Reluctantly, I leave, feeling inside me the weight of that tiny chaotic universe where my heart lives. Ready, so ready, to go bang.

AS SOON AS the elevator door opens, I see it: a bright white paper taped to my door. It's a letter from my next door neighbour, Mrs. Slater, signed by five other tenants whose names I don't recognize. *This is to remind you*, it says, *that DOGS ARE NOT ALLOWED in this building and we have now informed the landlord.*

My hand is shaking as I try to slide the key into the deadbolt lock. Grommet does not come, but the smell hits me and I gag:

sour vomit and diarrhea on the kitchen linoleum that I nearly step in before I snap on the light.

Grommet's on his side on the living room carpet, panting hard, froth like sea foam on his black lips. "Oh, shit," I cry, running to him as he struggles to stand. His legs are shaking, but he licks my face with a paper-dry tongue and gives a weak swish of his tail, then groans before collapsing near a pool of yellow bile by the couch. "I'm sorry, I'm sorry, I'm sorry," I sputter, as I release his head to the carpet, weeping harder before I catch myself, needing, right now, some control.

Even a half-dead Grommet wants food so when I hover an open jar of peanut butter near his nose, his eyes flicker open and he moves towards it. Slowly I lead him, leash on, into the hallway and even onto the elevator where he upchucks another small bit of bile before we hit the ground floor, go outside to my car.

9.

"I COULD HAVE killed him," I wail to Angie on the phone the next morning. The radio is on in my apartment, the D.J. speaking softly, introducing each classical music piece. Grommet's asleep on his bed. I've been awake all night, and only just got back from the emergency vet clinic where they took blood, put an IV on him and watched him while I dozed in the waiting room. It was quiet, apart from a guy who burst in around five a.m. with a cat wrapped in a soiled white towel. He left an hour later, waking me with a blast of cold when he pushed through the door. Stunned, he paused in the parking lot, staring down at the empty towel in the grainy blue light of dawn. The vet told me how lucky I was. No permanent damage. But I felt his eyes on me as I walked my groggy, slow dog to the car.

"You're doing your best," Angie says. She sounds like a machine, like I've put a quarter in the slot and those are the words that come out. I hear bottles clinking, imagine her pushing them back into their cardboard box.

"How's Matt?"

"Still sleeping."

I worry the skin on my forehead, pinching it, letting it loose. Then I tell her about the letter that was posted to my door.

"Mel . . ." she says.

"What?"

"That might have been something to consider before you got a dog."

I don't need this. The lecture. I told you so. What did you expect? I don't say anything when there are other things I want to ask her: Who is Owain, and how can I see him again?

"I have to go," Angie says. "The house is a mess and I have to go get Ellie. I'll send Matt over when he wakes up."

"What for?"

"Goodbye," she says, and sets down the phone.

part four

1.

DAISY BELIEVED human beings belonged to tribes according to their eye colour, and since we both had hazel eyes, we were on the same wavelength. She made me practise a meditation where we sat cross-legged, our knees touching, and stared at each other. Eventually, her features grew grainy and soft, like a TV with static. When that happened, she said, we were seeing each other's deepest essence. Often, I turned into a small child or a skull, she told me. For me, she became a lion or an old man. If you can get closer to that primordial part, she said, you'll attract your best reality, the one that will teach you what you need to know.

Lara thought she was full of shit.

"If we attract our own reality," she said, "does that mean people magnetize blankets full of small pox or AIDS or sexual abuse or cancer or concentration camps..."

She fumbled for her smokes, which had slid into the couch, and even though I lifted my hands to press them over my ears, she wouldn't stop. "...Or a murderous wife or a random fall in the woods that kills you," she hollered, so I would hear, and then the lighter snapped.

I stared at her. She glared back. I wouldn't let her take this away from me. Very calmly, I said, "Maybe there's something we still need to learn." I meant her, me, Matt. Even my dad and her brother, who'd died for their own mysterious education, of a gunshot wound, a tumble into a crevice in the woods.

"No guff," Lara said. "No sting, no honey, but that's the law of nature, not each of us somehow responsible for all the crap in our lives."

I didn't answer. She sucked on her cigarette, and I waved the acrid smoke away, wondering what I'd see in her if I gazed deeply into her black eyes.

DAISY AND I spent more and more time together. Eventually, I gathered my stuff into a couple of boxes and a duffel bag and moved out of Lara's. I left my job at the ice cream parlour and busked outside the art gallery, collecting change in a hat while Daisy did dance routines that she thought were amazing but which were truly bad, I knew, because of my mother. At night, most nights, we crashed at her friend Darryl's tiny, dank apartment off Cordova, near Chinatown.

Seasons passed. Autumn, then winter. The damp grey sky closed in on me for a while, and it was tempting: the bloom of joy on people's faces that I witnessed after the quick slide of the needle. Now and then, when I found myself plunging under the surface, I made my way back to Lara, and in April I knew I needed to see her one more time before Daisy and I left for California.

When she opened the front door, she eyed me up and down, then stepped back, gesturing into the house. "Go have a fucking shower."

There was tea waiting when I finished, and a salmon sandwich. I asked her if the fish was farmed, and she rolled her eyes, didn't answer. I knew it was, and I tried to resist, but my hunger got the better of me and soon I was cramming the bread and fish in my mouth. I talked around the delicious mash as I told her our plan to head to Northern California where Daisy's stepfather lived. We'd stay for a while, help him with his gardens, learn to live off the land. It seemed like a dream after the hard city, the constant rain, the sadness I kept seeing, trying not to. Lara studied me as I talked, her face steady and analytical, not giving anything away.

"How?" she asked.

"How what?"

"How will you get there?"

I thrust my thumb up.

"Oh, yes," she said. "Two young women hitchhiking through the States. What could go wrong?"

That winter there'd been posters all over the city, pinned to library bulletin boards and growing soggy on telephone poles, of Clarisa MacLeod, a twenty-year-old tree-planter who'd disappeared while hitchhiking to Nelson. Nothing bad like that would ever happen to me, Daisy told me, because I was too evolved. I didn't ask her about the hard stuff I'd already been through because that would mean I'd have to tell her about my parents, what had happened. It was a relief to let my own past go. I felt like I was becoming someone new, a person who was easier to live with; Daisy had even given me a new name. We'd done a ceremony at Wreck Beach where we burned a piece of paper with Melony written on it in gold sparkly gel pen and scratched my new name — Turquoise — deep into the sand, then filled in the grooves with sea shells.

"Turquoise?" Lara said. "Like the rock?"

"It's highly protective against negativity," I muttered, but I didn't meet Lara's eyes.

"Have you talked to Matt?" she asked after a moment. I flinched. "How will he find you if you start going by another name?" I couldn't tell if she was serious or making fun of me. We sat there for a while. There was a bag of chips on the arm of the couch, not quite empty, and I mashed my fingers into the crumbs at the bottom, licked off the salt. Lara took the last drag of her cigarette, then stabbed it out in the giant glass ashtray on their coffee table. Big tobacco, I thought, the brainwashing they do, and I looked at my friend with pity as I picked up my cup of mugwort-mint tea.

"I have one last exam," she said.

"So?"

"So maybe I'll come."

I laughed, a quick surprised cough that jolted my cup so the hot liquid splashed on my leg, soaked through my hemp pants, which were dotted with stains. "You hate her, you hate me, and now you want to come."

"I don't hate you, Barnett. I can buy a car. I can drive."

She lit another cigarette. I eyed it; I eyed her. Despite my best intentions, like I was still a little bit who I had been, back with her, back in high school, I reached out for a drag.

"Besides," she said, handing over the smoke, "it's an adventure."

2.

IN MY ROOM, I pull the curtains and climb into bed. When I pat the blankets, Grommet jumps up, circles twice, then settles, curled into a tight ball. I want to haul him up to me, stretch him out so I can feel his heart beating against mine, but I don't push my luck. Instead, I settle for moving my feet close, and he shifts his head, rests his chin on my ankle. We sleep, then, through the morning, all the way until around noon, when my phone rings. Grommet starts barking while my landlady leaves a message, and I have to listen hard to hear her telling me her husband is out for the day but to go talk to her. I groan, swing my legs out from under the covers, and sit there for a few minutes, Grommet growing tense and alert, before deciding. I might as well get it over with.

I bring Grommet because I'm hopeful, thinking that maybe Mrs. Mehta is an animal lover. We take the elevator, and the vomit's still there, dried to a dark green grime. He comes easily this time, as if he knows he has to stick close to me, that the stakes are high. It's a relief not to hide, but nobody is around, not even in the lobby.

The sounds of a television grow louder as I walk down the first-floor hall, until I recognize the goofy babble of Barney, that purple dinosaur, singing a stupid song about colours: *Orange! It's the colour of an orange!* When I knock, the sound abruptly fades and there are two little kids clustered behind Mrs. Mehta's legs when she opens the door. They're the same height as Grommet, and when they see him, they shriek and run deeper into the apartment, hiding behind a blue couch. Grommet's ears flatten against his head. He looks up at me. He's still not himself, and slobber dribbles from his panting mouth, but that might also be caused by the smell of frying butter. His nose twitches at the air. Mrs. Mehta watches all of this, and I expect her to reach her hand down, let him sniff her fingers, but instead she closes her door a bit, and I can see that she's afraid.

"This is the dog?" she asks.

I nod.

"You can't get rid of it?"

Grommet lies down because I'm not moving. "I don't want to."

"You can't have a dog in the building. People are complaining."

"What about the other one? The yappy one on the tenth floor."

She shrugs. "I don't know about that."

I look down at Grommet — his brindled black and copper fur, his dark face, wrinkled forehead, wide back. "Well, I guess I'm moving out then."

Mrs. Mehta nods easily at my decision, pulls at a bit of dried dough that's stuck to her thumb. "You can have until mid-May," she says, and points. "But it has to go right away." Her eyes are on me, not Grommet.

"Him," I say.

"Pardon?"

"It's a he."

"He goes."

"If we're quiet, can we ..."

She crosses her arms, and my eyes are distracted by the shimmer of a gold ring, but I can see that she's scowling.

"All right," I agree, although I've got no idea where he'll go, unless I drive him to another town, another shelter, and leave him there to regress, to lose that much more trust in human beings. For sure, Liv won't take him. I guess I'll sleep in my car if it comes to that. It's not like I haven't done that before.

Mrs. Mehta smiles and tells me to wait. She turns, letting the door swing shut, and when she comes back she's holding a grease-stained paper lunch bag. Grommet's nose swings higher, sniffing crazily. I smell curry, and it reminds me of the meals that Liv brings for her dinner at the shelter. "Samosas," she says. "Not for the dog. For you."

"Thanks." I reach for the bag, but she pulls it away, lifts it almost over my head.

"Not for the dog," she repeats, before she gives it over, lets me go.

Outside, in the parking lot, I sit on a bench bolted into the rock. I eat the tender, warm pastry, the spicy filling, and watch Grommet watching me, tracing the movements of my fingers to my mouth. Feed him as normal, the vet had said, so I hesitate for only a moment before letting him lick my fingers, then setting a chunk of potato on the ground for him to gobble up. I wipe my greasy hands on my jeans, try to figure out what to do.

HALF AN HOUR LATER, Matt finds me, still sitting there, still trying to come up with a plan. When Grommet sees him approaching, he's up in a flash, springing forward so aggressively that he lurches back on his collar, and once again I envision the chain that held him, rocking the tree to its roots. But instead of barking, this time he just lets out a long, low growl, which I choose to see as progress. I reach out and press a finger on his tailbone, trying to make him sit. He doesn't.

"So this is your famous new mutt," says Matt, taking his sunglasses off, revealing the brightness of his blue eyes against his ashen face. A shadow of whiskers spreads over his chin, and his hair's growing long, I notice, curling like little wings over his earlobes. There's a single samosa left, and I toss the bag to him, but when he opens it, curious, I see him swallow and lean back, and I remember him retching last night, gagging, as he stumbled towards the bathroom.

"Feeling good, eh?" I say, then flick my finger between him and Grommet who's still on alert, still ready to rip this new guy's face off, his lips trembling against his teeth. "Give it to him."

As soon as Matt reaches into the bag, Grommet shuts up, carefully observing as Matt sets the samosa down on the ground.

"This is my brother," I say, before I let loose on the leash. Grommet inches forward, then gulps down the pastry in a single swallow. He looks up at us and belches, making Matt smile. "Indian food as a training tool," he says. "That's new."

He sits on the very end of the bench, three feet away, fine by me since I'm still a bit angry. Probably Angie's sent him up to apologize, but what's the point of that? He was drunk. I'm fine. It's fine. I'm about to broach the subject, tell him in advance that it's okay, shrug away my hurt, when he pulls a pack of Camels out of the deep pocket of his green army jacket, slides one out and lights it with a fancy silver Zippo. I stare, my mouth gaping open, unable to find words. Matt, smoking. My brother, who won first prize in a Cancer Society art competition for his collage of rotten lungs, surgeon general warnings and magazine ads of sexy people smoking under a watercolour wash of red, who would lecture my father whenever he lit a rare summertime Colt.

He ignores me, gazing straight ahead like nothing strange is going on, focused on the pull of the smoke, the steady inhale and exhale. Exaggerated brackets have formed around his mouth, I noticed when I first came back, as if he's several years older than twenty-five, just turned.

"So," he says. "Things are very bad."

It's a statement, not a question. I nod anyway. Angie probably told him about my wailing phone call, but slowly it dawns on me that he might have something to tell me. About Angie?

My niece? Or maybe, I think, a shiver of cold fear spreading through my gut, about my mom?

"The UN's pulling out."

"What?"

"Even Dallaire has to go."

Rwanda, I realize. He's talking about that, about a crisis that's so far away it hardly seems real to me, especially because, for us, it's unfolding on the television set. I don't know what to say. Matt's hand is resting on his knee; he looks down at the building ash.

"It's hard to just watch," he says, and taps the smoke so the pillar shatters, light as feathers, light as air. But what else is there? I think. What else can we do? If I were my mother I would nod eagerly, and we'd start making some sort of plan. That was probably what had happened, all those years ago, when Matt came home for the summer beaten up, our mother ill after she'd driven to Toronto to get him. Maybe they'd gone to a protest, a demonstration. Cops in riot gear. Batons swinging. But why wouldn't they tell me about it? A wave of exhaustion crashes over me. I look down at Grommet licking a mashed green pea off the ground. He crawls under the bench, tucking his head between my ankles, and I reach down to touch his ear.

"I have to move," I say. Gently, I tap the side of my shoe against my dog's arm, near the small grey patch of bald skin where they'd shaved him to put in the IV. "I need to find a place where I can keep this guy."

"Oh," Matt says. "You mean my place."

I hesitate. Then, as if he's already told me he wants to help, as if we're on the same side, I say, "Maybe if you told Angie his story."

"I don't know his story."

I start to tell him, but he holds up his hand, palm out.

"You're not the only one who isn't paying attention," he says. "It's exhausting. This fucking apathy."

Matt's jaw is tense. He pulls out his cigarettes again and when he offers them to me I shake my head and say, coldly, "I don't smoke." Like we're strangers, like we've just met. The lighter flares, and his eyes skim over the parking lot, my apartment building, taking it all in like it's just a big mural. His knee jerks up and down, blurring the print of his work boot in the beaten earth around the bench. I stare at him, this alien wearing my brother's skin. After a minute, I say, "Can I ask you something?"

"What?"

"What did you mean about my being always in the dark?"

He whips a glance at me. "What? When did I..."

"Last night."

He shakes his head. I don't wait for him to dismiss it, make his excuse for not remembering. Instead, I blurt out my next question: "What happened to you and Mom that time she drove down to Toronto to get you?"

He sucks on the cigarette. As he exhales, he says, "I told you."

"No, you didn't."

"Food poisoning."

"That was mom. You had these..." I gesture at my face.

He looks sideways at me. "Midge, that was how many years ago? It was a stupid kid thing. I was a stupid kid. I don't want to..."

"What did you and Mom talk about that day?"

"What day?"

I bug my eyes out, lips pressed together, my face saying you know the day I mean. The day I graduated. The last day of normal life.

"Why?"

"I'm in the dark."

"You know what happened."

I nod. My mother's instability. My father's affair. She pleaded guilty. Case closed.

"Or are you finally getting ready to talk to her?"

I shake my head, fidget on the hard planks, my rear end growing sore.

"Because that would make sense," Matt says, nodding steadily, agreeing with this version of reality. He lifts the cigarette to his lips, again and again and again. Beneath me, Grommet's started farting, and I wave my hand against the smell, but Matt pulls his cigarette away from me, scoops the drift of smoke with one hand.

"When did you start that anyway?" I ask.

He shrugs. The silence yawns open between us. Finally, I get to the next thing I want to ask him. "Your friend Owain," I start.

"A bad influence," Matt says, and flicks the butt away. Grommet's head leaps up and I wrap the leash twice around my hand.

"He's a writer?" I ask.

"Songs. Little ditties. He's no Bruce Springsteen."

Maybe Matt doesn't know him that well, I think. Maybe Owain keeps quiet about his talent. Maybe we'll pack my car and move to Nashville, buy a ranch, and he'll get discovered at the Bluebird Cafe. "Mel?" Matt says. He's standing now, without me even noticing, holding something out, a tiny scrap of paper.

"Mom's phone number," he says. "At the prison. You need to talk to her yourself."

But I don't take it. It stays there between us, flapping in Matt's fingers until he scissors them open, lets it go. The paper flashes across the parking lot like a scared little animal, still wearing its white winter coat.

this has nothing to do with you

THERE'S EVIL in the world, our mother said to us once. We were at the dining room table, the TV on in the corner of the living room, David Brinkley delivering a special bulletin about a bombing in Beirut. Carnage on the screen, soldiers standing on the remains of shattered buildings, a crater opened in the centre of the city from the truck bomb blast. After she spoke, her eyes studied Matt's face as he watched the screen over her shoulder. Her wide forehead was lined with slight wrinkles, worry lines, although I wouldn't have called them that then. They were just part of who she was. She tapped her fork against the edge of her plate and drew in a breath to say something else, but my father pushed his chair back and walked into the living room to snap off the television set, to close us in to our immediate surroundings. Frankie, who'd been lying beside me, waiting for dropped macaroni noodles, bits of ground beef, scrambled out of the way, and I felt the air shift, felt the danger in Matt swinging his gaze over to my dad. Eye contact. Hackles up. I pushed a green bean into my mouth, mashed it with my teeth, swallowed the cold pulp, felt it drop inside my body.

"Sit up," my mother snapped at me. I'd slouched down, on my way under the table where I knew I could safely hide out with the dog.

3.

MATT'S TRIED TO get me to do things before. When I was out in B.C., he attempted to convince me to come home, phoning again and again through the fall, over Christmas, and into the wet winter before I moved out of Lara's. He gave me lengthy reports about where things stood, and a lot of details I can't remember anymore because I would zone out, following Daisy's advice to only let in what sustained my soul, to resist negativity. I'd answer just enough to make him think I was listening, and it was easy until he'd start saying things like, *She misses you. She asks about you. She wishes you'd come home.*

It's not like I hadn't seen her.

I'd seen her. Once, at the jail in the Soo. The clanging doors opening and slamming shut, the eye-watering odour of chemical cleaning solutions overlain with cigarette smoke.

My mother pale and drawn and very skinny. How could she have lost so much weight in only a few weeks? Her hair unwashed, a fat lip turned a splotchy purple, and a black eye.

Matt didn't react to her face at all, which told me that the injury wasn't new. It dawned on me that some of her injuries might have been inflicted by my father or his girlfriend as they fought for their lives. I thought I might throw up. Just in case, I stood beside a green metal wastebasket in the corner, its riveted seam dented like someone had tried to pry it apart. One of the guards came over to me, and I looked down, studied how the bright black of my new Chinese slippers had been muted by the parking lot dust. I listened to Matt's calm voice, explaining things to her, and what I wanted, more than anything, was to leave. To vanish into the peeling paint on the concrete wall. To blow away like dust. My father had been in the ground for two weeks by then and our house was filled with a weird silence.

"But you're going back?" I heard Mom ask Matt. "To school?"

Matt said something about her lawyer. He was all business, his voice clipped and clear in his explanations of procedure. He should have been wearing a pinstriped suit, silk tie, polished brogues. Him being in that role gave me the strength to try to sit down across from her, but when she reached for me, her fingers ticked with tiny cuts like she'd been counting the days off on her knuckles, I pulled away, put my hands in my lap, felt them trembling. Her eyes filled with tears. The chair's rubber feet screamed as I pushed back, got up, went through the door when the guard opened it.

That was the last time I saw her.

My name called out in her sad, desperate voice, hanging in the air as I ran.

4.

IN MY APARTMENT, Grommet goes immediately to his bed and lies down. The vet had said he likely wouldn't be himself for a few days. As I was paying the bill — five hundred dollars that I didn't have, that I had to put on the credit card I got a month ago — he told me to make sure my medicines were locked up, because of course I'd lied. Of course I'd told him Grommet found the Gravol on his own, digging into an old cosmetic bag under the bathroom sink. I make myself an instant coffee with lots of cream and sugar and open the newspaper to the classifieds.

My father taught me to take the path of least resistance. He gave me that advice a couple times, once when I was worrying about whether to stay on at my job dishing out fried rice and chicken balls at the Three Aces or try to get some dog-walking clients. I thought the experience would look good when I applied to university, but I also needed money, and I was talking about it one night, and that's what he said. As usual, Matt had an opposing opinion.

"The path of least resistance leads to crooked rivers and crooked men," he muttered, without looking up. A silence fell, and I could feel the energy crackling off my brother and father and I braced for combustion, but nothing else was said. Later, I heard the van fire up and the crunch of gravel as Dad backed down the driveway. The path of least resistance probably led him straight to her, to Celia, who was at his work every day around noon, in the cafeteria at the refinery, dropping mounds of mashed potatoes onto his plate, blonde hair piled under her hair net, her eyes flickering up to meet his. Was that what happened? Did she lean across the counter to ladle gravy on his roast beef and whisper, I want you. I want you right now.

Or maybe the other way around.

Who knows.

What I do know right here, right now, is that there's lots of resistance. Not a single path seems clear.

WHEN I CALL the numbers in the ads, everyone tells me the same thing about the fact that I have a dog. "No pets allowed." They hang up without a goodbye or a good luck, as if I'm already guilty, as if I've already damaged their place.

I'm just about to call Liv. I'm just about to pick up the phone and dial her house, not the shelter, since it's Sunday, her one day off. In my head I'm making up what I'll say, something to do with my own inadequacies, how sorry I am, or maybe that I have cancer, that my brother's unwell, that my mom has cancer, that she's in prison. *I guess I never told you, but she murdered my father, and now she's dying, and now I have to go to her.* There's a lump in my throat, formed from sadness and shame, and I know I might not get through the conversation without breaking down but maybe that's good, maybe that'll help her forgive me faster. My hand is hovering over the phone when it rings.

"Is he still there?" says Angie.

"Who?"

"Matt, of course."

"No," I say. "He left ages ago."

She sighs. "He didn't tell you, did he?"

"Tell me what?"

"I sent him up there to tell you about Owain."

I clutch the phone, press it closer to my ear. He's married. He's got an STD.

"He's got a friend who fosters rescue dogs."

"What?"

"In Massey."

"You're lying."

"Why would I do that?" She seems annoyed. "No, sweetie," she says, off to the side. "Put that down." I hear the clunk of the phone against the kitchen counter, and when she comes back the sound of Ellie's cooing is as close as Angie's voice. "She's got two of her own and a pack of rejects. She lives on a farm. Well, kind of a farm. In a farmhouse, anyway, in Massey."

Massey's a tiny blot of a village on the Trans-Canada Highway, a forty-minute drive to the west. I wonder why Matt didn't tell me. But he had seemed focused on larger issues.

"I thought you should know," Angie says. "Just if you decide he's too much, that you've taken on more than..."

"Okay," I say, noncommittally, as if this isn't a sort-of miracle dropped into my lap. But I don't want her to think of me like that, like I'm making stupid mistakes, and I'm still not sure. Liv had used the word *relinquish* and I don't want that. It'd only be temporary, just until I find a new place, where the two of us can more easily live.

"And it gives you a reason to call Owain."

A smile twitches on my lips. When I don't respond, she says, "I figured the two of you weren't down there having a *Donkey Kong* tournament."

"No," I say.

"You like him?"

"Maybe. I don't really know him."

"Me neither," Angie says, over the sound of the microwave beeping, a bottle heated up for Ellie. "He showed up here one day asking for Matt, and the two of them disappeared downstairs, like teenagers." Irritation sharpens her voice but then she says, more softly, "But he seems interesting. Unique, like you."

I feel flattered, and for a split second a memory surges to mind of my mother, sitting on the side of my bed, advising me not to give myself away so easily to guys who didn't really want me. Not sex, she didn't mean sex, she meant emotionally. How needy I was back then. I'd been stood up and was trying to convince her to drive me to the show to see if I could find him.

"I don't know," I say, because suddenly I'm not sure, remembering what Matt told me. Maybe Owain was claiming to be someone he isn't. A writer, he'd said, like he had half a dozen novels under his belt instead of a few songs.

"You're young," Angie says.

"I'll see."

"Take a chance."

I wish she'd stop.

"When did Matt start smoking?" I ask her.

"Oh, God," she says. "Ages ago. He quit at New Year's, before you got back, but lately..."

"Really?" I am stunned.

"Got a pen?" she asks, and she recites Owain's number before I can answer. I scurry to grab the nub of the pencil I'd been using to circle apartment ads and scrawl it directly on my counter top. "Call me back," she tells me before hanging up the phone.

I DIAL RIGHT AWAY. I'm nervous, I'll admit it. Things had been pretty hot the night before and we might have even had sex if Angie hadn't shouted downstairs, reminding me where I was. In their basement, on a couch from my childhood, that Grommet was waiting. Owain answers after a single ring and hollers, "Yo!" I hear music blaring and wonder if it's his band practising, but the sound dials down immediately, volume adjusted.

"Owain? It's Mel."

"Mel," he says. "Mel, Mel."

I flinch. "Matt's sister."

"I know. I know who you are."

His voice is gruff, flirtatious. I feel heat pool in my belly as I pick at the coil of the phone cord, smiling. "Angie told me maybe you could help me?"

"Help you . . ." he says, sounding confused.

"With my dog? Your friend?"

"Oh, right!"

"So he can?" I pluck at the cord. "Or she?"

He chuckles. "That eager to ditch him?"

"No," I say, and feel my face flush.

"But you're giving him up."

I'm not sure if I am or not, but I'll deny it. At least until some perfect dog person comes along, able to give Grommet a home he'll love, lessons in self-confidence. "I don't know," I tell Owain honestly, then explain about my apartment, getting caught, how I have to move.

"You're looking for a place?"

"Know any?"

"Might."

I nod, then he says, "I already talked to Sophie, though. She's got a full house, six or seven dogs, a couple cats, even some lizards."

"Oh." I finger the corner of the newspaper, start thinking about calling more places, lying this time, moving in with Grommet until we're caught.

"But she said she can take him Wednesday."

My disappointment turns to a bloom of relief. Then, just as suddenly, I'm not sure again. I look over at Grommet, belly up, the toenails on his back foot clicking against the glass door as he runs in his sleep.

"It's not permanent," I say.

"Better not be."

I smile. I like that Owain's said that, and I like it even more when he offers to drive me out there himself when I ask him for directions. After we make plans for him to pick me up at my place on Wednesday, I say, "Bring cookies."

"Dogs love me."

"Or even better, a sirloin steak."

He laughs. I stall, hoping he might turn the conversation to the previous night or ask if he can come over right now to try meeting my dog in advance. But he says, "I've got to jet," and then he's gone.

"Just a few more days," I whisper to Grommet when I set down the phone. Then I just sit there and watch him, my heart a lump in my chest as he sleeps, back legs jumping, eyelids fluttering as he bounds through an open meadow in his dreams.

5.

ANGIE'S READING *Wherever You Go, There You Are*. She saw the author on *Oprah*, she tells me on the phone Wednesday afternoon, when I'm waiting for Owain. Then she spotted the book in Coles as she was leafing through a fishing guide for Matt's birthday.

It's true, my brother enjoys fishing now, but I'm not quite sure how that happened. He did as a kid, we both did, venturing out with our father into the vast landscape of forests and lakes full of pike and rainbow trout and whitefish way down deep. In the summer, the three of us would set out in the boat and drift, dropping lure-weighted lines through the green strata of sunshine and sediment. Our family gathered food from the land: fish hanging on aluminum stringers and ducks shot out of the sky when Matt and Dad went hunting. He did that too, for a while.

My mom helped as well. She taught me to slice open the fish bellies, remove the guts, cut the flesh into careful fillets we'd dredge through a batter of soft white flour, spices, and beer. The mallards she butchered on a wooden chopping block with a trough around its edge that would quickly fill with blood.

When he was fifteen, Matt stopped going on excursions with my dad. Normal, right? For a teenager. But my dad seemed to take offence, as if Matt was judging him, his hobbies, and that was when the fighting really started, when the two of them couldn't seem to talk to each other without the conversation turning violent. I was only eleven, but he didn't take me out anymore either, even though I'd always thought I was my dad's favourite. It bothered me, but I didn't say anything, because you didn't do that in my family. What would I have said? My mother's depression and tricky distance shut me out, and my father was the one who should have been accused. You never could though. If you said, This hurts me, he would find a way to convince you that it was all your fault.

"You should read it," Angie tells me, on the phone.

"The fishing guide?"

"No," she says, drawing out the word. "This book."

I roll my eyes. I hear that every day, all day, talking to the librarians and eager readers at my job. They rave about the bestsellers of the moment — *The Bridges of Madison County*; *Men Are from Mars, Women Are from Venus* — and I nod and smile, but I've got my own reading to do — *The Hidden Life of Dogs*, *Gorillas in the Mist* — and buried at the bottom of the pile, its uncracked spine turned away from the bed like it's some sort of secret, *My Mother My Self*, sent by my aunt from out West.

"Seriously, Mel," Angie says, and I hear her fingers scratching through the pages. She starts to read and what she says — "'If we hope to go anywhere or develop ourselves in any way, we can only step from where...'" — reminds me vaguely of Daisy, so I quietly set down the phone. I turn away to open the freezer, pop ice out of the tray, and drop the cubes into a glass, and they crackle as I pour myself some bourbon.

I don't want to talk about a stupid book, about advice I should learn to follow. Not now, not while I'm waiting for Owain to bring Grommet and me to my dog's new home, not while I'm exhausted from the whole situation, from last week, and from the past three days when I've hurried home at lunch to take him outside, before leaving again, closing the door while he started howling over the sound of my TV.

Yesterday, after a meeting with Teresa that ran to half past four, I came home to find that he'd chewed through the other leg of my bookshelf, letting loose another avalanche of books and knocking the porcelain figurine of St. Francis to the floor.

I did not speak. I stared at the shards, then walked straight into my bedroom, slammed the door and screamed into my last remaining intact pillow as Grommet began to bark. When I calmed down, I went and mixed myself a drink, stepping around him, because he was stretched out on the linoleum. I downed half of it in one go. "It's time, buddy," I told him. "We're not doing each other any favours." Then I called Owain, to make sure he hadn't forgotten.

"No way," he said. "I'll be there."

Angie's still reading when I come back onto the phone. When she finishes, I ask, "Is that a riddle?" about the quote I've only partly heard.

The book closes with a thunk on her end. "I just think you'd get a lot out of it. I think your brother would too." She hesitates, then asks, "How did he seem to you the other day?"

Intense, I think, but then Matt's always been intense. Once again, I remember him and my mother, in front of our house on the day of my graduation. Her covering her face with her hands. Him clutching her arms. Did the conversation really go like that or have I imagined it? Maybe he was just talking about school, wanting to change his major yet again, which would mean a few more years before he could graduate. I suck on an ice cube, appreciating the sweet sting of the alcohol and the cold in my mouth, and my words come out sounding fat and blunted when I talk around the object.

"Okay, I guess."

A vacuum seems to form on the other end of the line, as if Angie has suddenly disappeared. I realize that she's waiting, breath held, hoping for me to say more, to fill in the blanks. There is more I could say. He seems different. But different from whom? He's Matt, a guy who's been smoking for years, it turns out. Maybe I don't actually know him that well at all. I glance at my watch. It's 4:52. "He'll be here soon."

"Okay," she says. The moment has passed; I've pushed it past. "Try to have a good time."

Like it's a date, like I'm not giving up my dog. I look at Grommet, black head cocked to one side, staring at me, quizzical, his lips drooping in an anxious frown. I can't answer her;

I think I might cry.

"One more thing," Angie says. "Can you babysit for us on Friday?"

I nod, noticing now how Grommet seems a bit fatter, probably from the meaty bones I've been giving him to try to keep him contented, which don't work anyway, that he won't touch until I'm home, and then he'll lunge at them and spend an hour licking out the marrow while I need to get him outside for a walk.

"Mel?" Angie says.

"Yeah. Sure."

"We'll need you here by five. It's our anniversary."

There's something in her voice, something like sadness. "What are you doing?"

"Don't know. Figured we'd try."

"Try?"

"Try to have a good time," she says again, and then tells me goodbye.

6.

OWAIN'S DRIVING A black Chrysler minivan with rust eating the wheel wells. There's a Grateful Dead skull sticker on the bumper that someone's tried to scrape off. I grip Grommet's leash with both hands to keep him from barrelling into Owain when he gets out and comes around to the back of the van. He's wearing a green and blue plaid shirt unbuttoned to show off his Nirvana *In Utero* concert T-shirt and black jeans that emphasize how skinny he is, how easily Grommet could knock him over. Upstairs, on the way out, I saw Mrs. Slater in the hallway, a mesh shopping bag hanging from her forearm, banana ends poking through the weave. It might not have been an accident that Grommet got away from me and galloped towards her, slathering in excitement, moments before she slammed her apartment door. I heard the heave of her breathing as I clipped his leash back on, heard her hollering, "Keep that thing away from me!" What happened to her, I wondered, but by now my curiosity's been erased by the effort of holding Grommet, his back legs bucking as he attempts to get free. "Shhh," I keep saying, as if that'll make any difference at all.

"So, here's your buddy," Owain says, as he opens the rear door. Grommet's ears are pressed back; he's showing his teeth. I stand with one leg on either side of his rear end, knees ready to squeeze his hips to help hold him back. Owain flicks his eyes towards the dog's face, then away, then back again.

"Did you bring cookies?" I ask.

"Mmm-hmm," he hums, crouching down, turning sideways and opening his mouth in a yawn. With his platinum hair, black jeans, big brown work boots with the loose yellow laces, he looks a bit like he's doing some sort of performance art piece, but then he digs into his pocket and tosses an orange bone-shaped biscuit into the space between us. Grommet's ears pop up at the sound of it landing, and he pulls me close enough to sniff the treat, but doesn't eat it. Then Owain creeps closer, nudging the biscuit, and Grommet gobbles it up. We do this for a few minutes, Owain stepping gradually closer, until finally, finally, he's able to extend his hand and feed my dog another cookie, and Grommet takes it and actually licks his thumb. I'm smiling; Owain is too. He moves around to the end of the van and pushes aside a rusty shovel and a milk crate holding a bag of fertilizer, and when he gestures into the space, wide open because the back seats have been removed, Grommet leaps up.

THE VAN SMELLS like stale cigarette smoke and something sweet like the residue of a fruity perfume. There's dust everywhere, coating the dashboard and the glove compartment and the cup holders. Before I get in, Owain reaches over to grab a couple cassette tapes, a map book, and a metal pencil case off my seat and tosses them in the back. When I put on my seat belt, I feel grit on my fingertips and immediately crank open my window to let in some fresh air.

As we weave our way out of the city, Grommet fills the silence, whimpering, barking at people and dogs on the sidewalk, but he calms down when we merge onto the Trans-Canada. In the outer lane, a transport roars by, and Owain veers away, pointing the van for a split second at the deep ditch with its far side sloping up onto the open rocky terrain that surrounds Norbury. My stomach lurches, but he doesn't even seem phased. He shifts in his seat, tugs at the inseam of his jeans, then jerks his head towards the back.

"So how old's the monster?"

I wish we wouldn't talk about the dog. I wish he'd tell me about the songs he writes or whatever his job is, or how he knows Matt, or the places he's been. But he's waiting, so I say, "No idea." And then, because I have to, I tell him Grommet's story: the chain, the tree, the cigarette burns, the good Samaritan, his first owner who didn't work out.

I hate telling it though. I hate telling it because people act like it's unusual when it isn't. They ooh and ahh; they hold their fingers over their mouths. I can see their motors running, how they start thinking that they might want one of their own, a rescue case. They praise too much. Like you're some sort of hero which, obviously, I'm not. I know all this because before I got Grommet, that was me. Now I get it. Now I know that I'm just another part of Grommet's story, and my role might only be as the second person who tried and failed to give him a good home.

But Owain doesn't do any of this. He doesn't really respond at all, and I wonder if he's even heard me. Instead, he nudges a cassette into the player and a guitar lick starts up, but then he turns the volume down. "Music or CBC?" he asks.

"Music."

"Your brother's all about the CBC."

"I know."

"There's so much bad news." His mouth tightens, and I notice how thin his lips are, like two pink lines. "Sometimes it's too much," he says, glancing between me and windshield. "You know what I mean?"

"Sure," I say, remembering Lara, something she'd said to me once about how I should count my lucky stars to be in a position to choose positivity. Lucky's not a word I'd use to describe my circumstances, but I know what she meant. That I didn't have to walk three miles every day to haul water, that I didn't live in the midst of a war zone, that I was healthy, that the accident of my birth made me white and able, at will, to block out the world, like my dad used to, snapping off the news on the television set.

It was my mother, not him, who focused on the broader suffering. He couldn't take it. But it could also have been that he just didn't care, was totally intent on his own needs. I don't want to be self-absorbed like that, yet sometimes it's too hard to look outward. I'm thinking all of this, and about Matt, how he can swing in the opposite direction too, unable to see the simpler needs right in front of his face, when Owain says, "I guess you would," and my hackles go up. Dread surges through me: the feeling I get when I realize somebody knows my story, is looking at me with pity. But Owain seems to play dumb. He glances at me, at how my face must look. Pinched and unsure.

"What?" he says. He jabs a thumb towards the back. "I mean with how hard it's been with this guy." I study him, assessing. His eyes hold mine. "What?" he asks again. I shake my head, then turn towards the window, relief flooding through me. It's easier when people don't know, when I don't have to question how they see me. That's what I said to Lara the night before she and Daisy and I left for California, when I told her not to say anything, and finally confessed the truth: that what Daisy knew about me was that my brother had died, had fallen into a crevice, hit his head, had not been found for a whole winter. Lara looked at me, her mouth yawning open in shock, then clamping closed in anger, head shaking back and forth, furious that I'd steal her and Pete's story. I expected that she wouldn't want to come anymore, but what she said was, "Then I guess I get to be you."

"You and Sophie," Owain says, interrupting my thoughts. "You've got that in common."

"What?"

"The love of animals." He glances at me. "The tender hearts."

I struggle not to smile. We sit inside a warmth spreading between us. My fingers twitch to reach over, to touch the skin on the back of his hand, but I don't. Instead, I ask, "How long has she been doing this?"

"Rescuing critters?"

I nod.

"A long time," he says. "Since she inherited the farm."

"How do you know her?"

"Long time family friend."

"Did she come from Wales too?"

"No. She's Russian. Well, Canadian, but her dad came here, after the Second World War. When I was a kid, she was Aunty Soph, the coolest adult at the Christmas parties." He nods at the highway ahead of us. "You'll see."

MASSEY ISN'T MUCH of a town. We drive past a grey and white clapboard building with its paint peeling, a red brick bank on the corner. Owain turns off the highway onto a street called Limberlost Lane, between a townhouse with a rusty metal rocking horse sitting on the lawn and a neat bungalow with colourful whirligigs spinning in the garden. For ages we follow the road, beyond where the asphalt crumbles into gravel, then cross a wide farm field and ascend to the top of a forested hill. From there, I can see the house. It's almost glowing in the warm light of the early evening sun, and half a dozen dogs stand poised near a long, covered verandah. It's a farmhouse, shabby, two stories, the roof covered with worn shingles smooth as onyx. At the end of the driveway, the surname Bronski is printed in black stencilled letters on the side of a rusty mailbox. The name seems familiar, but I'm not sure why.

The dogs run towards us, barking and leaping around the tires as Owain pulls into the yard. Grommet's whining and barking too, pushing against the windows, wanting out. When Owain parks, we're immediately surrounded. A border collie, a brindle cattle dog with one brown and one blue eye, and a scraggly white Shih Tzu with a pink tumour swelling out of its fluffy white hair crowd around my door. I reach for the latch but Owain touches my knee.

"Wait," he says, a tiny smile on his face. It's like he's got a surprise.

The front door of the house swings open and a woman comes out. Sophie, I assume. She marches to the verandah stairs, claps her hands three times fast, and calls the dogs' names in a long chant — "Oliver, Mowat, Stella, Hazel, Mumford, Guido, Trotsky!" Amazed, I watch as they scamper away, disappearing through the large dark doorway of the barn on the other side of the yard. Owain grins, a sparkle in his eyes.

"Wow," I say. Even Grommet has shut up, astonished by her control. He'll want to chase right after them, I know, and there'll be nothing I can do to stop him, but maybe this woman is really the answer. Maybe she can help me give him another chance.

7.

I'D EXPECTED SOMEONE tall like Owain, but Sophie is short and stocky. She walks briskly across the porch, gazing at us from under strawberry-blonde hair that's cut so crudely it sits on her head like a wig, tufts sticking every which way. Apart from a red flush across the bridge of her nose, her skin is pale, and her clothing takes me aback. Neon yellow parachute pants, a grubby white T-shirt with the words *I'm With Stupid* atop a fat red arrow that points to the oily gleam of the windows over the porch. I think I see a face hovering behind the glass, but it quickly pulls away, withdrawing into the darkness inside the house.

Grommet's going nuts, bouncing around in the van behind us, barking towards the barn where the other dogs are slowly creeping out to stand in the shadow cast by the roof. He lets out a long, loud whine; I wonder if he made that same sound inside my apartment when he was left alone.

"Let me see him," Sophie says through Owain's open window, coming up beside the vehicle. She doesn't even look at me, and I feel a deep twinge, as if all of this is getting settled without me. But he's mine, I suddenly want to yell.

"KEEP HIM THERE," Sophie says to Owain as the trunk opens. Grommet is trembling and trying to push out of the van, but Owain blocks him, even holds him by the collar. I stand aside, arms crossed, hoping Grommet doesn't go for him, sink his teeth into his wrist. Sophie's doing the thing, darting her gaze away and back to the dog then licking her lips. I almost roll my eyes, because I already know that, how dogs yawn at each other and show their tongues to ease tension, de-escalate conflict. All you have to do is watch them at a dog park. But once Sophie stops, Grommet does something weird. He actually sits down, his tail wagging, like he's more interested in her now than in all the other canines. She steps right up to him and he doesn't even flinch as she touches his shoulders, gently picks up one of his ears, which is pebbled with frostbite scars, touches the spot of a burn scar on his shoulder, the ring of tough skin around his neck almost hidden now by thick, new fur.

"Beautiful boy," she says, and finally turns to look at me, inquiring, curious. Her eyes, a pale, white-blue, seem almost luminescent. "Separation anxiety?"

For a second I think she means me; it takes me a second to find my voice. In the gap before I can speak, Owain starts telling her Grommet's story. When's he's done, Sophie squats, looks into Grommet's face. "Poor big beast," she says. "You didn't deserve that."

A clunking sound comes from the verandah, and when I look over, I see a young man walking with a cane towards us. One side of his cranium is ballooned out and bald, and his right eye bulges, wet and bloodshot, like half of him is in mourning.

"Hey, Teddy," Owain calls, and lifts his hand in a wave.

"It's Ted now," Sophie says. "Just decided that yesterday; might not even answer you."

But the boy calls out a greeting, limps closer. From across the yard, the Shih Tzu trots towards him, a move the other dogs interpret as release, so they race for us and Grommet. They're bounding around barking, and Grommet seems to be both shrinking back and tugging against Owain's grip on his collar. His tongue steadily circles his lips, and he lets out a shivering yawn, head quaking.

"All his shots?" Sophie asks me. "No mange?"

"Yes," I say, then "no."

"How's he with dogs?"

I shrug. We put him out a couple times with the other rescues at the shelter and he did okay but he was standoffish, and once pinned down a basset hound.

"Well, he's got to learn sometime," Sophie says, glancing from Grommet to me. "But we'll keep an eye on him, split them if they start to get aggressive."

To Owain, she says, "Go ahead and let him go," and when he does, Grommet leaps out of the van like he's set on flying. He lands in the midst of the fray, the other dogs spinning around him, turning to start a chase. Soon Grommet is struggling to stay on the cattle dog's heels, then he gets the lead, the wind flapping at his lips, spittle flying as he circles past. Mere moments at his new home and he already seems happier than he ever was with me.

"Out of the garden," Sophie screams as they hit a patch of dirt near a gnarled apple tree whose limbs are spotted with a white confetti of early blooms. "Gotta fence that in," she says, and then I feel her hand on my shoulder. "He'll be all right."

"I don't know what I'm doing," I mutter.

"That makes" — Sophie glances around — "four of us. Day by day, take what comes. Right?" she says to Owain. He's lit a cigarette; he blows out a stream of smoke, nodding.

"When are you going to give that up?" asks Sophie, but Owain just grins, like he's pleased with himself. His eyes connect with mine, and I feel an instant pulse of pleasure, a

this has nothing to do with you

warmth I savour. It's nice here, I want to tell him. I like her. I smile back, then turn again to Sophie.

"Are they all rescues?" I ask.

"Two are ours." She points towards the blur that's the Shih Tzu. "Trotsky was a show dog, and one day he fell off the groomer's table, broke a toe, and that was it. Instantly retired; instantly abandoned. And Guido" — a slender, long-legged, greyhound mix, running like a gazelle — "was found out on the highway. Teddy brought him home."

"Ted," says the teenager, sticking his hand towards me. When I take his palm, it feels dry in mine.

"Tea?" Sophie asks, squeezing my shoulder once again.

Owain holds up his cigarette. "Be in in a second," he says, and Sophie nods, then glances at Ted who's kicking one of the tires on the van, right hand stuffed in his pocket, staring down at the ground. Sophie leads me onto the verandah and around the corner of the house.

Trotsky is waiting for her on a muddy straw mat by the back door. She scoops him up, and the pink tumour on his back seems to wobble. Inside the kitchen, she kicks off her untied runners and hands the dog to me, smiling when my arms come up instantly, without hesitation. His hair is long and shaggy, and he really needs a bath.

"Is it terminal?" I ask, as she steps over to the sink to fill a metal kettle.

"What? Life?" She chuckles.

"His condition."

"Yep. He's a trooper though." She looks out the window at Ted. I follow her eyes and see him and Owain entering the barn, surrounded by the dogs. I meant Trotsky but I'm not sure if Sophie knows that.

"Where are they going?"

"Probably just getting Grommet settled," she says, then opens the cupboard above the stove as Trotsky wriggles to be set down. I place him gently on the worn linoleum. "Regular or some sort of zinger?"

WHILE THE KETTLE clatters on the stove, I ask to use the washroom. Sophie points into the den area attached to the kitchen and says, "Through there, upstairs, second door on the right." I walk past the couch, over it an ugly painting of wispy orange boats in a harbour, and spot a collection of photographs on a shelf beside the corner woodstove. There's Owain as a boy with a mullet, and Sophie, standing between a woman in a teal blue skirt suit and a teenage girl with white-blonde hair who's half turned away from the camera, arms crossed, shoulders slouched, either angry or shy. She looks vaguely familiar to me too, and I take it as a sign, this swelling sense of déjà vu, that I'm exactly where I should be. That's what Daisy would advise.

Sophie's got the tea made when I come back. It's set out on the round kitchen table — a full china set, white with orange and pink roses and gold trim. She's put out a plate of sugar cookies too, and she gestures at a chair and asks, "What have you tried?"

"Tried?"

"With your boy. Any training? Is he food motivated?"

I pick up a cookie and snap it in half, then tell her about my struggles with Grommet. Mostly I talk about the damage he's done, and when I explain about my couch, she laughs so hard she snorts.

"He must have had fun with that," she says, pouring me a cup of the orange pekoe, now steeped. "I wonder when he realized."

I can tell she already loves him, and I feel a spasm of uncertainty. Can he be saved, or will he be happier here, want to stay?

this has nothing to do with you

131

I take a couple gulps of tepid, milky tea, not sure what else to say, so I ask her about the house, how long she's lived there. We chat about leaky foundations, bats in the attic, the need for a new roof. Things I know nothing about.

"My father left it to me," she says, refilling the tiny creamer from a jug in the fridge. Over her shoulder, through yellowed lace curtains, I see Ted and Owain coming out of the barn. They're talking, heads close together, and it reminds me of Matt and my mother, out on the road, sharing their secrets.

"My grand inheritance," Sophie says, swinging her arm through the air. "Perfect place for a middle-aged woman and a teenage boy." I can't tell if she's being sarcastic. Her face looks flat as she takes a drink, holding her teacup delicately in her large hands, each fingernail a clean white moon, then quietly says, "And you've got a brother."

I'm about to ask how she knows that through the mash of sugary crumbs in my mouth when the boys come in through the front door, Grommet with them. When he sees me, he bounds over, racing along the length of the den, and jumps up to plant his big paws on my knees and grab the cookie out of my hand. I jerk away, and have to shove him back as he thrusts his large head towards the plate full of treats.

"Well," Sophie says, setting her cup carefully in its saucer. "I can see we've got our work cut out for us."

IT'S HARD to leave him. Night's coming on and Sophie walks me over to the barn so she can show me where Grommet will stay. There's a large puffy bed, a couple of rips in it that have been duct-taped closed, and an old ice cream bucket full of fresh water, an aluminum pot for his kibble. A few of the dogs have followed, and Sophie scoops up Trotsky once again, then shuts Grommet into his kennel by closing the wooden gate. He jumps up to look over the side as we walk away. I hear him howling after me, and I brace myself, turn away, push at my wet eyes with the knuckle of my thumb. Sophie touches my elbow, guiding me back to Owain's van.

"I'll let him out as soon as you're gone," she says. "He'll have some supper. He'll be just fine. You can come back whenever you want, help me teach him. Learn how to do it yourself."

It's good, it's all so good, but what I feel right now is the large dark press of failure, the quiet cracking of my heart. How I couldn't do it: change my life, make his better. When we drive away, I blow my nose on the scrap of a napkin as I watch Ted and Sophie in the side mirror, waving. Then, Sophie puts Trotsky down on the ground, and he seems to just disappear in the dust.

part five

1.

IT WAS MY MOTHER who wanted a dog, who complained about loneliness, about needing something to do. The puppies showed up in a black and white photograph on a poster in the IGA, and my mother brought up the idea one evening at dinner. I was nine, just turned, Matt twelve. It was October, around the time that my father had decided to take over my mother's mirrored dance area. He'd bought a big TV, our first VCR, and furniture too, the couch and loveseat that's now in Matt's basement, purchased second-hand.

Had he asked her? I don't know.

She hadn't used the space in a while, not like before, when I was seven and he first put up the mirrors to make a studio so she could try to teach. Back then, she'd been down there all the time, hustling upstairs in the evening in her tight black leotard ordered from the Sears catalogue to hastily prepare inadequate suppers of fish sticks or grilled cheese sandwiches. Late at night I'd sometimes wake to the soft distant strains of piano music, which would then lull me back to sleep. She had a couple students, but they didn't last long. They quit when they realized there was work involved, according to my mother.

When she suggested the puppy, my father wiped his mouth with a paper napkin left over from my birthday.

"I'll walk it," Matt said, and I nodded fiercely, but my father ignored us. He picked a bit of chicken out of his teeth.

"Or you could get a job," he said. "Get some more money coming in; help out around here."

My mother was silent. What kind of employment could a professional dancer find in Hixon River? Anything, was what I thought at the time. She could have tried giving lessons again, not been so mean to the students, become a bank teller, learned to repair shoes or arrange flowers.

Anything other than what she did, which was to sit for hours, reading mysteries with cracked spines or fat hardcovers from the library, or knitting, the steel needles moving steadily in her hands to produce a drape of lacy fabric over her knees. Once I came across her like that while I was doing my chores, lazily dragging a cloth soggy with chemical spray over the wooden surfaces. She looked up as I launched a storm of dust into a shaft of light, and it was like she was caught in a trance. This was years later, long after that dinner when Matt volunteered to take care of the dog, which we did get, which we called Frankie. Her hands slumped into her lap, the needles jabbing upward like defensive quills.

"My past is everything I failed to be," she said. I didn't answer, but she kept staring at me so I grunted in a sort of agreement even though I didn't understand.

Now I think I know what she meant.

She was a dancer who didn't dance, not like she wanted to.

I'm a lover of dogs who couldn't mend my own dog's broken soul.

I imprisoned him, nearly killed him, and the only solution was to send him away.

"IS THIS ALL you and Owain talked about?" Angie asks.

"What do you mean?"

I look down at the tissue that I've been tearing to bits. She sighs, stands, and tries to pass me the bag of sour cream and onion chips she's been holding. I shake my head, not hungry. It was Matt I wanted to talk to, who Owain had brought me to see because he said he needed to talk to him too. Angie told us he wasn't around, and Owain left, and now it's nearly nine, and almost time for me to go.

"It's just..." she says, then hesitates before her words rush out: "You tried. It didn't work out. He's in a good place now."

A good place. The same thing the minister had said. A better place. Than our house, he'd meant. With his kids. Our home. Our family. Alive.

"I mean the dog," Angie says. "I mean you tried, and that's great, but you can't get dragged down like this. Life just tumbles along, and you just have to go with it. Here's this guy" — she swings her arm, gesturing at an invisible Owain — "why not give it a shot?"

I hadn't given it a shot. I hadn't asked him anything on the drive back. The whole way I'd been trying not to cry. He put on music, cranked it, tapped his steering wheel frenetically so all I felt was annoyed.

"Life shrinks or expands according to one's courage," Angie says.

"Is that from that stupid book?"

"I don't know where I heard that." She wipes her hands together, so vigorously that crumbs scatter across her knees and the sound is like applause echoing through the quiet living room. I think of my mother again, dancing in that empty space, usually alone, no audience. Had Matt watched her? Angie crosses her arms.

"Are you mad at me?" I ask.

She sighs. "Honey," she says. "I just don't know how I can help you."

I want to say: you could have taken in my dog, you could have let Matt have him, but I don't speak.

"Have you thought that maybe it's depression?"

My head snaps up; I stare at her.

"They have drugs now," she says. When I don't answer, her voice drops as if she's sharing a secret. "It's genetic, you know." Her gaze has fallen to the floor and when I follow it I see the Jägermeister stain from where Matt had dumped half the bottle, right in the middle of the room. I slip off the couch.

"It didn't come out." I touch the brittle weave; it still feels sticky. "Do you want me to try?"

Angie shrugs. Her bottom lip trembles, but she disguises it with her hand, pushing more chips into her mouth. From down here on the floor, I see the shadows under her eyes, how dark they seem, how deep. I'm about to ask if she's okay, but the moment's filled with the sound of Ellie through the baby monitor, her cries edged in static. Instantly, Angie's out of the chair, running up the stairs. Left alone, I stretch out on the carpet like a dog, my face beside the stain, smelling the faint sweet treacle of the spill, wondering what to do now.

2.

THE NEXT MORNING, I leave my apartment easily and arrive at work on time. I stay through lunch, eating a cheese and mustard sandwich at my desk, scanning into the Os. Oddities is my favourite file so far, and in it I find an article about a man who claimed to have captured a cast of a sasquatch footprint and one about a two-headed calf born near Massey. The mention of the town makes me wonder about Grommet, how he's doing, how he slept, and I itch to call Sophie, but I don't. Instead I spring out of my chair while the scanner's gathering the latest image and go to the lunchroom where I pour coffee in a mug covered in a storm of orange, yellow, and blue butterflies that Josie gave me for Valentine's Day. I dump in powdered creamer and mix clear the clumps, and I'm still stirring when my coworker Ruth walks over to the fridge.

"You know that stuff kills rats?" she says, bending to reach for a yogurt. The heavy buttons on her blouse weigh her shirt down so I can see right down her top to her tan bra. I smile tightly, dig into the can for more powder.

Most of my colleagues know about me, about my family, about what happened. I swear it affects how they talk to me. Everything out of Ruth's mouth is about death or illness it seems, disguised in a helpful way, like she's trying to prevent future grief. It's annoying, her exaggerated concern, the constant mentions of dangerous food, acid rain, lead tests on Norbury soil, and even things from long ago like how many locals died during the Spanish Flu. She knows a lot about the hardships that people have endured.

"Hey," I say to her now, quieting the rattle of my spoon. "What do you know about Russian immigration to Norbury after World War Two?"

this has nothing to do with you

She nods thoughtfully, pulling the foil off her raspberry yogurt. "Sure," she says, mixing in the murky red water on the top. "They came here to work in the mines or with lumber, mostly displaced people who opposed Stalin or found themselves in Germany after the war. A few families became very well established. The Belokopytovs, the Bronskis."

There it is. I knew I'd heard the name before. "Bronski?" I ask, digging for more.

"Big philanthropist; the patriarch, I mean. He gave a lot to social justice organizations in the city. There's a plaque." She points and I follow her finger through the lunchroom door, past the circulation desk, between the stacks and my windowed work area, to the magazine section. Beside a TV on a rolling cart, there's a gold engraved plate beside a photograph. I carry my coffee over to take a closer look. Peter Sacha Bronski gave a hefty donation of Russian language materials back in 1973 and his portrait looks like a male version of Sophie: the same wide face, the same pale blue eyes that seem luminescent, even in black and white.

MY APARTMENT'S SILENT when I get home. No scramble of claws, no dog overjoyed to see me, no disasters. Just a plate of cupcakes with pink icing waiting outside my door. We are all happier now, says the attached *Thank You* card, over my neighbour's loopy, cursive signature. It makes me angry, how she thinks I made my decision because of her, how she doesn't bother to express any sympathy or well wishes for Grommet. But I eat the cupcakes anyway, all three of them, chewing the sweet vanilla cake, sucking the buttercream frosting off my fingers.

I turn on the TV to get some noise and flip from a soap opera to the *Oprah Winfrey Show*. She's interviewing a woman about past lives. It's the kind of thing I think Angie might like, that my father would have called hooey, the way he'd dismiss anything that bumped up against his simple vision of the world, like the time the Chinese dance troupe was coming to the Soo and my mother wanted desperately to go.

"It's food, Al," she'd shouted. "Food! And you're denying it, so I'll just continue to starve!"

Her bedroom door slammed and shook the whole house. Even thinking about it I can feel the hard knot in my stomach. It wasn't like her to argue like that, and I could see the rage building in my dad. It was January 1990, and Matt had gone back to Toronto a few days earlier, after the Christmas break. My mother's emotions had been up and down since September when he had moved south again for school, and she'd started occasionally erupting as if something inside her had been smouldering, and Matt's leaving had fanned the flames.

I remember that fight. The way they screamed at each other. My father refusing to give her the money, simply because she hadn't asked him nicely enough, didn't appreciate him, or other reasons I forget. It went on over several days, and Matt gave me advice that seemed to conflict: keep your head down but make sure she's eating, stay out of the way, but also hide any extra pills. She had a full prescription of Valium in her bedside table. I knocked out fifteen, left her five, but she didn't say anything about it. One morning, she had bruises around her wrists that she seemed to want to show off, raising her hands often to punctuate her speech, waving at people we barely knew when we went to the grocery store. I tried to keep my distance, stayed a few feet behind her, focused on cereal labels and figuring out what we needed, but there wasn't any point. Anyone who saw us knew who we were: mother and daughter, Crazy Bernie and Mel Barnett. Most people kept their distance.

In the end, I bought the tickets. She brightened, cleaned the house, even went through her closets and donated some clothes to the charity shop. Then, a week before the performance, the show was cancelled because three of the dancers had defected in Montreal, and she sank hard, blinds drawn against the blue winter sky, her bedroom cast in hazy darkness like the space behind a stage.

My father said it was just as well. There were rumours about impending layoffs at the refinery. Strangely, though, he found the money for us to go to Florida. They took me out of school for a week and we drove all the way, spent hours and hours in highway silence, my mother and me watching the landscape shift to green. In our motel room, she acted pretty much the same as at home: drew the curtains, slept a lot, while my dad toured flea markets and car shows or drove along the beach, eyeing the women in their bikinis. Sometimes he took me with him, other times he left me on my own and I went hunting for shells, sharks' teeth, diamond rings, whatever lost treasure I could find.

MY APARTMENT'S STILL wrecked. I spend a bit of time trying to clean it before picking up the phone to call Josie. The line's busy, so I keep working, wiping Grommet's nose prints off the glass door, stacking books to hold my chewed shelf together, gathering a deck of cards he scattered all over the floor. After an hour or so, I try again but it's still busy. Finally, eventually, I get through, and Josie answers like we used to, when the three of us were teenagers and knew who was calling.

"Stalker."

"Hi," I say.

"Oh! Mel! Hi."

"Who'd you think it was?" I ask, although of course I already know. I know who she's been gabbing to for over an hour. The whole seven months I lived in Vancouver, Josie kept saying she'd visit, fly out for what she called a "girl's week." I'm not sure what that would have been like: her painting my filthy fingernails or attempting to braid my matted hair, the flimsy dreadlocks I tried for a while to create. I worried too that she and Lara would try to do some sort of intervention, locking me up until Daisy moved on, but I needn't have been concerned. Josie was just jealous, and still talks about how she should have come out, joined us on our road trip, but of course she never would have. Bruce would never have agreed to her crossing an entire continent, flying free, and actually I'm glad she didn't come, didn't see me like that. It would have been much harder to have the two of them on my case. Even still, I want to ask how Lara is, I want to know, but my pride won't let me, so instead I ask how Bruce's bite has healed. It's been over a week since it happened; this is the first time I've checked.

"Sorry I didn't call earlier," I say, and then I tell her about Grommet, how he trashed my apartment, how I have to move out.

"Where are you going to go?" Josie asks.

"I don't know."

"You can always come here. You can stay with us."

The thought of that — moving back to Hixon River, dragging my ill-mannered dog past Bruce every morning, being stared at by curious townspeople — fills me with dread. "I'll figure it out," I tell her, nudging the edge of the newspaper, opened to the classifieds. There are a few I haven't called.

"Have you started looking?"

"Yeah. Sort of."

"I could help you this weekend. I'm heading there."

this has nothing to do with you

"For what?"

"Doctor."

"When?"

"Tomorrow. Does that work? I could meet you at the library. I'll cab it over."

"A cab?"

"Bruce needs the truck."

I don't say anything.

"He has to work," Josie explains, because she knows me, knows how I'm sitting there wondering why he can't ride his bike for once so she doesn't have to take the Greyhound from Hixon River. I pick up the deck of cards and split it in half. "He has to get between job sites and I might not be able to drive back anyway."

"Why not?"

"They might have to break it again." I imagine her lifting her injured wrist like we're back in class and she's eager to answer a question. "They don't think it's set right. We'll see."

"Okay," I say, and then she asks me where Grommet's gone, and that leads me to telling her about Owain. She's got a lot of questions — do I like him (maybe), what's he do (I don't know), what's he look like (cute, a little bit like Corey Hart) — and as I'm answering her, I stare at the blank square of the next day — Friday, April 29 — on my calendar, feeling like I've forgotten something. Cards tumble out as I shuffle: the ten of spades, the three of hearts, the joker, upside down.

BY THE TIME I hang up, it's late, nearly eleven. The phone rings almost instantly. "Stalker," I say.

"You talk a lot," a voice says, then imitates a busy signal. "Bleep, bleep, bleep."

"Who is this?"

"I'm hurt." The sucking in of smoke, the exhale.

"Owain?"

"In the flesh. Well, sort of. Well, I could be."

That makes me smile. He asks me what I'm doing right then, right now, and I shrug, then agree to meet him at a bar up the street from my building even though I have to work in the morning. I hang up, change into my favourite paisley peasant blouse and the fringed leather jacket I found at a second-hand store a couple weeks ago, a pair of jeans that are ripped at the knees. My hair's growing very slowly, but I do the best I can with it, shape it into a sort of pixie look, then put on some lipstick and slip out the door of my empty apartment, feeling free.

3.

MY FRIEND LARA bought a car, I tell him.

I'd been in Vancouver for seven months, through my eighteenth birthday in September and the Christmas holidays, when I watched 1940s movies on the television set that popped when too much white came on the screen, and ate canned ham on my own in Lara's apartment. She stayed for the holidays as well, but her parents flew out, and the three of them drove to a rented ski chalet in Whistler. They tried to convince me to go, but it was the first one, the first Christmas, and I felt like the only way I could cope was to pretend it was just an ordinary day. Really, I should have been with Matt. He mailed me a tiny present which turned out to be a piece of the Berlin Wall tinted green and blue from old graffiti. It sat on a square of cotton batting in the kind of box used for Mexican jumping beans, and I stared at it for a while, then thought about phoning him, but when I tried to figure out what I'd say, I imagined a wind tunnel forming along the line, all the emotions I hadn't expressed cycloning up in a nanosecond. Pass, I thought.

I don't tell Owain this, the part about Christmas. Instead, I start with the car, the lemon-yellow 1972 Toyota Corolla with manual transmission that Lara bought for five hundred dollars. She was worried about stalling it at the border, so before we left we did a few practice runs, lurching through morning traffic on Venables, all the way up the long sloping street to our regular Italian coffee shop, where she ordered an espresso to fuel her nerve. I could tell she wasn't sure the trip was such a good idea. The night before, she'd finally met Daisy and had to ask her to put on clothes when Daisy came out of the washroom, freshly showered, and sat cross-legged on the couch totally naked. "Square," Daisy muttered, like we lived in the 1950s, and Lara replied with one word: "Hygenic."

At the border, I sat in the front seat, my hair still long but clean and tied back in a ponytail. I'd removed the many beaded necklaces and braided hemp chains that I usually wore and dressed in a simple white button-up blouse that I found at Value Village. As we rolled up to the guard, Daisy started muttering a meditation chant in the back seat, and Lara hissed at her to shut up.

I met the guard's deadpan gaze as Lara explained what we were doing: driving to Northern California to visit family.

"Whose family?" the guard asked.

"Mine," Daisy said, leaning forward between the seats, smiling. I held my breath. He handed us our driver's licences and waved us through, and I felt like we'd gotten away with something even before I saw Daisy working her hand under the waistband of her billowy pants, lifting her bum to help her

dig into her crotch. "What are you..." I started to say, turning around in time to see her pull out a plastic baggie, her face
beaming with pride.

Lara's eye widened. She shouted at Daisy's reflection in the
rear-view mirror. "You brought pot through the border? Are you
fucking insane?"

Her hands clutched the steering wheel, knuckles whiten-
ing, while Daisy stared at her, then slowly swivelled her head
to bug her eyes out at me like she and I were on the same side.

"That might have been a bad idea," I said. She slumped
aggressively back in her seat, crossed her arms, stared out her
window like a twelve-year-old. "Holy Goddess, you two. It's just
a stupid line some man drew."

We drove for a long time in silence, Lara fuming, moving
us south towards Oregon. In the back seat, Daisy used Lara's
California guidebook to roll joints, one after another. In Eugene,
we stopped at a health food store, and Daisy asked some kids on
skateboards if they knew a nearby place where we could crash.
They drew us a map on the flyleaf of the book Lara had picked
up from the store's free shelf, and Daisy gave them a couple
joints before we headed out of town into snow, to find a place
called Cougar Mountain.

4.

THAT'S AS FAR as I get. Owain's listening, his hand curled
around a pint of beer, but I see his face pinch up as he stifles
a yawn. I shake my head, aware that I've been babbling on, not
letting him get a word in edgewise.

"I'm talking too much."

He doesn't deny it. "Eventually you got to the desert?" he asks.

I nod. "Arizona, where I lived in a cave for a while."

"A cave?"

"Yeah."

He's grinning, lips slick from the beer. I twist the stem of my wine glass and look into his brown eyes. His face is pale except for a flush of freckles across his cheekbones that I hadn't noticed before, and his dark roots are showing under his bottle-blonde hair. He seems vivid and alive against the heavy, dark wood of the bar and the empty tables. Even the overweight bartender's pale in contrast, nearly frozen, one hand slowly stuffing a white cloth into a glass as he stares up at a TV suspended from the ceiling, showing the eleven o'clock news. All I have to do is slide my eyes over there, away from Owain's face, to see the world that's holding Matt's attention right now. I know what it looks like. Earlier, I'd seen images on my own television: an update on a shooting in a cafe in Toronto and a story about South Africa's first free elections. The long, snaking line-ups for the polls, a son carrying his father to a voting station.

"So I guess you like adventure," Owain says.

Do I? It had seemed less like adventure at the time and more like life simply unfolding. I shrug. "Sure. You?"

"Never been anywhere." He draws out a cigarette, the motion sending a ripple through the purple silk shirt he's wearing. "Well, once I went to New York City for New Year's. Watched the ball drop in Times Square."

"That must have been fun."

"It was okay," he mumbles, as the waitress appears, carrying a large coffee can. Silently, she empties the black plastic ash-tray on our table then drops it back down with a clatter. In the flicker from Owain's lighter, I see him looking at her and notice how flat her face is, unresponsive, even when I lift my empty wine glass, gesturing for another drink.

"She's got attitude," I say.

"Tammy," he says, but under his breath, like it's a secret. Then he says, "Tammy, Melony," moving the alliteration around in his mouth like a lozenge. Something throbs in me, a tiny red caution sign. I ignore it, and laugh. The wine's made me hungry for more of what had happened between us the other night, has made me want him.

"What about you?" I ask, leaning forward to try to catch the drift of his gaze.

"Attitude?" he says.

"No." I twirl my empty wine glass, trying to think of questions, then start with, "How do you know my brother?"

He spins the ember of his cigarette against the ashtray's edge. "Work."

"The MNR?" It's surprising. I can't imagine his silk shirts under hip waders. But Owain shakes his head.

"I'm an independent contractor. Matt's been helping me out. Me and Ted."

"Ted?" I ask as Tammy arrives with my wine. It gushes over the sides when she sets it roughly down, practically dropping the glass. I wipe at the spill with my fingers, lick off the sour liquid. I'm not a big fan of wine, but I felt like that's what I should order, that it'd be safer than bourbon. I'm trying to figure this out. Matt knows Ted? "Helping you with what?"

Owain doesn't answer. He's suddenly distracted by a bleeping sound that draws his eyes to the slim grey screen of his pager.

"Back in a second," he says, and I watch as he heads towards the brightly lit hallway where the washrooms are, huddles against a payphone.

this has nothing to do with you
149

"Drive you home?" he says when he comes back. I look at my nearly full drink. He swallows the last foamy dregs of his pint, then gathers his cigarettes and lighter. I'm not sure what's happening, but suddenly our date is over and I guzzle the rest of my wine, wipe a dribble off my bottom lip, then follow him out to the van.

OUTSIDE THE BRIGHTLY LIT lobby of my building, I ask him if everything is okay. I feel overeager, the alcohol combusting inside of me, burning a fuse, and I desperately want him to kiss me, come up, stay the night. I take a breath, then reach over and touch his leg.

"The dog's gone," I tell him, as if he doesn't know. He looks down at my hand, then lifts up my fingers, one at a time, squeezing them gently.

"My turn for a rain check."

When I don't move, he says, "A buddy needs a favour, that's all."

"What kind of favour? Can you go and come back?"

He smiles, the lop-sided flirty grin I'm getting used to. Then we're leaning into each other and his mouth tastes like the pink and green mints we fished out of the bowl by the cash register when he paid.

"I've never met a real live cave woman before," he says.

"Go and come back."

He throws his head against his headrest and groans. "Can't. Wish I could."

I want to ask him when I'll see him again, what will happen next. I want things to be clear, planned out, written down, easy, but I bite my tongue. Slow down, Lara used to tell me. You don't want to look desperate. I feel desperate though; I always have. When I push open the door, the overhead light comes on, and I see that he's already got his hand on the keys, is ready to start the vehicle and drive away.

"Wait," I say, one leg hanging out of his van. "You didn't tell me how Matt's helping you and Sophie's son."

"Ted's her nephew," he says. "Not her son."

The pager beeps then, and we both look down at the cup holder, where it's rattling like a trapped bug. "I'll call you later," Owain says, and he's gone before I reach my building's door.

5.

MY APARTMENT IS quiet and dark, high above the sulphuric pools of light in the night city, but not high enough to reach the stars. It's 2:03 a.m. when I wake, dreaming of my mother's hand on my brow, her touch like water dropped on a drought.

"Don't do what I did," she told me once.

I knew what she meant, knew her story: how she rode the train all the way from Saskatoon to Toronto, disembarked wide-eyed and only eighteen at Union Station. She was a dancer, gifted, everyone said, and her parents had sent her east to be a star. But the handsome set builder with the shocking red hair that gave its apple shade to my own got in the way. He peered at her from within the imaginary worlds he built of cut lumber and nails, cast his shadow over the stage. Right from the beginning, he wanted her to quit, couldn't stand it when the attention pivoted to her, and she tried to break up with him, but he wouldn't let her. He got what he wanted, my father, and what he wanted mattered the most, from his choice of ice cream flavour (rum and raisin, which I hate) to what I wore to where we went on vacation.

"But he was very handsome," she told me, a sad slanted look on her face. Confusion too, like she was working out a dream, pulling on its strands.

They were married at old city hall, the red brick building near the Hudson Bay store in downtown Toronto, on August 27, 1968. She wore a grey wool suit borrowed from her roommate. She was only a few weeks along, but she'd already put on enough weight that she had to leave the skirt's hook and eye unfastened, and she sweltered in it, the day was so hot.

"Don't do what I did," she said, sweeping my ordinary auburn hair out of my eyes. Don't worry, I remember thinking. I never, ever will. I would never have stayed with him; I would have broken it off as soon as I saw what he was, what he wanted from me, to take over my life.

Maybe that's what happened.

Maybe that morning, as dawn began cracking the night's dark shell, she finally fully understood what exactly she had lost.

Days. Years. A life.

And she blamed my father because he'd taken what he wanted, then decided to start over, leaving her in the lurch as he heaved himself towards happiness with another woman.

Because he was happy.

At my graduation dinner he talked boisterously down the length of the table to Josie's father, Frank, while my mother, clashing horribly in her burnt-orange bolero jacket and pink dress slacks, cut cooked carrots into half circles, pulled the skin off her chicken, ate only the green salad served in its own bowl. The only time my father met her eye was when they gave me my present, a watch with a brown leather band, a face like veined granite, delicate gold numbers and hands, and the words *Carpe Diem, Love M and D* engraved on the back. The feel of it:

that heavy, cool metal in my hands. Josie leaning over my shoulder to look. When I went to B.C., I left it behind, but I think Matt probably kept it. It's somewhere at his house, still in its box, the battery drained long ago, stuck on the distant hour of some forgotten day.

THERE'S A STABBING PAIN in my chest, and I can't catch my breath. When this happened before, in B.C., I thought I was having a heart attack, and it was Lara who talked me clear of it, Lara who'd been there once herself, stuck in a hinterland of grief. She knew what to do. I pick up the phone beside my bed and hover my finger over the number pad before realizing that her number's not in my head. Do I even have it? My address book isn't in my bedside table or in the junk drawer in the kitchen, and all the while I'm looking, rifling through old bills and expired video rental cards and dried out pens, I'm calculating the weeks, months, years since we last spoke. Almost exactly two cycles around the sun since I stood by the charred wood of that extinguished fire, breathed the pungent sage smoke, watched her walk away. No matter how much I want to, I can't just call her up.

There's another number beside the phone, scrawled on the back of a receipt. I dial it, forgetting about the time, and it barely rings before a voice answers, calm, wide awake, like she's been waiting.

"Sorry to call so late."

"I'm a night owl," says Sophie. "You must be too."

I'm not, though. If anything, the first morning light is what I like best, glowing like a clean slate, not the grainy texture of time past midnight.

"How's Grommet?"

"Sound asleep in the barn."

I'm silent. "Everything okay?" Sophie asks.

I fight back tears, not even sure what's brought them on this time. I should be feeling better about things but here it all is, the deepest currents churning to the top, cold and briny, full of crap. I wipe my nose with the back of my hand, and my snot feels freezing.

"Oh," Sophie says, surprised. "He'll be fine. Dogs are amazing creatures. They adjust to how they're treated, and sometimes, when they adjust to being treated poorly, like Grommet did to that bastard before you, that's what they know. It's tricky to get them back on track. But he's a smart boy. He'll be fine. You'll see."

I blubber for nearly a full minute, unable to speak.

"That is why you called?"

"Yes," I manage.

"Nothing else on your mind?"

I shake my head, then mutter, "No."

"Why don't you come out tomorrow? We can do some training."

"I have to work."

"Okay," she says. "Another time."

"Yeah."

"Soon, though."

I nod, then thank her and hang up. This is the second time I've cried in front of her, and I feel embarrassed, but it's helped, her words, and I'm able to return to sleep, although I dream. I dream that I'm in an unrecognizable living room with Angie, and there's a body we have to deal with, that we try to stuff into the kitchen garbage under the sink, but he springs out, too big to fit. We're trying to figure out what to do — call 911, the police, a funeral home — when the guy starts moving, flopping around on the floor like a fish, waxy skinned and blue in the face. He's a stranger, he isn't anyone I know, and I wake with no resolution, just a heavy sense of dread in my belly. Right away, I call my boss.

"I'm not feeling well," I tell her.

"Yes." She drags the word out, waiting.

"Maybe it's the flu."

She sighs, and I hear a tapping sound like the end of a pen hitting her desk.

"Second Friday in a row calling in sick, Mel."

"Sorry," I mutter.

"Are you sure you're happy here?"

"Yes," I lie. The truth is that I wonder that all the time. I don't feel like I'm doing anything meaningful. Does anyone even care about two-headed calves, buildings constructed fifty years ago, ancient car accidents, miners' strikes long since resolved, enough that it's important to preserve them for all time?

"All right," my boss says. I don't bother thanking her because she's already hung up.

6.

IT'S A GORGEOUS spring day and the sun is just beginning to burn off the night's cold mist when I reach the top of the hill near Massey. A faint thread of grey unwinds from Sophie's chimney, blurring into the blue sky. Through my cracked open window, I smell pine and wood smoke and the earth opening up, that pungent, rich aroma of thawing mud. The barking of dogs rings through the valley. Happy, I think. The word Teresa, my boss, used. Yes, I could tell her now, in this moment. I can't look too closely, though, or the feeling will evaporate.

GROMMET NEARLY KNOCKS me over when I get out of the car. I crouch down, rub his shoulders, haul him close. "Grommy," I say, laughing as he licks my face, pushes his cold nose into the corner of my eye. Sophie comes out of the barn dressed in tan work pants and a faded red polo shirt, her thick arms crossed. She's smiling. "You changed your mind."

"Yes." I stand, wipe my slobber-wet hands on my jeans.

"He misses you."

"I miss him."

"Any luck so far?"

I cock my head, questioning.

"On finding another place?"

"Not really," I tell her. "Most places won't take dogs."

"Don't tell them about him."

Grommet runs off, and I watch him push into a trio of other dogs by the apple tree, sniffing. One of them pees on the trunk, and then they all do, taking turns.

"They'd just find out."

She shrugs, then lets out a loud whistle, and all the dogs come running.

SOPHIE USHERS THEM into what she calls their apartments — those individual kennels at the back of the barn. Then we bring Grommet into the yard to work on his training. Before we pass through the wide door, Sophie pulls a fanny pack off a nail pounded into a beam. The sun throbs through the tops of the trees, warm enough that I take off my jacket and toss it on the hood of my car.

"Dogs are social beings," Sophie says, as I'm walking back towards her. "They want to do what you want. That's what thousands of years of domestication gets us."

She's got the fanny pack strapped around her waist, and

she's holding a small plastic box in her hand. A clicker, she calls it, and she explains that the only training she's done with Grommet was to charge it. This means that she gave him a whole bunch of treats, one after the other, punching it again and again so he'd associate the sharp, short click with a reward. It's obvious that Grommet knows what's happening. He stands close to her, his eyes on her hands, eager, waiting for cookies.

"The trick is to be as clear and consistent as you can with your instructions and don't expect Rome in a day." She looks at Grommet. "Now, let's see what you can do." She waits a beat. "Sit."

He stares at her. She says it again. I think I see a flicker of understanding in his eyes. He starts to lower his rear end toward the ground, and as soon as he makes that motion, she hits the clicker and digs into the fanny pack.

"That was an approximation," she says. "Not a total sit, but the first step towards the sit. You reward for that, those baby steps, and then make your way closer and closer to the behaviour you want."

She does it again.

"I think he's had some training," she mutters as Grommet gobbles down another treat. She angles her eyes towards me. "From you?"

I shake my head.

"Well, somewhere along the line somebody cared about him."

She takes a couple steps back, says the command, and I watch Grommet shift his feet forward and slowly lower his butt. By the third time, he immediately plunks his rear end onto the ground and she clicks when he's made contact.

"There," she says. "You've got your foundation. Want to try?"

I fumble the clicker, drop a handful of dried liver bits that Grommet sucks up. I take some more from her, try again. When

I ask Grommet to lie down, he does nothing. Three more times, I repeat the request, and he stares at me, as if challenging, as if pointing out that I don't have what it takes. Sophie's fingers brush my elbow, drawing my attention.

"Rule number one," she says. "Don't take it personally. It's not about you. If he doesn't know what you want, how can he give it to you? You have to show him what you mean."

She holds a treat near Grommet's nose and lowers it, and I remember, years and years ago, my dad doing something similar with Frankie, except that he'd push him into the postures he wanted and not offer any rewards beyond a gruff pat on the top of the dog's head. He always said he wanted the dog to listen to him out of complete loyalty rather than a lust for food. As soon as Grommet's neck extends, moving towards the cookie while stretching out his front legs to lie down, Sophie hits the clicker. Then she takes him through it again, rewarding him as he stretches his front legs out. Soon, he's lying down, and the sound of the clicker punches the air. "Jackpot!" she cries, and gives him a dozen treats, one by one, from the fanny pack. He's excited and smiling, I realize, recognizing that I haven't seen him grin like this before, his mouth open to reveal a line of pink flesh under his heavy jowls, eyes squinty. When he's standing again, she says, "lie down," and he immediately presses his belly to the ground. She clicks, then leans forward, speaking with a voice gone breathy and excited, "Where's your ball?"

He whips his head around, hunting. "Go get it!"

Grommet takes off as she unbuckles the fanny pack. "Eventually you've got to mix up the rewards, especially with him. He's a smarty-pants. He'd just stop doing anything unless you had a cookie right there with his name on it."

"He didn't know how to play before," I tell her when Grommet drops a tennis ball at my feet.

"He's a fast learner. I saw him watching Mowat. You play with him. I'll grab some drinks. Iced tea okay?"

"Sure." I whip the ball across the yard and Grommet scrambles to get it, already a different dog from the tense, damaged creature I first knew.

SOPHIE COMES OUT of the house with a tray. A pitcher of iced tea, glowing amber, and a plate full of sandwiches cut into triangles. I follow her into the yard behind the house, to a white table and chairs near a lilac tree that's beginning to bud. The sun is high, spread over a lawn that's still more dirt and lumps of yellow snow than grass, and we settle into the iron chairs. She tips the pitcher, pours tea into a glass decorated with images from *Star Wars*. Luke Skywalker brandishing his light saber, little green Yoda in his burlap robe. *Mother's Pizza* it says around the bottom. I expect the tea to be sweet, but it isn't, and the sudden bitter tannins surprise me.

"Where's Ted?" I ask, and Sophie glances left. I see the glint of greenhouse windows past a grove of trembling aspens behind the barn; the trees' new leaves flicker in the breeze.

"Out and about," she says.

"Owain said he and Matt are working on some project with him?"

"Did he?" She pushes the plate of sandwiches towards me, some on white bread, some on brown. "Tuna fish. I put a bit of onion and pickle in there as well."

When she pulls her arm back, she drops her hands into her lap and I realize she hasn't even poured herself a drink. She looks over my shoulder towards the scrubby bush beyond her house, a wide slope of pink and grey granite. "He keeps himself busy," she says. "Wanders off, hikes the back forty, works in the greenhouse a lot. I don't use it, never had much of a green thumb, and he's got a good crop of seedlings started. Tomatoes and peppers, that sort of thing."

For a second, I think she's talking about Matt. It would fit him, disappearing like that, focused on a self-made project, although I can't imagine him gardening. When we were kids it was always me out in the backyard, watering the strawberry plants and tender annuals my mother planted then forgot about while Matt was typing articles for the *Hixon River Gazette*.

"He has a condition called Proteus syndrome," Sophie tells me, reaching for a sandwich. "Born with it. You were probably wondering."

"Oh."

"He's still a teenage boy, though. I give him a lot of freedom. Figure he can make his own mistakes, learn his own lessons, and I'm always here when he wants to work things out."

I nod as she takes a bite. A car goes by on the road, heading for Massey. We hear it but only see a cloud of dust as the vehicle climbs the hill. Grommet stands, watching the drift, expectant, thinking it might be coming here.

"Were Ted's parents sick too?" I ask. "I mean, he's your nephew, right?"

"Owain again?" She raises her eyebrows, and purses her lips, amused. I feel like the question is not only about what he's told me, but also how. Were we lying down, was it pillow talk? With both shoulders, I shrug, and pinch away a smile, pretending to wipe my lips. She shoves the rest of the sandwich into her mouth, finishing it, and some part of me relaxes. I take another myself, realizing how hungry I am.

"My stepsister's by birth. She was only seventeen, couldn't handle it, took off." She lifts up the pitcher of iced tea, questioning, and I push my glass over.

"Where did she go?"

Sophie studies my face, then pours. "I was angry for a long time," she says, not answering my questions. "Then I started wondering, would I have done any better?" She hands me my drink and I take it, swallowing the thick mash of bread and fish, washing it down with the cold tea. Sophie's eyes are on me as I glance away, and I feel her staring at me, but then when I look again I find that she isn't. She plucks a hunk of pickle off the table, pops it into her mouth. It feels like a lesson but maybe it isn't one, maybe she doesn't know more than she's letting on, isn't offering me advice on how I should think about my mother.

"You know what I mean," she says. "If I had her life, her experiences, her upbringing."

"You didn't?"

She shakes her head. "Her mom married my dad. I was pretty much grown by then."

I nod, guzzling the drink that isn't sweet enough, wishing for sugar. Beside me, Grommet suddenly stands up from the bed he's scratched into the dirt. He twists his head towards the house and starts barking. Relieved, I flip my attention to whatever he's got in his sights. I don't want to talk about people who do bad things, who disappoint. In the driveway, there's a new dog, black and sneaky looking, crouched low, tail between her legs. She's appeared out of nowhere. Surprised, I say, "Where'd you come from?"

Sophie twists around to look. "Oh," she says, standing. "That's Hilda. She must have got off her chain." She gestures at Grommet. "Take him," she says, and I grab my dog's collar, hold tight.

Hilda creeps towards the verandah as Sophie shuffles towards her, turned slightly sideways, carrying the wedge of a sandwich. Nervous, the dog scampers, her gaze locked on

Sophie and even from that distance, I can see the whites of her eyes, how scared she is, what dog behaviourists call whale eye, I've learned. Sophie crouches, tosses a scrap of bread and fish onto the ground between them and Hilda inches closer, sniffs it, then ferociously gobbles it down. Grommet bucks, wanting freedom. I appease him, let him lick my fingers then give him an entire quarter sandwich of his own.

Sophie throws more food, moving sideways towards the house, building a path. Soon I hear paws clattering on the verandah, then the slam of a door. Moments later, Sophie comes out through the back door off the kitchen and looks at me, her cheeks ruddy, her pale eyes pulsing with light.

"We've been trying to rescue that dog for three years," she says, then springs into action, spinning her bulky frame back into the house while I stay outside with Grommet. He's edgy, prancing around the perimeter of the house, jumping up to sniff at the window screens. From the porch, I can hear Sophie on the phone, saying "stray dog...check her over...shots...this afternoon?" — and I realize she must be calling the vet. Finally, she comes outside.

"I've got to get moving on this girl before Ostranik shows up looking for her. Can you hold down the fort?"

"Sure," I say. I've got nothing else to do, nowhere to be. Sophie carries the lunch things back inside while I put Grommet into his apartment, give him a cookie, then walk to the house where Sophie's got Hilda on a leash in the kitchen. I move too quickly, letting the screen door slam and Hilda hangs her head, then pees a bit on the linoleum. There's an open sore on her side that's matted over with dirt and dried blood.

"Poor girl," I mutter. I'm tempted to touch her, but I don't.

"The vet's in Hixon River from the Soo today, and she can see me at one." Sophie glances at her watch, a kid's watch, I notice, with a yellow band, Goofy on the face. Hixon's about an hour's drive west, and it's already a few minutes past noon.

"Can you stick around until I get back? I might need you to run her into Norbury."

"Okay," I say, and Sophie smiles, then grabs her purse off the counter, a boxy brown leather bag stuffed full, worn white on the seams.

"If you're up to it, there's also laundry to be done, and if you can let the dogs out and clean up any accidents in the barn." I nod at her instructions, already pressing a sheet of newspaper onto the urine on the floor, and then she's gone, leading the cautious dog to her truck and calling back through the open window: "And keep an eye on Trotsky."

TROTSKY JUMPS OFF the couch and follows me around, waiting at the top of the stairs to the stone-walled cellar when I bring a load of blankets down to the washing machine. The duties remind me of my volunteer job at the shelter, and I do everything Sophie's asked, picking up some poop in the barn apartments and hosing down the concrete floor while the dogs play outside. When the washing cycle finishes, I carry a heaping basket out to the verandah, and I'm clipping clothespins to a yellow blanket with a tattered satin edge when the dogs race down a trail between the greenhouse and a wide bare garden that's been tilled and is ready for spring planting. They come back encircling Ted, who's talking to them about something he found, a perfect patch.

"Hi, Soph," he calls.

I pull the blanket aside so he can see my face. "Hi," I say, smiling.

He stops, jabbing the tip of his gnarled walking stick into the ground. He's got a backpack on and a wide-brimmed hat, one side squeezed over his head. In his hand is a long rolled up tube of paper.

"What are you doing here?" He looks around. "Where's my aunt?"

I fill him in as I pin up the last blanket, then push the line out so the laundry catches the breeze. Then I ask, "Out for a hike?"

"Yeah."

"Gathering food?"

He shakes his head.

"Oh, I thought I heard you say you'd found a good patch."

He looks away. "Blueberries, but they aren't ready yet."

Well, duh, I think. There are still patches of snow in the shade.

"Anything to eat?" Ted asks, walking towards the back door. I tell him about lunch and follow him inside to put the kettle on like I live there.

"When's she getting back?" he asks, piling sandwiches on a plate, then sitting at the table.

The flat white numbers on the ancient avocado stove say 3:37. Josie will soon be at the library, might already be there, waiting for me. "Soon, I hope."

He stuffs bread into his mouth, chews with full cheeks.

"So you like gardening?" I ask, trying to start a conversation. My hands grip the back of a chair. Behind me, the burner coil's starting to glow, the kettle beginning to rattle.

"Yeah," he says, and takes a drink of water. He's filled the same glass I used, that Sophie left beside the sink. Trotsky stands with his front paws on Ted's knee, and Ted lets him lick his finger, feeds him a sliver of fish.

"And you know my brother?"

Right then the kettle starts to hiss, and I hesitate, waiting for him to answer, but when it starts screaming, I turn, shut the stove off, start opening cupboards to find the tea. "Owain said he's been helping you, that the three of you..."

"He's been helping us map our land," Ted says. "There's eighty acres out here and one corner's up against an old mine. We want to know what we've got."

"Owain said..." That he was involved too, that he was an independent contractor. Ted interrupts me. "Owain's a landscaper," he says, as I pull out a box of Red Rose, stacked on top of a dozen boxes of various kinds of herbal teas. When I turn around, he's staring down into Trotsky's face. The little dog is lifting his paws, one at a time, performing all the tricks he knows to try to get more scraps.

"You're going to landscape eighty acres?"

"We need money," Ted says in a rush. "I know it might seem surprising, but rescuing and training dogs? Not so lucrative."

What then? Reopening an old mine? Stocking a pond? Starting a fishing camp? Any of those projects makes sense. Natural resources stuff. Matt sharing his knowledge of the area, his maps, his expertise. My fingers shuffle through the tea bags.

"So you met my brother through the MNR?"

Ted sighs, and I hear the clatter of his chair as he leans back.

"Last fall," he says. "He came to meet Sophie."

I turn around. "So, Sophie called him?"

Ted shakes his head, then abruptly stops. His mouth opens and closes before more words rush out. "I don't know. All's I know is he showed up here one day." He lifts both hands like he's surrendering. Maybe Sophie called him. Maybe Owain told Matt about her. Maybe my brother offered his services, volunteered to help. I'll ask Owain, I think. An excuse to talk to him. Tell me about the work you're doing, I'll say. Maybe I can help. Ted stands and carries his plate to the sink, washes it and sets it in the rack. I turn away to pour boiling water into the mug.

There are words on it that have worn down to nothing but green speckles scattered over a pockmarked happy face, bright yellow but scarred. Tea blooms out of the bag, and when I look up at the sound of the dogs, I see Sophie driving into the yard. It's time for me to go.

part six

1.

THERE WERE OTHER hippies on Cougar Mountain. In a hot
spring blurred by a mist of rising steam, we found them. "Hey
there," a woman called out as she kicked off a pair of black
winter boots and dropped her towel to climb naked into the
steaming pool. Meditation beads hung between her swaying breasts, and the men, one balding, his long white hair
held in a wispy ponytail, curved their eyes around her body.
Somebody lit a joint, and I watched one raised hand pass
it to the next over the surface of the water. I looked at Lara,
her arms crossed, each hand clutching the opposite elbow,
and then over at Daisy who'd already taken off her faux-fur
coat and was working on the sash of her skirt, the button of
her jeans.

"Turquoise," she called, using the name she'd given me. On
the drive through Washington, she'd tried some out for Lara:

Dolores, she suggested — it means "sorrows" in Spanish — but Lara hadn't responded, still angry.

"Coming," I said. Lara gripped my elbow.

"Where are we supposed to sleep?" It was cold, snow heaped around the fat tree trunks, and our car wouldn't keep us warm. But I didn't want to think about that. I wanted to live for the moment, plunge into the hot bath.

"Come on," I said, and grabbed Lara's fingers, tried to pull her along with me. She stayed rooted where she stood.

"No fucking way."

"We'll figure it out. Somebody'll put us up."

"That's what I'm afraid of."

Daisy called my name again. I looked at her, already naked, her small breasts bobbing, her face lit with eager excitement. I knew what she'd say, if she stood in my place. I turned to Lara. "You know this fear is totally your own construction."

She glared at me. "Yes," she said. "I'm constructing a choice to not flash my tits at a bunch of pervs." I didn't answer her. "Turquoise," she added, her voice pressing on the name, sarcastic. She cast her gaze up into the tall, dark pines around us, the stars clotting the sky. A lot like where we grew up. "What's that even mean? That you're so very blue and beautiful, with your tragic dead brother and all."

I barely heard her. I was already walking away. When I stripped my clothes off, everyone cheered, and somebody passed me a bowl of hash after I eased into the water, letting the heat sink into me like sunshine. Deeply, I drew in the thick smoke, and when I next looked over at the trail, Lara had gone.

WE ENDED UP in a renovated school bus that night, all three of us, Lara silently following me when a man named Mason led us back to his place. She and I slept on a plywood floor that was blood stained from a baby born the previous summer, our sleeping bags too close to the small, pot-bellied stove. Lara kept pulling them back so they wouldn't catch fire, waking me over and over, although it was already hard to sleep with the sounds of Daisy and the old guy having sex on a raised bunk at the end of the bus. His grunts, her high-pitched squealing. Whenever I slivered open my drug-swollen eyes, I saw Lara's face, close to mine, her hands covering her ears, her eyelids jumping around. I could tell she wasn't sleeping. Her face like that was a familiar sight. How many sleepovers had we had together? We'd known each other since we were eight. For a while, I watched her, and eventually the stiffness in her face relaxed, her lips dropped open, her breathing deepened, and then I could sleep.

2.

IT'S JUST AFTER FIVE when I get to the library, and it looks like it's going to rain.

"Shit, shit, shit," I mutter as I park across the road, hoping my boss has already gone home, that Josie's still waiting for me. Inside, I avert my eyes from Henry, who's sitting at a small round table flipping through the newspaper, because I know if I say hello he'll drag me over for a conversation about botany or local history that's all one sided. Past him, Josie's on the couch in the magazine area, her head nodding into sleep, a copy of *Chatelaine* winged open across her knees. Her arm's in a sling.

"Hey," I say, touching her shoulder. Her eyes blink open; a smile creeps across her lips. Her hair is wild around her face, tangled and unruly like it's been since her mom stopped weaving it tight against her scalp in braids.

"How long have you been waiting?"

"Not long. An hour."

"Shit, Jose. Sorry."

"That's okay," she says, rubbing one of her eyes. "I just sat down and had a nap."

I gesture at her arm, at the sling knotted behind her neck. "What happened?"

"Not much. They might have to rebreak it, but they couldn't do it today."

"Why not?"

She bites her bottom lip, and a smile flickers in her mouth, but from behind me, I hear Ruth talking to someone at the circulation desk. When I glance over my shoulder at the windows that surround my area, I see Chrissy, one of the pages, standing in front the book repair area, holding an art gum eraser, staring straight at me. She lifts her hand to wave, and I answer with a quick smile before looking over again at Ruth, head down, stamping books. At least she hasn't spotted me.

"Can we talk on the way?" I whisper. "I'm supposed to be sick."

OUTSIDE, GREY CLOUDS are pushing in, edging out the blue sky. We park at my apartment building as the first drops of rain start to fall, ticking against my windshield. I turn around and grab the groceries I'd picked up after dropping Hilda off at the shelter, then rush around to help Josie out of the car. All the way from the library I've been telling her about my day, about the dog and Sophie, about seeing Liv again.

Arriving like that meant I had to tell Liv what I'd done, that I'd found Grommet a temporary home until I could figure things out. She listened, nodding slowly, then crossed her arms and shrugged. "Well," she said. "As long as you know what you're doing."

I do, I told her, and she seemed to relax as I went on about how good Grommet was, how happy, how it feels like there's hope.

I'm happy too, I realize, as I'm gushing it all out to Josie on the elevator, talking so fast that her face looks startled, her eyes shifting around as she tries to keep up.

In my apartment, Josie drops her backpack on the couch and tilts her head at the crinkle of garbage bags under the blankets. The arms are hollowed into pits of yellow foam. I see my place through her eyes: the chewed-up bookshelf leaning against the wall, the splintered remote control, the filthy carpet I haven't yet fully cleaned.

"Wow," she says. "He did a number."

I set the grocery bags on the counter and stick a bottle of wine into the freezer to chill. I'm starving—it's nearly six—but when I turn to ask Josie if she wants to order a pizza instead of cooking I see the red light of my answering machine flashing insistently, and my stomach drops. Fuck, I mouth, silently, pinching the bridge of my nose.

Angie's voice in the first message is light, a sing-song. "I'm sure you're on your way but just checking..."

In the second one I can hear the tremor of irritation — "Where are you, Mel?" — before she drops the phone in its cradle. I push my face into my hands as Matt comes on, his tone cold, all business. "We called somebody else. Get here as soon as you can."

As soon as I can. Believing, I suppose, that something important must have kept me, that there was nothing to be alarmed about. Because it's me, I think. Because it isn't out of character, because this is what I do: let people down just by treading the path that seems correct at the time.

this has nothing to do with you

I let out a long, ragged sigh. "Jose," I call, because she's gone into the washroom.

"Yeah?"

"Change of plans. We've got a babysitting job."

3.

OWAIN ANSWERS THE DOOR. We push inside, Josie and me, soaked from the run from my car in the driveway. He's got a beer in one hand and Ellie cradled in his other arm. She's clutching the collar of his plain black T-shirt. He's dressed casually this time. No silk shirt. Worn jeans, ripped at the knees and mismatched socks, one black, one blue.

"Nice of you to show up," he says, as I'm stripping off my leather jacket, which smells, I realize, like wet dog. I drop it on the floor, on top of an old pair of Matt's converse sneakers, the red ones he used to wear when he came home from the big city. I haven't seen them in ages. I reach for my niece.

"Were they really mad?" I ask. Ellie giggles, spits up a milky bubble, then grabs at my earring.

"You could say that." He leans against the top of the railing that goes downstairs. "They called a few other people before they settled on me. Angie didn't seem very happy to give me the gig." He chugs on his beer, a bottle of Canadian with the silver label half torn off. "I offered references."

"Where were they going?" Josie asks, pulling a hanger out of the closet, struggling to slip it into her coat sleeves with one good arm. Owain sets down his drink to help her.

"It's their anniversary," I say, into the baby's face.

"Which one?" asks Josie.

"First," I say, then mutter, "I think," but neither of them hear.

"Ah," says Owain. "Paper." He leans into the closet, then picks up my coat and hangs it up as well.

"How do you even know that?"

"What can I say? I'm a romantic." He grins at me; I feel my blood rush. Then his eyes are on Josie as he extends his hand. "I'm Owain."

"Sorry," I say, uncurling Ellie's fingers from my earring one by one. I slide the silver bangle off and shove it in my pocket. "This is Josie."

"What's three years?" she asks, and I give her a look. She's playing dumb. It isn't like her to not know something like that. Owain casts his eyes towards the ceiling, thinking.

"Leather, maybe? Maybe wood?"

"Leather." I look at Josie. "That'll be an interesting challenge for Bruce."

She shrugs. I don't mean it as a jab, but she's probably taken it as one. I wonder how Lara acts with her now, if she's still trying to get Josie to dump him like we did back in high school, one afternoon spending our whole spare period writing out a list of all the things Josie would miss out on: one night stands with strangers, spontaneous trips to exotic countries, other stuff that mattered more to Lara than Jose, I knew. Lara taped it to Josie's locker and Josie stared her straight in the eye as she crumpled it into a tight ball, bounced it off Lara's forehead. And that was it, we knew. We'd lost.

"Who's Bruce?" Owain asks.

"Husband," I say, jerking my head towards Josie.

"Really?" He looks at her and I read his face. That's a shame, he's thinking, so I shove past him, carrying the baby up the short flight of stairs to the kitchen to get myself a beer.

this has nothing to do with you

"Drink?" I call down to Josie, but Owain's saying something to her, and she's distracted, and when I repeat myself, it's like she doesn't even hear me.

"Jose?" I holler, annoyed.

"Yeah?" she says. "No, thanks."

I stare at her for a second.

"Painkillers."

I turn away, remembering suddenly that I forgot to pull the wine out of my freezer, wondering if it will be ruined.

IN THE LIVING ROOM, Josie sits on the couch and holds out her good arm. I lower Ellie to her, and she gobbles the baby up in the crook of her elbow. She leans down and kisses her soft forehead, caresses her velvet skin with her thumb, and I see how Ellie looks at her, alert and curious, laughing and engaged. It's like I can already see the person she'll be, and I wonder if this is what my mother saw from the beginning in Matt, remember her raising a toast of fizzy champagne mixed with grape juice at his Grade 8 graduation, smiling, a smear of cherry lipstick colouring her front tooth as she called him our future prime minister. He won a provincial speech contest that year and got to go to Ottawa. He was president of the students' council. He was already so handsome, and even owned two suits, those miniature polyester ones with the elastic neckties. It's been a long time, I realize, since I've seen Matt in a suit. I drift over to the dining room to look at their wedding picture, hung in a silver frame beside the china cabinet. Matt grinning, his hand on the handle of the knife, while Angie stands behind the simple white cake, body turned to him, one finger touching the tip of his nose. Her silk dress gathers the light of the sunset and seems smeared with hues of pink and orange. Everything glows, except the dark row of pines between them and the lake, and

Matt's navy-blue suit, its colour flowing into the black plastic handle of the knife so you can't see the divide.

I wonder if they still have those clothes, if they're upstairs in the closet, if Angie's wedding dressed is vacuum sealed and put away for Ellie to wear one day. I can snoop, I realize, sliding my eyes over to the china cabinet, which I've never looked inside, not even when I lived here, and when I open the door, the hinges sticky and squealing, I find all the good dishes I ever ate on or out of: my mother's porcelain punch bowl, those small dessert plates that were out almost every Christmas, the cornflower-etched sherry glasses, touched by her lips after supper each night, an act I thought alarmingly pretentious, incredibly fake, by the time I turned seventeen. Quickly, I close the door, and the instant I do, the phone rings.

"Probably Angie," Owain says, coming back in through the sliding glass door, carrying the smell of his cigarette. He twists around the door jam, grabs the phone off the kitchen wall before I can reach it.

"Barnett residence," he says, and as soon as I see the confused listening look on his face, I know exactly what he's hearing. By the time he says "accept" — as in yes, I'll accept the charges — I'm already running up the stairs towards the bedrooms.

"Mel," he calls, and I shout back, "Bathroom."

I lean against the closed door, my heart beating hard. After a minute, I open it a crack to listen as Owain talks to my mother, telling her things about me, even saying something about Grommet, then laughing at a joke she's made. It's Josie who spots me, who stares up from the couch with a challenge on her face, but all I do is shut the door again and sit on the floor. I'll stay in there all night if I have to, to avoid both talking to her and whatever Owain will say to me afterwards: how nice

this has nothing to do with you

my mother is, how he didn't know she was in prison, and what did she do anyway? Unless he already knows.

"Mel," he calls again, but I ignore him. I sit on the floor until enough time has passed, until he must have hung up, and then stand up and stare at myself in the mirror. There they all are, drifting within my own features: my mother's wide forehead, my brother's narrow nose, my father's auburn hair, impossible to escape.

IN THE MEDICINE CABINET I find pills. Codeine, sedatives, sleep aids. Digging deeper, I discover a bottle of Prozac with Matt's name on it, dated from February. I cup the orange container in my palm, stare down at it, and when I shake it there's a rattle. Depression, Angie said, just the other night. Is that what's happening? Is he sinking? Like Mom, who refused to take anything, who treated herself with whatever she had on hand. Her nightly tipple, brandy left over from Christmas, the prescriptions she got after each of her parents died. Valium to quiet her shaky nerves, other medications to help her cope with grief. Percocet for bad cramps. I put the full bottle back, tucked into its hiding spot behind a comb tangled with Angie's blonde hair and a bottle of Tylenol 2s.

Now I want to open every drawer, but the rest of what I find is ordinary. Across the hall, in their bedroom, there's dental floss, a watch with a cracked face, condoms, a stack of books on his bedside table. A John le Carré spy novel, a tattered paperback copy of *The Razor's Edge*, poetry by Ralph Waldo Emerson. Angie's side I leave but I do find her wedding dress hanging at the far end of their closet in a garment bag that I unzip. Gently, I touch the smooth silk, watch it shimmer in my fingers. When they married, I was out West, and I didn't even know. If he'd told me, if I'd called, would I have come back? I would have brought only dirt with me, the soot from our riverside fire, bugs I tried to avoid by shaving my head, my body's sweat and grime. Even now, part of me is surprised when I drop the pure fabric without leaving any marks.

"What are you doing?" Josie asks, from the doorway. She looks straight at me to avoid seeing the private, unmade bed, the dresser heaped with Matt's shirts and jeans and folded underwear, Angie's pink jewelry box that plays a tinkly version of a classical tune when the ballerina slowly spins.

"Looking," I say, shutting a drawer.

"What for?"

I pick up a framed photo of Ellie as a newborn, her face flushed and wrinkled, eyes squinting. Behind the baby, out of focus, Matt's smile shows all of his teeth.

"Where's Ellie?" I ask.

She jerks her head towards the hallway, the living room at the bottom of the stairs. "Owain's got her."

I set the photo down, trying to match the edge of the frame to the line in the dust where it was sitting.

"You okay?" Josie asks, and I shrug. I don't want to talk about it. She opens her mouth to say something, and I know what's coming: you have to talk to her eventually, how long are you going to do this, you'll be better off if... I cut her off.

"Matt's keeping secrets," I say.

"What kind of secrets?"

"Fucked if I know."

She nods, and I can tell that she doesn't believe me, that she thinks I'm making it up. After all, put Matt and me side by side, examine our history, and you'll see who's more stable. So instead of humouring me, helping me dig through the dresser drawers, she pushes optimism into her face, smiles and asks, "So, that's the guy?"

this has nothing to do with you

"Yes," I tell her, but my tone is flat, because I'm not sure what to think of him either. He didn't exactly pull me into an embrace when I arrived. Then again, up until now my closest male companion has been a psychotically needy dog, so maybe my standards have been set a bit high.

"He's nice," Josie says, "but he smokes." She wrinkles her nose.

"Matt smokes."

"What?"

I nod. "One of the secrets."

I can tell by her face, by the dull expression of shock, that she remembers too. The lectures he gave anyone sucking on a cigarette, including Pete and Lara standing out back of the high school when the three of us were in Grade 10, our two brothers about to graduate. It was Pete's fault Lara started. The rebel, the outcast, with his eyeliner and his earrings, the bruises the bullies gave him.

I don't know why I'm thinking about Pete when it's Matt I need to worry about. I shove past Josie to head downstairs and feel her following me. The radio's on in the living room and Owain's swaying around with Ellie in his arms, singing *today is the greatest.* I don't stop, but I do look back to see Josie's reaction at this sweet scene, expecting her to be smiling, giving him her approval, but instead she seems stunned, still flummoxed, I suppose by what I've told her about Matt. How radically things can change. How careful we need to be.

DOWNSTAIRS, the door to Angie's room is still locked. Before last week it wasn't ever closed, at least not while I was around. I've been in there a dozen times, hanging out with Angie as she trimmed or permed her own hair or attempted to do something with mine as the stubble on my shaved head started growing in. I try the knob, press my hand against the cool wood. What could be in there? All of Matt's secrets, but what are they? We've been through the same things, were raised by the same parents, are only different in how we dealt with them. Matt, pushed up against the wall, our father's forearm pressed against his chest, telling him calmly to mind his own business, to butt out of their marriage. When was that? Some summer he was home or maybe earlier, before he left, when he first started bucking our father's control. Matt asking for something different off the menu when it was usually quietly decided what we would eat after Dad gave his order. Eggplant parmigiana, bright orange beside the mucky brown of three hot turkey sandwiches. The first time that happened, my father wouldn't let it go, kept making snide comments about Matt being such a man, having a mind of his own, until the argument escalated beyond reason, and there we were, pulled over on the side of the highway, half-way home from the Soo, Matt told to get out and walk the rest of the way. Of course, he didn't. Of course, my mother made enough peeps and calming sounds to get us going again, with Matt in the back seat belted up tight, shamed for having his own preferences. I drag in a breath, wishing my mind wouldn't go to those places, wishing my brother got out of the car that night, that I followed. That we walked together to a nearby farmhouse and put ourselves inside the welcoming, lit windows I liked to watch slide by in the darkness on that long drive. Not what actually happened. Not my mother eventually firing that single, searing bullet, the freed compression of a rage I've never fully understood.

"There's no one in there," Owain says, from behind me. I turn around. He hands me a new beer, not the one I've forgotten about, warm by now, lost upstairs.

"How do you know?"

He shrugs, takes a drink, gives me that smirk. His eyes drift over to the couch and I follow his gaze, remembering too. Yes, I want that again, but right now I'm more concerned about getting into this room than the distraction he's offering.

"Josie wants me to trim her hair," I lie. "I'm looking for Angie's scissors."

"Oh, yeah?"

He stuffs a hand into his pocket, rocks back on his heels, casually dangling the bottle from its neck like we're at a bar, waiting for the band to go on. Why did he rush down here, I wonder, and I think of what I know: Ted, Owain, and Matt. In on something. "You know where the key is." He doesn't answer. "What are you guys trying to hide?"

Upstairs, I hear Josie thump across the floor, singing a song to Ellie. Taking over, I hope, putting the baby to bed. Owain guzzles the last of his beer, and I wonder how long we'll stay like this, at an impasse. I step close, so close I can smell the last hint of his cologne, worn away from whenever it was applied, the sweet odour of old ash.

"He's my brother," I say, into the warm hollow of his neck and his empty bottle drops to the cushioned, carpeted floor. His hands go to my waist, slide under my shirt, and when he hits bare skin I suck in my breath. I want it to happen, for him to lead me over to the couch, touch me, until Josie hollers down, interrupting us. At the thought of her, I pull back, press my hand flat on his chest like I'd done to the door, and he draws away. For a moment, I expect him to lift up the key, grinning, like he's found it under my clothes, like it was on me all this time. A magic trick. But then he pushes his fingers into the pocket of his jeans and says, "I've got a better idea." A baggy holding a fat green marijuana bud dangles between us. "Let's get this party started."

4.

THE MOON IS FULL. It sits in the sky staring down, hard as bone. The rain has faded into a soft spitting that ticks against the metal eavestrough. In the triangle we've formed, I take a drag, two, from the sticky, slim joint, and quickly remember why I don't smoke pot anymore. Instantly, the caverns of my mind seem to widen, and creeping out is all this agony. My mother, my father, my damaged dog. And, Matt. Of course, Matt.

"Back in a sec," I mumble into the bramble of conversation between Owain and Josie. She's telling him about Bruce, about his job as an electrician, the new seniors' home he's working on. Her voice sounds flat and ordinary because she declined the joint, holding up the baby monitor through which we could hear Ellie's even, sleeping breaths. I'd taken it eagerly though, ready for escape, rationalizing that it might help me understand, inch closer to my brother's hidden world. Pot's medicine, the hippies out West always said, before toking to a point of oblivion, me included.

I step off the deck, walk a few steps on the soggy lawn before I realize that I don't have any shoes on. The grass is crunchy with a hard frost. At first it matters, is actually hilarious, and I laugh a long time before I stop caring. Or maybe it's that the cold grounds me, distracts me from the ache in my chest. Complicated grief, Lara had called it once, a term she'd learned from Pete. Because of him, I mean. Thinking I can escape it, I run. Towards the forest at the edge of the grass, towards the tall pines, their red, flaking bark lit luridly by the bright moon. Ignoring the needles stabbing into my bare soles, I enter the trees. From somewhere, a train whistle blows, or I hear one, anyway, and under my feet, I feel its rumble, imagine it carrying my mother, a young woman, north from Toronto. Matt inside her, nothing but splitting cells, the stem of a spine, a featureless, flat face. My father there, as well. Gone now. A storm that's settled. Absorbed into the earth on the day we buried him, Matt and me and half the town standing amongst the chattering jays in the graveyard, the bugs bad, wishing we'd sprayed ourselves down with DEET.

By the time I hear Josie's shoes cracking through the forest — and I know it's her, from the hesitancy of her tread, the sound of her voice quietly calling my name like she doesn't want to attract any ghosts in the dark woods — I'm practically drooling. My butt on a damp fallen log, my hands clutching my temples.

"Here," I say, because I know she doesn't see me. She stops.

"Here," I say again, and she turns to the sound of my voice and comes toward me, transforming into a solid shape in the mottled light, her sling glowing white.

"Angie called," she says.

"What did she..."

"Just to check in. She wanted to talk to you, but I told her you were in the bathroom."

I groan, anticipating consequences, what my sister-in-law will say. Josie fumbles for my knee, pats like a grandma. That's what we called her in high school, that's her nickname in our yearbook: Granny Jose.

"You okay?" Josie asks, and I sputter. I never sputter; I try never to let anyone see me cry, because I hate it, hate the pity that rolls over us like a tidal wave. But this is the third time in forty-eight hours. I lean my head on Josie's shoulder, and my eyes are a sudden hot mess of liquid. She slides an arm around me and rocks me, side to side. We've been friends for so long that she doesn't even ask what it's about, because she knows that if she did, I'd just pull away, fumble for logic, dismiss it, and then I'd be back where I started: stoic, shut tight. Instead she lets me cry until I'm finished, empty. I want to talk, to say something, but my tongue is so dry it feels like a wad of something, secrets that are still melting down.

"Do you want to go inside?" Josie asks, because I'm trembling.

"No, but it's okay. I can't stay here forever."

We don't move though. We stay on the cold tree trunk, in the dark, my toes losing feeling until Josie says, "I wish I could take you back, you know. I wish we could go back to before and stop it all from happening."

Turn time around so the fish food drifts up in the air to Matt's pinching fingers, drops into the small orange can. The minivan speeding backwards from our house, Josie robot-walking out of her mother's arms, folding, butt-first, into the vehicle. Lara picked up again at her uncle's, reversing past the crime scene, into the night while that single bullet whizzes out of my father's heart, seals up the wound on his girlfriend's neck. All that blood lifted into their veins.

And my mother, shuffling in reverse through the empty house, laying down alone in her bed, her deadly rage absorbed by blankness, by the disappearing dreams in her head.

How far back would we go? Rumbling into oblivion, until my mother and father had never met, were never even born, had never come to be?

"Would you still marry Bruce?"

She hesitates, then pulls me closer, and I press against her warmth. "Probably."

I don't respond.

"He's good with kids," she says.

"Bruce?"

"Well, we'll see. I wanted to tell..."

"Are you out there?" Owain shouts towards our hiding spot in the woods. I can see his face in Ellie's lit window as he hollers through the screen. "I think she needs her diaper changed!"

this has nothing to do with you

Josie bolts upright, onto her feet, and the whole scenario is suddenly so ridiculous that I start laughing and can't stop, not even as she tugs me over the rough ground, stumbling over branches and tree roots to the soft carpet of the lawn. But then we hear Ellie scream, a sort of furious shriek, and hand in hand we run to the house.

JOSIE'S LEFT THE back door open and a white moth is flitting around the brass chandelier over the dining room table. As soon as we get inside the phone rings and I'm expecting it to be Angie, calling back, trying again to talk to me so I suck in a breath, coming down by now, my nerves settling like branches at the end of a storm, and lift the handset.

"This is the Cornwall Prison for Women..."

I itch to hang up, but I'm slow and hesitate long enough that the stranger's voice asks again. Accept or deny. Surprising myself, I say, "Accept," and in an instant, there's my mother.

"Mel," she cries. "Mel, I'm so... Please don't hang up. Don't hang up."

She's breathing hard, almost panting, and I feel the same sudden stillness that came over me as a kid when I encountered her panic. How I'd freeze, wait to see what would happen, try to shrink into the wall. Now, I speak. "Mom," I say, and lean my forehead against the wall, close my eyes, focus on the galaxy of light inside my eyelids instead of the ache in my chest.

"How are you?" she asks from far away.

The baby monitor is on the kitchen counter, and through it I hear Josie and Owain talking to each another, Josie making my excuses. "She's just really high," she says, and then there's the ripping sound of Ellie's diaper coming off and Owain making a gagging sound, gulping like a frog. His footsteps echo in the hallway and then down the stairs, and then he's in the kitchen doorway. I have not answered my mother's questions, but it doesn't matter. She's talking, telling me she hasn't been well, that her lawyer's been trying to reach Matt. None of this do I need to hear, I think. Finally, she says, "Mel? Are you there? Are you there?" I hang up.

5.

OWAIN CRASHES ON the downstairs couch while Josie and I go to sleep in my old room, the guest room I stayed in for two and a half months when I first came back with Matt from Arizona. We whisper a bit about Owain, about whether I should sleep with him or not (I should), and also about Lara. "She's moving back," Josie tells me casually, as I'm drifting into sleep, and I fumble for words, when, where, but the pot is still in my system, swinging me out into a warm, deep current, and I let it take me. I don't surface again until noises start up in the house, Matt and Angie arriving back, doors opening and closing, the clunk of high heels hitting the floor. Harsh words, too. An argument, Angie's tears. It's almost two a.m. according to the bedside clock, and I listen until the rooms turn silent, then push back the quilt and pad out to the living room and down to the front door. There's a large wooden key with hooks on it screwed to the wall and, like I thought it would be, it's there: Matt's ring of keys.

None of them work. I try each one, careful to separate them so they don't clink together and wake Owain. He's sleeping with his face turned to the back of the couch, fully clothed, without even a blanket and I think about grabbing an afghan out of the closet in the laundry room, spreading it over him. As I consider this, looking over, I see the heap of things on the coffee table: his wallet, the baggie of pot, his lighter, his own set of keys, five of them on a ring attached to a large golden *O*. Team Org, I think suddenly, the stupid club that Lara, Josie and I had started as kids, named for Pete's nickname for us: Grommet. Exchange the *A* for an *M* and flip it around. Hand extended, I creep over to grab Owain's keys. The smallest one slides into the lock on the knob, turns it cleanly with a quiet click.

I don't know what I was expecting, but it isn't this. A blast of light hits me from a lamp above a dozen green seedlings, and I quickly close the door to keep the sunny glare from waking Owain. There's that smell again, the sweet, skunky odour, bringing back a hundred memories of my time out West.

On the counter that once held hairbrushes, hand mirrors, a basket of scissors, a dish of barrettes and elastic bands, there's now a mess of other stuff: a small kitchen scale, plant clippers, a box spilling shiny plastic baggies, a stack of dot matrix printer paper with a list of names and numbers printed out in pale grey ink.

The bottle of Barbicide is still there, shoved to one end of the counter, luminous in the bright light, reminding me of Matt's old tropical aquarium. As if it's beckoning me, like a crystal ball in which I hope to see my future, I step towards it and plunk myself down in that other familiar object, Angie's barber chair, unbolted from the floor, shoved into the corner.

This is now Matt's spot, I see. A cup of forgotten coffee sits on a table beside the chair, the cream a scummy pool on its surface. There's an ashtray full of butts, a can of air freshener, a yellow tea tin stuffed with cash, another pill container. I pick that up, see my mother's name on it, recognize the prescription. Amitriptyline. The bottle rattles, but when I open it, I see tiny green seeds. They roll into my palm. In the mess of soil and dust and hair clippings stirred up from moving the furniture, I know they'll disappear, and I drop them.

They bounce off the linoleum, scattering around the corner of a book with a bright red cover that's shoved under the chair. There's a pen sticking out of it, holding a place.

I nudge it with my toe like it's a carcass and I'm checking for signs of life.

It flips open to the spot marked by the pen and I see Rwanda written in large black bubble letters, white in the middle, like looking through bars.

Under this are dates and notes scrawled in Matt's boxy handwriting:

April 7: Major-General Roméo Dallaire using the words "all hell breaking loose" on the CBC.

April 14: a reporter from the BBC stating there was "a deliberate plan to massacre Tutsis."

On April 27, Matt's scrawled: *the Pope says genocide,* and yesterday, April 29, my brother wrote, *two years of fighting in Bosnia to get body count of 200,000 — figure could be exceeded in Rwanda in just six weeks — from the Globe and Mail.*

I FLIP BACKWARDS, moving into the earlier part of the book, looking for whatever else Matt's written, unabashedly snooping. Most of the pages are blank but at the very beginning I see a date, *November 27, 1993,* and words at the top. It's a letter to someone who won't ever read it.

Dear Dad.

I'm not sure. I close the journal, readjust, sit cross-legged, holding it on my lap, looking down at its red surface. I think of the wide stain of blood we'd driven out of town that summer to see, needing to plant our feet in that spot, the place where our father had died. After the crime scene tape came down, after the owner of the campground had tried to clean it and failed. Slowly, I open the cover; slowly, I start to read.

It's three o'clock in the morning and I can't fucking hack it. I'm downstairs. The baby keeps crying keeps crying. I shouldn't have left her, but I have. She's going to knock on the door any second and tell me to get my ass upstairs, drive Ellie around the block, and I should do it without being asked but I can't. I can't move. Gravity is dragging me down. Gravity is you.

My counsellor told me to do this as if it would help. As if I can somehow move on with my life by telling you how much I fucking hate you, how much I think I fucking hate mom more. How much I hate myself. How much I hate my invisible sister. How I can't live like this anymore, seeping out this toxic poison, ruining anything that's beautiful in my life.

Ang keeps telling me to try to just remember the good times. Like when I was six, and you taught me to carve, and I took to it like a house on fire. I sanded that thing until my fingers were all red and worn down, and I still have it. I don't know what it is. A horse or maybe a dog. It doesn't even matter anymore. Just a lump of useless wood I should burn. But fishing, at least that's something good you gave me. Along with all the bad. Putting me in places I never should have been. Sitting with her at that goddamned clinic. But that's my fault too. I went, and later if I hadn't been so fucking stupid. If I'd stopped for a minute and tried to see through you, and if I'd listened to what she said, didn't dismiss her like you always did, like you taught me to do. There, there, dear. Shut up and take it.

You told me about Celia like I was some sort of buddy, like I should have been happy for you, like I was supposed to buy you a fucking beer.

But because I'm such a patsy, a goddamned member of the

Justice League, my moral compass cranked me in a different direction and look what fucking happened? The ship crashed on the rocks and sank. No survivors except Mel.

Innocent Midge, who, like an idiot, I tried to align myself with that night, turning my back to what I'd set in motion, never thinking Mom would...

Murder you, I expect to read when I turn the page. But the words that stare at me sit all alone like the title of a book I've yet to read. They say: *do what she told me she would.*

My breath stops, feels like it won't come out again. What I want is to rush upstairs, shake Matt awake, look down into his face and make him talk to me.

He had known? Done nothing? Said nothing? What does he mean when he says he turned his back on what he'd set in motion? How had he had anything to do with it other than the same way I did: as witness, accidental victim?

The rest of the letter I don't understand at all. The clinic? Does he mean the hospital after her suicide attempt? And when had Dad had told him about Celia?

My head is spinning. The glaring light is beginning to hurt my eyes, and when I look up at the door pushing open, I'm somehow not at all surprised. I even hope it's Matt so I can show him what I've done, how I've invaded his space, so he can start explaining all the things that he's keeping from me. But I also don't want it to be him. I want to move this vignette of time backwards as well, peel my fingerprints off this book, put myself back in bed.

Instead, it's Owain. He stands in the doorway, the darkness a thick cloak on his shoulders.

"So now you know," he says, quietly.

I nod. "Now I know."

6.

"IT'S NOT A BIG DEAL," Owain says. "A few plants; a small and loyal clientele."

He doesn't fill in the other details, about Ted's role, Sophie's land, because I'm shaking my head, waving my hand at him to stop. We're sitting in the rec room, the door to Angie's former home salon shut behind me, seamed with light. The way the aquarium once glowed inside Matt's bedroom. Owain waits for me to speak.

"Does Angie know?" I ask.

"I don't know."

"He's got a baby!" I say. "It's illegal. He could go to jail." The thought is so absurd — Matt and my mother both in prison — that I actually let out a dark chuckle, but Owain ignores me.

"Booze was also illegal," he says, and he's off, launching into the argument I've heard a hundred times before. Hemp industry, William Randolph Hearst, corporate greed, the damage that alcohol does. None of this matters, not to me, because while I'm, yes, a little bit upset to discover that my brother's becoming a drug dealer, the real kicker is that other bit of news. How he'd stood on the dock, watching the sunset with me, while all along it seems he knew what our mother was thinking. What had they said to each other, down on the street, in front of our house, on the morning of the day I graduated?

"Watch her," he'd said to me on the phone just three months earlier. "She's so angry. She's so angry she's out of her mind."

I thought he was wrong. I lived with her. She was calm.

Calm like ice over deep water, I realized later. Most dangerous when it starts to thaw.

IT'S AROUND SIX A.M. when Owain leaves. He stands a few feet away from me, the distance crowded with my past, and cups his keys, tosses them in the air so the *O* glistens in the thin light through the basement windows. He's already begged me not to say anything to Matt, told me how my brother had insisted that I never know. Little Midge, fragile Mel.

"Call me later?" he says, and I nod, although what I'm thinking is, Why can't you call me? After he's gone, I stretch out on the couch, staring at the door, and slip back into the relief of sleep until I'm woken by the CBC, by Arthur Black's steady, friendly voice like that of a visiting uncle. I wish he was one; I wish I had a normal family; I yearn for that.

Matt's already in the kitchen. He's standing at the window, looking out, his hair shaggy around the collar of his bathrobe, nearly a mullet. For a second, I'm tempted to go up to him and tug on the dark locks, ignore everything I know, say something instead about reliving the eighties. Have things be friendly and casual, even tender. But I don't. From the doorway, I ask if there's any coffee, my voice rough from last night's smoking. It's a stupid question. The coffee pot is right there on the counter, filling up. When he turns, I catch the bright red streak of a cardinal flying across the yard behind him. I pretend to be more tired than I am, rubbing my eyes, crossing my arms tight. I'm fully dressed, having slept in the clothes I wore to Sophie's house yesterday: jeans and a long-sleeved top with lizards bleached onto it that Matt bought on Queen Street in Toronto and gave to me for Christmas one year. He doesn't seem to remember the shirt, doesn't give it a second glance.

"Morning," he says.

"Good time last night?" I don't know what else to say. There is a wall between us that's been hardening for years.

this has nothing to do with you

He shrugs.

"Now there's a ringing endorsement for marriage."

"Midge," he says, and it means: don't start, stay out of it, mind your own business. But it's a bit too late for him to shove me away. I know that; he will soon. He slips the pot out of the coffee maker, replacing it with a cup to catch the drips, then fills up two mugs, pushes one towards me. Green pottery, home-made, with fish carved into the glaze. I bought it for my dad on the Grade 8 Toronto trip.

I don't even touch it. Matt gets the cream out of the fridge, then scoops in sugar. His spoon clatters, but I hear how it stops when I say, "I talked to Mom yesterday."

He hesitates. "About time."

"She explained some things."

This is how I'm going to play it, I had decided in the wee hours.

"Why didn't you tell me?" I ask him.

"Tell you what?" He drinks his coffee, his face stiff and calm, and for a second he looks so much like Dad that my stomach drops. That cold reserve, the rage underneath. Not from Matt, I plead silently. Never from him.

"You know," I whisper, but he waits for me to go on.

"She told you," I tell him. I can hear my voice quaking because it's so hard to talk about it, to make that time real again with my words.

"That's what you talked about, the morning of my grad, and I've asked you, but you've not ever told me. Why won't you talk to me?" I look down at the floor before the tears start. I shove them away with my fingertips, don't let them out.

"I do talk to you."

Slowly I shake my head.

"Midge," he says. He steps closer, but he doesn't touch me.

"Just because I don't tell you what you want to hear, that doesn't mean I don't talk to you."

His voice is soft, patronizing. I glare at him, suddenly feeling like I'm six years old, my anger dismissed. A memory of my father and me, sitting on the stairs, me quaking with rage about something, and him insisting that I tell him I love him. Matt holds his mug in both hands, lets out a sharp sigh.

"Why didn't I tell you?" he says. "I don't know. How many times did she say she was going to do stuff? Kill herself, kill him, kill that cunt." The sharpness of his voice makes me flinch, and he twists towards the counter, drops his coffee roughly enough that it slops over the side. "And then it actually happened, and if I had told you . . ." He pauses. "One word, Midge. Say it with me." He annunciates each syllable. "Premeditation."

That morning, those long hours spent at the station, my mother hidden away in a cell. "Did you have any idea?" the policeman asked, when they finally ushered Matt and me into separate rooms. I sat at a table so clean it gleamed. I couldn't speak; all I could do was shake my head, the officer watching as he tapped his pen against the table's edge, examined my face. The bristles on his chin were a mix of red, silver and grey, and the silver ones shone when he cocked his head. "Can you tell me what your parents' marriage was like?"

What was their marriage like?

A shimmer of dizzy exhaustion had spread through me. Somewhere a clock ticked against the silence. It was around four; I hadn't eaten all day. The night before seemed like a happy dream. I didn't want to talk, and I can't say what I answered because I don't remember. Now I know what I'd say: they never should have been together, never should have had kids. In my mind, I spin back the reel to that moment on the stage when they met. The story I'd always heard about how my mother stumbled during a dance rehearsal and my father walked over to check on her. He was holding a hammer. I've imagined this as if I was seated in the audience, watching a scene from a play: how he shifted the blunt instrument to his other hand instead of putting it down, then reached forward to help her to her feet.

"She pleaded guilty," I say. What we knew, what we confessed to, wouldn't have mattered. Matt shakes his head.

"There were the charges to consider, the sentencing."

"Why did she do it?" I whisper. I've asked this question so many times, it slips easily out of my mouth, like a sigh.

"Have you ever been betrayed?"

I shake my head. "I have," he says, and I know he means by me, by how I left. Does he really hate me? But I can't ask him that. Matt lifts his cup to his mouth, then lowers it without taking a drink. "What else did she say?"

"Nothing," I tell him. He watches me like he knows I've been lying. He didn't tell me because he doesn't trust me. I reach for the cup of coffee and turn away, grab the rolled newspaper off the kitchen table and carry it into the living room. The TV's on, muted, showing President Clinton at a wooden podium. I shed the front section of the paper and dig deeper to find the classifieds, to see what's available for moving on, for finding a new home.

part seven

1.

WHEN WE DROVE into Mendocino, Daisy leaned between the two front seats, giving Lara directions. As we got closer, creeping down a dirt road through the forest, she let out a long, excited trill that reminded me of Frankie eagerly whining whenever he spotted another dog through the car window. "Here, here, here," she said, waggling her finger at the last driveway. Daisy's stepfather popped out the front door when we pulled in, wearing a full apron that said *Make Food, Not War.*

"I'm roasting an artichoke," he said, after Daisy skipped over to him. He looped his arm around her shoulders, his mouth relaxed in an easy grin, his green eyes bright.

"This is Turquoise," Daisy said. "And Dolores."

Lara shook her head. "It's Lara." She spoke at the same time he did. Their words echoed. I laughed, then pinched my lips shut when Daisy gave me a look.

"What?" Lara said.

"How interesting." His eyes twinkled as if a spell had been cast. "I'm Larry."

"And I'm starving," Daisy said, tugging his hand to haul him inside.

WE HAD A GOOD MEAL that night. Grilled portobello mushrooms, couscous, the artichoke. I'd never had one before and Larry showed me how to drag the thick leaves through a dish of melted butter, scrape the flesh off with my teeth. We had wine, too, and Larry told us about the pots he was firing in his kiln.

"I'm using copper carbonate to get that red glaze," he said, and rubbed the fingertips of both hands together like he was discussing a risky, important scheme. "They should be gorgeous, like beating hearts."

"I'm an artist too," Lara said, reaching for a piece of powdery Turkish delight.

"What medium?"

"Multimedia right now. I've been building ocean tableaux, using tinted resin to really make it look like water."

She went on, and I was just as entranced as Larry, listening to her describe her work, realizing that she didn't really speak much about it anymore. At least not to me. But then Daisy's glass tipped over, spreading a flood of red wine across the table, and we all leaped up and tossed our napkins over the puddle. Daisy burst into tears and ran out of the room. I heard the springs of a bed accept her thrown weight, and sat there, stunned. I'd never before seen her cry.

Larry looked towards the hallway where she'd disappeared, his bright, friendly face turned serious. The napkins were heaped on the dessert plate, sopping wet, the powdered sugar clotted red. It looked like we'd performed surgery.

"I think I'll go out for a cigarette," he said calmly.

"Can I have one?" Lara asked, and together, they left the house.

DAISY TOOK ME to the beach the next day. Larry had to work, delivering produce for a nearby farmer, and his Jeep was already gone by the time we walked out to the road. Lara stayed behind, drinking coffee and reading on the porch. She'd said good morning to both of us, but Daisy was ignoring her.

"Where's your mom?" I asked, as we walked. I couldn't see the water, but could smell it and hear it, so I knew it was close.

"Where's your mom?" she repeated, like a challenge.

Silence fell. She led me through a stand of cedars, along a trail of shattered seashells, and then the ocean came into view. I stood there, staring out at the broad horizon, breathing in the briny scent, letting my head fill with the wave's roaring rhythm. It reminded me of home, of the big lake a short walk from our house.

"You know," Daisy said, her voice sharp like a crow's call. "I really don't know how much more negativity I can take."

"What do you mean?"

"Your friend."

"Lara?" I asked, as if there was someone else. Daisy squinted her eyes, levelled her gaze at me, challenging.

"She's got a lot of junk inside her. It's toxic. It's infecting us both." She laid her palm over her heart. I stared at her, reluctantly nodding, but into my head popped the Lara from Grade 12, how she turned to me during an assembly about drunk driving in the spring and said, "It was my dad who identified him." She looked down at her hands, at the many silver bands and gemstones collected on her fingers. "By his clothes, the stuff he had with him." Most of the rest of her brother had disappeared. Eaten by scavengers; rotted away.

this has nothing to do with you

WE STAYED ON the beach for a while. Smoked a joint, then meditated. Daisy's face turned soft and bright like the good witch from the *Wizard of Oz,* and I wondered what that meant, if it was a sign I should ask Lara to leave, then stay with Daisy and her stepfather, who seemed so nice. I was still trying to decide what to do as we walked back, but then I saw Lara's book abandoned on the verandah, and Larry's Jeep parked outside the house. Smoke was pouring out of the chimney in the studio, and Daisy took my hand, led me over. Inside, it was a million degrees and sweat sprang to the surface of my skin before I even saw them, Larry and Lara, embracing beside a shelf full of blue-glazed mugs. His face over her shoulder, his hand rubbing her back. When he opened his eyes and saw Daisy, he abruptly pulled back, then slowed his motions, wrapping his arm around Lara's shoulders like he had with Daisy the day before. Lara dabbed at her eyes like a 1940s movie star, and leaned into him.

"She was just telling me," he said. "About the murder, her mother's trial. How she's made a mistake running away, how she has to get home."

Lara and I stared at each other. Daisy didn't even seem to hear. She had already turned around, hands blindly shoving, pushing me aside so I lost my balance and upset a bookshelf with my hip. A small ceramic sculpture of a devil dropped to the floor and shattered, and when I turned to run after her, fuelled by my own anger, I heard its pieces crunching underfoot.

IT WAS EXPECTED that I go with Lara. She couldn't do that long drive by herself, all the way home to Northern Ontario. And what was I supposed to do? Accuse her of lying, of stealing my story? You started it, she would have said, and it would have all unravelled, the truth, my past spread out on the table to be dealt with, like Daisy's spilled wine. I tried to talk to Daisy, but she locked herself in her room as if I was the one who'd betrayed her. A sign tacked into the wood said, *Love and Light Zone, Enter and Be Transformed* in childish purple handwriting, but a sharp scrawl of pencil said DO NOT above the *Enter*, added in some teenage rage or even twenty minutes earlier. A colourful rainbow, painted with watercolours, arched over the words, bubbling the paper. I left her in there; I turned to go.

Larry apologized for her as he walked us to the Toyota. "She's had a hard go," he said.

Who the hell hasn't, I thought.

I HAD NOTHING TO SAY to Lara. I sat in the car seething, slumped down in my seat, arms crossed as she wove the car through a grid of streets. Finally, she stopped, reached across my lap to pop open the glove compartment, and pulled out a map.

"What now?" I snapped. "You'll drive me back to Hixon River, drop me off like a lost puppy?"

"Maybe."

Lara backed up and turned around. We went another way, and when we rolled up to a red light at a *T* intersection, a woman on a bicycle rode by, the crown of a pineapple sticking out of her basket. She waved at us, but only Lara waved back. I thought of Daisy, how she'd opened doorways for me into magical ways of thinking, how she'd been so different, how she'd allowed me to be somebody else. I missed her already.

"It's not just bullshit, you know," I said. "I do hold certain beliefs."

"Like what? The earth is actually a zoo created by aliens?"

"Shut up."

"Or that you're the reincarnation of Cleopatra?"

Irritated, I turned away.

"Or maybe that your brother died so you could learn some lesson about what you owe the people around you, that you can't just abandon them."

I stared at her. Her eyes flickered over the road in front of us, thick forest on the other side. We could turn either right or left. Left meant north, back towards Canada. B.C., Ontario, Matt, my mom.

"Not everything we magnetize is bad," I told her, my voice too loud, nearly shouting.

"I see."

I twisted in my seat to face her. "We can attract good stuff too. We can wish for it."

She didn't answer. I shut my eyes tight, like when you're a kid and you want to see colours. "Universe, I wish for direction. Where should we go?"

A blue jay dropped from a pine bough on the far side of the road and swooped up into the limb of a closer tree. It squawked, scolding, as we waited for the light to turn green, and then a vehicle came into view, speeding through the orange, passing in front of our faces. A green VW with a bumper sticker pasted to the side window that said, *I'd rather be in Sedona, Arizona.*

Lara and I looked at each other. I wiped my palms together as if I'd completed a difficult job. Smug, pleased with myself, I said, "Well, then."

She flexed her grip on the steering wheel. Our light had turned green, but she didn't move until a car behind us beeped its horn.

"Fine," she said, and swung right to follow the van.

2.

AT MY APARTMENT, I call the numbers in the classified ads, ignoring the ones that say *No Pets*, while Josie has a shower. When the water stops, and she opens the bathroom door to let out the steam, I bring her a cup of tea, set it down on the vanity. She's wearing my bathrobe, and her injured arm's tucked carefully against her midriff like an invisible handbag's hanging from her elbow.

"There's three we can look at," I tell her as she leans into the mirror, pushes at a pimple on her chin with the pointer finger of her good hand.

"Okay." She glances down at the mug. "I already had tea at Matt's."

"I thought you'd want some more."

"One's enough, but I could really use some food."

I bring the cup back into the kitchen, drop bread into the toaster, and put out the peanut butter, crack open the jar of homemade strawberry-rhubarb jam she brought.

"Eat fast," I tell her. "Our first appointment's in half an hour."

I HAVEN'T TOLD Josie about Matt, haven't wanted to talk about it, to go back to that night on the dock, his lies of omission. It's too much to take in right now, that and my mother's voice in my ear for the first time in nearly three years, that needy, pleading tone. Part of me feels bad for hanging up on her, for not finding out why she'd called. But she'll phone back, I figure. She'll talk to Matt. Matt will figure it out.

If I tell Josie, I know she'll just try to get me to do what she thinks she would do: have a heart-to-heart with Matt, rush down South to take care of my mom, things that seem impossible, like trying to remember what forty below feels like in the middle of a humid heat wave.

What's real right now is the broad impasse between him and me, how we're looking at each other across such a distance. Both of us out on that ocean he wrote about, post shipwreck, floating alone. I'm not the only survivor. He's one too. Why doesn't he think he is?

The only thing I can focus on right now is hunting for a new place where I can bring Grommet, where I can make that idea of my life work out. I can't even deal with Josie, who's gone quiet, who seems to have something on her mind, so I ignore her, start the car and turn up the music when the cassette flips over, playing *Linger* by the Cranberries. It's a good song, upbeat, and it helps to give me a bit of hope, so I sing along while Josie stays silent, staring out her window like we're doing something really difficult, like the time I took her to the Soo to get her wisdom teeth out because her mom had to work and she needed a driver. Her arm must be hurting, I think, or maybe she's spaced out on pain killers. Finally, I turn the music down, reach over and poke her leg.

"You okay?" I ask.

"Just tired."

"Did you sleep okay?"

She shrugs.

"Did Matt say anything to you?"

She glances at me. "Like what? I only talked to him for two minutes."

"How'd he seem?"

She sighs. "Like Matt."

I consider saying something else, telling her about the pot, about the apparent grow op that I don't know what to do about, but I know it would lead to more questions and I have to follow the house numbers, hunting for eighty-two.

"This is it," I say, pulling to a stop outside a large house on one of the oldest streets in the city. It's painted a bright, fresh forest green. A wooden toboggan leans against the front step even though most of our snow is gone. There's a big tree in the front yard and a screened-in porch where I can imagine reading, Grommet stretched out at my feet.

"Looks promising," I say.

THE APARTMENT'S in the basement. The walls are painted a sickly pink and a worn red rug with the white weave showing is spread out on the concrete floor. The ceilings are so low that Josie and I have to duck to enter the bathroom and the bedroom. It's ridiculous, moving around the bare lightbulbs like we're giants, while the landlady, who's barely five feet tall, pretends not to notice. She stands at the bottom of the stairs that go up to her kitchen stating the rules in a clipped accent. No parties, no drinking, definitely no drugs. She'll need first and last, and a damage deposit. Smoking is okay, she says, which is obvious because the place reeks and the ceiling panels are stained an ugly yellow. "But no pets."

Josie and I exchange a glance.

"You got a cat," she says, and lifts both hands, palms out. "No way."

"A dog."

"A dog! He lives inside?"

I smile. "Well, yeah."

Her head's already swaying back and forth. "No way," she repeats. "Once you got to clean up piss and shit for a whole week you learn your lesson."

"I wouldn't do that."

"The dog's like her kid," Josie says, but the woman's already turning around, her slippers slapping against the wooden steps as she climbs. I take a last look, as if I really wanted the place, as if Grommet wouldn't be wailing his head off, trapped down there in a different kind of cold and dark, even worse, I think, than being tied up outside.

THE NEXT ONE, shown to us by a man with large round glasses, is full of mould. As soon as he unlocks and opens the door, the smell hits us, and we all shuffle back. A humidifier is on inside, feeding a collection of tropical plants, their thick leaves glossy and huge, an acorn-sized lemon growing on one branch. He pulls a narrow, antique sofa away from the wall to reveal a flush of green spread over the back of the upholstery and the cream-coloured paint. "Oh my God," he says, pinching his nose, obviously stressed. I feel sorry for him, and when we leave I wonder if the place might have actually been an option. After being cleaned up, of course. Josie's still quiet, picking at her sling. By now a bunch of the threads are unravelled at the edge.

"You'll have to sew that," I say, turning onto the highway, heading north. She pulls her head back, studies it like a canvas.

"I'm thinking I'll embroider it, or maybe you could knit me a new one."

I smile although I don't knit much anymore. My mother tried to teach me once, but I found it more an exercise of frustration than anything else, trying to avoid all those unintended yarn-overs causing accidental holes.

At the Iron Rail — a tavern on the edge of the city where chopper bikes are lined up and the twang of AC/DC drifts through the windows — I hit my turn signal. The apartment's next door, over a small engine repair shop, and the windows rattle as the downstairs mechanic works a power drill. I'm not thrilled, but other than the shop, the place is surprisingly quiet, and it even has a balcony overlooking a wide rock cut spotted with birch trees. I start to get excited but even it's not an option, it turns out.

"Can't do pets," the landlord says, jostling the cupped keys in his palm. He sounds apologetic though, and when we're outside, standing by our vehicles, he says, "Hang on a sec."

He pulls a black phone, the size of a brick, off the passenger seat of his truck and punches in a number. He talks for a bit, then jots an address on a notepad, tears out the piece of paper, and hands it to me. "Good luck."

"I'm tired," Josie says again in the car. "And I want to get the two o'clock bus." It's nearly one.

"Just one more stop," I tell her. "This could be it."

Maybe I still believe that if you wish for things you can get them. When I wanted a dog, Grommet showed up, and when I needed help, there was Sophie. And now Owain, right when I'm lonely, when I think I could maybe start letting someone in. So it strikes me that this might just be the perfect place, found with serendipitous good luck, as I drive us back into the city. And then, when we located the building, I realize it's right around the corner from the library, so close to my work that I can walk.

THIS LANDLORD'S DRESSED in a rumpled suit that looks slept in. He extends his hand to shake both mine and Josie's, then leads us through a doorway beside a furniture store and up a flight of stairs. The apartment is beautiful. Full of light from the big window that overlooks the street. It's got hardwood floors, even a fireplace with white and teal tiles around the hearth. When the landlord flicks a switch, orange and blue flames leap out of a fake log and I laugh. I love it.

"How much?" Josie asks. When he says the price — seven hundred dollars a month — my heart sinks. She looks at me, silently saying, let's go, but I pretend not to notice.

There are two bedrooms, one with a small ensuite bath, and a big kitchen with new appliances, including a large microwave.

"Look, Jose," I say, running my fingers along the edge of the glossy black stove. "When you're finally done with the Brute you can move in here with me."

As soon as the words are out of my mouth, I regret it. Way to go, Midge, I think to myself. That nickname — the one Lara gave Bruce back in high school — hasn't come out of my mouth in years. From the main bathroom, done in tasteful grey tile, I hear her footsteps ringing down the stairs.

"Think about it," the man says, and hands me an application form that I know I can't fill out. Maybe I can live with Owain, I'm thinking as I head back to my car. Maybe we can get married, sleep with Grommet stretched out between us, shove him off the bed whenever we want to have sex, run him in the woods on Sunday mornings...

Josie's waiting by my car, arms crossed, cheeks ruddy. There's a tense line across her forehead that I haven't seen in a long time. I stare at her for a second, then unlock my door. "Do you want to go get a coffee?"

She shakes her head, quick, curt, and I get in the driver's side, lean over, and pull the lock up. "Is your arm hurting?" I ask, as she gets in.

"No."

I stare down at my hands in my lap. I have a dozen excuses at the ready. All I have to do is tell her about last night, about Matt's journal, let her know what's on my mind. Instead, though, I do what I know I should, even though it's hard.

"I'm sorry I said that about..."

"It's not that," she blurts out. "Well, it's partly that. I just wish...I wish you'd get your shit together."

"Jose," I say, and am surprised by the sound her name makes, high pitched, like a bird chirping for its mother. She doesn't look at me. All I see is the back of her head, her messy blonde hair. She shakes her head, prods her tense forehead with her fingertips. "I'm sorry. I'm just tired. Last night was tiring. So much drama."

My hands clench the steering wheel. I stare straight ahead like we're already on the move, heading down one of those long, straight roads Lara and I travelled through Nevada. Flat desert, pale grey all around us, nothing for miles, too much room to think.

Silence fills the car. It's 1:32, and there's not much time to get across town for the bus. I start the car, hit my signal, and we drive for a bit before she speaks. Quietly, her voice heavy like she's making a confession, she says, "I'm pregnant."

"Jose!" I swing my head to look at her, but she doesn't meet my eye. Her smile's small and clenched. I crank the wheel to pull over and end up turning into the Donut Line and parking outside the front door. "Jose," I say again, the sound broken by the start of a sob that I swallow, shove down. I push a knuckle against my lips. She giggles, then smiles broadly, turns to me with light in her eyes and I open my arms to hug her, hold her tight.

"Ouch," she says, pulling her sore arm away. It's her tears that are spilling now, and I see she's already got a tissue in her fingers. It's coming apart, into pieces of lint that she wipes on her cords. It's been a long time since I saw her cry. For her own stuff, not my parents, not Pete. She's a mess, as messy as at that Grade 9 dance when her first boyfriend dumped her for Crystal Forester, who was drunk on a mix of root beer and gin, a manic redness covering her whole face, crawling up her bare arms like a rash.

this has nothing to do with you

"Why are you crying?"

"I don't know," she says, and laughs, wipes at her eyes with her fingertips as if trying to gather her tears. Then she calms, suddenly, and covers her face with her hands. A hush builds until a few old men, laughing, raucous, wearing plaid wool jackets, one in a hunter-orange cap, push through the swinging glass door. Duck hunting season, I think, even though it's spring. And then I think of my dad, of the scent of autumn coming off him when he returned from a hunting or fishing trip, when he was happy, when we could take a break from watching him, from waiting for his anger.

Josie wipes the heel of her hand against her cheeks, pushing streaks of mascara towards her temples. I hold my breath until I know I won't cry.

"When are you due?" I ask.

Her eyes jump like candle flames. "December fifteenth. A baby for Christmas." There's pure joy on her face now, radiating freely. She's so bright I can barely look at her and I pick at the cracked vinyl on my steering wheel while she talks about when she found out, who she's told. My mind drifts, thinking about Grommet, about driving out to Sophie's, about finding out more about Matt. But then I hear a familiar name and I look at her, attentive.

"I told you last night," Josie says. "She's moving to Peterborough." She looks at her watch, peering at the tiny square in its face that shows the day of the month. "She's probably already there. I want to wait. I want to tell her in person."

"Why?"

"To see the look on her..."

"No. Why'd she move back?"

"Oh. She said she missed home, and she got into a graduate program there."

Lara, all of a sudden just a seven-hour drive away.

"She's worried about you," Josie says. When I don't answer, she goes on. "June. The anniversary." I stare straight ahead. "That you're home for it now."

"Wood year," I mutter. "Is it wood?"

Josie shrugs, watches a woman walk by with a toddler who's dragging her stuffed bear on the ground.

"Matt used to carve things out of wood," I say. I've been trying to remember that thing he made, the crude animal he wrote about, but can't. It must be hidden in a box. Then my father's coffin pops to my mind. That slick oak, shining with the sky's reflection. The one Matt chose on his own because I wouldn't help.

"Trees are also made of wood," Josie says. "And sticks for dogs and paper for writing letters."

She reaches over and squeezes my wrist. I feel the hard gold of her slender ring, and it seems wider, more solid, than I know it is.

"I really am happy for you," I tell her, but my voice sounds mechanical, insincere because of the effort to maintain control.

"I know."

AT THE BUS STATION, Josie hesitates before she gets out of my car. Something is still floating between us, unsaid, and I watch her eyes drift across the windshield, trying to catch sight of it. I don't help her. I'm anxious to get on with my day.

Plus, I don't think I've done enough, haven't gushed enough, haven't asked about names and her mother's reaction and baby showers and all the rest. Didn't immediately squeal with joy like the best friend in the movies, and start right then, right now, knitting booties and blankets. I guess I'm tired too. I guess I still don't trust the future, not even hers, when everything seems to point to her being happy, despite my own opinion.

this has nothing to do with you

"There's the bus," I say. It's pulling in, a row of ghostly faces peering out the dark windows, eager for their smoke break.

She gives me an awkward sideways one-armed hug. "Call me later?"

"Or you call me."

"Love you," she says.

"Love you too," I respond.

MY APARTMENT'S QUIET. I lean against the door when I come in, and see the flashing red light of my answering machine pulsing in the shadowy kitchen. It makes me groan and close my eyes, afraid of whose voice I'll find. More of Matt's bad news, more accusations, more of my failures, of Angie's concern. But when I step over and hit the play button, hoping for Owain, I'm surprised to hear my Aunt Doreen, calling from Saskatchewan. "I've been trying to get ahold of your brother," she says. "Your mom or her lawyer need to talk to you because..." I push stop. The sudden silence is broken by the dim, distant barking of that dog on the upper floor, the sound drifting down through the building.

Why can't she get in touch with him?

Maybe I should phone him, I think. Talk to him. Try to.

But the thought exhausts me, what he'll say, how he'll deliver the day's news like my own personal anchorman. How I'll have to skirt around the knowledge I now have, trying to find a way to ask him what he's up to without outright asking.

Why can't I just tell him, just ask him? Matt, I know about your new career, your anger at our parents, at me. How you've been keeping all these secrets. I went in your private room, scattered your pot seeds, read your diary. I saw the condoms in your bedside table, the unused antidepressants in the bathroom.

I imagine the look on his face, his blue eyes bulging. That would be it, I think. He'd be so mad. More than he already is.

My finger's still hovering over the answering machine. I pull it away. I'll listen to the message later, I tell myself. I'll deal with it then. Right now I've got other things on my mind.

The mess of newspapers is spread across my counter. Half a dozen apartment ads circled, crossed out. I pick up my pencil, put a slash through the ones I've seen. Where am I going to live? Now, no matter what, I don't think I can stay with Josie. I love her, I do, but it was hard enough putting up with her in wedding-planning mode; all she'll want to talk about now is the baby. For a second, I imagine hanging out with Bruce in his garage, just to get away. Maybe he and Grommet could learn to get along, a dog bed in the corner by his mechanic's hoist. How long could I listen to talk about engine repairs and hockey though? Besides, living in Hixon River, where my history hangs everywhere, a gallery of images I can't avoid, would gradually wear me down.

Perhaps I could rent a room at Sophie and Ted's, help out with the dogs. I could learn about training; it'd be like an internship. But would they want me there? Wouldn't I interfere with the business they've got going with my brother? Maybe I could join them, quit my job, help out, make a bunch of money. Yeah, I mutter into the afternoon's silence, our whole family could end up in prison. The loud laugh I let out echoes in my apartment, surprising me, and I shake my head, wondering again how Matt can take that risk. Daisy's voice comes into my mind. It's just a plant. And Lara's, too: yes, like cocaine, like potatoes and wheat before fermentation, like a lot of things that can potentially destroy your brain. "While you're busy self-medicating," she said to me once, "I'm attempting to actively live my life."

I suppose I could say the same thing to Matt.

But what would he say back?

"While you were busy running away . . ."

this has nothing to do with you

"I'm back now," I'd tell him. Like it or not, I'm back.

I glance at the phone but don't pick it up.

Matt's secret could have been revealed to me out at Sophie's, I realize. Ted could have slipped up, told me about it yesterday. Maybe it's him I can talk to about it. I change my shirt, put on a fresh pair of jeans, grab my car keys and go.

3.

THE MORNING MY MOTHER told me about my dad's affair, I found her in the living room, frozen on the velour chair, her eyes red. It seemed that she'd been crying for hours, even days. But when her head started turning towards me, I hustled away, went downstairs to call Matt. I knew something was coming; I felt afraid, so I ran.

"They're on the outs," Matt told me. Now I know he already knew the whole story, but he didn't explain about Celia. Maybe he wanted to leave that task to my mother. Instead, he gave me instructions. Watch her, he said.

"What are you doing today?" I asked, changing the subject. Wishing that, like him, I lived far away.

"Working on an essay, then going down to the clinic."

He meant the Morgentaler Clinic, where he volunteered to escort women through a group called Operation Rescue — the members read out loud from the Bible, sat on the asphalt, blocked access. Sometime that winter my mother had told us about it, standing in the kitchen with my father's fried egg on a spatula.

"I hope he's paying as much attention to his school work," he said, and my mother drew herself up and threw the egg.

The yolk smashed against his shoulder, sprayed yellow across his shirt. None of us moved. My father dabbed at the stain, sighed like she was simply a toddler he couldn't control.

"Then go see a band, maybe get laid," Matt said, on the phone.

"Matty," I groaned.

"Midge," he said. "The world is huge. You should see this city. You should come visit."

I told him I would. I wanted to. What would I find in his metropolis, I wondered, what version of myself? As I wandered upstairs, I was thinking these things, growing excited, but then my mother stopped me when I was almost past, almost in my own room.

"You know it's not easy being aware of every mistake, every inadequacy, every single way you're wrong and unwanted and ugly," she said. How could I walk away from that? I sat down on the couch across from her, and stared at my hands. My fingernails, painted black like Lara's, were bitten right down. I wondered how much polish I'd ingested over the years, if flakes of salmon pink, neon green, midnight black were cluttering up the soft walls of my intestines. It was after eleven, almost noon, and my mother was still wearing her housecoat, the belt torn from when we'd taken in a black lab puppy a few years earlier and my mother couldn't handle it, almost had a nervous breakdown. It's a puppy, my friends said, disbelieving, and I shrugged along with them, judging her, when the truth was I'd watched and laughed as he zoomed around the house, as he chewed up half our shoes, harassed Frankie, bit at our fingers with his sharp baby teeth. We left the housetraining to my mother. At first we'd named him Reginald but changed it to Spaz. At seven months, he went to a friend of my father's from work. Later, we saw pictures of him, and he looked happy and calm and grown up.

this has nothing to do with you

She started to talk. She pressed her fingertips against her forehead and told me how my father's proximity, the fumes coming off him, had started giving her headaches. How she'd finally asked him who he was dressing for, and he turned to her and said, "You might as well know now."

I sat there, listening, a coldness in my belly. For so long we'd hammered together our existence as a family, rushing around to make everything suitable for him, just for him to abandon us. Everything was falling apart. I could practically hear the floorboards caving in, the shingles slipping free. Soon we'd be standing on air.

My mother's face looked soft and puffy, smeared with shadows that looked like streaks of dried clay. She reached down to her ankle, squeezed her fingers around the bone, slid her hand up her bare shin. I could see the ghost of the dancer in her, in her body, so slender, too skinny, and wished suddenly, fiercely, that she'd get up, get dressed, go running. Move.

"You could dance," I said, my voice shrill. "You could move to New York City. You could do anything."

She smiled: a tight, small stretch of the lips you reserve for someone who's stupid. It's the look Lara gave me whenever I jumped on some impulsive scheme.

"I'm forty, my love."

"So? It's never too late."

"Sometimes it is."

Her hand flew up to clutch her hair. She coloured it herself, a dark brown, but there was a lot of grey at the roots now, I noticed. Looking closer, I saw how age had piled quickly on her face. I thought of women cursed in fairy tales.

"The bastard," she hissed. "The fucking prick."

I burned; heat surged into my cheeks. She crackled with an aggressive energy. I pushed the heels of my hands against my jaw.

"Mom," I said, in a small, scared voice.

"I could cut his fucking balls off."

In the weighty silence, she blinked, then opened her eyes wide as if we'd overheard someone else. She cleared her throat, touched her fingertips to her neck, to that vulnerable spot where we swallow and breathe.

Quickly, I left the room, left her. I went back downstairs and stood for a while, looking into the aquarium, which had become an algae-filled swamp. There were some tetras left that I'd tried to feed, but there wasn't enough salt, or something, and Matt had bagged up all the tropical fish the last time he came home and brought them to a friend. In my father's room, shirts on hangers lay piled on the bed next to a box of his underwear and socks and aftershave bottles. Two books, paperback Westerns, sat on the dresser. I didn't go inside. I closed the door and went to call Lara. I had my own life. I took to heart the other words my mother said to me during that conversation. I had to. The crevice, so deep, so close to my feet, had nothing to do with me.

4.

THE SKY IS HEAVY and grey when I get to Sophie's. There are no dogs in the yard, but they bark from the barn when I pull in and park with my car pointed towards the verandah. The windows in the house are lit. Yellow boxes against the overcast day.

"Hi," Ted says, when he opens the front door. He steps back and swings his arm, ushering me inside. My feet catch on a rag rug, and I look down, then up, consciously averting my gaze from his deformed cranium, but he doesn't notice. He's too busy closing the door. "We can't let the cat out," he says. "There's been an eagle around."

I haven't seen the cat before, but there she is: a scrawny tabby sitting at the end of the hall, cleaning herself, one leg stretched long like a dancer's.

"Did Matt send you?" Ted asks.

I hesitate.

I shake my head. If I was involved, would I be transporting money, or drugs, or both?

"Why would he?" I ask, prodding. Ted shrugs, an exaggerated poke of his shoulders up to his ears. He's wearing a pink polo shirt that's too big on his slender frame and cargo pants held up by a wide leather belt from the seventies, coloured orange and purple and green. When he turns away, taking long limping steps towards the back of the house, I follow.

"Is Sophie around?" I ask.

"Training," he calls over his shoulder, disappearing into a room on the other side of the staircase that I haven't entered. Inside, there's an enormous terrarium, six feet long, glowing like a stage set. Ted stands in front of it, the strong light flooding his face, creating shadows so he appears almost monstrous. Inside the glass box are cacti, spiky succulents, a painted cardboard backdrop of blue sky. Sand and a cedar-coloured log and red hunks of rock. The scene gives me a sudden, sharp longing for Robert, for my previous life down South. How much easier it was in a way, without these relationships to navigate. My days taken up by simple tasks: panhandling, selling sage smudges to the New Age shops, using the change to buy green peppers, blocks of cheese, occasionally an avocado. Bathing in the river. Keeping my head shaved. Staying high.

Ted plucks a dandelion bloom from a plate on the dining room table, drops scraps of the shredded petals onto a lizard crawling out of the log. I step closer to see the creature's mottled green and grey skin, the vivid yellow stripes along its back, its spiky armoured tail.

"We've had a death," Ted tells me. "Harold. This is Maude. Do you think she's grieving?"

Maude turns her beady black eyes on me, then climbs onto the log, gripping the edge of the wood with her long, sharp claws.

How would I know? I'm about to say, but Ted talks first.

"Ornate uromastyx. Rare. Like me." He grins, sweeps a hand over his bulging forehead like Elvis smoothing his pompadour. His lips are chapped, he seems to have no eyelashes, and his hair grows in dark brown patches over the boney bulge on one side of his head. The bald spots on his scalp are wine-coloured.

"Is there a cure?" I ask.

He shrugs. "Interventions. But they're a big hassle. This is just me. For life. Well, not much of a life." He makes a croaking sound, runs a finger across his throat. "By 29, they say."

I stare down through the mesh top of the terrarium at the lizard who's chewing while examining me and change the subject. "So, whose idea was it?"

Ted lets out a guffaw. "Um, God?" he says, and drops the rest of the dandelion into a cat dish beside a bowl of murky water.

"Not that."

When he doesn't answer, his eyes following the lizard as she crawls under an arch of red rock, I say, "It's okay. They've told me everything."

"Oh," he says. "The business." He exaggerates the *Z* sound of the *S*.

I nod.

"If they told you everything, why are you asking questions?"

this has nothing to do with you

I don't know how to answer. Ted grins, pleased that he's caught me. He tsks, wags his finger, then reaches into the terrarium for the water dish. I follow him into the kitchen.

"At least tell me how long you've been doing it."

"Why?"

"He's my brother."

"Who's your brother? I haven't got a clue what you're talking about."

I sigh, shut my eyes. "Did Matt tell you not to tell me?"

"Tell you about what?" He flicks his finger into the stream of water, waiting for it to cool.

"How did you meet him?"

"I told you. I didn't meet him."

"But you know him?"

Ted lets out a long sigh, rolls his eyes towards the ceiling, tin, the white paint flaking off. "He met me. He came looking for Sophie."

I nod, remembering. "Right," I say. "To talk to her about her land."

"No," Ted says. "Not that."

My eyes swim around the room, hunting answers. "What then?"

Ted stiffens. I see it. He turns away from the sink, shoves past me, delivering the fresh water to the lizard. I can feel the crackling of the nerve I've hit and am about to go after him, insist that he explain, when Sophie opens the door. Grommet pushes around her, prances wildly over to me, leaps up to get closer to my face.

"Down!" Sophie shouts, and he springs back, leaving large muddy prints on my top. I crouch down, let him lick my chin as I rub his sides, examine him, notice that the fur's nearly grown in around his neck, disguising that grey loop of skin. When I stand, Sophie's face has clenched, gathering wrinkles around her mouth that I've never seen before. Is it me? Should I have called first?

"He's a challenge," she says, walking over to fill the kettle, then turning on the stove burner. "Any luck on a place?"

I shake my head, reaching down to stroke Grommet's ear. He's settled already, is lying on his side, droopy jowls splayed on the worn hardwood floor. Quietly, Sophie mutters, "Here."

Grommet scrambles to his feet and crosses the room in a couple bounds.

"Good boy," she says, wiping her damp hands on the stretched-out hem of her blue T-shirt that's speckled white from splattered bleach, then looks up at me. "Some progress," she says.

When the water boils, she fills the teapot and carries it and a plate of cookies to the table. I reach for a fruit creme as she tells me how the training will help make him feel secure.

"If he knows he doesn't have to figure everything out, to be always on guard, hyper-vigilant, then he'll get calmer, but for separation anxiety..." She sighs. "That you'll have to tackle a different way."

"How?"

"A minute away, reward for good behaviour, build up. Like I taught you yesterday: approximations, rewarding him for getting closer and closer to what you want, not expecting Rome in a day. He's had a long time to learn his bad behaviours." She looks at Grommet who's dozing with his belly up, back legs splayed, leaning against the kitchen cupboards, and I can tell that if she were closer, her hand would be reaching down to touch. "His coping mechanisms."

"And that's the way to cure him?" I ask. The tea gurgles out of the spout as Sophie pours.

this has nothing to do with you

"Cure him," she says, but it isn't a question. It's a flat statement, as if she's setting the words between us so we can both take a look.

"It isn't that easy, I'm afraid. Sometimes the dog has associated aloneness with such fear that nothing will help."

What she says reminds me of my mother, but then everything seems to these days. I think about how much I left her alone, secured in her back bedroom, that cage she couldn't seem to leave, watching Peter Jennings' handsome face on the tiny black and white television and the final episode of *Dallas*. All the while making terrifying plans I didn't know about, plans she'd shared with Matt. There are much bigger questions here, I realize, as I think of Matt. His secrets. What he's doing in that basement room. What he knew about and when. Why he came out here to meet Sophie. The question's on the tip of my tongue.

"Sometimes," she repeats. "We don't yet know if that's the case with Grommet." If he's broken, irrevocably scarred, she means.

"What'll I do then?"

"Don't know, but I think you have to try."

I nod. "I know."

Sophie's cup lands with a clunk on the table, beside the plate of cookies and a deck of playing cards with the corners rubbed soft. "Do you?"

She gives me an examining gaze. She's waiting for me to give up, I think, and then I think of other people she must have seen give up. Her own stepsister, dropping deformed Teddy as a baby into her care.

I haven't touched my tea. A hunk of chewed jam from the cookie is stuck in my teeth. I pick at it as Ted comes back from the dining room, where the lizard lives, and walks over to the freezer.

"Will you stay for the funeral?" he asks, as he pulls out Harold's body, holds him in both hands. The creature's lying on a plastic bag, and he looks like the other, the live one, but his once lemon-yellow stripes have turned a pale grey, the spikes on his tail grown frosted, those quick eyes now white marbles. I didn't even know him, but I burst into tears.

"Oh," Sophie says, half standing. The movement sloshes my tea, and some of it spills over the side in a miniature wave. She waggles her finger between Ted and the sink and he slips the dead lizard back in the freezer, turns to toss a cloth to Sophie who mops up the drink.

"Sorry," Ted says.

I shake my head. It isn't him. It isn't his fault.

"What's going on?" Sophie asks.

I shrug. What I want to do is beg: tell me everything, let me stay with you. But I don't talk. Not for a long time. Needy, I think. Like Grommet. We're made for each other.

Across from me, Ted leans against the counter, looking nervous. He puts his arms behind his back as if he's already been arrested. I flick him a pitying glance.

"How did he die?"

"Natural causes," Sophie says. "Old age."

I look straight at her. "Why did Matt want to meet you?"

Her eyes dart away from my face, then return. Abruptly, she leans back in her chair, and Grommet looks over, expectant, anticipating change. I know how he feels: the morning my mother told me about Celia, the morning the cops came, five a.m. this morning reading my brother's confessions. Sophie sighs as if my mental recounting has tired her out. I push the heel of my hand against one damp cheek.

"That is a question for your brother," she says, crossing her arms to grip each shoulder.

this has nothing to do with you

"And what's the answer?" I push, but she shakes her head. Probably she's right. The questions aren't for her or Ted or Owain or Lara or my mother or anybody else. The questions are for Matt, even if I have to force him to give me the answers.

As if contented that it's settled, Grommet lies his head back down, lets out a rumbling sigh.

5.

THE FIRST THING I do when I get home is pick up the phone to call Matt. I don't even take off my shoes, and I track dust from Sophie's yard across the filthy red carpet. I'm like a dog on the scent, circling an area where something's hidden, like Frankie in the springtime when he'd wander through the forest behind our house, tracking the earth until he found the right place to dig, resurrecting cow bones he'd buried the previous autumn. Matt's been hiding things all over, and I know I'm not done finding them.

Angie answers, and she sounds like she has a cold, nose plugged, voice thick, but I know she isn't sick. Before I can ask her if everything's okay, she says, "Did you find a place?"

"No."

"How's Josie? Matt says she hurt her arm."

I hesitate for just a second, but I know what this news will do: deflect any anger she might still have at me for screwing up, probably make her happy. "She's pregnant," I say, pumping extra enthusiasm into my voice.

Angie gasps, surprised. "That's wonderful! When's she due?"

"Mid-December."

"A Christmas baby." Her tone is soft and slight and dreamy. When was Ellie born? I realize I can't actually remember. Sometime in the summer, I think. As her aunt I should probably know that, and I feel the expected stab of guilt. We talk for a bit about Josie, how excited she is, how they'd been trying for several months, and when the conversation peters out, I ask, "Is Matt there?"

There's a scraping sound of food being pushed off a plate before Angie says, "I don't know where he is."

This is strange. It's past suppertime, just after six. The news should be playing in the background. He should be in his chair or on the downstairs couch, paying close attention, sipping a beer. Suddenly I remember the wine and I stretch the phone cord around to the fridge, open the freezer and find the green bottle, flushed with cold, the cork held on the end of a frozen gush of red. I pull it out, stand it in the sink, press my fingertips onto the frosted surface of the glass.

"Did he say anything..."

She laughs, a dry chuckle. "He isn't saying much these days. Not to me anyway."

I hesitate. I don't want to break Matt's confidence, even if he doesn't know that I'm becoming aware of his secrets. I grew up learning to not talk about things, to hide my troubled feelings, to pretend everything was fine. I wonder if he's counting on me to maintain the illusion. But usually this game of make-believe was how I coped with my parents, not with him. With him, I've almost always been honest, and I assumed he was too. Or that's what I thought until yesterday.

"Are you there?" Ang asks. I pick one question. The easiest. "Has he said anything to you about Sophie? Sophie Bronski?"

"Owain's friend?"

"Yeah."

Angie shakes her head. I hear her earring tapping against the phone. "The first I heard of her was last weekend. Why?"

Because he tracked her down last fall, went to find her, and nobody will tell me why.

"She's nice, is all. She's got a great place out there. Grommet's happy."

"That's good." Her voice is dull, distracted. I hear the plates clanging, sliding into the dishwasher, water running, then the TV coming on. "He might be at Owain's," she says, and I hesitate.

"Why would he be there?" I'm fishing. What does she know?

"Mel," she says. "I'm tired."

"Okay," I say, my voice small.

"Let me know if you talk to him," she says, and hangs up.

"HENDERSON," Owain says when he answers the phone. His last name. If I were five years younger, I might be scrawling that name—Melony Henderson—into the rubbery skin of a binder. It seems strange to think I was ever so young, a kid to roll my eyes at. Because *as if*, I think. Somehow I already know that Owain isn't the happily-ever-after type, but I can't help but like him. His sparkle. How he makes me feel. Lighter. Like he breathes helium into my mouth.

"Hi," I say.

"Who's this?"

I'm stung. "Mel." You moron, I want to add.

"Oh, hi. Hold on." He muffles the phone with his hand, but I can still hear voices, male, a blurred thumping, then footsteps, and the squeal of door hinges when he comes back on.

"Are you busy?" I ask.

"Never too busy for you."

I grin, his words sparking a thrill of pleasure. I push my hand against my belly, under my coat which I still have on.

"I'm looking for my brother, actually."

"Oh, hold on. I just came from there."

"From where?"

From downstairs. Just a minute." The phone clatters onto a surface and when he returns, a couple minutes later, he says, "He's gone."

"Did he go home?"

If he did, I'm thinking I'll just walk around the corner to his and Angie's place, meet him at his front door, but Owain doesn't give me an answer. Instead, he says, "What are you doing right now?"

This derails me, the attention. I told myself I only wanted to talk to Matt, but now there's Owain, the memory of his hands on me, his mouth, how I wondered if it was even still an option.

"Nothing," I say. Then, "Sorry if I was a bit of a drama queen." I remember Josie's voice crackling over the baby monitor, making excuses for my breakdown, and I pull a hunk of the melting wine off the bottle's spout, pop it into my mouth.

"I don't mind the drama."

"Perfect," I say, around the sting of icy wine. I'm about to add, "then we're a perfect match," but that's too much, too soon, so what we're left with is a long awkward silence. In the distance, I hear Radiohead groaning *so fucking special* and I ask him if he likes the band and we talk for a few minutes about music. Finally, he breaks into the middle and blurts out, "So, do you want to do something?"

Something. I wonder what that means. Climb the bare rock overlooking Ramsey Lake, smoke a joint, toss rocks into the water's depth, crack open a few cans of beer. Or maybe that's my fantasy, acting like I'm sixteen again. I see them, I see them all the time, those crowds of teenagers, drifting by the library, taking the hills on their skateboards, like Matt used to do, used to tell me about doing, in the middle of the night in Toronto when he first moved away.

this has nothing to do with you

"Okay."

"Pick you up in half an hour," he says, and hangs up. I feel a stab of guilt when I set down the phone, wondering where Matt's disappeared, what dark street he's wandering right now, but I shove that feeling away. It's actually a relief, taking a break, letting Matt be, to instead get ready for a date.

I shower, push my short hair around under the blow dryer, apply mascara, then lipstick, while thinking about Marcos, the last guy I was with. He worked with me at the ashram near Sedona, a job I got the second year I was there, when the cold weather came on, cooking garbanzo bean curries and spicy stews with in season prickly pears. We slept together three times before he pulled me aside in the kitchen to whisper to me that he was actually married, that he'd left his wife in Detroit but was thinking about convincing her to come join him. I was holding a large slotted spoon and I lifted it, thought of hitting him, then threw it clear across the kitchen so everyone turned to look. The director called me into his office that afternoon and said something about my negative energy, told me I'd polluted the space, so I went back to Robert, to living in the cave, helping collect bottles, dive dumpsters, visit the food bank every month.

This has nothing to do with Owain, I realize, except that I know he's the next one. My legs are shaved, the smooth, naked skin still so odd to me after several years of not bothering, my best bra and underwear put on under my clothes. I'm thinking about tonight, but I'm also wondering about the future, whether I can actually invest in someone, have an ordinary life, even fulfilling. The fact that Owain seems to have no job other than drug dealer drifts off in the distance, into the blur of my concern about Matt. It's simple. I just don't look over there.

When the intercom buzzes, I hit the button and tell him I'll be right down. Then I fill my mouth with slushy wine and leave.

"WHAT DO YOU want to do?" Owain asks, when we're sitting in his van.

"I don't know. You asked me out."

"True." His hair is freshly slicked back, and I can smell the spicy musk of his cologne, the same kind he wore at the eighties party. Patti Smith is playing on the tape deck, that song about love's desire that I wouldn't even know if it weren't for my brother mailing mixed tapes to the boonies of Hixon River. Owain rolls his window down and lights a cigarette, and, impulsively, I reach for a drag. We sit there for a couple minutes, the only sound the crackle of the orange ember as it flares in front of our faces as we pass it back and forth. It makes me lightheaded; my head swims. I'm ready for an adventure, to be cracked out of myself, severed for a little while from my past. "Let's take off," I say, as he crushes the butt against the outside of his door, drops it to the pavement. "Let's just drive."

"Head down to Mexico?"

"Sure."

He grins.

"How much money do you have?" I ask.

A sideways glance. "Plenty."

I should have known. The tea tin stuffed full of cash. Is that why Matt's doing it? The money? Does he need it? Owain pushes the gear shift into drive. "I know a place," he says, and hits the gas pedal before I even respond.

this has nothing to do with you

6.

IT'S A CABIN, dark and far. On the drive, Owain stretches his arm across my lap and reaches into the glove compartment to pull out a silver flask. I unscrew the cap, gulp down a few swallows of sharp, stinging whiskey, almost cough it up as he laughs. The van rumbles down a road paved with broken asphalt then lurches onto gravel, thick forest on either side, and I feel like I'm back there, in my life before. All that's missing is Lara and Josie in the back seat, maybe even Bruce and Matt and Pete. The six of us, heading to a party at the black cliffs, bathing suits on under our clothes, ready to take the two-storey leap into that deep, gushing water, our feet nudging the sunken architecture of mossy logs before we push back up, swimming hard towards air.

Owain hits the blinker at a driveway I can't even see, swings right, and the headlights sweep over a woodpile stacked along a wide verandah. Ahead is the lake, the water oily and dark, marked with thin sheets of grey ice. The first stars are scattered across the sky like spilled salt. Toss it over your shoulder, my mother always said. To avoid bad luck.

"What place is this?" I ask Owain.

"Otter Lake. A buddy's camp."

He shuts the car off. The silence of the night sinks around us. I turn to him.

"This all right?" he asks.

"Yeah," I say, then nod.

"Let's get a fire going," he says, and I follow him, wishing I'd worn a warmer top as he crouches down on the verandah and fishes with one hand behind a red metal ash bucket. He pulls out a lozenge tin, flips it open, and there's the shiny brass key.

THE INSIDE OF the cabin is colder than outside, and it's pitch black. I wait for my eyes to adjust, suddenly thinking of Matt, of the time he drove me out to the woods near the boom camp, where loggers once floated fat tree trunks to the mill. It was night, nobody there. Early spring, the cold coming up out of the rocky earth, like now. He led me into the trees and I followed, his flashlight illuminating a wide path, our feet crackling on the earth.

"Here," Matt said, positioning me in front of a tall white pine. He slid the light over my eyes so I was blinded then snapped it off. I called his name, but he didn't answer. Now I'd think it was like an episode of the *X-Files*, that he'd been suddenly swallowed into a creature's underground cavern but back then, 1985 or so, I'm not sure what I thought or felt. Fear, I think, until he spoke.

"Can you see anything?"

Everything was black, even my hand in front of my face. He told me to wait. Gradually details started coming clear. Tree trunks, the patterns of pine needles and birch bark, even an owl, perched on a low branch. Then Matt smiled. The small movement drew my gaze and there he was, his teeth almost glowing, his face so bright it seemed impossible I hadn't seen him before.

Now, the kitchen counter comes clear, the table across from it, the wooden chairs with rounded backs, the boxy green couch. There's hardly any moon, so the water through the two large windows looks vast and empty, like outer space. When Owain touches his lighter to a lamp on the wall, the room draws in, tightening around us so we could be drifting, a million light years from home. The glass orb glows, warming the space, and I hold out the flask, which flickers in the new light. He bolts back a swallow, stares at me.

We both know why we're here, and when he comes to me, I help him pull off my jacket, raise my arms so he can strip off my shirt. He's so warm I want to crawl further into him, and he lifts me up against him, carries me to a bed where the sheets are so cold they feel wet, and I gasp as my skin hits the quilt.

"I THINK I MIGHT like you," I say when we're done. Lying in the freezing bed, his fingers stroking my shoulder, squeezing slightly to feel the shape of the bone.

"Uh oh." He pulls his arm out from under me.

"What's that mean?" I slap his thigh beneath the covers, and he twists away, reaches for his pants on the floor to fish a pack of Camels out of his pocket, the same brand I saw Matt smoking. But instead of a cigarette, he draws out a joint, rolled tight, the paper bright white in the burst of flame. "Your old friend," he says, and blows sweet smoke into my face.

I know what will happen. It's so cold in the cabin that I'll start shaking, shake extra hard, the trembling so bad that I'm sure the springs that screamed beneath us will start shrieking again.

"Dancing skeleton," Robert had said to me the first time it happened with him in forty-degree weather. "Your body trying to come to terms with back then."

Owain pulls his hand away. "Suit yourself," he says, and takes a deep toke. I watch as his face relaxes, his eyes growing soft.

"Is that from Matt's plants?" I ask.

"They aren't Matt's." He sucks on a finger, presses the guttering tip.

"No?"

Owain peers at me, sideways. "You're not going to get me talking about that," he says, scratching out the rest of the joint in a glass ashtray on the bedside table. "I told you last night. You're not supposed to know. He didn't even want me to . . ."

"What?"

He's sitting up now, hands clenching the edge of the bed, turned away.

"What?" I ask once more.

When he doesn't answer, I press my hand against his naked back, run it down the knobs of his vertebrae. "Do this?" I ask, and when he turns around to kiss me, I taste the sweet smoke on his tongue.

"THAT WAS NICE," Owain says, when we're finished. I'm still on top of him, my breasts mashed against his chest, and he reaches under me, between my thighs, to pull off the condom. When the space opens between us I feel the cold rush in, so I cling to him, not wanting to move, but he pushes me aside, gets out of bed, walks over to the wood stove.

"Finally, a fire," I say.

"Well, if you'd stop distracting me."

He chops kindling off a log with a hatchet, crumples newspaper.

"Whose place did you say this is?" I ask, moving my hand over the damp patch on the sheets.

"A guy I knew from high school. He lives in South Carolina now. I keep an eye on it for him."

"How old are you anyway?" I ask.

"How old are you?" I hear the striking of a match. "Never mind; don't answer that."

I sit up, pull on my shirt, stuff my bra in the pocket of my jeans. "Do you think they'd rent it to me?"

He shoves a log on top of the pyramid of split birch and crumpled newspaper I'd watched him make.

"Still looking?"

I nod. "This place is a bit far though." I look up into the open, shadowy rafters. "And spooky."

"You should have told me sooner. I've got a downstairs apartment but now it's rent —" He stops talking abruptly, leans sharply forward, blows on a weak flame. I watch him.

"Downstairs?"

He glances at me, his eyes flickering across my face.

"What?"

"A downstairs apartment?"

He spouts his explanation: "I've got a house. My grandmother's. She died last winter. Perfectly fit. Fell and cracked her head on an icy sidewalk. Terrible shame. Only seventy-seven. Not so old..."

He's babbling. Downstairs, I'm thinking. The echo of that word. "You said Matt was downstairs."

Owain stares into the fire. It's caught now, the paper combusting, and his face and naked chest glow orange. He's so still, he could be cast in bronze. I remember what Angie had said, how Matt hadn't come home for dinner, how she didn't know where he was.

Owain lifts his hand, reaches towards me. "Mel..."

"Matt's moved into your house?"

"Fuck," he says, pushing a palm against his jaw.

"Does Angie know?"

He doesn't want to talk about it, I can tell, but I stare back at him, waiting. Finally, reluctantly, he nods. "That's where he went tonight. To tell her."

"To tell her what? That he's leaving her? They're splitting up?" I turn away, then back. Owain spreads his hands, palms out.

"They have a baby!"

He shrugs.

"But he'd rather play gangster," I say, angry now, my voice rising. "With you."

"It isn't like that. It's not a big deal. I think..."

"What?"

He stands up, marches towards me, starts gathering his clothes off the floor.

"You need to live your own life, let your brother live his."

"His double life, you mean?" I look away. "Fuck," I say, to myself, thinking What is going on? Dressed, Owain shoves through the screen door, and in a second — as I sit there, grinding my teeth, furious, trying to figure out what to do — I hear the sound of him pissing off the side deck. He's done a shitty job of the fire. The flames are already petering out. I get up, go over, and slam the stove door shut to deprive it of oxygen, to extinguish it fully.

this has nothing to do with you

part eight

1.

AT FIRST THE VAN won't start. Owain pulls a flashlight out
of a box in the back and pops the hood to take a look. There's a
tension between us that reminds me a bit of Lara and me, stuck
in the desert outside Las Vegas. The day before, we'd driven
for hours and hours, stopping only a few times, for bathroom
breaks and gas, once at a church food bank where a fat bearded
man dressed entirely in camouflage stared at Lara for the whole
half hour we spent waiting, his eyes dropping from her face to
her chest, like he was concentrating, like she was a flat sheet of
water he could pull something out of.

It got late, Lara still driving, flipping between radio sta-
tions to try to find something other than classic rock or country.
We passed through Las Vegas, and the lights of the strip were
swimming in the rear-view when I climbed into the backseat.

"Don't you bail on me, Barnett," Lara shouted.

"I'm not," I said, although I was. I stretched out. The upholstery still smelled like Daisy, like the patchouli oil she dabbed on the acupressure points on her wrists. I heard the crackle of the bag of Oreos we'd mostly finished for supper, then the blinker, and felt the car bump off the road to a stop. Sleep dragged me down, too tempting, like the darkness of a winter blizzard.

"This is your fucking fault," Lara said in the morning, so mad she was pacing, dust lifting as her boots scuffed the earth. She was dressed in the same clothes she'd worn for two days: jeans she'd cut into shorts at Larry's, a blue tank-top, a dirty white shirt tied around her waist. That morning, after eating a few handfuls of dry Cheerios and drinking gritty, strong coffee made on our camp stove, she'd put the car in reverse and tried to back out of the dirt clearing onto the side road she'd turned onto in the night. The tires dug into the soft sand and spun. With the car in neutral, we tried to push it but we weren't strong enough.

"You're the one who drove off the road," I said. There was no one and nothing around, and I could feel the sweat building under my clothes.

"I wouldn't have had to if you hadn't fucking abandoned me."

"How's that?"

"You went to sleep!"

"I couldn't help it."

"You couldn't help it. It's the will of the universe. Everything happens for a reason. I had to abandon my brother. I had to ruin my best friend's life." By the last word, she was screaming. When she finished the desert silence hummed hard in my ears, almost painful. A trio of hawks circled far above us, dots on a clear blue sky.

"I ruined your life?"

She climbed up to sit on the hood of the car, boots planted

on the dented chrome bumper, arms crossed against her belly.

"Yes! No. Sort of." She huffed out a sigh, looked down at the ground. "Let's just say that things would be a whole lot different if I didn't have to look after you."

"You don't have to look after me!"

She stared at me. Memories swam between us: me, arriving at her place when she'd barely started her new life, then the junky apartment where I stayed when I wasn't with her, Daisy's and my scheme to hitchhike to California, how Lara interfered.

"You don't," I insisted and turned away, looking out at the desert, wide and shimmering, stretching to a dark ribbon of hills. I hadn't asked for her help. She didn't have to give it. The only thing I'd needed was a place to run to when I had to get out of Hixon River. After that, she could have let me be. Lara gazed out at the dirt road we couldn't reach, a few metres away from our car. Finally, she started talking, and I closed my eyes, wishing she'd stop.

"When Pete died it made no sense. None. Eventually I just had to accept the horrible random chaos of it."

Shut up, I wanted to say. Shut the fuck up.

"At some point, I figured out that it would be a bit like sobriety for an alcoholic. Every day I'd get up and I'd have to carry this big thing, and carrying it would be all I could do. I couldn't change it." She pushed at her palm with one finger, rolling something loose, a bit of dirt or dust from breakfast. "But it took me a while to stop being so angry, to stop acting out."

"That's what you think?" I said. "I'm not doing what you want me to, so I must be acting out?" I made quotation marks with my fingers. She was just like Matt, I thought. Wanting to control me, to do what he thought best. When I'd last spoken with him, he begged me to go home. My mother would soon be sentenced, had pleaded guilty. No excuses, just the truth: Yes, I killed two

this has nothing to do with you

237

people. There would not be a trial, but still Matt wanted me there, to play the role of supportive daughter, sit there in my best dress, cry for leniency.

Fuck that, I thought, and Lara said, "You can't just abandon your past."

"Look who's talking."

"What's that mean?"

"Who moved two thousand kilometres away from Hixon River?" I said. "As far as she could get?"

"That's different."

"How?"

She looked at me like I was stupid, like I couldn't figure out the algebra.

"There's something out here for me," she said. "A life." I felt a surge of anger. I didn't want to be there anymore. I barely wanted to go to Sedona. If I could have chosen any place right then it would have been back in time. Grade 9, maybe, the year before Pete died, stupidly excited about a Friday night dance, somebody's house party, a bonfire on the beach. Still eager for the days ahead, for the world beyond that small town, a life that couldn't be anything less than perfect.

Lara looked down at her fingernails, at flaking red polish left over from an end-of-semester party. The colour flashed brightly, a surreal hue in the dun-coloured world. She lifted a hand to wipe at her eyes, trying to disguise the motion. I did not speak. I stood there wishing for shade, wishing the sun wasn't pulsing so brightly, stripping everything bare, and for Daisy, too, with her simple explanations and diagnoses, her ready medicine to combat negativity. My throat hurt; my mouth felt dry. When a tow-truck driver finally got there, called by someone who'd spotted us from the main road, he pulled us out as easily as if we hadn't actually been stuck at all.

"EARTH TO MEL," Owain says. We're outside my apartment building; we spent the whole drive in silence after he fiddled with the distributor cap, got the vehicle started, told me that it happens all the time. I sit there, not wanting to leave the van.

"Did you want to sleep here?" he asks, gesturing at the open area behind our seats, the shovel and a bag of fertilizer off to one side. "There might be room for you to stretch out."

I undo my seat belt, trying to find words but as soon as I open my mouth to fumble something out he holds up his hand. "We had a nice time," he says. I hear what he doesn't say: let's leave it at that. And what's that mean anyway? This is it?

When will I see you again? I want to ask but I know what that'll be.

Too needy.

Even this — stuck in his vehicle, wishing he'd bring me home, or come up to my apartment so we can start again — is too much. I open the door. Suddenly all I want is to get away. I wish Grommet was waiting for me, that warm, loyal body, with problems I could tend to, clean up after, at least work doggedly to fix.

"Goodnight," Owain says, hands gripping the steering wheel, not moving to draw me close for a kiss. "Goodnight," I repeat, and climb out.

2.

TWO WEEKS TO GO before I have to move out, and no new place in sight. The coffee gurgles in my kitchen the next morning as I flip through the newspaper again, hunting for ads I might not have noticed, one that says, *Destructive, anxious, incurable dogs welcome!*

this has nothing to do with you

Did Matt seek out a place, I wonder, or did Owain simply give it to him? Take him into his basement, show him around, suggest, Why don't you stay here, bro? Was there a lease signed, and what did Matt tell Angie? Out on my little balcony that holds cracked clay pots crowded with dead geraniums from the previous tenant, I wrap my hands around the heat of my mug and look down at their house.

It's a little dark block in the dim early morning, as quiet as all the other places along the street. Angie's alone over there with Ellie, and I should go see her. Shower, dress, grab my jacket, and walk over, but I don't know if I can deal with what she'll say, with her anger towards Matt.

Really, he's who I need to see, and it's he who gets my allegiance. I know that. But what would Owain think if I called his place so soon after last night, when it's not yet even nine o'clock in the morning? That I'm using my brother as an excuse to talk to him again? That I can't keep away?

And what am I going to say to Matt? I tick the questions off on my fingers, imagine asking them, picture his face. Closed and cold like it's been lately, repeating what he said to me yesterday: "Just because I don't tell you what you want to hear, that doesn't mean I'm not talking to you." What does he think I want to hear?

Answers. The ones that he's not giving.

"What were you and Mom talking about?" That was a question I often asked as a kid. After he brought her ice cream in her room and the two of them stretched out on the bed to watch television. *60 Minutes*, a documentary on TVOntario. I never felt like I was invited, and if I'd gone downstairs I would have had to wedge myself into the silence surrounding my father as he stared at his own shows: *MacGyver*, *The A-Team*, *Quantum Leap*, even *ALF*. I'm not sure why my mother never trusted me.

Maybe because I was an accident, because I came along after she figured out the mistake she'd made, that prevented her from escaping. Matt had been her ticket out of Saskatchewan, but me? I guess I was just another trap.

In the kitchen, I pour myself a second cup of coffee, add cream and sugar, and stare at the phone. The red light is blinking on my answering machine again, but I don't want to hit the play button, to listen to everybody's demands: my Aunt Doreen, Angie, maybe even my mother, because if my aunt has my number now, Mom probably does too. Instead, I go into my living room and look around at my stuff, the piles of books stacked against the walls, the chewed bookshelf, the knick-knacks that weren't broken by Grommet, and I decide that I might as well do something towards my future. I might as well pack.

There's nothing on TV. I only get three channels and one's playing a gardening show while the other two air church services. Instead, I flip on a radio station that's replaying Casey Kasem's weekly countdown from the day before, and that's how I spend the morning: packing with no idea where I'm going or where I'll end up next. It feels familiar. It feels like the numb, uncertain time after my dad died, when Aunt Doreen stayed with us, to help us get ready to sell the house. Every day Matt would assign us tasks: box up my parents' wedding china, sort through the books, empty out the junk drawers, wash, fold, and bag both of our parents' clothes.

While we worked, my aunt told me things about my mother, things I didn't know. How she was born when her parents were older, her mother nearly forty and my grandfather just past that. The pregnancy came a long, long time after they'd given up any hope of having their own child, so it felt like God had handed them a gift.

"What about you?" I asked my aunt, and she shrugged quickly as if shaking off the memory of a heavy load. She was adopted, she explained. Born out of wedlock to my grandfather's cousin. They'd agreed to take her in but when Bernadette came along, when Doreen was six years old, it was like she ceased to exist.

"They gave your mother everything," she said. "Dressed her up like a little princess. It was all right there for her, laid out on a silver platter."

Thousands of dollars spent on dance lessons, shimmering silk costumes, pointe shoes custom ordered from New York. It was expected that she'd be famous, that the city would one day have a sign posted at its limits. *Home of Bernadette Kolanko.* That her parents could enter their old age reimbursed for their efforts, grown pudgy on pride.

"But it was never going to be like that," my aunt told me as we worked in the kitchen, cleaning out the cupboards. Behind a broken open sack of flour, I found a pile of dried-out potato bugs, and I listened while sweeping them up.

My grandfather was a piano tuner, she told me. He tightened the wires, tapped the keys, manipulated how the instrument spoke, and expected to do the same with his women. As soon as she could, my aunt left home, married a trapper, moved to a place called La Ronge. She had no children, and when her husband went through the ice one winter, she ended up on her own in Prince Albert, working at the Giant Tiger, taking night courses in accounting.

"I've always envied your mother," she said, her hands growing still, her eyes hovering over the brown checked wallpaper. "She got to live a little, at least to try to follow her dreams."

She took a breath, then pushed the soapy cloth into the vase she was washing.

"But it makes sense to me now that the first guy who offered her romance would be the one who'd get her, and that happened to be your father." She wrung out the washcloth. Brown water trickled out. It was one my mother had knit that had turned from fancy cotton lace into a rag.

"Why didn't they send someone with her?" I asked. "To Toronto?" It was the 1960s. Shouldn't she have had a chaperone?

My aunt nodded. "Mom was supposed to go, but she broke her leg. If she hadn't been so clumsy, you probably wouldn't even be here, definitely not Matt." She gazed out the window at the birch trees. "She felt terrible about that for years."

I stared at the black and taupe beetle husks in my hand and reimagined the story I'd been told over and over of that moment when my parents met. Instead of my father rushing from the wings to help her when she stumbled during rehearsal, there's my grandmother, springing out of her velvet seat in the front row.

Poof, I think. I'm gone. Poof, my mother's famous, living the life she was prodded towards, the dreams she abandoned.

I WORK LIKE THIS for a few hours. Nothing but me, moving through my place, riding the elevator down to the basement storage room to bring up more boxes. When my fragile items are wrapped, using sheets from the newspaper, and the books boxed up, I look over at the empty shelf. All that remains are the things I've been avoiding. A photo album and *Detection of Poisons*, the box that holds my mother's letters, both of them partly chewed by the dog.

First, I flip open the album, and there's Lara. Sitting on the ground in the forest by the beach, a silver can of Coors lopsided in her hand, that grin that showed a lot of teeth, that used to embarrass her when we were young. Back then she'd cover her smile with her hand, fingers up, palm turned downward, knuckles knocking against her nostrils, but this time wasn't like that. She was laughing, mouth wide open. The trail through the woods visible behind her, trodden to the cedar roots, a weave that regularly tripped people on their way to the fire spot, so one Saturday night, late, Josie went down first, and Lara and I followed, our shirts wet from spilled beer, laughing while someone snapped the camera.

I pull out the photograph and stare at it for a while, thinking about how Josie is starting the rest of her life, how Lara's about to move back East. Both of them firmly on their paths while I'm still tripping on the roots, planting my face in the mulch of last year's leaves. Not the girl in the picture anymore, but not who I need to be.

Most of the photographs are swimming under the cellophane skins, come loose from aging glue, and when I flip the page, one of them slides out and stops me. It's a black and white picture of me and Matt, taken when I finally went to see him at university. My hair fills half the frame, a fresh spiral perm teased within an inch of its life. The two of us dressed to go out, crowded onto the single bed in his residence room, an R.E.M. poster taped to the concrete block wall behind our heads.

I stare at it for a long time, remembering.

Remembering Matt and me, our bond more than blood, more than survival in our difficult family. How interesting he was, always wanting to explore, push into places that seemed off limits, even forbidden: the dark forest without a flashlight or the kiln at the shuttered mill which we broke into one night to watch lightning flare sulphuric across the high concrete walls. Sharply, suddenly, I miss him, miss who he was, who we were. I shove the picture into the back pocket of my jeans, thinking that right now I could go to him, bring it, lay it down on a surface in Owain's basement, make him look at it and say, "Remember?"

But maybe I'll catch him when he's high, his eyes swimming up out of that alternate reality, whites thick with a pinkish scum. He'll just ask me what I'm doing there.

And what would I answer? "I'm here to help you."

"I don't need help," he'll tell me. Blunt, stubborn, withdrawn. Like I was with Lara.

So I'll stand there, flapping the photo against my knee, trying to figure out what to say to bring back my brother, the one who taught me to drive, who'd snap off the headlights to see the stars while we coasted the empty highway late at night, who'd take me snorkelling at the beach near our house, opening up that underwater world, alive with darting silver minnows, green-and-gold pumpkinseed fish, even the occasional ancient turtle flapping its wrinkled fins, swimming hard towards the sun.

Remember that? I can ask, although I don't think it will work. He'll listen without response.

He might be too far gone. Maybe those memories mean more to me than they do to him, and if that's the case, what can I possibly do?

I lay the album aside, turn to the other hard object, the shellacked book made into a box. I don't open it, not right away. Fully thawed, the bottle of wine is still in the sink, and I pour myself a glass, then go back, touch the holes in the corner made by Grommet's gnawing teeth, take a breath, flip it open.

Inside, Lara's spidery handwriting stares up at me from when she forwarded the letters to Matt. Others — the ones I received when I lived out there — are dirt stained, stuck together with wine spills, ruined. Hand trembling, I pluck out one of the envelopes and hold it up to the light like to an x-Ray. When I open the seam, the letter won't come out, and in my effort to unstick it, I end up ripping the paper, watching my mother's sentences split apart. Anger overtakes me, a sudden, frenzied surge, and I tear the unread letter to pieces, scatter the scraps across the floor, stare down at the words glaring up from the carpet: Matt, blame, father, fault, beautiful, you.

For a long time, I sit there.

Like a person in the woods. Lost. Doing what they're supposed to do. Staying in the same spot, waiting for rescue, suspecting it won't come.

3.

IN THE MIDDLE OF the night, my phone rings. The sound turns into a siren, a cop car chasing me as I'm driving up a steep canyon road, unable to steer. Look at that, Angie says, from the back seat, pointing to a swarm of vultures blackening the sky but I can't take my eyes off the road, off the sheer drop into red rock. It's a relief when I'm dragged into waking, recognize the sound for what it actually is. I stumble into the kitchen. The clock on my stove says 3:57.

"Midge?"

"Matt?"

"Midge, things are bad." His voice is low, like he's whispering, like he's gone somewhere to hide.

"What do you mean?"

He sucks in a breath, and I imagine the swarm of smoke inside his lungs, the space gaping open in his head. Is the fear that fills that space the same for him as it is for me?

"We aren't doing anything. It's all over."

"You and Ang?"

"No direct military action."

"Where are you?"

"Why's that matter?"

"At Owain's?"

He doesn't answer.

"Did you talk to Angie?"

"I'm not calling about that." His tone is sharp, impatient. "Why's everything have to be about that?"

"About what?"

"Emotions." The word spat out, mocked. I swim around my sleepy mind, afraid of his anger, as I once was of my dad's. If this was my dad, what would I say? Nothing. I'd tiptoe away. Instead, I suck up my courage.

"I'm worried about you," I mutter. "So's she."

"Spare me, Midge. Try spending two years not knowing if your sister's dead or alive."

I rub my forehead, wondering how many times I have to apologize, and then, if I actually ever have. "I'm sorry," I start to say, but Matt cuts me off.

"Something has to be done. The moral imperative is to act. I thought you'd care."

"Of course I care!" What I don't say: it's the middle of the night, I have to work in the morning, have you left Angie, I'm worried about you.

"The UN is turfing their legal obligation."

"We aren't the UN," I say, too loud, my fingers flicking from my chest out into the air, gesturing towards him, hidden somewhere in the city. Down below the light is on at his house. Angie, up, on her own, comforting Ellie.

"What about . . ." Your wife, your daughter, your own threatened family, your fragile mental health. Me. He doesn't let me finish.

this has nothing to do with you

247

"You sound like Dad," he spits.

I don't answer. The clock grinds into the next hour. Four a.m. The sky already growing lighter, the distant smokestack becoming visible on the horizon. A plume tinted pink like candy floss.

"I know about the pot," I tell him. "About Owain and Ted."

"Good." I hear the snap of a bottle being set down. "One less secret."

"Do you want to tell me about that day?" I suck in a breath. "What you said to Mom?"

"You know our foreign affairs minister called it an African problem? Said it's got nothing to do with us. Do you agree with that?"

Like he's a journalist, focused on a story, pressing a mic into my face. Like I'm somebody important.

"I don't know how I can help."

"It's simple," Matt says. "Don't turn away."

He hangs up; I'm thrust back into the silence of my apartment, that steep drop in my dream coming close, and I push my face into my hands.

Everything's worse in the middle of the night, I tell myself.

In the morning, I think, Matt will go to work, to his office with the green and blue map pinned to his wall, stuck with clusters of coloured tacks.

He'll sit at his desk, stare at the framed photograph of Angie, him, and me, the one taken in February when I first got back. My hair an auburn bristle on my scalp; Ellie in my arms and an expression on my face like I don't quite know what she is, how to hold her.

He'll pick up the phone and call people. He'll get his life on track.

IT'S A RELIEF TO GO to the library. A relief to have something to focus on outside of myself. In the staff room, Ruth finds me dumping a heaping teaspoon of powdered creamer into my coffee and this time she doesn't say anything. I sip as I prod a week-old newspaper on the table, flipping through to find the classifieds. "Have you been following the news?" she asks, sliding a sliced bagel into the toaster oven. I think of Matt early this morning, filling me in, and the words are there, in my mouth: my brother's fixated on our inaction, I'm not sure what to do. And the rest: he's left his wife, he's growing pot. But like a stressed dog, I shake it off, hackles settling, tension dispersed.

"Good weekend?" I ask, and it's like I've broken a spell. Light flashes on the knife as she digs into a brick of butter.

"Took the grandkids to the nickel museum."

"I haven't been there in years," I say, letting the paper slump. Grade 4, the year Josie first arrived, her father transferred to work at the uranium refinery.

"Exactly the same," she tells me. "And you?"

Like a movie montage, I play mixed up scenes from the weekend in my head. Friday night, Matt's journal, his secret room. My time with Sophie, apartment hunting, Josie telling me she's pregnant. When I hit Saturday night, I'm overtaken by a quick surge of desire then uncertainty. But of course I keep it simple. I don't give her any juicy details. My brother's abandoned his family and is apparently writing letters to our dead father. My mom phoned from prison after I had a breakdown out in the rain, but I only talked to her for a minute, long enough to refuse her once again. "Busy," I say. "A friend came to visit; I babysat my niece."

"Ellie," she says. It sounds like she knows her. There's a smile on her face, like she's pleased that my brother and I are apparently healing, that new beginnings are possible for people like us. I sip my sweet coffee, staring over the edge of my mug. She stops scraping the blade of her knife when she talks, her voice gentle and patronizing. "That's nice," she says, and it irritates me, but I also feel weirdly proud, like I've finally done something right.

ON THE WAY to my desk, I think about that school trip to the nickel mine. Josie, Lara, and me turned together like the petals of a tight bloom as we rode the rattling metal elevator. The darkness deepened the further down we went and when we finally stopped, a couple hundred feet underground, the only light was from a flickering fluorescent tube on the wet, black wall, and the yellow beams from our mining helmets. The warm air smelled of earth and a fresh, metallic tang, like copper. I could hear Josie breathing in my ear. She gripped my hand, crushing my fingers together so hard that it hurt.

A man with black dirt smeared on his cheeks told our class that the city of Norbury stood on the edge of a crater formed by a meteorite striking the earth a couple billion years ago.

"Could that happen again?" Josie blurted, interrupting, and there was silence as the adults' eyes connected in the shadows all around.

"Well, yes," said the man. "It actually could."

"But it won't," our teacher added hastily. We all laughed, but I remember thinking, How can you possibly know?

MY DESK HAS BEEN tidied by the person who was in for me on Friday. Pens collected and put back in their holder, books stacked on the filing cabinet, and my keyboard even wiped down. Two piles of purple folders sit on either side of the scanner, one with a yellow sticky note on top that says *Finished*. The other, I assume, is where my replacement left off, and I see that she got all the way into the *P*s, finishing the fat files on *Ore Mining and Organizations*, and a slender one titled *Organ Donations*. I'm about to flip open the next — *Philanthropists* — when I look up and see Angie on the other side of my interior window, Ellie in a carrier on her chest. She's gazing around the library like they've popped through a portal and she's not quite sure where she's ended up. For a second, I think of hiding, of crawling into the space under my desk, waiting for her to go away. But her eyes swim across the length of glass and connect with mine. I smile; seconds later she's standing in the doorway.

"Bad time?" she asks, her face tight and nervous. There's a rash on her chin, dotted with red blood like she's been scratching away the scabs.

"You okay?" I ask, pulling a chair over for her from the book repair desk. A tremble starts in her bottom lip, and I hand her a box of tissues, but she doesn't take them. She lets the tears roll down her face, dropping onto Ellie's fine hair. It's turning auburn, I realize for the first time, seeing the flush of orange under the fluorescent lights, and I reach out and cup her warm scalp, ruffle the delicate growth. She gurgles, bounces her chubby arms, flashes her blue eyes over my face.

"Matt's quit his job," Angie says. My fingers freeze on Ellie's tiny digits, her small wrist.

"What?"

"He says he wants a different career."

What career? Selling drugs, or something that would actually make sense? As a kid, he dreamed about joining the foreign service, travelling the world, helping people, and it's never seemed right to me: him boxed up in that MNR office or heading out into the woods on his own. Empty wilderness is not his natural terrain. The city is. Downtown shelters, protests, places where people take a stand. I nod. I understand, but I'm not sure about the way forward, about what Matt's told her, if Angie knows.

"What's he's going to do?" I ask, holding my keys out for Ellie who's fussing now, kicking her legs. She grabs the shiny ring. Angie shakes her head.

"What's he told you?" I ask.

"I can't deal with this," she mutters, pushing her fingers into her messy hair. Her mascara has smudged from crying; it looks like she has bruises on her cheeks. "He's writing all these letters."

"To who?" I ask, thinking of the one to our father, and all those blank pages in his book.

"Politicians. Chrétien, the UN secretary general." She squeezes one of Ellie's dangling feet, and I feel it in my own hand, the tiny appendage like a plump sturdy bird. "He keeps writing them, asking them to listen to Dallaire."

Ellie tugs on the keys I'm holding out, and Angie sniffles, then says, "I get it, I do. It's awful, it's horrible, and I love that about him, his concern for people, for the world. It isn't that. If it was just that..." She takes a breath.

I nod, I feel exactly the same, and an overwhelming sense of helplessness too. Don't turn away, Matt had said, but how does one not?

How does one keep watching, with no power, with no control? Is it enough to simply witness?

"He won't talk to me, he's living in this basement. He's quit his job. He's..." Her voice fades out as she pushes a Kleenex against her face. Ellie stuffs the key inside her mouth, and I take hold of her wrist, try to pull it back but her face crumples, ready to cry, so I leave it, let her suck on the cold metal. Imagine her driving, and if only, I think. If only we were there already, in that future, all the hard things resolved. My teenage niece driving us out to a movie or dinner, Angie and me in the back seat, poking Matt in the shoulder whenever he bossed her around too much. A happy family.

"I guess I'll have to go back to cutting hair," Angie says, after she blows her nose. "If I can find someone to watch her because he can't. He's moved out."

I don't say anything. "You're not surprised." She hesitates, then leans forward, gazing sharply at me, looking for a reaction. "Have you talked to him?"

"No," I lie.

"But you knew."

I nod. "Owain," I say. I hesitate, then lean closer. "We slept together," I whisper, and press my lips together, waiting for her reaction. I want something else. A break, to talk like normal sisters-in-law but Angie just stares at me. Her face looks flat and numb. The tears have stopped. The only sound is the baby, gurgling as she pulls the metal object out of her mouth, then puts it back in.

"Owain and you," Angie says.

I nod.

"So you're in on it too?" Her eyes are questioning. My mouth opens and closes. Before I can find an answer, she sees what Ellie's doing and grabs at her hand, hauls out the key, wet with spit.

"Ellie, no! Dirty, that's dirty!" She glares at me. "How could you let her do that?"

The baby's shrieking breaks the silence as I'm fishing around for explanations, trying to understand what's happening.

Hold on, I want to say. Stop everything. You know? About the drugs, the seedlings, those tender new plants waiting for sunshine and space, the sandy soil on Sophie's eighty acres. And what else?

Angie leaps to her feed, bouncing Ellie in her arms, comforting her. Several of the library patrons swivel to look at us from the stacks. One of them shoves a book back, possibly to be lost forever, the Dewey Decimal number misaligned, but I don't have time to check. Angie dashes out my office door without saying goodbye, heading for the exit with my wailing niece, leaving me feeling like I've somehow betrayed her, and I'm not even certain why.

5.

TERESA COMES OVER to check on me. "Everything okay?" she says, sticking her head into my room. Her eyes drop to a couple of balled up tissues on the floor, and I pick them up, toss them in the trash can, and say, "Just peachy."

She stands there, waiting for more. What can I say?

All I've got in my mind is Matt, sitting in that dark basement I've never seen, doing what? Chain smoking? Watching the news? Reading the newspaper? Getting high? Pruning the new plants, starting others from seed? Writing long letters to our dead father that will never get sent and others, desperate to address injustice, inaction. Is he at least sending those?

Or maybe he's sleeping, and is that what's happened? Did the fatigue from being a new father shake up his brain, stir loose a chemical soup he inherited from Mom?

I won't know until I talk to him, but I can't right now.

Teresa's eyes are still on me, so I flip open the next file, the one labelled *Philanthropists*, and then watch through the windows as she walks away, heading back to the circulation desk, and her office on the other side.

Inside the file, there's a stack of partial furniture ads that make no sense until I turn them over and see that they're obituaries of important community donors. Thomas Frederick Martin, who met his maker in 1978; Lu Nguyen, who passed suddenly in 1967; Gladys Navue, who died after a long battle with cancer in 1989. One at a time, I scan them, and put a tiny checkmark in the top right-hand corner when I'm done. Rarely do I read them, because if I did, the job would take forever, so I simply scan, move to the next, then the next, then the next, but this time, when I pick up the brittle, yellowing article on top of the pile, dated 1988, I stop. The headline reads *Community Father Dead at 79*, and there's a large familiar photograph of a man with a clipped goatee, fedora, wide bow tie. The wide face, the pale eyes. It's the same person in the picture on the library wall. Sophie's dad.

Survived by two daughters and a grandson, the article says. None are named. Sophie, her stepsister, and Ted, I assume, as I settle into my chair to read the rest of the article, learning about the war, about a long walk to Germany's American zone, about emigration. When I'm finished, I stand up with the file, to flip the article onto the plate of the scanner, but something falls out. A rusty paper clip and a slip of newspaper that flutters like a moth under my desk, flying far to the back. On my hands and knees, I crawl under to retrieve it, and when I turn it over, that's where I stay, inside that small cave, because it's another obituary. This one for Lucille White. Leaving son Theodore and stepsister Sophia to mourn her loss. Celia. My father's mistress.

this has nothing to do with you

I'M STANDING, with no memory of having gotten up. The obituary is three years old and brittle, but I stuff it in my pocket without caring if it breaks. My desk, I leave as it is, the purple file open, loose clippings spread out. Quickly, I gather my things, my purse, my jacket. Teresa's on the phone in her office when I walk by, but I don't even stop. She says something to me, loud, then rushes to her door, calling me, but it's too late. I'm already outside, in the cool air, running across the road to my car, heading for Matt.

6.

THERE'S ONE PROBLEM. I don't know where Owain lives. I find a payphone, pump in a quarter, but of course Angie doesn't answer, and neither does Owain. When the coin drops for the second time, I fish it out, tap it against the glass wall as I'm thinking, then use it to call Sophie after looking her up in the tattered phonebook. Somehow it seems amazing that her number's right there, in black and white on the tissue-thin page, after I'd scanned the dozen Hendersons, but found no O. As soon as Sophie picks up, I jump to my request: I need to know Owain's address. It's an emergency, I say, babbling about how I have to talk to Matt, how he's left Angie.

"Slow down, slow down," she says, and she's right, because there are things I should be asking her. But how can I? My mother murdered her stepsister. A lump forms in my throat, blocking speech. Silence fills the phone line, buzzing in my ear, but there isn't any silence at all, actually, because Sophie is speaking to me; I have to calm myself down in order to hear.

She's telling me about Hilda, about how she isn't doing well at all at the Norbury shelter, how Sophie can help her at the farm, that Grommet needs to go. Details that seem secondary to my current concerns, strangely foreign, a far distance away. Where I am is on the edge of that puddle of blood in the campground, the wide red stain that won't ever disappear, that formed in her landscape as well, I now know. I close my eyes, lean my forehead against the filthy, smudged glass of the phone booth.

"Please," I creak, and Sophie must hear something desperate in my tiny, quiet voice because she says, "76 Boreal Drive."

"Do you need directions?" she asks, as I hang up.

I know exactly where it is. Just a few blocks from my place, down a street where I walked Grommet plenty of times to reach a clearing so he could run through the trees, set free.

OWAIN ANSWERS THE front door in nothing but his boxer shorts. His eyebrows shoot up in surprise when he sees me, and I think I see a flicker of fear cross his face. "I'm here for my brother," I blurt out.

"Oh," he says, and jerks his chin towards the driveway to my left. "Around the side, under the car port."

There's no bell, so I try the doorknob, find it unlocked, let myself in. Ahead of me, a short staircase leads up to what I assume is the entrance into Owain's place. The basement's to my right, and at the bottom of the stairs there's a plastic shoe-mat filled with filth from the spring melt, and a closed door that I knock on once, tentatively, then with more conviction. Silence pulses through the blank wood though, and I'm listening so intently, leaning my ear in, that I jump when Owain talks to me from the stairs.

"Maybe sleeping?" he says, but I ignore him, press my mouth to the crack in the door and call Matt's name. Still, there's no answer. Maybe Angie was wrong, I think. Maybe he's at work and everything's fine, or at least not as bad as she said.

Owain's in his kitchen, cracking the cap off a Labatt's 50 on a bronze bottle opener that's fastened to the wall. "Want one?"

"It's ten in the morning."

He shrugs and guzzles a third of the beer, then sets it down. I'm still trying to figure out what to do, am about to ask him where he thinks Matt might have gone, when he steps abruptly close and puts his hands on my hips, kneading his fingers into my waist. I'm startled, remembering how things ended the other night, unsure how to read him, so I press my palms against his chest and pull back a bit.

"I thought it was just a good time."

He shrugs, gives me that grin. "We can't have more of a good time?"

I don't answer, although what I'm thinking is yes, yes, I do want more. Slowly, he leans in to kiss me, but before his lips meet mine, I spit out one of the questions that I need to ask.

"Did you know about Sophie?"

He goes still, his face close to mine. He's warm and I'd rather push against him, close my eyes, crawl into this intoxicating burrow, but there's too much I need to know.

"My family," I whisper against his neck. "Do you know about my family?"

"Yeah."

"Sophie's sister."

"Stepsister."

"Did you know her?"

He shakes his head. "Never met her."

"You knew about my dad?"

He nods. I feel his head move. His lips lower to my neck. I don't say it: my mother. How he chatted with her on the phone, without judgement, like she was anyone, a waitress, a woman at the till in Giant Tiger, his girlfriend's mom.

"You never said anything to me. Nothing."

"Matt told me not to."

I pull back so I'm facing him now, bug my eyes out at him. He lifts both hands, palms out. "What?" he says. "I just do as I'm told." He grabs his beer off the counter, says, "I guess he thought since you just got home..."

I turn away, grasp the edge of the kitchen sink, stare through frilly yellow curtains at the backyard. There's a station wagon at the end of the driveway, abandoned, tires flat, a worn green tarp covering a load of stuff spilling out of its open trunk. Along the fence, there's a garden bed filled with bent tomato cages holding the yellowed plants from a previous season. Some landscaper, I think, taking in the details as I seethe, irritated with my brother, his silence. What was the point of him coming to get me, dragging me out of that cave, if he was just going to keep me in the dark? And, more importantly, what is he even doing? Serving a voluntary sentence on behalf of our mother, the gun in her hand, that bullet slicing Celia's neck, opening a valve. Trying to make amends? I shut my eyes, cling to the ugly green counter.

"How did Matt meet Sophie?"

"Tracked her down, I guess, but I don't know what they talked about."

"And then you thought you'd like to screw the murderer's daughter."

"No!" I hear the bottle clatter back onto the counter. I turn around to see him wiping his wet lips with the back of a hand, and I study him. Creepy, Lara might say. His interest in me. How she glared at all the gawkers who showed up for my father's funeral, standing on the sidelines. We could have sold hot dogs, she muttered later on.

this has nothing to do with you

But is it creepy?

Who am I to judge?

He tips his eyes down, pushes at the linoleum with his bare toes. "Honestly," he says. "I just think you're hot."

7.

WE SHED OUR CLOTHES in the kitchen and do it around the corner on the living room couch. After, breathing heavily, Owain has two apples of red on his pale cheeks and we lie there, wedged side by side, cushion buttons hard against my spine. This close, I can see a dark mole on the underside of his chin, faint spidery veins on the side of his nose, his long spidery eyelashes, dark brown like his eyes.

"Are you actually a brunette?" I ask, pinching a lock of his bleached hair. He opens his eyes, smiles, then twists away from me to sit up. I pull a crocheted afghan in clashing colours of pink and mustard yellow off the back of the couch and stretch it over me as Owain perches naked on the cushion's edge and reaches for a pack of cigarettes on the coffee table. It and the couch and a giant TV are the only items of furniture in the room. On the far wall are three bright squares from missing paintings, revealing the wallpaper pattern of gold pillars and twisting ivy that's faded everywhere else. He taps the pack against his naked knee, noticing me looking.

"My aunts and uncles took all the old lady furniture, but the only thing I need is that," he says, nodding towards the huge box in the corner with its flat screen.

"And your music stuff?" I ask. His eyes flash toward my face.

"Yes," he says. "My guitar."

But I don't see a guitar, just a few tortoiseshell picks on the coffee table, next to a notebook open to a rumpled page. Several scribbled stanzas cover it, with a single scrawled line near the bottom. I want to lean closer, see what it says, or ask him to sing me a song, but then there's the crack of a match into flame, and he starts telling me what a technological marvel the TV is, with its rear projection, stereo sound. I zone out, pull the soft blanket up to my chin, feeling like I could stay here all day, cocooned, avoiding Matt, my job, Sophie, the dog. I'm almost asleep when Owain clicks on the remote control and Toni Braxton jumps into the room, running through a French estate holding up her heavy skirts. We watch one video after another — the Beastie Boys, Soundgarden — with him sitting at the other end of the couch, my feet in his lap, nudging his penis. I like this, I want this, neither one of us talking, as comfortable as a couple, but when I hear the side door open and footsteps going downstairs, I tense, then automatically start sitting up. Owain grips the coffee table book in his lap, about volcanoes, that he's using as a surface for rolling a joint.

"Whoa," he says, and I stop. There are delicate piles spread out on the book's hardcover, pungent tobacco rolled out of a cigarette and bits of dry green buds. "Sorry," I mutter, as he mixes the materials together with his fingertip, and I watch, already smelling a mist of sweet smoke drifting up through the vents.

"It isn't about you, you know," Owain says, as he works the joint into a tight tube, then pops it into his mouth to wet the seam, smooth it down. "What he's doing."

"What's he doing exactly?"

He pauses, staring over at the picture window that faces the street, that's hidden by pulled brown curtains. Dust mites dance in the brightly lit crack. "Living his life, finding a different way. Unconventional, maybe, but it's his choice."

this has nothing to do with you

I stare at him as he uses his cigarette — smouldering in a black plastic ashtray, like the one the waitress from the bar the other night had dumped out into a coffee can — to light the spliff.

Shifting the book with his free hand, he turns sideways and holds it out to me, but I shake my head, my arms crossed tightly around my naked breasts, my body already faintly trembling. He sucks in smoke, holds his breath, creaks out the words. "He wasn't happy."

"Happy?"

Owain sucks on the tight tip of the joint and studies me, I guess because of how I've said the word. Like an accusation. Who's happy? I'm thinking. Least of all us, Matt and me. That was something we never saw growing up, not really, not much, not without consequences. When Matt was happy, my dad would challenge him, drag him down. Same with my mom. I saw that enough that I didn't even bother feeling good unless my father was in an upbeat mood as well. I read the predominant mood, then fit myself into it. The only time I was happy was when I felt free: Lara, Josie, and me soaring down Cemetery Hill in neutral, ice-skating on a patch of cleared-off lake, drinking so much stolen rum the stars spun in blurry circles while we laughed and laughed. But then, I think, I felt a bit of that the other day, floating down the hill to Sophie's, towards that yard full of dogs. Although even that, I now realize, is not untethered from my past.

Owain flicks through the channels, passing infomercials and a news show, a blip about Bosnia that blinks by so fast, barely registering. I feel a sudden urge to ask him to stop, but he ends up back at Erica Ehm, showing clips of Kurt Cobain talking about his music, his eyes shining, that shaggy blonde hair, the worn jeans, the plaid shirts, and I'm ready to talk to Matt.

When I move, the book tumbles to the floor. The rest of the pot and tobacco scatter across the worn hardwood. On the splayed open pages, I see figures from Pompeii: a person cradling a loved one's head, a family turned to stone.

"Shit," Owain says, staring down.

"Sorry," I say, although I'm not.

He leans back into the couch, leaving the mess, his hands dropped, palms up, on his naked thighs. He grins at me. "Well, when I'm desperate I'll know where to look."

MATT'S RUNNERS ARE outside his apartment, kicked off on the dirty shoe tray. I knock, but he doesn't answer so I try the door and the knob twists freely.

"Matt?" I call, stepping inside the dim space, led by the light from an aquarium against the far wall. It's filled with murky water, plastic plants, drifting strands of soft green algae. A fake anchor encrusted with tiny snails sits on a bed of dirty pink pebbles. The filter's humming, so I know it's on, and I see half a dozen tetras flashing silver like floating dimes.

"What do you need, Mel?" Matt asks out of the darkness, startling me. I jump, then spin around, working to locate him. There's an orange ember floating over the wide bulk of a couch, and in its faint light I see his face. "Here to see Owain?"

"No," I say, and I sound like I'm twelve. Like I should be crossing my arms, jutting out a hip, embarrassed by my big brother pointing out the boy I like. But of course we're way past that.

"You," I say. "I'm here to see you."

"You should have let me know. I would have prepared some tea."

It's a stupid joke, and I don't laugh. I stand there, not sure what to do, watching as he leans forward, stabs his smoke into an ashtray on a wooden spool once used for fat hydro lines, now turned on its side. He hasn't asked me to stay, would probably prefer if I left, but I take a seat on a green velvet chair and rest my elbow on one of the ornate wooden arms.

"I found out some things," I say.

"Yeah, you told me."

"Not that." I wave my hand, shifting the smoky air, a mix of sweet marijuana and regular tobacco. I look around for windows to open, but they're on the other side of the room, over the kitchen area, blacked out by dark curtains. Matt finding his place out of the light, just like our mother did. My throat clenches, and I try to quietly clear it, in order to push on.

"Other things. Things I think you could have let me know about."

He does not speak. He sits quietly, like a spirit I might overlook.

"I know who Sophie is now, and I know about Celia." I look down at my lap; I hate using her name. "You found out about her too, who she was, that her family lived nearby, and you tracked her down, and last fall you went to see her."

He still won't speak, and I wonder if he's taking in my words or if something's blocking his ears. That little kid game, a memory of trying to pull his fingers off his head, force him to hear me. I lean forward, impatient.

"Talk to me."

"You're a regular Jessica Fletcher."

"So Sophie knows about us?"

But I know she must. I recall the sharpness of her gaze when I asked her about Matt, when she instructed me to ask him about why he'd gone to meet her. How could she have known and still have treated me like I was simply a stranger, existing outside of the story, not involved? I feel like an idiot. Bawling about my stupid dog when all along...

I press on. "Why did you go? Are you trying to make amends?"

"This isn't AA, Midge," he says, glaring at me. The light from the aquarium is on his face, pressing a blue tint onto his cheeks that makes me look away because it reminds me of the dream I had the other night. That strange man's body, the dilemma Angie and I shared, both of us mute and numbly puzzled, trying to figure out what to do.

"What is it, then?"

He snatches a book of matches off the coffee table, lights one, touches the flame to the black wick of a candle, drops the spent match in the ashtray. A shell, I see now, its inner iridescence dulled by grey ash. Surrounding it are other things: a pile of newspapers, a stack of photos, a beer bottle with a hole knocked into the bottom for smoking hash, a crossword puzzle, half done, a paperback copy of *Future Shock*, fanned open.

"And now you're here," I say. "You've left Angie and your baby and quit your job, and now you're living in a basement, dealing drugs. Mom would be so proud." I expect Matt to tell me to shut up, but he doesn't. There's the papery, dry sound of yet another cigarette coming out of his pack, and I wave my hands, trying to clear a space in the smoky haze built from his tiny, desperate fires. The only hopeful thing in here is the tinsel-like glint of the fish, those mirrored fragments of our past.

"And now Angie knows about the pot."

He shrugs like it's no big deal, and I think about Owain's lecture on marijuana prohibition, can easily imagine my brother delivering the same speech. I lean forward, wanting to stand up, shake him.

"Matty, what is going on with you?" I ask, but he still doesn't answer. He sits there like he's frozen, except for the movement of his knee, jerking steadily, and I want to get up, go over, still him, steady him, but I grip my hands together in my lap. I can't remember the last time I touched him, hugged him, held him, with affection, I mean, not the headlock he put me in at the eighties party. Maybe after I saw him approaching from the mouth of my cave. That day we walked arm-in-arm to Robert's, Matt carrying my pack on his shoulders, believing we were over the worst of it. Grief burns in my nose and I push my fingers against my cheekbones, afraid I might start to cry.

"Clinton's speech the other day," he says. "Did you hear it?"

I shake my head.

"Patronizing, useless. Pretending to care. No action to back it up. How does that help?"

There are square holes cut into the newspapers, I notice, a stack of clippings nearby, and his red journal's there too, the pen stuck in its pages, holding his place. He sees me looking and says, "I've got ideas. I tried to tell Angie. But she doesn't want that. She wants me to keep my mouth shut, do my job, bring home the bacon."

His voice is escalating. A spray of saliva with the last spat words.

"Forty years of that? No thanks."

"She's worried about you."

He pushes his hand against his jaw, rubs the bristles of his new beard.

"And I am too."

His eyes jump up, his gaze attaching to mine, and I think about what I read in his journal. That moment he shared with our mother, out on the street in front of our house. The details, hidden from me. I close my eyes. I don't look at him as I speak, can't.

"Dad told you. You knew..."

"How do you..."

"It wasn't your fault," I blurt, even though I don't really know all the details. So many are hidden.

Smoke streams through Matt's nostrils. He shakes his head. "Please don't do that."

"What?"

"Pathologize me, like my concerns can't be real, like it's all about my psychology, like it's somehow made up in my head." Aggressively, he taps his left temple.

"I don't think it's made up."

"You think it's more about me, some sort of deficiency in me." He slaps his chest hard, hitting bone, scaring me.

"I didn't say that."

"You know who else was like that?" I stare at him. Slowly, steadily, he nods. "That's how he treated Mom. Held her down, belittled her dreams, mocked her concerns about the world."

I've never been able to argue with Matt. Not when he got started, spinning his logic, building careful arguments. When he was older, if our father bothered taking him on, even he would lose, eventually abandoning the discussion to retreat to the downstairs television set. He should be a lawyer, my mother would say, if politician wasn't in the cards. This time, though, I think I have a point to make. A winning thesis. That's how he treated you, too, I could tell him, but Matt's on a roll now, and I can't get a word in edgewise.

"This has nothing to do with me," he says, lifting a leg to kick at the heap of papers. "It has to do with right and wrong, with morality. We should all be talking about it all the time, in lunchrooms at our jobs, in bank lineups. Instead we're..." His voice peters out. My head is swimming. I feel a pressing wave of helplessness. How can I talk to him if he won't — can't? — dig through the present to look at our past. Upstairs, the phone rings. Owain's voice, an easygoing rumble, breaks the impasse between us, and Matt lunges for the remote control, turns on the television, starts flipping from a commercial for pest control to a foggy soap opera flashback, searching for news, I gather, for somebody to tell him what's happening outside this dim room, right now. His face is lit, mouth set in a scowl, eyes deep-set and dark.

"Why are you being like this?" I ask.

"Like what?"

"Like a jerk to me."

"I'm a jerk?" he says, emphasizing the pronoun. I hear the accusation and to retaliate, I say, "What about Ellie? You know: your daughter?"

It doesn't work. His face, staring ahead at the TV, gives nothing away. I stand up, step closer, wanting to find him, to dig down under the layers of smoke and obsession with the news to locate my brother. He doesn't even seem to smell like himself anymore, that sweet, musky odour that was him, that, if he died, I would try to breathe in from his clothes, like I did with my dad's. I took one of his plaid work shirts out West with me, wore it for a long time, until it smelled more like patchouli and pot and my own old sweat. One evening, I buried it under a wide rock in Oak Creek with Robert. We smudged the area; I said a prayer. None of this have I ever told Matt.

I let out a long, ragged sigh. Exaggerated, childish. The couch is in the middle of the room, and I move behind it, hovering behind Matt's head. If I could see our reflections in the television set, my own would be faint, indistinct, just a layer added to my brother, the two of us somehow combined.

"I guess I'll talk to you later," I say, and poke his shoulder. It feels boney, too thin.

"In a while, crocodile," he says, like nothing's happened, like we're little kids. Like a thousand miles aren't still stretching between us.

Upstairs, before I slip out the side door, Owain finds me.

"Sophie's hoping to see you," he says, rubbing his palm against the fuzzy dark hair on his naked chest. To get Grommet, I remember, and I groan and lay a hand across my forehead. Where will I put him? And what will I even say to her? When I take my hand from my face, Owain's still watching me. He steps down to where I'm standing by the side door, slips his hands around my waist, and nuzzles against me.

"See you soon?" he says. I nod, feeling myself flush.

"Everything is going to be all right now," he says in a sing-song voice, holding me, swaying me back and forth. I lean against him, appreciating his warmth, his solid frame.

8.

I HIT THE ROAD. It's what I need right now: to take off, to get out of Dodge. With my foot heavy on the gas, the car speeds out onto the highway, threading through the tall rock cuts, soaring over the moonlike landscape that's been stripped bare by acid rain. Devoid of vegetation; the small lakes to the east clear as glass and empty of fish. Sterile, without complications, without life.

I'm thinking I'll skip Sophie's, maybe go see Jose, but then I start fantasizing about truly running away. Blowing past Limberlost Lane, right through Hixon River, heading to the Soo to cross into the States, driving south, south, south, then west, to find my way back to Arizona, to Robert. Deep down I know what that is: a step into a past I'm already done with, where, I realize, I won't actually fit anymore. A wave of grief hits me, and all of a sudden I'm crying so hard I have to pull over and it's just like the days and months afterwards when my eyes would skim over a picture of my parents and I'd think, no. Just that, but all capitals: NO. No is back in my mind again, but this time about Matt, about how I seem to be losing him, and what can I do? I sit there, my face in my hands, until a tap on my door makes me jump. Through a smudge on the glass from Grommet's eager nose, I see that it's a cop.

"Everything okay?" he asks, as I roll down the window.

"My dad died," I tell him.

He takes a step back, subtle, that slight, familiar recoil, and I see his face start to calculate the questions to ask. "A long time ago," I blurt out. "He had a heart attack," I lie, so I won't have to get into details, use the name of it, alarm him. Murder.

"Oh," he says. "I'm sorry."

"It's not your fault." I wipe my nose on the cuff of my sleeve.

He looks behind me. "A transport could come flying around this curve," he says, advising me on my safety, offering care. "Better pull up a ways, or, better yet, find a coffee shop, get yourself off the road."

"Thanks," I mutter, and he nods. As I shift into drive, he stands there, watching as I pull out and go on my way.

I DON'T WANT to do this. See Sophie, collect my dog, sneak him back into my apartment building like the past few days haven't happened. But in Massey, my trembling hand hits the blinker and I turn onto Limberlost Lane. Before long, I'm at the top of the hill, looking down at the farmhouse. In the yard, my car door opens into a storm of barking dogs, Grommet muscling through to reach me. He growls a couple times to assert his claim, then leaps up, paws on my shoulders, and licks my face until it's soaked.

"Off," Sophie booms from the verandah. Immediately he drops away.

"You spoil him," she says, walking closer. She's wearing an orange vest over a pink shirt, the colours clashing so aggressively I have to glance away. "You can't do that. It'll only make things worse."

"What things?"

"Resource guarding, jealousy." She looks over at him. He's panting happily, leaning against my leg, but when her gaze shifts it's me she sees. My eyes red and puffy, I imagine, the skin splotchy around my mouth. The way she peers at me makes me feel like nobody's fully taken me in, not really, not for years, and the tears start pooling again. I can barely see as she takes my arm and leads me to the verandah, to a church pew sitting against the wall of the house.

"Take these two in there," Sophie says to Ted, who's standing on the other side of the screen door. He doesn't say a word as he leads in the greyhound, who's limping, I notice, and Trotsky. When Sophie's weight settles beside me on the bench the only dog left with us is Grommet, lying down on the planks and I nudge his back paw with my foot, trying to regain my composure, staring down at Sophie's rubber boots which are dusty like a wiped down chalkboard. I need to blow my nose, and I wish I had a box of tissues or a hanky like the ones my dad used when I was a kid, that he'd pull out of his pocket, that I'd give back to him sopping wet. When was that? When did I cry in front of him? When had he offered such care?

"Matt?" she says.

I nod. When I can speak, I say, "Why didn't you tell me?"

She sighs. "Which part?"

I look at her. "What's that mean? All of it, all the stuff I know now."

"It wasn't my place. He told me not to, and he's your brother."

"So?"

"So, I figured he knew best."

Anger, I feel. At Matt, his control. Sophie's looking down at Grommet, at how he's resting his chin on my foot so he'll know if I try to leave. "Protecting you," she says, and for a second I'm not sure if she means my dog or Matt. Believing he's still in charge, still the mediator, still the one who can make things easier for me. His little Midge.

"Well, you can tell me now," I say. "Your version, how it happened, and about..." Celia, I start to say, but my voice won't work, I know it. I push a knuckle against my lip and swallow her name, but Sophie doesn't seem to notice, is wiping her hands on her knees like she's getting ready to start a difficult task, stand up and go dig a trench or unspool a roll of chicken wire.

"All right," she says, and she starts to talk.

"Fifteen months after my mother died, my dad married Mrs. White. She was his housekeeper. She had one daughter, aged fourteen. Celia."

I can tell by the way her lip curls that this didn't make her happy.

"I was away, at my first year of university."

"You went to university?"

She glances at me, nods.

"I wanted to be a doctor, but I only got three years done. Three and a half. I was one of only four women in my class. But..."

"You left."

She looks at me with her white-blue eyes, so clear I feel like I can almost see her thoughts, at least the heavy regret that's still there. "You didn't come to hear that."

"It's part of it; you're part of it. I wanted to go to school too."

Her face is composed and quiet, still as granite, like Matt's in his basement, but I can tell she's struggling. Her lips open, then close, like she's sampling the sentences, and I shut my mouth, stop talking about myself and let her be, trying to be patient. Waiting, I gaze out at the yard as if we're anticipating a service, a serious one about forgiveness or evil, or maybe even a funeral. Finally, she continues.

"She was always wild, Celia was."

I remember the phone ringing at nearly midnight, my father explaining that it was work, an emergency, a yellowcake rupture or something, and how only later did I realize that it must have been her.

"Her own father was an alcoholic," Sophie says. "Ended up stepping in front of a train." Her gaze flickers over, to see my reaction, I guess, but I don't have much of one. The tears have stopped. I feel numb. "Hard things." I nod once, still listening.

"When she was sixteen, she got hooked up with this guy. Door-to-door vacuum salesman by day, sociopathic biker by night. That was Teddy's father. My parents tried to keep them apart. My dad bought this farm, thinking he'd fix it up, start some sort of a business, that Celia could help run it, thinking if he kept her busy enough, if she was far enough out of the city..." Sophie stares down at her hands, fingers laced together between her knees. "But she ran off. Disappeared. At first they were frantic with worry and then" — she shrugs — "what could they do? Life went on until..."

"Ted."

Sophie ignores me. The story's coming out on its own. It's like I'm not even there.

"That Christmas I was home. We chopped down a tree, a beautiful blue spruce, huge, and it was out of a picture book, the perfect family Christmas. I was even getting along better with my stepmother. Then out of the dark night, there she is, showing up with this baby." I glance beyond Sophie at the screen door but it's blank, Ted not there, or at least not visible.

"We woke up Christmas morning, and Celia was gone. My parents were old, my stepmother already diagnosed with cancer by that point. No one would have adopted him. Days later, we found a note, buried in the blankets in the laundry basket that was Ted's bed."

"What did it say?"

"What could I do?" Sophie mutters, ignoring my question. "I couldn't go back. How could I go back?"

She looks at me like I've challenged her, like I've asked her to defend her decision. Really, I'm thinking about Matt, making the same choice and how I took off. The silence is so abrupt that Grommet lifts his head, waiting for movement. Lines have deepened around Sophie's mouth, across her forehead.

"It said, *I'm sorry. You can change his name if you want.*" She swings her head slowly back and forth, a disbelieving smile sneaking onto her lips. "Like this beautiful kid was nothing more than a malformed dog you might or might not take out back and shoot."

I don't know what to say. I wait, but I'm impatient to hear it all, catch up to my part, my father's.

"But she came back," I prod. Later, I mean. Years after Ted's birth. A few years ago.

Sophie shakes her head. "No," she says. "Never here." She swings out her arm, encompassing the verandah, the barn, the whole eighty acres that Ted spends his days tromping through, living the life Celia gave him. I wait.

"Why'd she move to Hixon River?" Sophie asks. "I don't know. Sneaking closer to us maybe, trying to steel her nerve?" She snorts, glares out into the empty space of the yard like there's something there to judge. "It didn't work."

"Eventually she got a job in the cafeteria at the refinery," she says. "You know that. I don't know if she intended to make amends, to try to be a mom to her son, but she didn't. Didn't even contact me until she'd been living there, in that awful rented motor home out on the highway, for three months." She sighs. "And by then she'd met your dad."

I stiffen. Now the story's no longer the anonymous blur of someone else's life, a fuzzy soap opera flashback like the one that had softened the screen in Matt's apartment as he flipped through the channels. Now it's full, bright Technicolour, glaring and crisp. Sophie pushes her hands against her khakis, and I wonder if they're sweating, if she's getting more nervous the closer we get to the end. Do we even need to talk about that? The whizzing bullet, the spreading pool of blood. I want to get up suddenly, explain that I should be going, and as if she knows this, Sophie stands, and says, "Do you want something to drink?"

She doesn't wait for me to answer. I follow her inside, and we don't speak as she puts the kettle on, stands in front of the stove, her back to me, waiting for it to boil. Ted's nowhere to be seen, and I wander over to the shelf near the woodstove and look again at the framed picture of the woman in the turquoise dress, the young girl with her face turned away. I look closer, realizing now who they are: Mrs. White and Celia, and, yes, I can see the resemblance between this teenager and the pictures of the woman, my father's mistress, in the newspaper back then. Which I studied. Which I cut out and kept for a while, tucked into a photo album. Probably I still have it somewhere if it hasn't turned to dust.

At the sound of a drawer opening, I turn, see Sophie pulling out a silver flask. Gratefully, I watch as she drops a dollop of amber liquid into each of the cups, then carries the pot, wrapped in its cozy, over to the kitchen table. She goes back for a plate of cookies, and starts talking again as she sets them down, her voice seeming to boom in the quiet room.

"She told me about him," she says, "but she didn't tell me he was married, had kids. To be honest, I didn't care one way or another. What I wanted was for her to get her shit together and come see her own kid, take him back, give him his proper mother."

Sophie fills the cups with weak tea and I take a sip, absorb the welcoming, stinging warmth of the whiskey, then reach for a cookie that's shaped like a maple leaf, nibble at the pointy edges, and realize how hungry I am. It distracts me for a moment, the food and gentle blurring, so I'm barely paying attention as Sophie lifts the tea to her lips, sets it down without taking a drink.

"So then when she told me about the baby..." she says. I stare at her. The sugary dough clots on my tongue, turned bitter, like arsenic.

"Oh, shit," she spits, setting down her cup so hard that the liquid gushes over the rim.

Carefully, I put the half-eaten cookie back on the plate with the others. Make myself swallow. My voice is a tiny squeak. "Baby."

"Fetus. Not an infant, just a —" she's up on her feet, pulling a towel off the counter, cleaning up as she babbles, trying to somehow make it okay "— I thought you knew. You said you knew."

I stand as well. I want to go somewhere, get away, but where? Grommet's at the kitchen door, watching, and when he sees me through the dirty glass, he barks.

"Go lie down," Sophie shouts, and he barks again, then rushes around the corner to the front of the house, his big paws pounding. Another dog's joined him, I can hear, and through the walls come the growling, tussling sounds of the two of them at play. At least there's that, I think from somewhere far away, along the flimsy chord that still ties me to the present. At least my dog is happy.

Sophie empties my tea into the sink and replaces it with a shot of straight whiskey. I bolt it back and sit there, eyes closed, letting it quiet the edges of my nerves, then push my cup over for more. It feels like a hole's opened, and here I am, staring down, knowing I have to leap, wondering what will break my fall.

"She was..." I start but I'm unable to say the word.

"Maybe Matt..." Sophie says.

"Just tell me."

"You're sure?"

Of course not. No, I think of saying, fantasizing again about moving time in reverse: driving back to the city, avoiding the Philanthropist file, avoiding Matt's new place, going all the way to my time at the kennel, making the practical decision about Grommet so I wouldn't ever meet Sophie, but then my heart pinches as I imagine working my boring job, never meeting Owain, even Josie's embryo splitting into its cells, retreating into that armoured, lonely egg as the days tick backwards, and I burst into tears. Again. Because I have no choice, I realize; the only choice is to hear the truth, the whole story. Sophie nudges a damp towel over to me, and I pick it up but don't bother wiping my eyes. "Go on," I say.

"There isn't much more. She'd only just found out. That spring, early June. Called to tell me a few days before your mother..." Her hand swims through the air, making a gesture that's supposed to imply the unsayable, that horrifying final action. Sophie shakes her head, a weak wobble. "I got so frigging angry at her. There she was, so excited about this new baby, acting like Teddy didn't even exist. But you know, it was still early days. Barely eight weeks. No longer than..."

"That's supposed to make me feel better?" I bellow.

Her eyes drop. A dust of tea leaves is spread in the bottom of each of our cups, I see, and I wonder if she can read them, what mine might say. What advice they'd give.

"And Matt knew."

She nods. I think I get it now. The two of them, that morning, my mother and Matt. How I watched them from the house, saw her turn sharply towards him, close as conspirators. How I asked Matt what they'd talked about, how he brushed it aside, how he hasn't ever answered. Except in his journal, except in that letter to our dad. That was the bit of news our father had told him, wanting what? Congratulations? A twisted new closeness with his son?

I shut my eyes, trying to catch up to this new version of events. My dad would be a father for the third time, and this knowledge sent her careening over the edge. But how could she have done what she did, knowing a baby was involved, and how could Matt have told her, then left her on her own?

"It was Matt who put the pieces together for me," Sophie says. "Told me they were planning to keep it. They were peas in a pod, those two. How she walked away from Teddy, and how your father boasted to your brother, then demanded he not tell your mother, tried to swear him to secrecy."

But Matt disobeyed. Big surprise.

"He told your mom, and she was shocked, stunned." Sophie raises her eyebrows, stares at me. "You can imagine."

I feel myself stiffen; I pick up the remains of my cookie, snap it in half.

"Matt thought it would help her get moving, be decisive, call a realtor, make a plan to leave, and that's how he left her that night. She agreed that she'd spend that evening figuring out her options. He never expected..."

The trailer park, the police. Matt's face, so pale when we got to Josie's, him sneaking a drink. How I found him at the house: downstairs, pretending, hoping, I suppose, that nothing was wrong, that she was out for a walk, that any minute she'd be home and ready to make a plan. How he seemed to barely be breathing.

"So only you and he..."

"Yes, and Ted." She lifts up a spoon, uses it to point. "And now you."

We sit there, staring together at an invisible spot on the table. I can feel the story sorting itself in my head, falling into place.

"Only us. Not the police." The judge. The officials who decided what happened to my mother after she did what she did.

"Lazy coroner. Cause of death was obvious. It would have been worse for your mother if..."

"My mother?" I ask, voice high-pitched, slightly hysterical. "We're thinking about my mother when..."

I can't continue. I bend forward, clutching my waist, my head almost toppling the empty cup. Then Grommet's there, licking the salt off my face. Who let him in? I wonder. Sophie's squeezing the bridge of her nose, I see when I sit up to push back the dog. The soft skin around her mouth is trembling. It surprises me, her emotion, because I suppose I've been thinking that this is mostly my story, my tragedy, because that's how it's been for years. Living my life wrapped tight around the broken parts. But it was her stepsister. Ted's mom. Slowly, I reach over and touch her hand.

"And you didn't tell anyone."

She reaches for the teapot, refills both our cups. Passively, I watch, not caring either way. The heat has dissipated, the steam blown away. "I told them what I know to be the truth,"

this has nothing to do with you

she says. "We didn't have much to do with one another; she didn't care to have anything to do with her son. But I didn't tell them about her pregnancy because I didn't want Ted to know. I never wanted him to know."

"But he does now?"

"Yes."

"Who else? Does Angie?"

She shakes her head. "Matt didn't think she could get past that, if your mother ever gets paroled."

Deciding for her as well, curating our family secrets.

"Yes," I say. "Better a double murder than a triple."

Sophie eyes me. "It wasn't a baby," she says. "It was an embryo, a gathering of cells. I suggested that she get an abortion. There was Ted; there was you. Your family. If you want a child, I told her, I have a wonderful boy here who..." She stops, overcome, and presses her fisted knuckles against her lips. I agree with her, but still: my mother consciously killed a pregnant woman. My head swims.

"How can you be friends with us, after..."

Sophie pulls her hand from her face, reaches down to stroke Grommet's ear. "You couldn't have stopped her. Neither could Matt. She was a free agent."

I nod, leaning forward, hands clasped between my knees. I've never thought that, though: that I could stop my mother. I never felt like I had any influence over her at all, neither her nor my father. I guzzle the tea, bitter, sharply tannic because it's been steeping for so long, then set down my cup. Was she free? I wonder. Were we? I remember hiding out in my room, listening through the walls to the rumble of my father's rising voice, how afraid I usually felt.

"And free agents make mistakes," Sophie says. "But apart from that, there is something I've learned over the years, and

I'll put it like this: despite what you might think, your mother is more than the worst thing she ever did."

I don't know how to respond. It's as if she's speaking to me from across a wide distance, and in order to understand I'll have to cross that dry wasteland, nearly die. But that must mean she's already done that, crawled over, survived.

"And despite my fury at them both, so was my sister and so was your dad."

Tears well in my eyes again, then travel freely down my face. I don't bother wiping them away. I'm way too tired for that.

SOPHIE LETS ME SLEEP. Upstairs, in a room with plastic stretched over the window, the carpet half ripped up. There's hardwood under it; I can see the shiny spots of nails. I lie down, and it's like my brain doesn't want to work anymore, needs a break, because one minute I'm looking at the yellow water stain on the ceiling, and the next I'm gone. When I wake, Grommet's scratching on my door, the sun's hanging over the top of the hill, my stomach's rumbling, and I really, really need to talk to Matt, to try again.

On the kitchen table sits a box filled with Grommet's stuff: a bag of cookies, a filthy stuffed rabbit with one ear missing, a couple clickers. I heave out a sigh when I see it, because I'd forgotten this part. Hilda's on her way back from the shelter with Liv, Sophie tells me as she walks me out to my car. She's got some high needs, and Grommet does too. "He's had a lot of focus," she says. "It's somebody else's turn." I nod. I just have to figure it out.

Sophie reaches to hug me, and she smells like wood smoke and a tinge of something sweet and earthy, like apples in autumn. When she pulls back, she keeps her hands on my shoulders and their weight almost hurts as she peers at me, so intensely that I have to look away even though I'm listening.

this has nothing to do with you

"I'm just going to say this, okay?"

Reluctantly, I nod.

"Your mother's built herself a prison, and she'll be in it for the rest of her life."

"But she's alive," I mutter.

"Has she ever really been alive?"

I don't answer that. I don't know how to. She doesn't wait. She hauls me into another quick hug and then steps back, and there's Ted, appearing out of nowhere, awkwardly sticking out his hand. Seventeen, I think. Only a few years ago, I was his age, but it seems like another lifetime, a previous incarnation.

"Take care of your boy," Sophie says as I get in the car, and at first I think she means Grommet, but then I realize she might mean Matt. Her bright vest disappears in my rear-view, but I know she's still standing there, like an ember alive in the night.

part nine

1.

THE ROAD INTO Sedona wound down a pine-covered mountain, zigzagging in switchbacks. Lara drove, cranking the steering wheel and riding the brake as I braced myself against the dashboard. Through the trees, the landscape of red rock glowed, lit by the late afternoon sun, and I felt a sudden sense of euphoria, like something really good was about to happen. When we pulled onto the main street, crystals glittered in the New Age shops, and flute music drifted through the doors of busy restaurants.

"Oh, good Christ," Lara said. "Welcome to hell."

THAT NIGHT, we followed the hippies to Oak Creek. There were a few vans, an old Cadillac, some tents. Lara drove us further along, to a quiet spot, and we pulled in under a cottonwood tree that arced over the stream. There was a spot to have a fire, and while we were collecting sticks to burn, a shirtless guy dressed in striped jester's pants came by with a water bong, and even Lara took a hit. His girlfriend was smudging the place, drifting a burning bundle of sage. They'd harvested it in the hills in Utah, she said, and I bought one for a couple dollars in loose change that I dredged out of the car. Stoned, I left to find a place to pee, wandering further down the river. Up ahead, a thin grey ribbon unfurled from what looked like a pile of rags, but as I got closer, the details came clear: a canvas-draped shanty, a crooked wooden table, a handleless teapot sitting on a flat rock. When Robert emerged from the low hut, he startled me, and I almost burst out laughing when he straightened to his full height, because he was so tall and his shaggy white hair was a bright, unruly mop against the wall of orange rock that lined the creek. He wore a grubby tunic, his bare knees pointed sharply as he crouched beside a smouldering fire, prodding the embers with a stick.

"Greetings, fellow drifter. Can I offer you a snifter?"

Until he spoke, I wasn't certain he'd seen me. But then he held out a fragile cup, pink and white, with roses on the side. The gilded handle glinted. My lips were stuck in a smile. I was thinking of those kids' books Matt used to give me, about ordinary twelve-year-olds slipping through portals, as I stepped into his encampment and sat down on a stool, accepting the warm drink. He pushed a clay container towards me, and I used a small bleached stick to stir a glistening rope of honey into my tea.

"And from where do you hail? Freedom or jail?"

I took a sip. The tea had a bite to it. Hibiscus-cayenne, I found out later.

"Canada."

He nodded. "Canada's got lots of space. Maybe you can name the place?"

I didn't say Vancouver or B.C. or Ontario. Instead, I said "Hixon River," surprising myself. The name popped out as a question. He shook his head.

"I don't know that town, and I've been around." He tugged on the edge of his tunic, and I glanced down, saw his long toenails, yellow and curved, and felt a tiny prickle of fear. I reached down for a palm-sized stone, pretended to examine it, flipped it over to the brighter side, where it was wet.

"Are you on your own?" he asked. "Have you come to atone?"

"My friend Lara's right over there." I pointed upstream, although she wasn't visible. All we could see was the water trickling amongst the boulders, the wide shelves of sandstone.

"Ah, with all the others who have lost their mothers."

My mouth fell open a little bit. He watched me, his blue eyes glowing. Then he smiled, deepening the crow's feet that creased his dark skin.

"They are lonely souls although they like to gather, but I fend for myself because what matters..." He hesitated, lips moving in a silent chant as he searched for rhymes. My mind spat them out — ladders, shatters, mad hatters — but none of them worked. He frowned, and seemed to curl into himself, shoulders rounded, a faint flush building on his cheeks.

"Is to learn to transcend," I blurted, excited.

He looked up. "Or simply to mend."

We grinned at each other. I lifted my cup. "A toast to new friends."

"Where were you?" Lara asked, looking up from the fire she'd started. The air growing cooler as night came on, the sky a deep indigo, the first stars poking out like shards. She'd stretched a sleeping bag out on the ground and was sitting on it, cross-legged, a bottle of red wine in her hand.

"Where'd you get that?"

"I went and bought it," she said. "You can't just take off on me like that."

My high had faded, dragged to a thin wash of dull grey in my head. I sat down on the other end of the sleeping bag and reached for the box of crackers she'd pulled out of our food box, although Robert had fed me a bowl of chickpea soup.

"I met this weird man." I told her about Robert and described the cave that he'd shown me, where he said he sometimes let people stay. It had a waist-high platform for a counter, and a wide flat area that could be used as a bed, big enough for two, and it looked out over the river. "He said we could stay there, if the price was fair, which is free, just for me." I was grinning, but Lara didn't notice. She stuffed a hunk of sausage in her mouth and spoke through the chewed meat.

"What do you even know about this guy?"

I shrugged and picked up the sage smudge I'd bought. "Instinct," I said.

"Instinct?" Her voice sounded flat and mocking. I didn't want to tell her how I thought he looked like Matt, with his blue eyes, his height, his narrow face. Matt in forty years, I thought, as I pushed the tip of the sage against a glowing ember in the firepit and watched as it combusted, releasing pungent smoke.

She tipped back the bottle, guzzling. I reached for it, and when she handed it to me, I noticed her fingers, normally stained with colourful paint, now just grey, as if she'd been smudging a charcoal drawing, trying to get the shadows right. "Mel," she said. "You're telling me you want to go live in a cave that belongs to some stranger you just met?"

"It doesn't belong to him," I said, and she started laughing without making any sound. She leaned forward, then threw her head back and drew in a deep, loud breath before groaning, "What the fuck are we doing here?"

It was me she was laughing at, my life, the path I was choosing to follow. I don't know why she even came along. "You know you can go anytime you want," I said, giving back the wine. I blew on the sage, fed its smouldering tip, initiating a thicker, brighter burn.

"And just leave you here?"

I gestured at the fires around us, mere metres away. Someone was playing a guitar, and a woman was singing *Friend of the Devil*.

"There's lots of people around. Lots of potential friends."

"New friends."

"New friends for the new me," I snapped.

Lara stood then, stepped backwards. Unsteady on her feet, I saw, even though she was wearing her solid black army boots. When she spoke, her lips in the firelight looked bloody, stained a dark red.

"The new you who's so free since she decided to flee."

"Just like you," I said.

"I'm not free."

"No, but you ran first, and I just followed."

"I'm not running."

I raised my eyebrows. Wielding a knife right then, studying its shine, deciding whether or not to use it, how deep to cut. "So, you've forgiven yourself then?"

The smudge was still burning, and the smell was starting to make me feel sick. I tossed the whole thing into the fire, thinking that would eradicate it, but it only burned harder, with blacker smoke. Lara stared at me and I lifted my eyes to hers, and made a choice, sick of her trying to tell me who to be, block my path. "I still think you should have told them what you knew when you knew it," I said, opting to lunge.

this has nothing to do with you

287

That Pete had gone to meet that girl, I meant. The one his parents had forbidden him from seeing. A stolen bottle of champagne in his backpack. Lara knew, but when he didn't come home, she assumed they'd taken off, caught the Greyhound to Toronto, were having the time of their lives. She covered for him, even faked a note, waited days before she called the girl, a goth named Cynthia who went to a different school in another town. Cynthia told her Pete hadn't shown up. That weekend we had our first big snowfall, and the world had turned as white as her face right then, staring at me beside the orange fire, the orange world. I'd spent that entire winter telling her it wasn't her fault and now here I was, saying the opposite, casually, as if I'd thought it all along. She turned away from me, stumbled into a darkness riddled with cacti. I heard her throwing up, but I didn't go to her, didn't hold her hair out of her face.

I SLEPT ON THE GROUND, in Lara's sleeping bag. In the morning, a bunch of tourists in a pink jeep that said *Sedona Adventures* stopped to take my picture. A hippie in her natural habitat. The clicking shutters woke me, and I stood, then kicked at the ring of stones around the fire, covering the last of the embers. Sand sprayed; I felt the grit on my shin. Another day, I remember thinking. To get through.

Downstream, Robert was outside his shanty, shirtless, chopping something on his table, the knife blade flashing in the sun. Lara was gone.

She'd left without a hug, without a handshake, without even a glance back. Josie told me later that she'd phoned her parents from Sedona, had them wire her some money, then caught a bus to Tucson and flew to the Soo. She stayed in Hixon River for a few weeks; Josie helped her plant a butterfly bush at Pete's grave.

She left me the car, though. Hoping, I suppose, that I would come to my senses, drive home. But after she was gone, I cleared everything out and carried my stuff over to Robert's. That evening, he brewed us some magic mushroom tea, and I felt my past like something physical, a skin I had to work to scrape off.

Some hippies slept in the car for a while. Eventually, the tires went flat. Then, one morning, in the middle of winter, I woke to find the red rock covered by a rare white dusting of snow, the car gone. My passage back had closed.

2.

THAT PART OF MY PAST is a wall. I lean on it, let it give me stability. But now Sophie's revelation has dropped like a boulder into a sheet of calm water and the waves are rocking outward to the edges of my life. A potential baby. A half-brother or sister. A part of the story nobody's bothered to tell me, thinking what? That I didn't need to know? That it wouldn't affect my life?

THIS TIME, Matt answers the door. It's still dark inside his apartment, the large room built of shadows. But the fish tank glows, and a floor lamp beside the green chair is turned on.

"Celia was pregnant," I say, and he abruptly turns around, walks away, so I have to follow him. The news is on: a crowd of refugees filling plastic jugs from a broken water main, the camera closing in on a woman's face, a blue scarf hiding her hair. Dusty rubble all around. Bosnia this time. I wish he'd look at me.

"We pick and choose what we pay attention to," he says, dropping onto the couch. "Genocide dismissed as tribal conflict. Money and troops dumped on the war involving white people."

this has nothing to do with you

His hand trembles as he reaches for his cigarettes on the mess of the makeshift coffee table. The pile of newspaper clippings, three beer bottles, his journal, open now, a page filled with writing, and a stack of photographs, the one on top an image of him and Dad grinning, a stringer of trout stretched between them. There's an orange pill bottle, too, the bright plastic catching the light so it glows like a tiny lantern. My eyes hover over it, and I resist the urge to pick it up, read the label.

"And nobody can do a goddamn thing about it," Matt says. "Least of all me." He carries the overflowing sea shell ashtray to the kitchen, trailing a scattering of grey, but doesn't empty it. He leaves it on the counter. In the shadows, his face is pale and drawn. Defeated.

"I thought you were writing letters."

He shrugs without meeting my eyes. I reach for the remote and turn off the television set, and in the sudden silence, I hear Grommet barking in my car, marking time like a metronome.

"Celia was pregnant," I say again.

"I hear you've got your buddy back," Matt says.

"Why didn't you tell me?"

He doesn't answer. He stares into the sink, stuffed full of dirty dishes.

"You talked to Sophie about it."

"That was different."

"Why?"

He mumbles something. "Pardon?" I step around the couch, moving closer.

"Her, I can help," he says.

I don't understand. He helped me. He flew all the way to Arizona to get me, to bring me home. He gave me a place to stay. I put my hands on the edge of the counter, and we stand across from each other, at an impasse. He opens another pack of cigarettes, finds it empty, drops it. In another pack, he finds one left, and when he lights it, I reach out, take a drag. Our exhalations of smoke fill the space between our faces.

"As soon as you could," says Matt, "you just fucked off."

"I had to," I say, voice small, trying not to whine. "I couldn't stay in that house, stay until I couldn't take it..." He stares at me, waiting. "Until it was me who tried to kill myself."

It's true. It's true, because no one ever taught me how to plod through life, sort the daily tasks, stay busy instead of sinking or running away, as Matt somehow learned. In that quiet, horrible aftermath, with him helping our mother figure out her practical needs, there was no room for me. There never had been. As a kid, once, eating out, I'd accidentally sprinkled my spaghetti with hot peppers instead of parmesan cheese, and rather than call attention to the mistake, I ate it. Mouth burning. Guzzling water. No one even noticed. Leaving that fall had been a desperate leap of faith to find a place where I fit. I knew Matt could handle my mother, sift through the wreckage, salvage what he could. The ember of his cigarette flares a solid orange as he sucks greedily on the smoke, then offers it to me again.

I stab it out on a plate smeared with dried ketchup. "But I'm back now, and that's thanks to you. You've helped me. You can help me some more by telling me."

Firmly, he shakes his head. "That won't help you."

"Matt," I whine.

"Midge," he says, mimicking me.

I glare at him. The old nickname sounds patronizing, and, when I think about it, it always has been. Picked up from my mother calling me her little smidgen of life, before I was born, when I was barely anything at all.

"Celia was pregnant with our father's child," I say for the third time, annunciating each word, the sentence beginning to sound like the first line of a complicated novel or a spell, said thrice, a summoning.

"Did you even come to see me today?" Matt asks. "Or is it all about Owain?" His voice is clipped, biting, and I sigh, shut my eyes.

"You." Owain's van wasn't in the driveway. Matt turns around, opens the fridge, pulls out two beer, and slides one over to me. I haven't eaten since Sophie's, since that single maple cookie, and the alcohol will go straight to my head, but I take it anyway, twist it open, gulp down a long drink.

"It doesn't matter," I tell him. "I already know; Sophie told me all about it."

"They why are you asking me?"

I set the beer down harder than I intend. It cracks onto the counter. "Because you never told me, and I want to know why. I want us to be able to talk..."

"Talk. More talk."

"So you're not talking? Not to anybody? Not to Angie? Your wife. Remember her? Mother of your child." My voice grows louder in the quiet space, rising over the hum of the aquarium filter, the fridge.

Or only to Sophie, nearly a stranger, and to Dad, I almost say, remembering the letter. He doesn't answer, and I wonder where his words have gone, those insistent positions he took at the dining room table, prodding at my father's irrational anger, spinning out eloquent arguments when our father had only two words: you're wrong. Those discussions were never not personal, never just about NAFTA or Separatism or the war on drugs. Always, they were about who was smarter, who was right, and our father had to be right, would turn vicious in order to defend his superiority, twisting truths enough to make your head spin. Once I remember his voice booming — "Because I'm

lauren carter

292

your father" — before Matt stumbled through the sliding glass
door at the back of our house, bellowing "Jesus Fucking Christ"
into the quiet suburban night, overtaken by frustration. He ran
off into the woods, branches cracking, and I laid stock still on
my bed, belly hard, breath held, waiting to hear the loud whistle
of the train as it chugged through the forest, and when it came,
I felt a cold wave of fear.

I already knew bad things could happen: Pete, my mother
washing down that bottle of pills with a small glass of water.

"Where's your washroom?" I ask.

He points to the door beside the fish tank and I cross the
room, close myself in.

WE WERE A FAMILY that kept secrets, stayed silent in order to
pretend that everything was fine: my mother's depression, my
father's need to be in charge, how irrational he could be. Maybe
this is what Matt is doing, I think, as I stand in the bathroom,
staring at my face in a toothpaste-spattered mirror. Holding
himself upright in that old official uniform he'd tried to shrug
out of as a teenager. Nothing to see here, move along. It makes
sense to me, although it shouldn't. It makes sense to me the way
being tied to a tree made sense for so many years for Grommet,
and how now that he's free, he doesn't know how to behave. I
don't know how, simply, to talk to my brother about our childhood, our past, how to drag forward the details I've learned, lay
them out in a vivid display, force him to answer my questions.
But I have to try.

Through the door, I hear the TV come on again. This time,
a news anchor's talking about Rwanda, about the UN's delib-
erations. I know what Matt will say: they're going too slow to
make any difference. The last time I watched the news, I shut
it off quickly, horrified by the images: crowds streaming out of

the country, trying to escape into Zaire. A woman in a flowered blouse carrying her child on her back along a dirt road. A man in a red jacket, pushing his bicycle. Then, the people who'd been massacred . . . I close my eyes, dread filling me, remembering that page in my brother's journal, that accounting of the events over there, or what he's learned of them, anyway. Looking outward at a trauma so far past anything we've ever known, trying to figure out how to help, how to make the West accountable. It is very Matt, but Matt to an extreme.

There's evil in the world, my mother explained that evening at dinner before my father stood, exerted his control, shut off the television news. Sit up, she scolded me, as I slumped towards vanishing underneath the table. Then she stared at me and asked, "What do you have to run from, anyway?" I did not answer. I ate my meal, which I had cooked. Felt the chicken and green beans sit in my stomach, sustaining me.

Now, I look at myself in the mirror, my messy short hair, my work blouse wrinkled and dirty from Grommet jumping up. I feel a wave of helplessness that isn't unfamiliar. Before I leave, I slowly lift my hand to open the medicine cabinet and am overcome by the heavy rush of relief I feel when I find it empty of pill bottles, all the glass shelves blank.

MATT'S SITTING ON the couch when I come out of the washroom and Grommet is still barking, the sound penetrating through the walls. I take the chair with the wooden arms and look down at that stack of photographs. Him and Dad, happy, a stringer of fish. Has he been looking at that, forgetting, thinking it was always that way, that it could have been again if it weren't for him? Our father softening with the birth of his new son or daughter? I want to pick the pictures up, but I also don't. Don't want to flip through that slide show of memories.

The only picture I wish was on display is the one of Matt and me that's hidden in the pocket of my jeans, on my bedroom floor.

"You used to trust me," I tell him, both of us staring at a stream of commercials. Cleaning products, Marineland, a local furniture store. I say this even though I'm not sure anymore if it's true. "You should have trusted me," I say.

If he had, I might have stayed home. I might have started school. By now, I could be a vet, already practising. My life would be something else, something better.

"You have this fantasy that it would have helped, but it wouldn't have helped."

"How do you know?"

He looks at me, eyebrows raised, like we're talking about a fact that's obvious. "Come on, Mel," he says, lighting another cigarette from a fresh pack on the hydro-wheel table. "You're soft. You can't even handle a challenging dog."

I stare at him. "At least I'm not running away anymore."

Not like you, I mean.

"No?"

He takes a drag, and I whip my hand back and forth, waving a clearing into the smoke.

"And I don't get that," Matt says. "How you can be more concerned about a dog than thousands of people being slaughtered..." A hot flush rises to my cheeks, but he doesn't notice because he's pontificating now, waving his cigarette, delivering a lecture on colonization and Belgium and moral obligation. My cheeks burn, hot with shame, as I try to think of possible answers. Liv might say we respond to suffering where we can, how we're able. But I don't speak, too afraid that Matt will laugh at me, mock me. My neck is bent. I stare down, trying to figure out how to defend myself, what to say, and I remember.

this has nothing to do with you

I remember it too well. My father beating down my mother, explaining how she always failed.

"Stop," I shout, and he does. He clamps his mouth shut as if he's been waiting to be told. Grommet barks on and on while Matt flicks through the channels until he stumbles across a black and white movie, that one with the big house on the hill in San Francisco, the wife suspicious of her husband, one of my mother's old favourites. I watch it without watching it, my mind drifting, wondering if they screen films in prison and how they do it. A bed sheet hung from shower hooks, fluttering from the laughter of a hundred women? I wonder how she talks to Matt, if she holds him accountable, if she blames him, if they speak about what she's done.

I wonder what she'd say to me.

What did you have to run from, anyway...

"I knew about the gun," Matt says suddenly, as the orchestral music grows louder, as the woman sneaks downstairs in the night. "She mentioned it to me like a joke." He glances at me. "Mom did."

"How do you mean?"

"She said, There's always self-defence."

He drops his cigarette into a beer bottle, bends forward, folds his arms over the top of his head. I don't know what to do. I should go to him, comfort him, but I'm afraid. Is he crying?

"Matty," I say, and hear the pleading in my voice. He's right: I'm soft, I can't stand to see him like this even after I've begged him for the truth. When he looks at me again, his face appears flat, emotionless. There is no evidence of tears. His words come out clipped and factual. "I should have stayed with her, watched her, and I didn't."

"But you couldn't have known."

He smiles, a small cold crook to his lips. "But I did."

Our eyes meet. It feels like we're looking at each other for the first time since those hours immediately afterwards. That night and the next day and for a few days after that, I had anchored my focus on him like we were two people treading water, trying to stay afloat. He could have told me then.

"Is there anything else you haven't let me in on?"

He looks from my face to the aquarium behind me and the light catches in his eyes. When his mouth opens, I lean forward, expectant, like an animal detecting a shift, but right then there's a booming knock on the side door. Matt's gaze ricochets around his apartment, landing on a table in the corner of the kitchen that's piled with shoe boxes, baggies, rolling papers, a scale. I jump up, run upstairs, and there's a man at the door, breathing hard, his face flushed red.

"Is that your fucking dog?" he says, gesturing at my car.

Grommet's muzzle is pushed against the rear window, the glass covered in spittle. Even from a few feet away, I can see the shine on his teeth.

"I work nights, and I'm trying to sleep right there."

He jabs a finger towards the window on the second storey of the neighbouring house, then screams, "Deal with it." As he marches away, I feel myself trembling, and when I turn around, Matt's immediately behind me, looking over at my car.

"Did you find a new place?"

"No."

He sighs. "Little Midge," he says. I brace myself, thinking he's mocking, but then he smiles and reaches out to give me a hug. "Take care of yourself," he mutters, and turns to go back into his dark basement den, to shut himself inside.

3

RELUCTANTLY, I leave Matt's. I had been planning to ask him if I could stay, sleep on his couch, but the way he closed his door so firmly told me he wanted me to go. At my apartment building, I pull into my spot, and when I look across the parking lot at the brightly lit lobby, I see two people talking by the mailboxes: my neighbour, Mrs. Slater, and Mrs. Mehta, the landlady. It's like a joke. I almost laugh. I sit there, waiting, but they talk so long that eventually Mrs. Slater sits down on the wire shelf that holds the real estate papers, turning it into a makeshift chair, and I push my fingers against my forehead. I need to figure out a different place.

I could drive to Hixon, show up at Josie's, but Bruce will probably send me to a hotel. I could stay in a hotel, but payday isn't until Friday, and I'm already nearly broke. Angie's too stressed out, and I don't know if I can show up at her door, face her, knowing everything I know without spilling it all. She should know about Celia — that's my opinion — but is it up to me to tell her? Then there's Owain, but he wasn't home. Thinking of him, though, brings to mind the cabin we went to, with the key tucked in the lozenge tin. One night, I think. That's all I need, and tomorrow I'll have the whole day to figure out my next steps, not to mention talk to my boss, make my excuses for ditching work.

Grommet has settled since I joined him in the car and now seems exhausted. He stretches out on the back seat, going belly up as soon as I work my way out of the city, around the giant hump of rock in the centre of town that holds the water tower. I had watched when Owain drove us out there, and I follow Highway 10 to Lantern Lane and then onto an unnamed dirt road that winds along the shore of Otter Lake. The cabin's at the end. When I get there, an hour later, I discover that I'm not alone. The windows glow orange; Owain's van is parked beside the verandah.

I don't want Grommet to bark, so I just let him out. He trots down to the water, gulps a long drink. There's music playing, some sort of jazz, and I follow it to the cabin. Anxiety prickles in my stomach. I already think I know what I'll find, but when I push open the door, there it is, the scene I've been dreading.

A blanket laid out beside the wood stove. Long dark hair, a slender waist, the knobs on a woman's naked back, and Owain underneath her, his eyes widening when he sees me.

He nearly knees her in the face as he fumbles up, shouting my name, hauling his plaid boxer shorts over his erection. The woman swings around, and I see her breasts, her tight dark nipples, her face. I recognize her. She's the one from the bar, who served us that night, who plunked down my glass so the surface sloshed, spilling wine down the sides.

Tammy, he said, then recited my name next to hers.

Now he shouts, "What are you doing here?" I don't know how to answer. It seems crazy: I was going to squat at your friend's cabin. Does he think I've been following him? Grommet's trotting fast towards me, his claws clicking along the wooden verandah and I don't know how he'll react, so I quickly slam the door, the deadbolt clicking shut, and feel the blast of Grommet's breath on my hand. "This way," I tell him, and together we run back to the car.

It takes a few minutes for the tears to come, for that sickening feeling of betrayal to bloom in my belly. I'm already in the car — Grommet behind me, the tires spitting gravel as I blindly reverse — when I start to sputter.

Owain does not come after me. There are no headlights bobbing in my rear-view as I drive along the main road looking for a place to pull in. Finally, I swing into somebody's dirt drive-way, stop beside a collapsing A-frame a hundred feet from the lake, shut the car off, and sit there, sobbing. There's the fragile, cracking shell of my heart and a broadening understanding: my mother, sitting quietly in the orange velour chair, explaining the flimsy surface truth she knew at the time. An affair. Another woman. Happenings she believed had nothing to do with me. But they did. I was also cast aside; I also didn't matter.

4.

PINK LIGHT WAKES ME, soft as sugar candy snagged in the pine trees, and a loon cries out across the melting lake's mot-tled surface of silver and blue. Reluctantly, I open my eyes, then shut them, stabbed through with pain from the memory of that other waterfront morning at dawn. Matt in the van, my friends slowly coming to consciousness. I wonder if I'll always be there, living those few hours over and over. The hours before I learned that I'd lost my whole family: Matt, who spun into action, who left me behind, who didn't tell me what he knew, and both of my parents.

My mother, Bernadette, who my father — Al — called Bernie. I always thought this sounded better than the syncopated rhythm of Bernadette Barnett, but she hated the short form, fought it, although her opinion didn't make a difference. She got the name he wanted her to have, and eventually she just accepted it, I always thought, but deep down maybe she didn't. Maybe part of her kept struggling to defend her own interests; in the end, it was enough that my father had betrayed her with another woman, but then there came the final, decisive blow.

Another being, like a ticking bomb; that tiny, determined heart no bigger than the spark on a fuse.

GROMMET PUSHES his big head between the seats and licks the tears off my cheeks. I lean back and let him until he's tired of it and barks at the door. He pees on the trunk of a felled birch tree when I let him out, then kicks his paws in the dirt and fallen leaves, and I follow him down to the collapsing dock, cup icy cold water into my palms, wash my face, then try to clean the marks off my blouse. I've got no idea what time it is, but I'm about an hour's drive from town, and I need to go to work, explain about yesterday, try to make amends, while Grommet stays trapped in my car, ignoring his breakfast of half a dozen dog biscuits set out on the seat beside him.

"Be good," I tell Grommet, like that'll help at all, like the dog's had a chance to learn the difference between good and bad. It's early, just past eight, but Teresa's car is already in the parking lot, and maybe it'll help for me to show up keen and eager — eager to apologize, anyway. I smooth my pants as I walk towards the library's back entrance, noticing how muddy my shoes are from the short walk down to the lake. At least I have a brush and a tube of lipstick in my bag and was able to fix myself up a little bit, although my hair's greasy, and I need a shower, and my clothes look like they've been slept in because they have. Also, I reek of cigarettes from the time spent in the smoky box of Matt's apartment.

I'm planning to go to the break room, pour Teresa a cup of coffee if it's brewed, but two things happen. Grommet starts barking before the library door even shuts behind me, and Teresa pops into the hallway, drawn by the noise.

"Mel," she says, and maybe I imagine it, but she seems to obviously look me up and down. "Come chat with me." She turns around, and I follow her into her office, settle into the chair near her crowded desk. She moves two stacks of books so she can see me and sets her forearms on a pile of photocopied annual reports, clasps her hands. Attentive, I think. Ready for my confession. I feel the muscles tighten in my back, resistant.

"So, what's going on?"

I widen my eyes, slide my gaze away then back as if I'm not sure what she means. "Oh," I say. "Yesterday."

"Yes. Yesterday." She unlaces her fingers, crosses her arms.

"A bit of a family emergency."

"Well, you ran out of here like a bat out of hell. I expected at least a phone call."

"I know." I rub my face, feel grit in my eyelashes, push my palms against my pants. "I'm sorry."

Teresa studies me, waiting for more, for at least a hint of an explanation. When I don't speak, she leans back, and I see the shimmer of her blouse, white like mine but much cleaner, in the grey screen of the box of her computer monitor. We sit there for a long time, Grommet's barking pulsing through the walls, but I don't think she notices.

"You're in early, so that's good."

I give her a quick smile and stand, assume she's dismissing me, but before I turn away I notice my file's also on her desk, opened, the pages ruffled like there's information in there, like there's something to discover.

BY TEN A.M. Grommet's howling in the parking lot, and there are complaints. Ruth sees me in the staff room, scans me from my head to my filthy shoes and says, "What the hell happened to you?"

I'm beside myself, don't know what to do, and I think how good it would feel to tell her all of it, because I know how much she'd love to listen. The secret love child, murdered in cold blood, my life like a thriller novel, plus Owain, his shocked face, that naked woman straddling him. But right then, Teresa sticks her head through the door and says, "Mel, my office!"

Her head's in her hands, wedding ring shining, fingernails, I notice for the first time, bitten down to the quick. "You can't bring your dog to work."

I hesitate. "Dog?" I try.

She tips her eyes up at me. "Seriously?" she says, then sighs. "Is it your dog?"

Hesitantly, I nod.

"You come in like this" — her hand lifts up and down, gesturing at my body — "after yesterday, give me no explanation, then I find out you've locked your dog..."

"I've got nowhere else..."

"Were you evicted?"

"No."

She stares at me, waiting, but what am I going to say? I brought a dog into my apartment when I know they don't allow dogs? When I don't speak, she pulls a paper out of my file. "You've called in sick several times, and one day, when you were supposed to be sick, you came here to meet a friend!"

I cross my arms, look down. The mud on my shoes has dried, and I'm leaving a powdery, brown dust everywhere. I wipe more off onto her emerald green carpet.

"I've reviewed this, and I'm sorry, but I can't continue to employ you. Despite what you say, I don't think you really care about this job."

She shakes her head, as if mournful, as if this is hurting her more than me. "I've very sorry. I know what you've been through."

"What's that?" I say, trying to make her say it. The pity's what I hate most of all.

this has nothing to do with you

Her mouth opens and closes without any words, giving me a tiny bit of satisfaction, but then she slides my time sheet over to me. She's crossed off yesterday's seven hours, which I filled in ahead of time, not expecting it would be the day I found out that my murdered father's murdered lover was pregnant. She's written in a two. Teresa taps on the spot on the bottom where I'm supposed to initial. I do, and she starts wishing me luck, saying something about offering me a satisfactory reference, but I'm already out the door.

It's kids making Grommet howl. Two of them on their bikes, tossing pebbles at my car windows. "Get lost," I scream, loud, way louder than I intend, drawing the attention of Mrs. Matthews who's pulling a stack of books off the back seat of her Cadillac. I wave, but her eyes bounce off me like I'm invisible. Is this how it happens, then? Is this the slippery slope towards ending up someone like Robert, coping by controlling your language, living in a creek-side shanty, puppeted by your past?

Grommet's hot breath is all over my ear and my neck in the car. He's panting, the whites of his eyes bright and obvious. I twist around to face him, scratch the base of his ear, and try to figure out what to do. I decide that by now, I don't give a shit. Mrs. Slater and Mrs. Mehta can gang up on me, escort me out themselves, call the cops, I'm still going to try to get back into my apartment, have a shower, change my clothes, finish packing my stuff, even call Josie. Because I desperately need to talk to someone who knows me, knows all of it, who will soothe me, comfort me, who will just listen to me cry.

part ten

1.

DAYS PASS, AND I LET THEM. Tuesday turns to Wednesday turns to Thursday turns to Friday. I hide out in my apartment like I once had in my cave, this time with Grommet to keep me company. I use only the stairs to sneak the dog out for walks at odd hours: five a.m., midnight, 2:30 in the afternoon when I can hear Mrs. Slater watching her soaps. I keep my television on as well, loud, and I love it when a dog barks so I can say, if she asks, that it was just a program I enjoy, being the dog-lover that I am, even though I suspect she probably knows he's back, and that my days are numbered. It feels like it did before, though, before I met Sophie, slept with Owain, learned about Celia and the baby, before Matt left Angie, buried himself in his own cave. It feels a bit like I'm caught in a repeating time loop, like that movie *Groundhog Day* in which Bill Murray's character can't move on until he learns an important lesson. And what is that lesson? I can't remember right now.

But I'm also making an effort, attempting to change my life. I answer newspaper ads for apartments and spend a couple evenings driving all over town with Grommet in the car with a knee bone, looking at one place after another. There's always something wrong. If they do accept animals, the rooms reek of old cat urine and stale cigarette smoke or, at one, the landlord looks at me with beady eyes in his greasy face, calculating how desperate I might be. Every time, I go home, climb up to the eighth floor, and ignore the flashing light on my answering machine. My aunt's message is still on there, I know, asking me something to do with my mother, and probably a couple collect calls from the prison, and maybe even Owain. I'm not ready to talk to anyone. I even told Josie to let the phone ring once, then call back so I know it's her, whenever she wants to talk.

"I never thought he was right for you," she said when I told her about walking in on Owain. "Way too — I don't know — too-cool-for-school."

"I liked him," I whined, remembering that last moment when he'd held me at the back door of his house and I felt some hardened part of me begin to maybe melt.

On Friday night, just a week before the deadline Mrs. Mehta's given me for moving out, after I've returned from taking Grommet for a long walk, there's a knock on my door. The TV's on to Much Music, sound cranked, and I'm on my hands and knees, wiping the close, crusty nap of the living room carpet with a damp tea towel, trying to erase the yellow stain from the night I fed him the Gravol. I scrub at its stiffness, full of regret, when the knock sounds again, and this time the dog hears it too and is up and flying towards the front door in a shot, barking so loudly that nothing will cover the sound. It's Angie, I see through the peephole, and I grab Grommet, clamp my hands around his jaw and try to quiet him before reaching to flip the deadbolt.

"Come in," I shout, and the door creaks open.

"Mel?"

The dog lets out a muzzled whine.

"Get in here," I say, because I think I can already hear Mrs. Slater on the other side of the wall, moving towards the hallway. Angie steps cautiously inside, keeping her back pressed against the door jamb, and when I release Grommet, she gives a high-pitched squeal as he stuffs his snout deep in her crotch before I can grab his collar, pull him off. I tell him to sit, and to my surprise he does, instantly, grinning, his tongue hanging out the side of his mouth, jowls wobbling. I lean into the kitchen and grab a treat from the box on the counter for Angie to feed him. He eats it off her palm like he's a horse and she wipes her hand on her thigh. She's dressed differently. A jean jacket, a bright red scarf, her hair a bit shorter, neatly trimmed and brushed carefully, gleaming blonde. She looks like someone else: not a harried mom, not my brother's worried wife.

"Where's Ellie?" I ask.

"At my cousin's." Beth. The Madonna look-alike. I wonder if Owain slept with her as well, if he'd been hoping for a repeat performance on the night of the eighties party. If I hadn't stuck myself between them, waited her out, would everything now be different?

"So this is Grommet?" Angie says, as I turn to fetch the bucket of cleaning water. "I thought Sophie had him."

"I had to take him back."

"What about work?"

I shrug.

this has nothing to do with you

"You quit?" Ang says. "What is it with you two? You and your brother. Peas in a pod."

Irritated, I turn away, pour the dirty water into the kitchen sink, watch the dog hair clot in the drain. The tea towel falls like a sloppy, dead fish onto the counter, and I leave it, grab the kettle off the stove burner and fill it to make tea. Some sort of zinger, as Sophie said ages ago, or what feels like ages. Angie steps deeper into my apartment, looks around, and I see it through her eyes. The piles of packed boxes, the filthy carpet, my couch still a mess of blankets and garbage bags, the constantly shedding cushion foam.

"Doing some redecorating?"

"Well, since *Architectural Digest* called..."

"Oh, you're returning their calls?" We both look at the answering machine, its steady blinking light. "I've called you three times."

I don't respond. I stand there, staring at my stove, listening to the clatter of the aluminum kettle as the burner heats up. What was that thing about frogs Matt told me, trying to explain why our mother wouldn't leave? How if you plunk them into boiling water they'll hop out, but slowly heat it up and they'll stay until they're cooked.

"So our mother's actually a frog?" I asked him, wondering if that made us tadpoles, even though I wasn't a kid. I was fifteen.

"No, stupid. Circle of certainty." He was in university then, first year, constantly trying to explain things to me I didn't understand, but never giving me enough information. Just like now, I think.

"Earth to Mel," Angie says, like Owain did the night he drove me home from our date at the bar, served by the waitress I found him with on Tuesday night. My tears start leaking and I push at them with my fingertips, and Angie's immediately behind me, shutting off the stove, handing me a rumpled tissue from her pocket, opening the fridge. "I think we're going to need something stronger than tea," she says.

I've finished the bourbon; all I've got is what's left of the once-frozen wine. She empties the bottle into a couple of glasses and we sit on the couch. "Good lord," she says as she perches on it and the garbage bags slip under the blankets. I laugh a little bit. Everything seems so weirdly fucked up.

"Tell me what's going on," Angie says, taking a sip.

"I don't know how much I can."

"Just fucking tell me!"

I've never heard Angie swear. Not once. I stare at her. "Just tell me," she says, quieter.

So I do. All of it.

The pot she already figured out, she says, fielding phone calls from Ted and Owain, sometimes in the middle of the night before Matt moved out. When she confronted him, fed up at not being able to use her room, he explained that they needed his help, they were poor, they'd lose their house if he didn't do what he could. He wanted this, he told her. He needed to do something good.

"What did you say?"

"I said, not in my house."

I nod, staring down into the wine. There are tiny bits of cork floating in it. It's terrible.

"He said Sophie was an old friend of your dad's," she says. "She's not?"

I shake my head, then take a breath and explain about Celia, Sophie's stepsister, and then, about the pregnancy. Angie groans and covers her mouth with one hand, and when she pulls it away the first sound she makes is my brother's name.

"Matt," she says. "He told your mom. About the baby. And he thinks that's why she killed them. He thinks it's all his fault." Her eye spring up to mine, shiny and clear. "That's what he can't get past."

It takes me aback, the succinct diagnosis. I've not been able to see it all so clearly, so simply, I realize, as blinded as I've been by the muddle of our childhood. How I failed him by running away, and my anger over his secrecy, how he's failed me too. Angie leans close.

"Why hasn't he told me this?" she says, pleading, as if she's actually asking, as if I'd know. I try. This time I try to figure it out.

"Maybe he's been protecting her."

"Your mother?"

I nod.

"She's his mother! She wouldn't want that!"

Angie bolts back the rest of her wine and stands up.

"What are you doing?"

"I have to see him."

"You can't..." I know he'll be mad at me, so mad, for spilling it all, letting out the secrets.

"Who am I, Mel?"

"You're...Angie?"

"I'm his wife. I gave birth to his child. We aren't living back then." Her arm swings wide, sweeping towards the glass door, beyond which she means the past. That landscape I can't stop staring out at, captivated by the details even as they shift.

"Come on," she says.

I shake my head. "I can't go over there," I say, in a tiny voice. I pull my feet up, hug my knees to my chest.

"Did you have a fight?"

I shake my head.

"I talked to him, and I had Grommet, and I needed to figure out a place to stay so I drove out to this cabin where Owain and I..." I explain it all, about walking in on Owain, about how I'd thought we were together. I push my forehead against my knees, trying not to cry again. He's a stupid loser, and Angie must think that too, so why would I cry over him?

"I'm sorry," Angie says. "But why would you go all the way out there?"

"What?"

"Why wouldn't you just come to my place? It's not like I don't have room."

I'm stunned. "You don't like dogs. That husky that mauled..."

"Husky?" She looks over at Grommet then back at me, puzzled. "I've never had dogs." I don't know what to say, and when I don't speak, she sighs, crosses her arms, leans against the wall by my front door.

"You and Matt," she says. "You make things so much more complicated than they have to be. It's like you look at the path of least resistance and just on principle you think, no, I can't do that. I've got to cross the quaking bog instead of this trampled little trail through a manicured park." She steps over to my answering machine and nods towards the flashing light. "It isn't that hard, you know. Just answer your goddamn phone. Maybe Owain's called you. Maybe you can at least have it out with him, tell him what a shithead he is, then move on."

I've never heard Angie talk like this. I stare at her, my face wide open, astonished. She pushes her hair behind her ears.

"I'm just done," she says. "I'm done with all the drama. Not that you and Matt haven't had drama you didn't choose. You're entitled to that, but you've got to figure out how to keep living, Mel. How to ask for help. Maybe even how to heal. Both of you do."

this has nothing to do with you

If there's any resistance left in me, it's gone now, and I'm a puddle on my torn-open couch. Angie goes to the bathroom and brings me a roll of toilet paper because the Kleenex box is empty, and we sit there for a while, with me sobbing and her watching me cry and rubbing my back. My tears are dropping over the side of the couch, on the clear spot I've scrubbed into the carpet. It's a perfect oval, like a portal, a place where I can stand and be transported somewhere else, somewhere better than here. But where would that be? The perfect future I'd fantasized about as a teenager? I've got no idea.

When I came home from the desert, I was surprised to find that Matt seemed to have actually found a normal life. A nine-to-five job. Busy with one task or another: shovelling his driveway, putting his baby daughter to bed, drywalling a mouldy patch they'd had to cut out of the laundry room. Suddenly, so fully, an adult. But his careful, organized life seems to have been an illusion, perhaps just what I wanted to see, hoping that some-day, without much effort, I'd get there too.

"Who's this?" Angie says, picking up the photo of Lara that's been out on my coffee table. It shocks me that Angie doesn't know. But why would she? Lara's no longer part of my life; I made sure of that. I look over at the answering machine, that insistent light like a throbbing memory that won't go away, that needs to be resolved. "I should listen," I say to Angie.

"Yes, you should."

THERE ARE ELEVEN MESSAGES. One each from Sophie and Liv, checking in, a quick "hey, call me" from Owain that makes me flinch, and two from Angie. My aunt's also phoned twice. The first time she just asks me to please return her call, and the second time her voice sounds urgent, and I can barely write down the details because my hand's shaking so hard, something about my mother, injury, a segregation cell. Angie takes the pen from me. "I've talked to her," she whispers, like Aunt Doreen's actually in the room. "That's part of why I came over." I wait, but she doesn't continue, listening instead as the messages click through. Two collect calls from the prison, and one from my mother's lawyer. And then, the final message, which must have been left when I walked Grommet early this morning or tonight, before Angie arrived. It's Matt. When his voice comes on, I feel Angie grow still beside me, listening sharply like we're in the woods, looking for a way out. Her hand on my forearm, squeezing.

"Midge?" he says, and his voice is harsh and deep, the way he sounds now with all the smoking. "Midge, you there?" Long pause. "Guess not," he mutters, and drags in a breath.

"I just wanted to say a few things…" Another pause. "I should have told you about Celia. I should have told you a long time ago. That would have been better, but I didn't think you'd be able to get past that. And you need to. You need to go to university, get on with things, live the life you want. But in order to do that, this is what you have to do. You have to talk to Mom. She isn't a duty or a responsibility, and it isn't your job to sort everything out for her. She knows that. But you just need to speak to her before it's too late."

This is not like Matt, this open admission of a mistake. Such clear guidance. He sounds like he's going away on a trip, like we're standing on the tarmac at the dinky airport in the Soo, like he's saying goodbye. "I don't want you to blame yourself," he says, and Angie's hands go to her mouth, layered, covering her lips. I can't look at her, can't look at the wide mirrored glare of her eyes, as I'm beginning to realize, as my own hands lift towards my face, covering, covering, disbelieving, wanting to hide. Angie starts keening, a long, high wail that makes me lean closer to the small black box to hear him.

this has nothing to do with you

"That's a trap," he says. "There be dragons." He chuckles, then mutters, "Take care of my baby, okay? Tell them . . . ." I can barely hear him, his voice fading, and all I hear is "love."

"Jesus Christ," Angie cries, and spins towards the door, running. Grommet barking, barking behind us as we fly out into the hall, door slamming, closing him in, the two of us racing for a car.

2.

MATT'S DOOR IS LOCKED. We knock, we knock, we knock, we knock. Angie starts pushing her fingers into the edges of the wood as if looking for a groove to start tearing it apart. It's when she screams Matt's name that Owain shows up, running down the stairs barefoot, wearing jeans and a T-shirt, his new girlfriend trailing him in a long, flowered dress that looks like a nightgown.

"Let us in," Angie shouts, her face a broad beacon, a searchlight sweeping the dark hallway.

"What's going . . ." Owain starts. Too slow, too dull.

"Just let us in," I scream, and he spins around, bends over and pulls a key out from the under the dirty shoe tray. Hands trembling, he twists it in the lock and pushes open the door and I reach around, flick the switch, blasting light into the room, illuminating the grime and dust I haven't seen before, the rot at the edges of the worn parquet flooring. Angie rushes ahead while I'm moving more slowly, terrified, that old trembling starting up again, and on the round coffee table, I see that the stack of photos has shifted, that the one now on top is a picture of Matt and Mom, the city of Toronto spread below them, as if they're floating.

I've seen it before. Taken at the CN Tower, that spring she drove down to the city to get him, stayed for a few days, came home on his birthday with her so sick, Matt bruised from the unexplained fight.

His bedroom door is closed but not all the way. A line of black waits to be broken.

Angie pushes through, and I brace for an outburst, for Matt's surprise, then anger. We've scared him, sneaking in like this, waking him up, but Angie is already shrieking his name, hollering, "Matt, Matt, in here, in here," and the others are moving around me like Lee Majors on *The Six Million Dollar Man*, so fast but so slow.

Tammy runs into Matt's bedroom, and Owain races upstairs, comes back talking fast into a boxy portable phone, telling somebody his address.

"What is it?" he shouts, as I'm sneaking up on the door to Matt's room, as I look in and see Tammy on my brother's bed, her hand under his neck, her mouth lowering to his, and I almost start yelling, wanting her off him, not my brother too, but Angie screams "overdose" into my ear, and it's then that reality snaps like a flag in a breeze and I see him: waxy skin, wedding suit on, lying on his back on the neatly made bed, an orange bottle toppled over on its side, lit like an uncatchable flame.

"Matty," I cry, and rush for him.

Owain grabs the back of my shirt to stop me, pulling it so tight that pain shoots through my shoulders and my breasts, and I turn around, haul back and punch him as hard as I can in the face. The phone goes flying, and Angie has to run for it as Owain's nose explodes in a spray of red blood and I'm gripping my head so hard, *so sorry*, so hard, *so sorry*, so hard it's black.

part eleven

1.

MATT'S DEAD when I wake up.

My eyes will not open. I cannot make them.

You can't make me. I know I am but what are you?

I'm seeing his pale face, paler than the white sand on the beach up the road from our house, than the silver angelfish named Garbo that fluttered in the light of his aquarium, than the whites of Grommet's anxious whale eyes.

Grommet, I think, and groan, and roll over, in whatever soft bed I'm in.

But then there's a hand on my forehead, pushing my hair back, so gently, strand by delicate strand. Mom, I moan. It's you. It was all an awful dream.

"Mel?" Angie whispers. My eyelids flutter but won't open. "Mel, he's okay, he's going to be okay." I push my face into the pillow, weeping, weeping, until once again, I can sleep.

IT TURNS OUT I'm anemic, dehydrated, and have a serious vitamin D deficiency. The sorts of things that happen when you don't take care of yourself, Angie explains when I wake up, after she tells me about Matt, who's over in another ward, the locked one.

"They're checking for liver damage," she says, leaning forward, her elbows on her knees, hands clasped. "And he's on what they call a seventy-two-hour hold."

"Can we see him?"

"Maybe," she says. "After the doctor does an assessment." She looks at her watch. "It should be soon."

I nod, and she drops her head, stares down at the floor. I put my hand on her arm, feel the tension in her as she fights not to cry.

"Where's Ellie?"

"Still at Beth's." I nod and rustle with my other hand to pull a box of Kleenex off the bedside table. My knuckles sting, there's an ache in the tiny bones.

"If we hadn't . . ." Angie says.

"I know."

She breathes out, sits up, pushes a tissue against her nose. Grey shadows tint the skin beneath her eyes. I wonder if she's slept. "Totally random accident of luck."

I think of Lara and me, that wish I made at the intersection that brought us to Sedona, that ripped us apart, that delivered me from her care into Robert's. "Maybe it was meant to be."

"We were lucky that woman was there too," Angie says.

"Tammy?" I spit her name; can't help it.

"She saved Matt's life." Her voice breaks; she has to clear her throat to keep going. "The doctor said that, said it pays to know CPR."

A memory yawns open in my mind and I groan, grip my jaw with my sore hand. "Did I really...?"

Angie nods. "You really did. The paramedics were extremely busy."

She glances off to the side, as if Matt's there, hidden behind a curtain, in a bed I can't see, and she's holding his ankle, staying connected. "But I made them work on my husband first."

Breakfast comes: slithery canned peaches, greenish-tinged scrambled eggs. I stare at it, my stomach roiling because of the anxiety over Matt and the other question I haven't asked yet, too afraid of the answer: oh, they took him away, owner neglect, you'll never get him back now... But all I have to do is say his name and Angie speaks around a piece of bacon she's nibbling. "He's at Owain's."

"Owain's?"

She nods. "I took your keys off you. He went and got him last night after..." Angie touches her nose. "He brought him back to his place. But..."

"What?" She finishes chewing the tough meat, swallows and seems to change her mind, gives a quick, curt shake of her head. It's something about Tammy, I expect. That she's there too, that she loves dogs, that she's a dog trainer, that she's actually even a vet, but I don't have time to prod because the nurse has come in, looks at Angie, and beckons. Angie stands, seems to waver. I grab her hand, squeeze it tight, then let her go talk to my brother.

I DON'T KNOW what they talk about. A lot, I'm sure. It's not until later that I see Matt, after the doctor releases me with a sheaf of prescriptions and a promise to eat regularly, avoid alcohol, drink enough water. I pull my clothes back on, and my sweatshirt's spattered with a fine mist of blood. I hate it.

this has nothing to do with you

This is what I did, it seems to say, and I feel awful, but also, deep down, a tiny pulse of satisfaction, like when Grommet bit Bruce, accomplishing what I felt I never could with words. Revenge. It reminds me of the only time I ever physically fought with my father, thrashing at him, scratching his face after he pinned my arms to my sides, tried to hold me still, contain me. This because I'd burst out of my room in the midst of a fight, when he'd boomed at my mother, "Why can't you just put a smile on your ugly face?" and yelled at him to leave her alone. "Mind your own business," he said, and I rushed at him.

My mother's mouth fell open in astonishment. I never acted like that; it was always Matt who leapt to her defense. I'd been the one who retreated, closed my door, buried myself in my closet, wishing the back wall would open up into another reality. Peaceful Narnia, where the moral compass was fixed. That was April 1991, and they were arguing over whether or not my father would actually leave. He already had though. He just liked to come back, squat in the wreckage of our house, play music in his downstairs bedroom, scavenge for whatever he could claim. "It's all mine," he told my mother, and I thought that he meant us as well, which is why I fought so hard to get out of his grip.

Angie's in the ward on the other side of the locked door, and when the nurse buzzes me in she takes my hand and leads me like I'm having trouble walking. My heart's beating hard, and when we go into Matt's room, I'm surprised to see him awake, a shaft of sunlight spreading from the window across his blanketed legs.

He smiles at me, his lips pressed together in that sheepish grin that says he's sorry for doing something so stupid, and I burst out crying. I hurry to the chair beside him, lean my forehead against him, feel the sturdy frame of his rib cage, his heart beating beneath, and let my hot tears seep through his ugly blue hospital gown so he can feel what he needs to feel from me.

"If I'd known you were going to react this way," he says, his voice mushy, the words slightly slurred. I lift my head, stretching a fine thread of clear mucus that I wipe away with the back of my hand.

"How the hell did you think I'd react?"

He doesn't answer. He's closed his eyes, laid his head back on the pillow, and for the first time I wonder about his reaction when he came home from seeing Mom in jail that day and found my note, left on the kitchen counter, pinned down with a sherry glass. *I've gone out West to stay with Lara for a while*, it said. *Good luck.*

Good luck. Like luck had anything at all to do with his future right then.

"Don't ever do this again," I say. "Don't ever leave me alone."

"You're not alone, Midge."

I look at him, at the brackets around his mouth, already formed from the tension of the past few years. He opens his eyes and focuses on the door that Angie went through, leaving us to talk. When he turns his gaze on me, I can see that he knows he's wrong. We are alone. It's him and me. No one else has been on our particular journey, known our parents, that landscape that formed us, the sinkholes and bombs. No one else can understand.

"Okay," he says.

"Promise?"

He flinches, I see it, a quick tightening, and I let it drop although it terrifies me.

"Promise?" I repeat, a high pitch to my voice I haven't heard in a long time, that sounds like I'm years younger than I am.

this has nothing to do with you

"I've been watching..." he starts. His voice is hoarse. He presses a fist against his Adam's apple.

"Too much TV?"

He shakes his head. "You can't shut off the world."

Don't look away, Matt had advised, but didn't you have to sometimes? If you could, if you were lucky enough that you could? Take a break, acknowledge your limited power, get stronger to fight another day. For a second, I feel a rush of expectation: great things will come of Matt. It's like, right then, I just know it. Like my mother always knew it. I reach out and squeeze his arm.

"Is it also..." I start to ask, but I don't need to say the words. I mean our past, always hanging between us. He pulls his arm away, pushes his fingertips together; I see that they're smudged with black ink.

"In part. And these very big questions I can't seem to find answers to."

"Like what?"

He lets his head sag against the stacked pillows.

"I'm tired."

"Tired?"

He gives me a wobbly smile. "Of the grief, the guilt."

"The guilt?"

"The guilt," he says again.

"You couldn't control what she did."

"I know." He looks at his hand, at the skin flushed under the wide, white tape, his blood bright crimson where it backs up a bit from the needle.

"There be dragons," I say, whispering, because it's hard to speak those words in a regular voice, repeating the message he left for me when he thought that he'd be dead by now. It feels wrong to bring it up, as if I'm poking fate, but his eyes jump

lauren carter

322

to my face, the whites yellowish, blood shot in spots, the blue still very bright. I push my lips together, forcing myself to hold back these fierce emotions so that I can sit here quietly with my brother. A memory springs into my head: the two of us, canoeing, Matt launching into song. His tenor voice drifting, a silver thread between the blue water and the blue sky, ringing off the stony shore. *There is a town in North Ontario...All my changes were there...* We sit in silence for a long time, the light from the window sliding across the bed until eventually Matt starts to cry. I've never seen him cry before. Well, not for a long time anyway. Not since we were both small. I grip his hand as hard as I can as his sobs bark out, animal-like, a creature let loose from his chains.

part twelve

1.

OWAIN ANSWERS his front door in a plush purple bathrobe. He's got a band of white tape across the bridge of his nose and one of his nostrils is encrusted with a fringe of black blood. There's a deep blue bruise under his left eye, the edge already glowing a faint, sulphuric yellow. I look at him, then point to my face, my lip in an exaggerated pout. "You should see the other guy," I say.

He doesn't smile, is too busy hauling Grommet back from the open door so I can step inside. I know what he's thinking: I'm a lunatic, too needy, a stalking psychopath who followed him out to his cabin to catch him in the act and then later chose that moment — *that moment* — to knock his lights out.

"I don't need to come in," I say, as soon as I'm inside. "I can just take him."

"Take him where?"

"To my apartment."

He stares at me, lifts two fingers to rub his face, forgetting the injury, then flinches. "You haven't been back there yet."

"No," I say. "And really, I can just take the dog." My voice rises because he's turning away, walking around the corner into the kitchen. I don't want to be there, don't want to accidentally run into Tammy, coming out of the bedroom or something. Is she here? I follow him anyway.

"Brace yourself then," he says, standing by the gurgling coffee maker.

"What do you mean?"

"I think he got a bit upset about being left."

I shrug. I'm used to Grommet's destruction. Right now I'm a bit irritated by him, though, prancing all around, over-excited to see me. He's thrown himself on his side and nibbles at my toes, at my sock feet, my unlaced running shoes kicked off at the door.

"Go to your spot," Owain tells him, pointing to a blanket on the floor in the dining room, and the dog rushes over and lies down. I pretend not to be impressed; I cross my arms as Owain pulls a second mug out of the cupboard, ready to refuse his offer of coffee. There's a huge bouquet of flowers tossed in the sink, wrapped in cellophane. Red roses mixed with baby's breath and greenery. When he turns around, holding a full mug in each hand, he sees me staring.

"From your girlfriend?"

"She's not my girlfriend."

I shrug and take the coffee, although I don't really want it and am slightly afraid I might throw it in his face and scald the bruising and broken nose I gave him. But I take a sip, pretending I don't care. It's too strong, and he hasn't even offered any sugar or milk. "How's your brother?"

"Alive." I flinch at my dismissive tone, but it's all I can give him, all he'll get. "Thanks to your girlfriend, actually. She's the one who saved him."

"She's not my girlfriend," he says, a red flush climbing into his cheeks. "I didn't mean for that to happen. She's an old..."

"Soul? Star-crossed lover?"

"Friend. An old friend."

"Who you happened to run into out at your love shack?"

"At the bar. I ran into her at the bar. I had too much..."

"Yep," I say, and set the mug down with a clunk. "I should go."

"You can stay down at Matt's," he blurts, and I belt out a startled laugh.

"No, sorry, bad idea."

I turn to leave and Grommet leaps up.

"Just..." Owain says. "Wait a second."

I cross my arms, feeling the tonk of my heart in my chest.

"She was here because she came to bring me those." The roses, he means. They're slowly drying out, several red petals fallen on the counter and the floor.

"It was my birthday, but I'm not interested, I'm not..." He hesitates. I wait, pick at a broken bit of Formica on the edge of the counter, peel it back, hope for it to break.

"You're going to make me say more."

I look at him. "I'm not making you do anything."

"Well, it was a mistake."

"A mistake?"

He grimaces, takes a slurp of his coffee.

I shrug. "We're not married."

He feigns surprise. "We're not? I thought it was our leather year."

"That was last year. This was our cheat-and-get-punched-in-the-face anniversary."

this has nothing to do with you

He struggles not to smile, then looks down into his mug. We stand there for a few seconds, not looking at each other.

"So I guess maybe I'm sorry," I say. "About that."

He shrugs, mutters something I barely hear. I step a little bit closer. "Pardon?"

"I guess I deserved it."

"Did you?"

He reaches out, pushes a single finger against the skin on my wrist, making a white mark that quickly fills with red when he pulls his away.

"How old are you?" I ask.

"How old are you?"

I harden my face against the grin that wants to come.

"I've been working on something," he says, moving around me, walking down the hallway. When he comes back he's got his guitar on, the teal strap slipped around his shoulders. It's the first time I've seen it. He strums a few chords, then stops. "You like eighties tunes, right?"

"Not really," I lie.

He smiles, then launches into a song.

A little ditty about Matthew and Melony,
two Canadian kids growing up in the rocklands.
Matthew wants to change the world for the better,
Melony wants to save all the dogs she can.

The final chord pulses through the kitchen, and in the silence that follows I blink hard against the damp in my eyes. Owain watches me.

"That's as far as I got," he says, and shifts, moving a tiny bit closer, the lush purple robe flaring open at his chest. I know I shouldn't. I know he's what Lara would call a pecker-puppet, led around by his you-know-what, but I do. It's the look he's giving me, the sweetness of the song. I'm a bee enticed by a rich, dark bloom, drawn in to collect what I can.

2.

WHEN I LEAVE his house, the dog pulling hard on his leash for the car, Owain tries to kiss me but I put a hand up, push him gently away.

"Now ask me out," I tell him. I'm thinking, we'll see. That's what my mother would have advised: slow down, don't hurry, *don't do what I did*, and the sting of betrayal is still with me. It won't so easily stop throbbing.

"Okay," he says. "Do you want to go out?"

"Maybe next weekend," I tell him. "I've got stuff to do this week."

He nods and withdraws into his house, and as I drive away I see him standing in the living room, looking down at his hands on the guitar, the smoke from a cigarette drifting around his focused face.

I'M GOING TO STAY with Angie, but I need stuff from my apartment. Clothes, Grommet's food and his bed, and the other things that Owain didn't pick up. Just to be safe, I leave Grommet in the car. This is a good thing, it turns out, because my apartment's been destroyed. The front door's wide open, and Mr. and Mrs. Mehta are both inside, turning slow circles in my living room.

Grommet's dug out the drywall on one side of the sliding glass door. Tufts of pink fibreglass insulation are scattered across the floor, clashing with the red carpet, mixing with a dust of plaster that's covering everything like a late spring snow. My boxes are torn open as well, *Detection of Poisons* reduced to chunks and soggy, torn bits of my mother's handwriting, and he's also wrecked my bed, the apartment's bed, actually, because the place came furnished. Feathers from the pillows drift like the remains of a chicken coop slaughter. It amazes me, after seeing how calm he was at Owain's, but then my brother also appeared calm in his hospital bed, his head still thick from my mother's old pills.

"It doesn't take much," the doctor had said to Angie and me before I left. "Luckily he opted for a conservative measure."

Unlike our mother, I'd thought, who'd swallowed nearly a full bottle that spring Matt found her spread on the bed like she'd been dropped from a height.

"How could she do this to us?" I asked Matt that day, outside the old hospital in Hixon River. My eyes still stinging, my nose stuffed full and burning, and Matt throwing stones, aiming at the lake's wide horizon so he wouldn't have to look at the smaller shine of the windows on the fourth floor, our mother behind one of them, sleeping it off.

"This isn't about us," he said, drawing his arm back, whipping a rock violently across the quiet waves. I waited for more, but no more came, and I turned around, faced the bulk of the dark brick hospital, thinking that he was wrong.

That June, my mother stayed in the hospital for five or six days. When she came home we moved around her like she'd been in a car crash, was bruised all over. Then, one day, for no particular reason, she baked a cake. She went to Stedman's and bought a piping bag and special nozzles and decorated the stacked sponge layers with yellow icing and pink and white roses, even careful leaves veined with a darker, richer green.

We ate it without celebration. It was just there, like an ordinary dessert. Like Pop-Tarts or an easy scoop of ice cream. My mother burnt a single candle on it, although I didn't see her do it. I just noticed the dots of hardened wax and picked them off, and it was then that I saw the name. Faint, a pink shadow on the yellow icing that spelled out Eleanor. She'd piped it on, then peeled it away.

"Who's Eleanor?" I asked Matt, but he shook his head, didn't tell me. Not then, and not later, when I learned that he'd chosen the same name for his own daughter.

"We just really like the name," Angie said. "Eleanor Bernice Barnett."

Now, the Mehtas' eyes are on me, waiting for me to speak but I can't meet their gaze. All I can say is, "I'll pay," and I fumble inside my purse to pull out my wallet as if I'll have enough cash on me to fix all the damage. A five-dollar bill floats between us, pinched in my fingers. "I'll pay," I repeat, then I fish out a pen, jot Angie and Matt's phone number on the bill, place it on the kitchen counter and leave with the two of them shouting at me to come back.

3.

THE BOAT SLAPS hard on the water as we travel out to sea, an open, blank horizon in every direction. My mother and Matt are in the bow, laughing, my mom with a scarf around her hair, the tail flapping, and my father's in the stern, operating the motor. "Not far now," he shouts, but I don't know where we're going. I'm alone on the wide, empty seat in the middle, and I want to ask him, but I can't talk over the noise; I can't possibly make myself heard. I'm starting to think that I might have to swim, that the vessel will break apart any second as it slams and slams into the wide building swells, the sound echoing, pulling me awake as I realize that it's Grommet, barking and barking because someone's at the door.

Angie's already at the hospital with Ellie and Matt, so I get up to answer, and it's Josie, dressed in a teal green top, her hair frizzed around her face, a bright panic in her eyes. She grabs me before I can catch Grommet's collar, tug him away from his explorations of her crotch, and hugs me so hard I can feel her bones and the flesh overtop, and I think of that miniature, peanut-sized potential human inside her that so many people would already miss if it were lost. Although it's hers. If she said, I can't do it, I'd be a hundred percent behind her.

"How are you?" she asks, pulling back. I shrug.

"I could have picked you up," I say, as the cab backs out of the driveway, the late morning sun sliding across its front windshield.

"Matt and Angie?"

"They're at the hospital."

"No, I mean are they okay?"

Slowly, I nod. "Actually, it's better now that everything's out in the open."

Saying this out loud makes me realize how true it is.

"Are you ready?" she asks, looking around the front hall for my luggage. Of course I'm not. I haven't packed. After I went to my apartment yesterday I brought the dog over here and tried to get him settled, fed him some cheap kibble from the corner store, then made all the phone calls I needed to, including an hour-long conversation with my aunt and a chat with my mother's lawyer. I talked to Josie then too, even though it was late. "Do you want to go on a road trip?" I blurted, and she instantly agreed.

"Someone should go," the lawyer had said, her voice softening as she added: "if there's concern, if you can manage it." Even my aunt has been preparing to fly east since she hasn't heard from either of us, has been trying to find someone to look after her three dogs and feed her chickens.

"Go," Angie said, when I got through to her at the nurse's station. "It'll be a relief for him." Before I hung up, I told her to tell him that I love him, because I realized that I hadn't said it, not for ages, not for years.

In the house, Josie follows me up to the spare room, Grommet tagging along behind us.

"Thanks for doing this," I tell her.

"No problem," she says, but that's not true. It's actually Mother's Day, and I've pulled her away from a celebration with her grandmother and her mom, three generations, with her carrying the fourth. They planned to take photographs, she told me earlier that week, by the bridge over the Hixon River where the town had installed a new fountain. But she only had time for a quick breakfast with them before the bus left for Norbury.

"To tell you the truth," she says, swatting Grommet's nose away from her bum. "I'm excited. Is that bad?"

"No," I say, hiding my anxiety by digging into one of the boxes brought up from Matt's basement. My clothes are still at my apartment, so this is all I've got to wear. A pair of acid-washed jeans, a hot pink T-shirt with RELAX across the front in huge white letters. Josie's mouth opens, in surprise.

"Seriously, Mel? We could just go the mall."

"And miss the chance to relive my glory days?" I say, holding up an old pale denim jean jacket with pouchy sleeves. The front is panelled with a thick cluster of safety pins, some of which have gone orange with rust, overtop of band names —

The Parachute Club, Sinéad O'Connor — scrawled in black magic marker.

"I hope they gave me a tetanus shot," I say, and Josie laughs. I look at her. She's beaming from the joy on her face, and I bask in it. I draw it deeply in. It was her idea to stay with Lara in Peterborough before I head off to the prison. She's called my long-lost friend; she's planned it all.

4.

GROMMET DOES WHAT Grommet does well — stretches out on the back seat as I turn onto the highway, this time heading southeast for the busier world of Southern Ontario instead of west towards Hixon River. Josie sets her white handbag neatly beside her clean running shoes and settles in, watching the blur of marshy rivers meandering towards Georgian Bay. Her sling is gone, I notice, but she's still babying her arm, cradling it, rubbing it like it's sore.

"I still can't believe you punched Owain," she says, as if there's a body memory in her own arm from the swing of my elbow, my fist making contact with his face. And why wouldn't there be? We've been friends for so long. Sometimes I'll be thinking about her and a second later the phone will ring, or I'll pick it up to blankness and she'll already be on the line. I haven't told her the full story about Owain though, what he said to me, that song, how we might start really going out, and I'm not quite sure how to do that. Instead, I smile and say, "Nobody can get between me and my brother." Then I ask, "Bruce okay with this?"

She turns away, but I can see the stiffness in her jaw.

"He's not the boss of me." Probably they had a fight.

"Well, tell him I appreciate it. Him not trying to hold you back, I mean."

Josie studies me. I know the look. Who are you, and what have you done with Mel? I pretend I don't see it; I pretend I've always been like this, so mature and compassionate and respectful of her relationship.

"It's just his mom made us a crib," she says. "Out of cherry wood, and it's beautiful and we had to rush it . . ."

Because I needed her, once again. I flash to their wedding, the table place cards that her cousin from Sarnia had set out for my mom and dad, not knowing. How long I'd spent sobbing in the washroom, how my face looked like a beetroot in those photos of the head table, how Bruce said nothing at all but had swept his hand across my shoulder blades at one point, passing behind me, acknowledging my presence.

At the time, it made me angry. At the time it wasn't enough. I retreated outside with the smokers until Josie's sister came to get me so I could help with handing out the cake.

"Names," I say to Josie, changing the subject.

"Violet?"

I shake my head. "Isn't that the bitchy kid from *Charlie and the Chocolate Factory*?"

"It's my grandmother's middle name."

I glance at her. "No offence."

"Well, maybe Laurel. For a girl."

"That's pretty."

"Lara attached to Mel equals Laurel."

"Oh," I say, surprised.

"I'm sorry," she says. "With everything that's going on . . ."

She fishes around in her purse, pulls out a tissue tinted blue from the bag's liner. I take it, wad the Kleenex against my runny nose. When I've recovered, I say, "What? You didn't like Laramel?"

She flings her hand against my knee, lightly slapping.

"Sounds like an anti-depressant."

"Shut up," she says, but I don't. I talk some more; I tell her what's going on, why the sudden rush.

"FINALLY," my Aunt Doreen had said, when she answered my phone call.

I didn't apologize. Instead, I told her about Matt, and she sucked in a startled breath. "Oh, no," she moaned, then asked how he was, and said. "Maybe don't tell your mom that right away. She's not in a great place."

Well, duh, I thought.

"Are you ready to hear this?" she asked.

No. "Yes."

My mother had helped another inmate write out a complaint about the conditions, Doreen told me.

"The conditions?"

"How things are there," she said, as if I needed a definition of the word.

"Well, if she didn't want to live like that, maybe she shouldn't have..."

"I'm not talking about having a yellow umbrella instead of a pink one in your pina colada. I'm talking inhumane stuff. Being openly mocked by the guards, toilets backing up, no heat, lice infestations..." She went on and on. Matt's stove clock said it was just after seven. Out West where she was it would be five or six, and I imagined the sunrise, flushing pink over the flat earth. Matt's alive, I thought. Matt's okay.

"... so then the warden put them in segregation," Doreen said. "And then you're talking the rattiest cells, limited human contact, electrical problems, no private place to talk to your lawyer..."

My mother's lawyer's voice had been so gentle, so calm. If you'd like to, she said, if you think you can . . . She meant going to visit. I don't have a choice, I told her. If my brother found out, he'd be roaring from the rooftops.

"And then it gets a whole lot worse," my aunt said. An altercation with a guard, inmates throwing urine, my mother on the sidelines but roped in, and all of them shackled and strip-searched.

"Treated like animals."

I heard the tremble in Doreen's voice, the shiver of anger, barely restrained, and I turned to the sink and ran my fingertips under a stream of cold water then put the phone down, rested my head in my hands. There was silence for a little while. Never in my entire life, the part I can remember, anyway, have I seen my mother naked. That's how modest she is, always locking the door when she went to take a bath, talking to me with the door between us in public washrooms.

"This is long distance, kiddo," my aunt said, her voice tiny.

I picked up the phone. "I'm here."

She sighed. "I think it would help a lot if you went to her, reminded her that you're still around, that you haven't turned your back on her, that she's still a human being."

By then, a numbness was spreading out from my centre, a feeling I recognized. Some days, back then, the autumn after the murder, this detachment was the only way I got through, dished out ice cream at my job, did the dishes at Lara's, got groceries. But I realized suddenly, so suddenly it was like the jolt of a surprising contact, that maybe that detachment wasn't exactly working. Maybe grief had been bullying me around, shoving me towards stupid decisions, for years, without my even realizing.

"I haven't talked to her in a long time," I said. "Really talk, I mean."

"You and Matt are all she's got."

"What about you?"

"I'm far away."

"So am I."

"Melony," she said. She drew in a breath, and I heard the tap of an earring as she pressed the phone close to her ear. "I don't know how much you know."

"I know," I said. "I know that Celia was pregnant."

In the aftermath, she and Matt had engaged in plenty of hushed conversations. I would walk into the kitchen to find her standing at the stove stirring tomato soup, Matt by her side. The two of them would go suddenly quiet before Doreen sang out, "Hungry?" like I was four years old. All that time they'd been figuring it out, going over the whole string of events, and I'd never had that chance. To hear it from my mother's own side, with all these secrets lain out like evidence in the longer, more complicated story. This was my chance, I realized. To hear the whole story laid out, to know all of it. This has nothing to do with you, my mother had said. Now was my chance to show her: yes, it did. "I'll go," I told my aunt.

"CELIA WAS PREGNANT?" Josie says in the car, pressing a palm against her own belly, her eyes wide. I nod.

"Oh, God." She turns away, and I know what she's feeling: a smaller version of my own response, that confusion over how to hold both things at once. Horror at what she did and a pitying love for her. I feel terrible about what she went through, but deep down inside there remains a tiny, furious voice: at least you're still alive. I can never shake the images I see: the gun in her hand. The bullet that lodged in my father's heart after opening Celia's artery, killing her quickly.

"We're so much more than the worst thing we ever did,"

Sophie had said to me, out at her farm. Deep down I know she's right but the worst thing still exists, it still has a place. It must still be discussed.

5.

JOSIE WAKES WHEN I turn off the highway at the Voyageur Trading Post, a restaurant and gas station my family would stop at whenever we went south to visit my dad's father before he died, or his one surviving brother, a big, gruff man named Thomas who told my dad he was gay and then we never saw him again. I feel sad about that, and think about looking him up. As soon as I pull up to the gas pump, Grommet's awake, his big head hanging over my shoulder. I fill the tank, then move the car to park near a strip of lawn with picnic tables and a trash barrel.

"The usual?" Josie asks, even though we've only done this drive together a few times, not counting a couple of school trips in yellow buses. Once with Lara, to check out universities, and another time, with Josie's mom, to go shopping for Josie's wedding dress in Toronto.

"Yes, please," I tell her, and she walks towards the building with its bright orange peaked roof while I clip the leash to Grommet's collar and let him out of my car. He pulls me over to the grass, skirting around a mud puddle with an edge of ice that looks a bit like lace, and a sudden memory surges to mind: my mother laying the hand-tatted lace tablecloth in the dining room at Christmas. It's so clear I can almost touch the fabric, feel the rough edge, see the stains from dribbles of sherry and the Swedish meatballs she usually made for Christmas Eve. We had our moments.

I hold tight to the leash as Grommet hauls me towards the edge of the forest. He sniffs at the mat of last year's fallen leaves and orange pine needles and pees on a rotten log, flushed green with moss.

I'm still thinking about those Christmases — about my mother opening the antique opal pendant my dad gave her one year and the time my parents bought Matt the fairy fish, about my own gifts of sea monkeys, a chemistry set, stuffed animals — when I notice a man, good looking, thick brown hair and bare muscled arms visible since he's wearing a rumpled Sex Pistols T-shirt. He walks towards a boxy white van with a large decal on the side that says Couch and Cookies Dog Training and Boarding. When he sees me, he stops. His eyes meet mine for a moment then drift down. It isn't me he recognizes.

"Hey," we both say at the exact same time. I'm pointing at him and he's pointing at Grommet. "Sunday!" he calls, and Grommet's tail starts to wag, sweeping the air. It's the trainer who came to the kennel that day, while I tossed a ball for Captain Jack, fuming and figuring out that Grommet had to be mine. So much has happened since then that I feel like I was a different person, imagining that this guy was my adversary, wishing Grommet would scare him off.

"It's Grommet now," I say as he approaches then tell my dog to sit. I have to say it a second time before he slowly plunks his butt onto the ground.

"But he was Sunday?" The man crouches down. I nod as he touches Grommet's shoulders, pulls back his fur to examine the rough grey scar looped in a perfect circle around his neck. He even affectionally pinches one of Grommet's jowls before Grommet yawns noisily.

"Looks like you're doing a great job. He was so anxious when I met him." I wish I could take credit. I'm about to tell him about

lauren carter

340

Sophie when a seagull lands on the grass and Grommet's up and lunging, hauling on my arm so I have to set my feet, hold tight to the leash.

"Work in progress," I say, straining.

He laughs. "Figured that. I've got a few of my own." He jerks his head towards the van, and I see a black dog with white on his muzzle sitting in the driver's seat, staring at us.

"I'm Brian, by the way," he says, and sticks out his hand. I shake it, tell him my name. He crosses his arms, sticks his fingers in his armpits, watching my dog.

"These mastiffs, though. Smart as the dickens but stubborn, minds of their own."

"Bred for boar hunting, so they had to have some independence."

He nods.

"Did you know they used to dress them in little suits of armour?" I tell him. I read that, after I first met Grommet, back when he was so very scared. I reach down, run my fingertips over the top of his sagittal crest and he casts his brown eyes up, panting now because he isn't sure what's happening, if I'm handing him over, if he has to expect yet another big change. "Like knights," I mutter, and when I look up I see that Brian's watching me. Our eyes meet warmly, and I feel a flush rise into my cheeks. He smiles, fishes a card out his pocket and hands it to me.

"If you ever need anything," he says. "Fellow dog lover." Then, he walks away.

"DID THAT GUY just hit on you?" Josie asks, appearing almost instantly as Brian drives away. She's holding two Styrofoam cups, stacked, and a white bag with grease spots on the side. The smell of butter and cinnamon makes my stomach rumble.

"I don't know."

"Who was he?"

I tell her about him as she sets the coffee and tea on the hood of my car.

"Fate!" she sings, pulling a hunk of the sweet bread off the roll, stuffing it into her mouth. I look down at the card. Brian Rowntree, it says. Dog Trainer.

Maybe, I think, carefully sliding it into the back pocket of my jeans.

6.

WE SPLIT THE DRIVING, but I'm back behind the wheel by the time we get close to Peterborough. Nerves are making my belly churn, and when Josie pulls out a few crackers from a plastic baggy in her purse, I expect her to offer me some, like I'm the one with morning sickness. Instead, she turns around and feeds one to Grommet, and in my rear-view, I see him take it delicately, using only his front teeth. "You'll have to tell me where to go," I say, and she wipes her fingers on the seat, pulls a folded piece of paper out of her purse.

"Directions," she says, opening it up. "To the gallery."

"Gallery?"

"Art gallery. I told her we'd meet her there." She glances at the red watch on my wrist, a Swatch watch with interchangeable bands that I've had since 1987 and found in one of the boxes. When I got it, opening the small, wrapped box at my fourteenth birthday party, she was there, and so was Lara, and we watched a rented laser disc of *Footloose*, drank Pop Shoppe cream soda, stayed up until almost two a.m.

THE GALLERY'S a big white building on the edge of a small, round lake. A huge iron tube sits across the front lawn, covered in recessed, wiggly trails that look like paths carved by carpenter ants. A sign posted beside it says *Arrival*, and I wonder if you're supposed to crawl inside it, where it would take me if I tried.

The art show's called *Transformations*, I read on a handout as we walk down a ramp lined with black and white photographs into the main gallery space. A picture window overlooks the lake, and on the opposite shore I can see the granite crosses and tombstones of a cemetery. It's the last day of the exhibition, the last half hour, and a dark-haired woman wearing a fuchsia and blue cable knit sweater, long out of style, stands by a ladder, ready to start taking things down. She smiles at us, at me in my acid-washed jeans, and says, "Just in time."

"We've got a friend in the show," Josie says.

"Who's that?"

"Lara Witmer."

The woman gestures to the corner of the gallery. "Powerful stuff."

"That?" I ask, pointing at a wide black box on a pedestal.

She nods. "Get up close," she says.

Josie and I move towards it slowly. I'm remembering irritating conversations with Lara's friends in Vancouver, how they plastered thick and gummy meaning on things that seemed so simple. This black box might be nothing but a black box representative of something only Lara knows. But once we're close, I see that each side's equipped with swimmer's masks to look inside. At first, all I see is darkness until Josie cries out, "Light switch." Then, suddenly, we're looking into a starry night over a cracked slab of granite, half of which is underwater. It's like being transported into the wilderness of our childhood, the big rock behind Lara's house where her brother had fallen to his death, lay hidden in a crevice for most of the winter. But it's different, too. There wasn't water in that forest, submerging the rock, or these schools of glittering fish, and the one lone angelfish with its drifting, translucent veils, hovering half in, half out of the crevice.

I've stopped breathing, I think, gazing inside, my face pressed to this plain outer wall, and it takes me a moment to realize that there are other features here too: Josie's eyes, visible on the other side, and another pair, as well, that last looked at me in hurt and anger in the desert. Josie screams, excited, and pulls back from the box, but I stay there for a few more seconds, on my own in this peaceful, magical place made by Lara.

7.

THERE'S A LOT I need to say. At first, though, we just look at each other, take each other in. She's wearing black boots that go up to her knees, velvet tights, a short red bolero jacket. There are blue streaks in her brown hair. Her eyes take me in too, and what I'm wearing, and she presses a knuckle against her grin.

"You haven't changed a bit," she says.

I roll my eyes; my face growing hot. "It's a long story."

The tremble starts in my bottom lip as she steps closer, holding out her arms, tentative. I want to spill it all right now, the apology I need to give, the fumbling explanation, but she doesn't let me. "Come here, you New Age bitch," she says, and pulls me into a hug.

"I HOPE IT'S OKAY," I tell her later when we're out at my car. She's got her fingertips up to Grommet's nose, is letting him sniff her hand through the open window.

"What?"

"His name."

She nods. "Josie told me."

She leans close and puffs the dog's name into his face so he can smell her breath.

"You little grommet," she says, and for a second it's like Pete's there again, using the nickname he gave us, that term he'd picked up for kid surfers, those not yet experienced at riding the steepest, roughest waves. That's who we were back then. Team Org. Grommet spelled backwards.

The dog whines, lifts a paw up towards her chin.

"I love him," Lara says, scratching him hard behind both ears.

8.

LARA BRINGS US to a bar. At first I don't want to go. I gesture down at the outfit I have on and explain how much Grommet hates being left in the car.

"Nobody cares," Lara says, and it takes me aback, because I hear old Lara, critical, and feel again the gap that had grown between us out West. My eyebrows pop up at the same time as she shakes her head.

"No. I mean about your clothes. But you can always borrow something."

"I'm starving," Josie says, and when Lara says we can eat there and even keep Grommet with us on the patio, I decide to not worry about what I've got on. Soon, Grommet's leading us through a fence at the side of a building while Lara goes in the front door. Josie, the dog and I pick a round wooden picnic table beside a chain-link fence blocking the steep drop to a roaring creek, and when Josie goes back to the car to get her jacket, I tell Grommet to sit. He's too anxious, though, his eyes darting around at the people, settling on a guy with dreadlocks who's leaning against the brick wall, smoking.

Above him, a huge sunflower has been painted against the deep blue brick wall. It's three stories tall, its huge centre stamen patchy and bird-pecked, the yellow petals like ragged ribbons. Decrepit but beautiful, like it would look in a field edging into autumn, and as I'm studying it, squeezing the fur on Grommet's neck to try to help him calm down, Lara pushes through the green base of the stem with a menu under her arm, three dark pints clustered in her hands.

"I took the liberty," she says, sliding a beer in front of me and another one over to where Josie will be sitting.

"Where'd she go?"

"To get her sweater," I say, as I study the menu.

"It is a little chilly out here." She pulls her shoulders in, crosses her arms. She's just got a jean jacket on, while I'm wearing an old green sweatshirt of Matt's, embroidered with the Ducks Unlimited logo. It doesn't suit me, though, and I can feel Lara's puzzlement, how she's wondering who I've become, because it isn't obvious, not by my clothes, anyway. But those conversations are long ones, and we've only just sat down. I push the menu over to Josie's spot, tapping the corner of it against the pint glass.

"Not sure if she'll want that though," I tell Lara at the same time as Josie comes back through the gate, tying the belt of a heavy brown cardigan. She sits down and looks from the beer to Lara, and Lara's eyes shift between Josie and me. I feel it, our old telepathy, that thick web of connection.

"No way," Lara says.

"Way," says Josie, and Lara shrieks, startling Grommet who lets out a single loud bark. I soothe him, patting his head and grinning as Lara leaps up, hauls Josie into her arms.

THE NEWS OF Josie's pregnancy seems to crack something open between us so we can easily talk. I order a huge plate of nachos, and we sit there eating, covering everything — Lara's career, the gossip from Hixon River, my destroyed apartment. When I tell Lara about Grommet biting Bruce she spits up some of her beer, she's laughing so hard, and then Josie interjects to tell her all about Owain, who I haven't even mentioned yet. When she gets to the part about him being a cheater, about my walking in on him and Tammy out in the cabin in the woods, I realize the equanimity. I am where Josie was, on the defensive because I actually still like the guy, so I take a deep breath and tell them about how good he is with dogs, what he'd said to me, an apology pretty much, the song.

Lara raises her eyebrows, peeling a slab of greasy cheese off a chip. Josie stares at me, her hand wrapped tightly around the mug of mint tea she'd ordered while Lara and I split her beer. "One verse?" Lara says. "And you're all agog?"

"It was pretty sweet," I say. I sound exactly like Josie, I know. She's beaming at me, and I can tell I've touched her romantic soul. I like the guy. I can't help it. He's easy. He's Mr. Right Now. We haven't brought up the fact that I did get to punch him in the face, although I'm dying to tell Lara that, but doing so will mean I'll have to explain about Matt, and I'm not ready.

Josie plucks a black olive off a chip, helps me change the subject. "What about that Brian guy?"

"Who's Brian?" Lara asks.

Josie tells her, and Lara nods, watching my expression. When I don't answer, she slides her hand over, touches mine, and the oil on her fingertips leaves shiny prints on my skin.

"You get to decide, you know. Don't let somebody else do it for you."

Bossy Lara, back again. But she isn't wrong.

I know she isn't wrong.

9.

I'M THE FIRST ONE up the next morning. Grommet lays his chin on the side of the bed that I'm sharing with Josie and groans, letting me know he needs to go out. Quickly, I dress, throw on my jacket, and follow him down two flights of creaking stairs to the street.

Lara's apartment's on the second storey, over a used book shop, around the corner from the bar we went to. We got to her place after midnight, Josie driving, and Lara offered to take Grommet today so I wouldn't have to worry about him. Josie asked if I minded her staying with Lara, and I said I didn't. She was tired, she told me, and I think the day will be easier on my own.

This means that I can go anytime I want but I'm not in a hurry. I let Grommet lead me by a factory on the river that's spewing white smoke that smells like burnt popcorn. We head across a bridge, and I pause in the middle, looking down at the water shifting this way and that, riffling in the shallows, gleaming silver where the pools are deeper. Last night Lara also told me that she's looking for a roommate, that there's a zoo just outside town that sometimes has jobs posted. I think about this town; I wonder what it'd be like to live here.

But would that be running again? Would I just be trying to get away from the hard things, from Matt and whatever he needs from me now? We'd had a good time last night, dragging out memories like we could somehow curate the past, wash the whole thing pink with nostalgia, and the feeling was so seductive.

But is it true, this feeling? This delight at who we were as kids?

Am I more that twelve-year-old, the little grommet, or the woman whose mother murdered her father? And can I figure out how to be both?

LARA'S UP WHEN Grommet and I get back, sitting on the sofa that faces the wide windows in her living room. The sun is just beginning to angle through the rippled antique glass, and the peaked roofs on the other side of the street look blurry.

"There's coffee," she says, as I unclip Grommet's leash, and he races over to her, toenails clattering on the hardwood. In the kitchen, I find a mug on the counter, the turquoise one covered in a lacy weave of vines spotted with pink blooms, that was my favourite out in Vancouver. I'd often left it on the kitchen counter, holding the dregs of my loose-leaf herbal teas, and the next time I went to get it it'd be back in the cupboard. Cleaned out by Lara, I assumed, who'd scraped the sloppy mess into the trash. Who did I think she was? My mother?

"Do you want more?" I call and carry the pot over, fill her cup, add a bit of cream from the carton in my other hand, just the way she likes it.

"Thanks."

"You're welcome."

Grommet stretches out in front of a tiled hearth that's holding the iron bust of a horse in place of a fire. Guard log, my dad would have called him. From the guest room we hear Josie talking in her sleep, saying something about dolphins, and we giggle.

"She's really happy," I say, pulling my feet up to sit cross-legged on the chair across from Lara, my back to the windows.

"She's wanted this for long enough. How's Brute?"

I shrug. "I think they had a fight, about her coming here."

"The more things change..."

"But she loves him." I remember the last time I spent the night there, listening to their quiet conversation, their laughter.

Lara rolls her eyes. "Lord help us."

And I think he loves her too, I'm about to say when she asks, "Do you want to call Angie?"

"I should, in a bit."

We sit there, quiet. Down below, a couple cars pass by. Back here, at the end of the night, my head swimming with intoxication and emotion, I cried and told her about Matt, his suicide attempt, his new business, his great impassable silence that had blocked me out and she'd listened to it all. It hangs in the room with us now like a sort of awkwardness, and I know that this is my moment to say the things that I need to say, my cue, my time to stumble on stage.

"Lara," I start, and adjust myself in the chair.

Abruptly, she leans forward and sets her mug down on the coffee table. It lands with a clunk in the hush of the room.

"Don't," she says.

"But I need to tell you..." I'm sorry, I'm about to say. For the car. For what I'd said. How I hadn't really meant it.

"No, you don't."

I look at her, puzzled.

"What you've got to do is let go of this complex you have like it's all your fault. You're actually a lot like Matt, just quieter about it."

I open my mouth to speak but she holds up her hand, palm out.

"I went along with you guys to try to get you to do what I wanted you to do" — she presses her fingers against her chest — "to try to pull you towards the path that I thought was the best one. We were both to blame."

"But what I said . . ."

"Yes, that hurt."

"I'm sorry."

"I know, Mel! Holy shit! You think I don't know? I've known for fucking years." She sweeps her arm out like all that time is spread around us in this tiny, old apartment. "Even Daisy . . ."

"What about her?"

Lara shakes her head. "I feel bad about that, about how much I hated her. But I guess I was jealous."

"Jealous?"

"You totally ditched me for her, and then once we got rid of her — well, once I did, thinking desperate times and all that — you instantly ditched me again, for that guy . . ." She snaps her fingers, like a magic trick, like a conjuring.

"Robert."

She nods, and her gaze swims up to the ceiling, over to the fireplace. "And that's when I got it, I think. It wasn't me you needed. All I was doing was keeping you trapped." Her eyes are on the mantle, on a photograph of her and Pete, his light hair dyed black, his thick kohl eyeliner, his arm around Lara, a little kid with her pink, plump face and ponytails, the way she was back in Grade 9 before she started to change. My eyes smart; all this time I thought I'd hurt her irrevocably, but she saw it differently. She saw it as me springing the trap, a necessary severing. I push at the tears, then smile, when she turns back to ask, "How was that anyway?"

"The cave?"

She nods.

"Dusty," I say, and she laughs.

I tell her what Robert said when he first showed me the space, the morning she left. The words come out of my memory like a chant. "This place can be your home if you really need to roam, but running away is a temporary measure that will never give you pleasure or a life that you can treasure."

"A New Age Dr. Seuss."

"I don't know about New Age. Wiser than that."

"Why the rhyming?"

"OCD. PTSD. Vietnam." I swallow the last cold bit of my coffee. "His son told me that. I met him once. He came there, tried to convince me to help get him committed, although I'm not sure why he thought I was so sane..." I toss my eyes up at the ceiling, considering.

"You didn't help him?"

I shake my head. "Maybe not the right choice; I don't know."

She nods, and I glance out the window, at the clouds pushing into the blue.

"I think of him a lot, actually." I look at her. "Road trip?"

"Ha, ha, ha," she says. "No."

"If he hadn't been there, I might still be..."

"Lost," Lara says.

"What's lost?" Josie asks, coming out of the guest room in bare feet, wearing a pale green night shirt with a teddy bear hugging a heart on it. She pulls a quilt off the arm of the couch, one I recognize from Lara's family home, and wraps it around her shoulders.

Lara doesn't answer her, and neither do I. "Tea?" Lara asks, standing up. I give my chair to Josie and sit beside Grommet on the floor, rubbing the velvet softness of his ears, pretending to listen as she talks about her dream. Instead, I think about how very soon I'll be face to face with my mom.

part thirteen

1.

THE DRIVE GOES QUICKLY, my car flying east on the highway. Pretty soon I'm there, the city painted with a wash of grey
from a rainstorm that's threatening to sweep in from the big
lake. There's still ice at the shore, and a filthy hump of snow
leans against the tall concrete wall around the limestone prison.
Everything's grey, like wet cement, like I could easily sink down,
get stuck here, and I gaze up at the hulking building like a
Victorian orphan staring down my fate.

In the visitor's parking lot, I get out, swing the strap of my
purse over my shoulder, swing my legs towards the wide metal
door. There's a lot of swinging going on, because I'm attempting
to get my momentum up, push past my fear, move forward, like
a pendulum. I might end up heading in the opposite direction.
This reminds me of a joke my dad used to tell: what do you get
when you play a country song in reverse?

You get your wife back, your dog back, your truck back...

Inside, all the faces are pale and grim. It's like something really bad has happened and there's a radio signal reporting news that I can't quite hear. I sign my name in a logbook, show them my driver's licence and my red-and-white social insurance card, and pass silently through a metal detector. Meticulously, a male guard pulls apart my purse, item by item, wallet, comb, and when he finds the clicker that Sophie gave me, his eyes tip up, questioning.

"It's for training dogs," I tell him, loud, overly loud, trying to press my voice through the gridded plexiglass. He turns it over in his fingers, then nods, runs his hand over the lining inside my bag.

"Call ahead?" asks a woman standing behind him, holding a clipboard. She's wearing a light blue shirt that's snug around her breasts, and she looks like she'd be more comfortable back in the eighties. Spears of pink blush angle up her cheekbones, and her blonde hair is feathered, glints of silver showing at the roots, and I'm thankful that Lara lent me some clothes, a pair of crushed velvet tights and a long black sweater so I could leave my own acid-washed jeans and out-of-style tops at her place.

"My sister-in-law did," I say, leaning forward to talk through the hole in the glass. Angie told me this morning that she called the prison yesterday, that Matt had asked her to, to give them the head's up so they could be ready. Ready how? I wondered. Did they have to clean her up, convince her to get out of bed, help her wash her hair?

"Angela Barnett?" I say.

"But you did not?"

"No, she called to let you know..."

"But you did not?"

"No."

lauren carter

The woman shakes her head as if I've done something really wrong, like I'm wasting her time. Suddenly I just want to cry. Do you know? I want to ask her. Do you know what's happening with me? But then I hear someone yell from deep inside the labyrinthine building, a raging holler, and while I turn my head sharply to the sound, the ensuing clanging, the others don't even react.

"You're here for Bernie," says the female guard, looking down at a paper.

Bernadette, I think to myself, but I nod as if it's a question rather than a statement. My purse is shoved towards me, all the items stuffed back inside, but no one's told me what to do, so I stand there, still waiting, until the guard jerks his head towards a collection of grey chairs, where a man sits with a jacket draped over his knees. His arms are heavily tattooed, and he's holding a fat paperback, the spine creased so much it looks like the book's about to split in half, fall apart. His eyes examine me the same as the others, distanced, suspicious. But we're on the same side, I think.

"How long have you been waiting?" I ask, as I take a seat.

"About thirty-five years," he says, his knee jumping and jumping like Matt's.

By the looks of him, that would pretty much be his whole life. I'm not sure what he means, so I just nod, face stern, as serious as a guard.

I SHOULD TELL YOU that my mother got life, with a minimum of twenty-five years. She was charged with second-degree murder and manslaughter, and she pled guilty. When the judge asked her if she had anything to say, she apparently spoke two words: I'm sorry. Like she'd tipped over a jug of milk or nudged someone on a crowded sidewalk. Matt told me this during the flight home from Phoenix. I stared down at the middle of the continent, gradually blanketed in white as we flew steadily north. The stewardess brought me apple juice while he talked, delivering facts, his voice clipped and businesslike as if we were preparing for a significant meeting, not getting me ready for the rest of my life. The bits he left out were the important ones, the things it would have helped me to know. But despite how together he seemed, I realize now, he was buckling under a weight, keeping his balance by shoving aside the heaviest part, the one that made him culpable, burying the corresponding emotion.

"Melony Barnett," a voice booms. It's the woman with the eighties fashion sense, calling my name as if I hadn't just spoken to her, as if the waiting room is crowded. I look up from my examination of the man's arms, the dagger dripping blood, a crude heart holding initials and the letters RIP, an eagle in the crook of his elbow.

"Here," I say, like I'm in school. I stand, heart revving in my chest, and fumble the key to the locker, drop it on the floor.

"First visit?" she asks, as I stuff my jacket and purse inside the small metal box, clang the door shut. Her sympathy is surprising, but I don't really want it. I'm fine, I tell myself. I'm just fine.

IN MY IMAGINATION, my mother is always dressed in orange. A bright prison uniform glaring against the grey, that neon my father wouldn't let me wear. But she's not. She's got on a long-sleeved plaid flannel shirt and, I see when she bolts up from her chair at the round table, jogging pants and ordinary running shoes. Her hair is long and loose, the split ends holding a brassy auburn dye, the rest gone completely grey. Except for a touch of glossy pink lipstick, her face is free of makeup, drawn, yellow-pale, but eager, her eyes dragging me close. There's a bruise on her temple, purplish-blue, the size of a walnut and a scabbed-over cut on her cheek.

I stop. I've come through so many doors. Loud clanging gates and sliding steel panels. If I need to escape, I've got no idea how to do it, how to get out.

"Melony," she says, half shrieking. Then she starts to cry, to weep, a wailing that echoes in the corners of the room and makes me look around like I'm thirteen and embarrassed. I take a deep breath. I can't go back. Forward is the only way.

2.

THREE OTHER TABLES in the visitor's area are full but nobody looks over as my mother cries herself out. I suppose they're used to it here. We've got no tissues, so she wipes her nose repeatedly on her sleeve as I sit down across from her. We haven't hugged. I don't know if it's allowed or if I can even unlatch my arms from being crossed over my chest.

"How's the food?" I ask, because I don't know where to begin.

She sniffs, then smiles; a tight, small smirk. I've forgotten how much she looks like Matt, especially now, especially how he's been lately, in Owain's dark basement, his features carved out of the shadowy space. "You mean the kibbles and bits?"

She spreads her knees, leans forward. Tears dried, suddenly tough.

"That's what they call it, like we're dogs," she says. "Calling us for our kibbles and bits. But I suppose that's what we are to them. No better than dogs." I follow her gaze to the corner, the guard staring straight ahead like she's somewhere else, just her body left behind.

this has nothing to do with you

I don't say anything.

"Where's Matt?" she asks, and I shrug, glance away. "Busy," I lie. "Being a dad." The words come easily. Gulls flitting across the surface of a deep lake. But she studies me, seeing something.

"Have you been getting my letters?" she asks.

I shrug.

"Do you read them, or do you just throw them in the garbage?"

We fall silent for what feels like ages, like a whole ten minutes, a third of our visit, and then I take a breath.

"I found out," I tell her. "About Celia."

She drops her eyes; I lean forward. "That she was pregnant, that Matt told you. He can't let it go, you know, and I think you have to tell him..."

"Sweetheart," she says, and the look she gives me is deeply pitying, the same one as when I'd confess my love for a boy who didn't like me, when I'd want something I simply couldn't have, when I told her she should go to New York, seize her life, become a real dancer at the age of forty. My heart lurches in my chest like it's gasping back to life and all I suddenly want is to bury my face in her lap, feel her fingers in my hair. It's my turn to start crying. I resist. I touch my eyes, holding in the tears.

"Things have been hard," she says.

Shut up, I want to say. Shut up!

Snot gurgles out of my nose and she glances around, helpless, the mother unable to provide. I think of Josie, dredging tissues out of her purse.

"Josie's pregnant."

She smiles, and I think I see her face brighten, like a curtain's opened to let in some sun. Those black window coverings in Matt's basement, I think, always closed. How I didn't see until it was almost too late. I push the back of my hand against my nostrils, stare into my lap, thinking I shouldn't have come.

"How's Ellie?" she asks.

"Good."

"Matt said they'd visit this summer." Her face tenses, gaze skimming across the tabletop, scarred with carved initials and angular hearts. "A while ago he said that."

I can't tell her about him; Angie asked me not to. What I say is simply, "Can you explain?"

This is a huge question, I realize, once it's out of my mouth. It could mean anything from the past two decades, my whole, entire life, or even earlier, her own childhood, her own mistakes. But she grasps the closest subject and says, "Celia." Then, crisply: "Lucille White."

She doesn't start with her, though. Or even with that spring when the air in the house thickened with tension, when my father moved downstairs, or with the night of the murders. She starts further back, in the winter of 1990, when I was sixteen, when I was worried about things like who would go with me to the Valentine's Day dance.

"That March," she says, arms clasped around her middle, speaking so quietly I have to lean closer in order to hear, "I found out I was pregnant."

Startled, I lurch back. "What?"

From across the room, a child giggles as if to punctuate the words, and my mother turns her head to look. When I follow her gaze, I see a woman with a ring of barbed wire tattooed around her upper arm, lifting a squirming toddler over the table to another woman with grey hair.

"That's Charlene," my mother says, but I don't know which one of them she means. I hesitate. It's a crossroad, a chance to help her change the subject or stay silent in order to nudge her down that other path, into the dark thickets, where the things I need to know, that I'm afraid to hear, are hidden. I don't speak.

this has nothing to do with you

I wait for whatever's coming.

Pregnant, I think, then no. No, no, no.

"Maybe it was stupid. To want it. I realize I wasn't in any shape..." She looks at me shyly, as if asking for disagreement, for me to reassure her, to tell her she was a great mom, but I can't. For her, I barely existed. She rooted herself in external crises: Chernobyl, the *Challenger* disaster, the famine in Ethiopia, the tanks rolling into Tiananmen Square; or buried herself in novels about easily solved crimes with neat endings, tidy denouements.

"Your father did not want it," she says. "And you know how he could be."

I look down at the floor, a memory springing to mind of my father sitting on the couch with his shotgun on his knee until my mother came around to giving him whatever he wanted. I don't remember what he wanted. I saw the scene in fragments, the sliver of the living room that could be glimpsed through the gap in my bedroom door.

A baby, I think. A seismic shift. Another life to tend and care for, to put before him. A baby brother or sister. I stare down into my lap, dread pooling in my chest. My mom's eyes are on me, digging, rooting around for sympathy, but I'm not there yet. I need to hear it all and am hoping for one single, easy word: miscarriage.

Only a few weeks along, she'll tell me, a fetus about as big as Josie's. Too small to be viable. It just slipped out of her. Regrettable, but nobody's fault.

Unless it was someone's fault, a voice suddenly shouts in my head. That winter, that March. We went to Florida. My mother slept all the time. It was a few months before her suicide attempt. My stomach drops to the tile floor, adheres to its dim sparkle. I'm frozen but I manage to squeak, "What happened?"

My mother shifts delicately in her seat, still a dancer, her slender body moving with grace.

"I was waiting to tell him. But he started noticing things. He was not a stupid man." She pushes the flap of an unbuttoned cuff against her nose. "I was sick, so sick, and that went on for a few weeks, and then he was home a lot of the time, because that was when his hours were first cut. Remember?"

I don't remember. Not much. Mostly how I tried to keep away, joined every club I could — band, volleyball, whatever play was having rehearsals — so I'd have reasons to stay after school, to take the late bus home. Lara and Josie picking me up for the show on Friday nights while my mother locked herself in her bedroom, watching the news, calling Matt so much my father yelled at her about the phone bill, set limits like she was the teenager, and me the free adult.

"So one day I told him. It was another chance for us, I said. We could move somewhere else, start again, go out to Saskatchewan, even, or even closer to his brother, whom I liked, or even maybe out to the coast." She's leaning forward now, as if trying to convince me. Her eyes bright and focused. "But he just stared at me," she says. "Like I was a freak, a thing in a cage at a zoo, and you know what he said?"

I shake my head. The movement is minuscule, barely consenting. A tiny smile sharpens her lips like a thorn.

"Why would I go anywhere with a mental case like you." Her voice goes gruff, lowered. I can no longer remember what he sounded like, I realize, can't tell if her imitation has even come close. I close my eyes, fighting the urge to bawl. "I couldn't even talk to him about it," my mother says. "We had no money. His job was on the line. He didn't want to be pushing sixty with a teenager underfoot. Him, him, him. Never once, not once did he ask about me." She slaps her hand hard against her chest, making a dull, hollow thump that draws the guard a step closer.

"What did you do?" My voice sounds distant in my ears, like someone else speaking from the far corner of the room.

"What would you do?" she asks, making my head swim, but she doesn't give me time to answer. "I told him I was going to have it, that I didn't care what he thought."

Abruptly, she stops speaking. Mouth slammed shut. Face full of subtle shifts, the ones I spent my childhood trying to read.

"And then?"

Still she doesn't answer. I have to prod her, pushing my hands across the table, poking her elbow with one finger. "Mom?"

"He picked up the phone. That one in the bedroom." Her eyes land on mine, and we're both back there, in the old house, in their old bedroom, with the long brown dresser and the orange chair, the small box of a black and white TV, the full-length mirror beside the door with the chips in the glass near the bottom. "And he talked into it, like he was talking to a police officer or a doctor, I don't know." Her voice deepens, mimicking my father's. "My wife's unstable, threatening our safety, threatening our daughter. I found a knife under her bed. I think she needs to be hospitalized again. She's a danger to herself and others."

She pushes her hands against her cheeks, flinches when her fingertips contact the bruise, then presses it tenderly like she wants the pain. "He would have done that, put me away, lied, taken you."

I sit there, stunned. Taken me?

My life, a whole other story, revolving around my father while my mother . . . What? Had the baby in the mental ward?

Raised her in poverty? Matt moving back, quitting school in this plot line as well, helping to raise the other Eleanor, while I stayed with Dad. It turns out I was a chess piece, a bargaining chip, a cog in their distorted machinery.

Across from me, her eyes fill with water like a miniature tap has been opened.

"I've never been very good at life. I've made a real mess..."

"Mom," I say. The only word I have right then.

"If it was a girl, I wanted to call her Eleanor. I thought it was a girl."

Those perfect sugary roses on the cake, I remember, turning sour on my tongue, how I'd stared at the shadow of the name, now my niece's. I sit back, realizing how much in the dark my brother's kept me, how much he's always known.

"Why didn't..." I start. Anyone tell me, is what I'm going to say, but my mother cuts me off.

"What could I do?"

Her eyes are wet and red, nose running freely. I look around for tissues, for help, for someone – a kindly nurse – to appear with a box of Kleenex, and then I spot the woman at the other table digging into her black purse. She pulls out a wad, raises it towards me, and I almost burst into tears myself as I scramble over and take them, mouth *thank you*. Mom snatches one up, flaps it like a surrendering flag when I drop them all in front of her.

"He told me to get rid of it," she says. "What could I do?"

I know what I would have said back then, remember how I'd suggested she pull herself together, return to dancing, move to New York City. Like a fucking movie. Like life's actually like that. I stare at the table's surface, scarred with a hundred statements of true, undying love – SP + EJH – and swim inside my confusion. That other potential sibling, a baby sister, or maybe a brother. I feel like I might be sick, like I'm on the edge of a tumbling free fall of weeping, but I haul in a breath of the musty, close air, and stuff the tissue into the wet corners of my eyes.

"Matt helped me," she says. "Drove us downtown. We got in quick enough. But the people..." Her hand trembles as she pushes a palm against her brow. "Baby killer, baby killer," she mutters, and I pull in a sharp breath, picture the protests Matt told me about, his volunteer job escorting women. The bruises on his face that spring when he returned home with my mother, who'd driven south to get him. How she'd been sick for days with what she called food poisoning. Those hours she spent in bed, blocking out the bright summer sunshine.

"And then not even a year later..."

"Celia," I whisper.

She nods. "Your father, man to man, bragging to Matt, my son, my..." Her voice breaks. Baby, she was going to say. "Setting him up, leaving it to him, knowing that he would tell me. The fucking coward."

She spits the last words, and I see that hatred in her, the same as the day she'd told me about the affair, how she'd hissed out her desire to hurt him, how she'd scared me. Now there's bare exhaustion on her face, the skin around her mouth gone white as ice, dark shadows under her eyes, and I think we're done, that this is it, the whole story lain bare, given to me to sort through. I feel like I'm forty myself, like years and years have passed while I've been sitting in this hard chair, listening, and I wish I could turn time back around, step into the darkness, open my mouth like a baby and gurgle to my mom about Owain, about the boy I like, protected from these hard subjects, but it seems my mother isn't finished.

"It wasn't even about her," she says quietly, talking to the floor. "Celia stepped in front of him; she tried to save his life."

My mouth opens. I stare at her. Her eyes clamped shut, her clenched jaw softening, a growing calmness like the one that must have helped her get to Happyland that night, drive through town to the forest on the other side, carry the heavy gun that had always been in my parents' closet, curtained off by the neckties my father didn't wear: skinny ones from the sixties, wide ones from the seventies. Once or twice I'd even shot it, when he took me and Matt to the dump for target practice. The punch in my shoulder nearly knocking me backwards, and how he'd laughed.

I drop my forehead onto the table, not caring what germs are there, left by fingers tangled in their own messy lives. In my peripheral vision, I notice the wide blur of the guard turning towards the motion, watching us, and I quickly sit up again, but my mother's oblivious, gazing down at her hands in her lap as if she's holding the past in her palms. Tiny bits of captured time, fancy beads strung on a line, jewels I've never seen before that are part of my inheritance whether I want to claim them or not.

"What am I supposed to do with all this?" I whisper. I feel like I have ice in my mouth, that sweet slushy wine Angie and I finally finished off before racing over to find Matt. He's in the hospital now, he almost died, and I can't talk to her about it even though it was because of her, her fault. She shakes her head, unable to answer, to offer any advice, and we sit there in silence, seconds ticking by on the round clock high on the wall that's pockmarked with spitballs. Finally, my mother slides her hands across the table to me and I look down at the terrain of lines, the arc of her life line, the forks in her heart line, remembering Josie, Lara and me reading each other's palms with a book from the library. When I finally reach out to touch my mother's hands, I find that they are very cold.

I'M NOT CRYING when I get in my car, but I am shaking. I pull the seat up close to the wheel, grasp it tightly as I drive through the high prison gate. Soon the churning blue-grey of Lake Ontario is sliding by, looking like crepe paper as I head out of the city. It's raining. A full-on downpour making the world look glossy in places and blurry in others. Water's thrown back from the fat wheels of the transport ahead of me, and my windshield wipers are flying, fast enough to turn the road to fog. I white-knuckle the steering wheel, thinking about everything my mother told me, trying to sort the mess in my head, imagining the culmination, that night. How the darkness had pressed in on her, so thick because there wasn't any moon.

She knew where they were, my father and Celia. Hixon River is a small town and there were rumours; she would have easily found out. It was nearly four in the morning when she left the house, her boots kicked off at the door, exchanged for lightweight leather moccasins chosen, I figured, so she could move more gracefully under the tall red pines during her last performance, my father's final act.

She threw handfuls of rocks at the trailer, one after another, until the two of them came out. First my father, then Celia, when my mother wouldn't leave. She didn't talk long. A witness said she heard voices — male, female, female — and then, almost immediately, the single shot.

Matt had told me these details on the plane. His face stiff, reciting facts, like a doctor reading from a file. The bullet had come to rest inside my father's left ventricle after it nicked Celia's artery, opened her up.

My dad lived for twenty minutes with his heart beating around the cold metal lump, while his mistress died in just a few, a spreading wave of blood my mother must have watched, sitting where they found her, underneath the pines, waiting for the police to arrive. I'm crying harder now, thinking of that, the shock of her mistake, the fear my dad must have felt, face to face with the wildness of my mother, a puppet with her wires cut, her limbs flailing.

Her anger.

After what my father asked her to do, what she'd done, and what he was leaving her for, the news that Matt had given her.

I pull over, sit on the side of the highway, the car rocking as other vehicles charge past me. This isn't a safe spot, I know, but I stay, sobbing, shaking, trying to reorient myself, to find a solid footing while it all washes over me, those heavy emotions that Lara told me, years ago, she simply, somehow, learned to carry.

I've made a mess of it, my mother said.

Yes, I should have answered. You did. The two of you. You really, really did.

There's more to say, I realize. I hit my blinker. I turn around.

4.

THERE'S A MOTEL close to the prison. The second *A* and an *N* on its orange neon sign are burnt out, so it's called the *GATEWY IN*. From the outside, with its fresh coat of robin's egg–blue paint and polished bronze door numbers it looks okay. The woman at the desk checks me in without saying much, with a minimum of eye contact, and in my room I discover a comforter pock-marked with cigarette burns and a rust stain on the grey carpet between the beds that I stare at for a long time, trying not to imagine how it came to be there. From the bathroom, I can see the lake through a small, high window and I stand on the toilet, looking out, trying to get up the nerve to call Angie collect, to arrange for me to speak with Matt. But what am I going to say?

Two embryos, it turns out, two potential siblings. Four endings instead of two. An entire nuclear family. There were so many other possible outcomes, other stilted futures, that my mind is spinning. My own life could have easily followed a few different paths: taken away by my father to live under his thumb while my mother and Matt raised the new baby, my mother locked up in a mental institution, or even my father finally conceding, the four of us moving forward as a bigger family, with me acting as older sister to a baby my mother would not have been capable of raising, too fragile, too inclined to lock herself away in her bedroom at every lurch in the road. How strange it is that the path that ended up unfolding is the only one that's given me my freedom. And here I am, thrashing around, making one stupid mistake after another, too scared to seize my dreams. I think of Sophie, having to abandon medical school in order to raise Celia's son.

I don't call Angie. The only phone call I make is to Lara to tell her I won't be back until tomorrow.

"All right," she says. "Everything okay?"

I nod. The words are too heavy; they're like wooden planks that have yet to be hammered in place. "How's Grommet?"

"We're playing Scrabble and he tried to eat an *O* and a *P* but I made him give them up."

"Gross!" Josie yells, in the background, and I laugh.

"Drive safe, okay?" she tells me before I hang up and climb under the covers with all my clothes on. I go to sleep with the TV playing an old John Wayne Western, the sound turned all the way down, his rugged face floating over a Technicolour desert. He's in my dream as well, guarding me, watching over me, like a dad I never knew.

5.

MY MOTHER'S SURPRISED to see me the next day. She's wearing the same clothes and looks pretty much the same: long hair pulled back, grey roots, the edges of the purple bruise on her face turned slightly more yellow. We sit there for a few minutes in silence, her eyes on me, mine moving between a coffee machine with an out-of-order sign on it that I didn't notice the day before and her eager gaze. She seems brighter, more alert, like she's slept better or eaten a good meal of the things she likes: fresh caught pickerel in beer batter, strawberries from the garden in July. I wonder if she'll ever taste those things again. When she gets out, she'll be sixty-five and I'll be forty-two. After a while, she clasps her hands together and sets them in front of her.

"Go ahead," she says, so I start, and the first thing I ask is, "Why did you keep all of it from me? Why hasn't Matt told me?"

She peers at me. A look that's so familiar, that I saw a thousand times growing up, and that often preceded her leaving the room, quietly shutting her bedroom door, hiding. My father letting out a long, ragged sigh, sometimes following her, sometimes not. Once he went into the bedroom and dragged her back out, wrestled her into the dining room chair, fed her forkfuls of the lasagna she'd abandoned until she had sauce all over her face. Matt yelling so my father finally threw down the fork and left, as if fed up with us. Where was I? Watching from a slight distance, trembling in my chair, an observer in my own home.

"What would you have done if you'd known?" my mother asks.

"That isn't the point."

"It's part of the point."

She's right, and I know it. But it's so hard not to look back, to connect the dots, to draw the trajectory and understand how it all unfolded. If I'd known the hidden details then, maybe I could have stopped her, I can't help but think, and that must be how Matt feels too, except that he did know the details. But none of us have that chance, I realize. Not even him. We aren't up in the treetops looking down. We're knee deep in the muck, blinded by the dirt in our eyes.

"I suppose I was trying to protect you," my mother says. "Trying to spare you, trying to help you." She's crying again, the tears making slow, shimmering paths down her cheeks.

"Why?"

She looks up at me, surprised. "Because I love you."

Her bright blue eyes are so much like Matt's, like Ellie's, that I feel a burn in my throat, missing them, wishing we could all be together at the same time. A family. Fractured, but still connected.

"I ran away," I say.

She nods. "Tell me about that."

So I do, and the story I tell her is all about me, but it has everything to do with her. With her and my dad and Matt and Josie and Lara. Even Celia and Sophie and Ted and Angie and Ellie and the siblings who did not come to be. In the back of my mind, long before I've arrived at his part in the story that I'm telling my mother for the first time, Robert's floating as well.

Where does another person's suffering end and yours begin? I asked him once, after I'd finally fully explained about my parents, about what my mother had done.

It's here, he said, laying his palm on my sun-browned arm.

It's in your own skin.

epilogue

ANGIE'S FALLEN FOR Grommet. This, I never would have predicted. At least not when I first moved back to their place, and she'd seemed so fearful, her hands hovering, ready to snatch Ellie away as the dog sniffed the baby all over, licked mashed peas off her tiny fingers.

Now it's Angie who tells me things: how mastiffs were once called nanny dogs and were bred to watch over children, how their ancestors hunted lions in the desert.

"Did you know that?" she asks me again and again, looking up from a library book pulled from the stack she keeps beside the couch, covering that Jägermeister stain we've scrubbed to a dim shadow. Every time, I say no, act astonished.

"Probably you knew," she says sometimes, catching on.

She's training him too, has taught him to reliably trot across the park to her when she calls "here," and to shake a paw, and to leave things he shouldn't pick up in his mouth, except for Ellie's dropped food, which he's allowed to clean up. It's amazing progress. I definitely see a difference in him, and I can't wait to see how far along he'll be when I'm home

373

again — at Thanksgiving, Christmas, during my reading week in February.

It's late August now, two months since Josie and I drove back from down South. Lara's been home for a visit, and I helped her paint a mural in the baby's room at Josie's while Bruce was away on a guys' fishing trip. We swam and ate barbecue and went to the Riverside, where Lara took a photograph of Josie and me under the *Ladies and Escorts* entrance sign. She stayed with Angie and me too, in Norbury, and we went to see Matt in the hospital before he got out a couple weeks ago. We reminisced about Pete, laughing at the fun times we'd had.

It's felt, in a way, like that other summer should have. The first one before I was supposed to go to university. Every time I look around — at Josie reading a magazine on her towel at the beach, that slight swell to her bare tummy, at Ellie waving her arms for balance as she walks across the lawn, at the big lake sliding by on my drive to Hixon or over to Sophie's, to help her with the dogs — I've been taking mental photographs, conscious that I'm leaving, that I might never live up North again.

My bags are packed with new clothes. All of the eighties outfits have been donated to the Salvation Army along with a bunch of other boxes from Matt's basement. I got rid of most of the stuff from my apartment, too. Owain, Matt, and I fixed it up in late May when Matt was out on a day pass and Owain and I were still together. We patched drywall and painted in order to pay back the Mehtas. Angie sent over a plate of cupcakes, too, decorated with icing piped to look like Grommet. Mrs. Mehta raised her eyebrows at those, but she couldn't help smiling when her kids shrieked with delight.

"Ready?" Matt asks me, pulling on a baseball hat and giving Angie a peck on the lips. He cups his hand over Ellie's soft head, then shakes her little hand as she blows her lips, spraying saliva across Angie's cheek. These days she's fidgeting a lot, wanting to walk all the time, and we've been watching her, that insistent, instinctual push towards growth.

"I'll be out in a minute," I tell him, as he carries our suitcases through the front door to my car, which is now Angie's and which Matt will drive back home. She bought it from me to help her get to her new job at C'est La Vie, a downtown salon where she'll work while Matt stays home with Ellie, finishing the courses he needs to get his degree. He's driving me south, to help me look for a room to rent before school starts. I got late admission, and I'm already enrolled in Animal Anatomy 1 and Human-Animal Relationships. I'm going part-time to start, so I can also earn money to help pay my way. Being down there will mean I'm closer to Mom, too, can see her more often, help her get psychiatric care, work with her lawyer. But it also means I have to give some things up.

"Thank you for taking Grom," I tell Angie. "It isn't forever."

"I know," she says. There are tears in her eyes, bright spots that spill, surprising Ellie when they land on her pudgy, bare legs.

"Oh, you," she says, and reaches out her free arm to pull me into a hug.

At the top of the stairs, Grommet lies down on his belly and crawls towards us, thinking he can slink down unnoticed.

"Stay," I tell him, trying to imitate Angie's gentle, firm voice, and he pulls his head back, looks at me with his large brown eyes, questioning. It's him, his expression, the same one he'd give me when we first met and I came and went from the shelter. It almost does me in, makes me want to change my mind, stay right there, live in Matt and Angie's spare room, making do. But I can't. The past few months have changed me so much.

I think Lara said it best after I returned from the visit with my mom, sat on her couch for an hour, told her and Josie everything, and cried until I felt emptied out. She was dressed in her studio clothes that afternoon: hemp pants smeared with a dozen colours, a stained man's undershirt, a handkerchief tying back her blue and black hair. "Now you're mourning," she said, pointing the thick bristles of her paint brush at me, holding it like a wand. "Now you're learning to live."

MATT SITS IN THE passenger seat of my car, reading the liner notes for *Nevermind* as we wind through the city streets to the highway. I turn east towards Southern Ontario, the drive he'd once done from Hixon River to go to university too. So many ghosts float between us, and I think we're finally getting comfortable with them, or at least used to their presence, but then he starts fidgeting, pushing in my car lighter, immediately pulling it out again.

"You're not smoking again, are you?"

"Trying not to," he says. "It was a pain in the ass in the hospital."

He's been out for eleven days, is on a new and better medication, is seeing a psychiatrist. I want to ask him what they talk about, but I know Matt won't tell me, know how private he is. I suspect, though, that it isn't only about our father but also about Mom. I hope so, anyway.

"The lounge?" I ask, remembering that room where I'd visited him. The closed glass door and the thick grey tinge to the air, having to almost yell over the roar of the filtration system.

"Awful, didn't want to do it, so I figured..."

"Seize the day."

He nods sharply, a sudden hardness to his jaw. That was an expression our father sometimes used, and it's as if he's entered the space between us, stepped close. I can almost see him: enthusiastic, cracking jokes, the life of the party when it wasn't just us, when other people were around, strangers to be courted and charmed. That's what my friends always said: your dad's so funny.

Matt's knee is steadily jumping. There are shadows in him of a person I don't know and there probably always will be, I realize.

"What about pot?"

"Easier to give that up," he says. "Need to be able to think in a straight line."

I nod. I know what he means. How pot snaps your mind wide open, how sometimes that can be good, and other times it's better to avoid those yawning rooms. But to each his own, I think. Like Owain, loose-limbed, easy going, who I slept with twice more when I got back from seeing my mother before deciding I couldn't handle the uneasiness I felt whenever his pager went off. We can still be friends, I told him, then I called Brian and we talked for two hours.

I know that Matt's given up the drug business too, is intent on finishing school, raising his daughter, and working volunteer shifts doing grounds maintenance at a local women's shelter that Angie's cousin, Beth, referred him to. Ted and Owain are still involved, though, and when I asked Sophie about it, she said, "I don't go in for moral absolutes."

"Besides, these are desperate times," she told me. She wanted Ted to go to university, to pursue his dream of being a biologist.

"Isn't he . . ." I started to ask.

"Going to die?"

I nodded.

"Yes," she said, and that was all.

this has nothing to do with you

In the car, I think of turning on the radio, listening for the hourly news, but we've already read this morning's paper. Despite an estimated death toll of nearly a million and the word genocide finally being used by the U.S. government, the media has turned its attention to the O.J. Simpson trial. This infuriates Matt, who is still writing letters, mailing them now, and who even had an opinion piece published in the *Norbury Beacon*, which Angie hung on their fridge. For a while, my brother and I drive in silence, the forest flashing by, birch and poplars already spotted with bright yellow leaves.

"If I could do it all over again," I tell him. "I never would have left. I would have stayed; I would have helped you with Mom; I would have tried to be a grown-up; I would have insisted you tell me the truth."

This is the statement I've been rehearsing, knowing we'd have hours to talk. But Matt shakes his head.

"Mom never wanted to tell you," he says. "Not anything. Even when she tried to kill herself, she wanted me to try to convince you she had an ulcer."

"An ulcer? That's nuts."

He nods.

"And you agreed?"

He stares straight ahead at the highway winding like a long grey ribbon through the rock cuts and spruce. "I did what she wanted," he says. "I always have." He looks at me. "But you know it all now, and that's good."

It's a little bit of praise, or it feels that way, and a smile tugs at my lips. I turn to look at the lake stretching out beside us. That blue swath, the distant horizon a long straight line I stared at so much as a kid, trying to write out my future.

"I think I left because I thought I could be free," I say.

Matt looks at me. "Well, you know what they say."

"What?"

"Freedom's what you do with what's been done to you."

A wave of grief rolls through me, sudden, unpredictable, and then it's gone. Matt stuffs a cassette into the tape deck. The Cure. *Kiss Me, Kiss Me, Kiss Me.* He turns it up really loud, and we sing along to *Just Like Heaven*, windows down, pressing forward. Back to where we were, but also somewhere different, somewhere better, a moment further from our past.

Acknowledgements

This novel grew out of my love and admiration for the novel *We Are All Completely Beside Ourselves* by Karen Joy Fowler so, to start, a nod to that beautiful book.

Thank you to my agent Samantha Haywood for supporting me and my work and for finding a home for Mel and Grommet, and to Anna Boyar and Kelsey Attard at Freehand for connecting with Mel and her struggles. Thank you to Naomi Lewis for being such a sharp, sensitive and intellligent editor, to Natalie Olsen for the gorgeous — and insightful — cover design, and to my publicist Rachel Sentes. Deep gratitude, as well, to editor Jane Warren who provided thoughtful and enormously helpful notes.

Huge thanks to the Manitoba Arts Council for the support of the Major Arts Award which enabled me to dedicate myself to this story for over a year. I am so grateful. Thank you, as well, to Lauren Wadelius and The Pas Regional Library, and to everyone at the McNally Robinson book store for all they do for the writing community.

Thank you to my mom, Laura Carter, for reading many drafts and being available not only for editorial work but also for conversation about plot intricacies and character psychology.

Thanks to Ian Williams for several valuable conversations and shared manuscript goals while we were both working on novels in Calgary. My deep gratitude to Robin van Eck and the Alexandra Writers' Society for providing me the space and time to work on this novel in their beautiful city and I'm appreciative of the many conversations with writers I connected with during my stay. Thanks to Micheline Maylor, as well, for writing-talk, friendship, rides, and outings (and dog therapy).

Appreciation also to Marguerite Pigeon who shared with me her story about the question "is there a paucity of tears?" which I borrowed, with her permission.

Also a shout-out to my high-school friends who may see shades they recognize within this palate: Stephen, Jen J., Elouise, Scott, Steve, Jen D., Gabe, John, Jonathan, Gord, and others... And thanks to Neil Young for the song *Helpless* which Mel remembers Matt singing in a canoe and which basically poignantly defines my youth.

The news reports about the Rwandan genocide and other world events were obtained from online archives as well as from episodes of *The National* which I viewed at the CBC in Toronto, with thanks to Darren Yearsley. Darren also screened *The Fifth Estate*'s "The Ultimate Response" for me. This episode exposed video of a male response team's night raid at the Kingston Prison for Women resulting in an inquest into the inhumane conditions, some examples of which I used within the fictional setting and circumstances of this book.

The quote "freedom is what you do with what's been done to do" is by Jean-Paul Sartre and "my past is everything I failed to be" is from Fernando Pessao. "Not by might but by spirit" is from the Hebrew Bible (Zechariah 4:6).

I want to express gratitude to my family-of-origin, including my father, and deep love and thankfulness to/for my late brother, Tim, my sister, Carey, my mom, my mother-in-law, Joy, and the rest of my in-laws, as well supportive friends and fellow writers Renee Kastrukoff, Erna Buffie, Ariel Gordon, Donna Besel, Sally Ito, Sue Sorensen, Marj Poor, Charlene Diehl, Amanda Walker, Patti Train, Angie Gallop, Nick Popiel, Dave Fleming, Wes Ryan, Julie and Ozgun Intepe, Conni Cartlidge, Amy Teakle, and, of course, and for always, my ever-supportive husband, Jason, and our own dog-children, belated Oliver and much-alive Mowat, who may or may not have inspired some of the antics within this book.

LAUREN CARTER is the author of four books. Her first novel, *Swarm*, was on CBC's list of 40 novels that could change Canada. In 2014, her short story "Rhubarb" won top place in the *Prairie Fire* fiction prize and appeared in the annual *Best Canadian Stories* (edited by John Metcalf). Her work has also been nominated for the Journey Prize and longlisted multiple times for the CBC Literary Prizes in both poetry and fiction. She grew up in Blind River, Ontario, and lived in Orillia, Ontario before moving to The Pas, Manitoba. She currently resides in the rural area of St. Andrews, Manitoba, near Winnipeg.